P9-DNS-957

WICKED HEART

ALSO BY LEISA RAYVEN

Bad Romeo

Broken Juliet

WICKED HEART

Leisa Rayven

St. Martin's Griffin ⚑ New York

East Baton Rouge Parish Library
Baton Rouge, Louisia

4379 1889

This is a work of fiction. All of the characters, organizations, and events portrayed in this novel are either products of the author's imagination or are used fictitiously.

WICKED HEART. Copyright © 2016 by Leisa Rayven. All rights reserved. Printed in the United States of America. For information, address St. Martin's Press, 175 Fifth Avenue, New York, N.Y. 10010.

www.stmartins.com

The Library of Congress Cataloging-in-Publication Data is available upon request.

ISBN 978-1-250-06598-8 (trade paperback)
ISBN 978-1-4668-7305-6 (e-book)

Our books may be purchased in bulk for promotional, educational, or business use. Please contact your local bookseller or the Macmillan Corporate and Premium Sales Department at 1-800-221-7945, extension 5442, or by e-mail at MacmillanSpecial Markets@macmillan.com.

First Edition: May 2016

10 9 8 7 6 5 4 3 2 1

This book is for all those who have been kicked in the face by love and gotten back up again. May your fragile hearts be warmed by the sun and soothed by gentle breezes, and may you one day hide behind a strategically placed tree which allows you to ninja-tackle love and junkpunch it right in the nads.

ACKNOWLEDGMENTS

I need to thank a million people who helped shape *Wicked Heart*. (Well, okay, maybe "a million" is overstating it, but there are lots.)

Firstly, to my amazing editor at SMP, Rose Hilliard, who pushed for Elissa and Liam's story and spanked me until I got it right; thank you for your amazing brain.

To my wonderful and pretty agent, Christina Hogrebe; I still get giddy when you tell me you enjoy my words. Don't see that changing anytime soon.

To my beautiful bestie, Andrea, who is my rock and my cheerleader: Thank you for making me feel good about my writing even when I'm pretty sure it sucks giant yak balls. Your positivity and love is one of the greatest joys of my life.

To my darling Caryn, who pushed me from the start to write all the words and write them well. You've always had faith in me, even when I abused punctuation and continued my ongoing feud with the question mark. (That's never changing, by the way. Question Mark knows what he did. I will never forgive him.)

To my A-list pre-readers, Natasha and Kristine—girls, you rock my world. Just when I was on the cusp of chewing off all my fingernails and getting super-drunk, you talked me off the ledge. Your incredible words of support and encouragement saved my sanity. One day, I will write fanfiction about a haunted vagina just for you. And maybe some dino-porn.

Enormous thanks to my spectacular husband, Jason, who puts up with my being distant and quiet while characters take over my brain. Who supports me when I lock myself away to rewrite scenes 1,827,381,273,621 times until they feel right. Who sees me writing in my pajamas at 3 P.M. with uncombed hair and a face lined with too little sleep and still tells me I'm beautiful. You're my hero, honey. Always and forever.

To my boys, Xanny and Ky. Little dudes, you make me laugh every day, you make me love more than I ever thought possible, and your beautiful souls make my heart smile and swell with pride. Thank you for allowing me to be your Mummy. Now give me topper tuddles. NO BAKEY! (You de bivvin' 'em!)

I would need more pages to thank the countless amazing bloggers and reviewers who support the crazy that spills from my brain, but please know that if and when I meet you face-to-face, I'm buying you a drink and smooshing the hell out of you. I've already achieved it with some of my faves (Vilma, Aestas, Nina, Kristine, and Natasha— I'm looking at you), but you ALL deserve smooshings, and one day, I will make it happen. Trust.

To the Filets and Pams—you ladies are my safe place and my therapy, all in one. Thank you for your awesomeness.

And last, but absolutely not least, thank you to every single reader who has picked up my books, read them cover to cover, and still decided they like me. You have no idea how incredibly grateful I am to you all. You validate my crazy, you make the process of writing incredibly worthwhile, and your amazing support and encouragement makes me cry happy tears.

I'm so blessed to have you all in my life.

Leisa x

WICKED HEART

O Lord, deliver me from the man
of excellent intention and impure heart:
for the heart is deceitful above all things,
and desperately wicked.

—T. S. Eliot

ONE

FOOL ME ONCE

Present Day
Pier 23 Rehearsal Rooms
New York City

Tingles up my spine. Blood hot and fast beneath my skin.

Goddammit. This isn't good.

Why is this still happening to me after all these years?

I'm not a girl who swoons easily. I'm really not. If I were to describe myself I'd say I was passionate but logical, fiery but methodical, spontaneous but organized. All of these traits might seem like contradictions, but they make me a damn good stage manager, and I'm not too humble to say that at the age of twenty-five, I'm one of the most respected show runners on Broadway. Producers know they can depend on me to stay calm in a crisis. I run my shows with military precision, and I demand strict professionalism from everyone, especially myself.

My rules for a stress-free work environment are nonnegotiable: Treat everyone with respect, be firm but fair, and do not *ever* get romantically involved with someone in the show I'm running. For most of my career, I've had no problem following my own rules, but there is one thing that can derail my equilibrium in one fell swoop.

Well, not so much one *thing* as one *person*.

Liam Quinn.

As I sit in the private cinema with my production team and watch the shirtless man on the screen take down an overwhelming number of enemies, I'm embarrassed by how hot my skin feels. How my breathing is shallow, and my thighs are pressed together. How I drink in every angle of his face and body. How I thrill to the flex of every perfect muscle.

But even more than that, I'm embarrassed how the passion of his performance makes me fantasize about doing passionate things to him. Not just sexual things, but they're certainly high on the list.

To put it simply, he makes me swoon like it's his damn job.

He's the only man who's ever affected me like this, and it's safe to say I hold it against him. It's inconvenient and rude.

He runs toward the gorgeous redhead on the screen and pulls her into a passionate embrace. The redhead is Angel Bell—recent cover model for *People*'s "Most Beautiful Women in the Known Universe" and basic all-round Goddess. Perfect body. Perfect boobs. Perfect face. She's playing a seraph princess. Liam is her scorching-hot demon slave. They've just about destroyed the world trying to be together, and now Liam's kissing her like he'll die if he doesn't.

Goddamn, that man can kiss.

I cross my legs and sigh. This is insane.

I'm not against being aroused in general, but being aroused by this particular man is a recipe for disaster. The last time I let myself have these feelings for him, it didn't end well.

I feel a hand on my arm and turn to see one of Broadway's most respected directors, Marco Fiori, leaning over. His eyes are bright with excitement, and it's clear I'm not the only one who's noticed Liam's . . . assets.

"Quite the specimen, isn't he?" Marco whispers.

I shrug. "If you like that sort of thing, I suppose." My raging hormones scream that we do like that sort of thing. We like it a whole helluva lot.

The only trouble is, we can't like it, because Liam's an actor, and we don't date actors. Also, in a few weeks, I'll be his stage manager. Also, he's engaged to his gorgeous costar.

Oh, and perhaps the most important reason is, once upon a time, we had a short but passionate-as-hell relationship and I've never recovered.

Somehow, I've managed to lock away the heartache he caused, possibly because I blame myself as much as I blame him. But the desire? That's still roaming free, storming through my composure like a bull in a china shop.

Yep.

This is going to be an interesting project. It will be a miracle if my professionalism and I make it out alive.

Half an hour later, after a thunderous climax in which Liam saves the world, then has panty-melting sex with his leading lady, the movie ends.

Thank *God*.

When the lights come up, we all head into the nearby conference room. Our production team is small and consists of our producer, Ava Weinstein; our director, Marco; the designer and the production manager; and finally, my assistant stage manager and best friend, Joshua Kane.

"You okay?" Josh asks as we take our seats at the table. "You're flushed."

"I'm fine," I say. "Just warm. It was hot in there, right?"

Josh shrugs. "It was pretty damn hot when Angel was topless in the bathhouse, but other than that, I was freezing my balls off. I think the A/C was set to 'Arctic Blizzard.'"

I pick up the folder in front of me and fan myself. Despite Josh's chilly nuts, my blush is set at "Surface of the Sun."

Josh smiles to himself.

"What?" I ask, defensive.

"Nothing. Just finding it funny that after all of these years, one glimpse of Liam Quinn can still turn you as red as my credit card balance."

"Shut up."

"I notice that wasn't a denial."

"Double shut up. And if you breathe a word of this to Marco, I'll rip off your icy balls and use them as earrings."

He laughs. "Marco doesn't know you two . . . 'know' each other?"

"No."

"Or that every sexual fantasy you've had in the past six years has revolved around Liam?"

I glare at him.

He holds up his hands. "Fine. My lips are zipped. But if you latch on to him in rehearsals and hump his thigh, I expect to be absolved of all responsibility."

"If I get close enough to him to do any humping, you will have failed as my platonic life partner. Just remember that."

"God, woman," he says with a frustrated sigh. "Keeping you in line really is a full-time job."

Even when my anxiety levels are higher than James Franco's, I love that Josh can still make me smile. This is why he's been my bestie since our sophomore year in high school. Predictably, we met in drama club. He was one of the few straight boys there, and even though we both loved theater, we weren't great at the onstage stuff. After our less-than-stellar acting "debuts," in which we played what no doubt came across as the world's most awkward lovers, we decided to tread the less glorious path of backstage crew. It turns out my talent for organization and general bossiness is a plus in theater, and it wasn't long before I became the school's youngest-ever stage manager.

For some reason, Josh was content to play Robin to my backstage Batman, and we've been a dynamic duo ever since. People are always confused that we're friends and not lovers, but that's just the way it is with us. Besties 'til the end.

"Okay, team," Marco says when we're all seated. "That was the final movie in the *Rageheart* series, starring Liam Quinn and Angel Bell, our soon-to-be leading couple for my fabulous reimagining of Shakespeare's *Taming of the Shrew*."

I love Marco's concept to update Shakespeare's classic comedy. His work is clever and current, and I've been a fan since I worked on his most recent Broadway hit. The play just happened to also star my brother, Ethan, and his gorgeous now-fiancée, Cassie Taylor. After we'd been open for a few months, Marco poached me to run this project. Of course, at the time I had no idea it would star the "Lord of My Underpants," Liam Quinn. If I'd had that little nugget of information, I would have run in the other direction. Working with a man who lights up my libido like the Vegas strip isn't my idea of a good time.

"Now," Marco says, "unless you've been living under a rock for the past few years, you'll know that Liam and Angel are Hollywood's current golden couple. They dated for a couple of years, then got engaged, and judging from their regular public displays of affection, they're revoltingly in love."

I remember the day I found out they were dating. I'd never felt so stupid in my entire life. Or so heartbroken. I thought we had something special, but those photos were proof that even men as spectacular as Liam Quinn can be fickle bastards.

Marco points to the folders in front of us. "Those dossiers will familiarize you with our stars. They contain their official résumés, as well as quirky facts, likes, and dislikes."

As if I need any of that. I've been cyber-stalking Liam for years. Not my proudest achievement.

"At the back of the dossier," Marco says, "is a copy of Liam's and

Angel's production riders." A production rider is a list of things companies are requested to provide to keep stars happy. The can range from the simple to the ridiculous.

"Please keep in mind that these aren't regular theater actors," Marco continues. "They're movie stars, so they're used to having all of their outrageous demands met. Let's try not to disappoint."

I sneak a peek at Angel's list.

Jesus, really?

It would seem Miss Bell's happiness depends on her dressing room being completely white—white carpet, furniture, drapes, and flowers. Her food and beverage requirements are straight out of the little-known best seller—*Gourmet Crap That Will Send You Broke.*

I flick over to Liam's rider. It lists only four things

Free weights

Wi-Fi

Chocolate chip cookies

Milk

I smile. I remember his fondness for cookies and milk. He used to taste delicious after eating them. Cookies and cream is still my favorite flavor.

Josh frowns. "Are we really providing everything in Angel's rider? I wouldn't even know where to look for a 'Columbia Daylily.'"

Marco laughs. "Of course not. With our budget, we can barely afford bottled water, let alone a private chef or personal trainer."

Our producer, Ava, clears her throat. "I'm currently in negotiations with Anthony Kent, Liam and Angel's agent, and intend on vetoing the more ridiculous demands. Anthony needs to manage his clients' expectations about the difference between working in theater and film. Movie stars have no idea about how humble theater budgets are. I fear Angel and Liam are in for a rude awakening."

"Liam's done theater before," I say before thinking.

Ava raises an eyebrow. "Really?"

"Uh . . . yes. It's right there on his résumé. Six years ago. *Romeo and Juliet*. Tribeca Shakespeare Festival."

Marco narrows his eyes. "Wasn't that the same production you and your brother were involved with? It was your first professional show, yes? You were only nineteen."

Damn that man and his elephantine memory. "Oh. Uh . . . yes. It was."

"So you know Liam Quinn?" Ava asks, surprised.

"A little."

At least, I thought I did. The man I knew was different from the short-tempered bad boy who now shows up in the gossip rags every few weeks.

"Will he give us any trouble?" Marco asks.

I shrug. "He was very professional as our Romeo, but that was before he became Mr. Big-Shot Hollywood Icon. Now, he has a history of aggression toward paparazzi. I haven't heard about him being difficult in a professional capacity, but it wouldn't surprise me."

Marco nods. "Agreed. In contrast, his fiancée seems so sweet in interviews it makes my teeth ache. I think we should all be prepared to tread carefully and massage some difficult attitudes."

For the rest of the meeting, I keep only one ear on the conversation as I think back to the Liam of Christmases past. He used to be passionate, attentive, and hot as hell, and he awakened a part of my sexuality I never knew existed. I should have realized it was too good to last. There isn't a man on earth as perfect as he was pretending to be.

Even after all of this time, I hate how he played me. And I still wonder why he did it. To prove he could? To make sure I had both feet firmly on the rug before he pulled it out from under me?

Whatever the reason, what's done is done. I can't go back and change things. But I can make sure Liam Quinn never gets the chance to fool me again.

TWO

MR. QUINN

Three Weeks Later
Pier 23 Rehearsal Rooms
New York City

I hear a barrage of screams. Either Liam and Angel have just arrived, or hundreds of people are being tortured right outside the building.

My pulse kicks into overdrive, and I take a deep breath as I remind myself to stay cool. I just need to detach my emotions. Compartmentalize. It's usually my specialty.

Not today.

Knowing he's near, my dormant romantic fantasies spark like half-lit fireworks, threatening to ignite all over again.

The screams downstairs get louder. They do nothing to help my state of mind.

I cross the rehearsal room and look out the window onto the street below. Sure enough, down on the pavement is a huge crowd of salivating women, and a few men. Climbing out of a black Escalade in front of them is the object of millions of sexual fantasies. My heart rate speeds up as the tall man with the perfect physique smiles and waves at his fans. He looks good. Better than he has any right to.

His sandy-brown hair is artfully tousled, and although a lot of men spend ages trying to emulate the look, what they don't realize is that Liam rolls out of bed like that. It only adds to his sex appeal. Any man who naturally looks like he's just gone ten rounds in the sack gets top spot on the hotness meter. His high cheekbones and square jaw bump him up even higher, and that's before we even make it to his lips and eyes. I thank the gods his crazy-beautiful blue-green eyes are hidden behind sunglasses, and that I'm too far away to get the full effect of the rest of his face.

Pity I can't say the same thing about his body.

I've never met anyone with a body like Liam's. It's my definition of perfection. Every muscle is defined and sculpted but not huge or bulky. Broad shoulders and a narrow waist. The best butt I've ever laid eyes on.

I didn't know I had a thing for muscles before I met Liam, but boy, I know now.

His T-shirt pulls tight across his shoulders as he reaches into the Escalade and helps a statuesque redhead out of the car.

Angel Bell. Beauty queen, socialite, fashion maven, and Hollywood princess. Daughter of Senator Cyrus Bell, and sister of award-winning journalist Tori Bell.

Josh appears beside me. "Angeeeeeeel," he whispers in a reverent tone. "Leave that muscled loser and let me love you. We'd make beautiful babies."

"Oh, ew," I say.

Josh leans closer to the windows to get a better look. "So you're allowed to lust after Mr. Tall-and-Ripped but I can't have an innocent crush on lovely Leggy McRedhead?"

"Josh, none of your crushes are innocent."

He chuckles. "Okay, fine. I want to do bad things to her. But can you blame me? I want to wrap those long legs around me and make her mewl like a kitten."

"Isn't she a bit vanilla for your tastes?"

"I have no idea what you're talking about. She seems like a perfectly nice girl."

"Exactly. You don't date nice girls."

Josh has a thing for actresses. More specifically, wildly ambitious actresses who are two neuroses short of batshit crazy. His girlfriends tend to have a lot in common with Broadway shows: They're always high maintenance and filled with drama.

"You're right," he says. "I usually prefer girls who challenge me."

"You say 'challenge,' and I hear 'scare the crap out of.'"

"That reminds me—tell me again why you and I have never dated?"

"Because we made out that one time in sophomore year and both thought it was weird as hell."

"Well, you thought that. I was into it."

"Oh, please."

He crosses his arms over his chest. "Elissa, I don't know whether you realize this, but you are a smoking-hot female specimen. Yes, I'm your best friend, but I'm also a man. Kissing a chick who looks like Scarlett Johansson's younger sister is going to give me masculine stirrings. Have no doubt."

I laugh. I really don't want to hear about his stirrings, masculine or otherwise. Josh is like my brother. Well, a brother I get along with.

I pat his arm. "Okay, let's drop the subject. We're on the clock now. Professional faces, please."

He nods. "But just to be clear, I can tell you my pornographic fantasies when we get home, right?"

"If you must."

I turn back to the windows to see Angel stumble in her heels. When Liam pulls her tight against him with a look of concern, the whole crowd *"awwws"* before getting back to their dedicated screaming.

"I love you, Liam!"

"Sign my arm!"

"Marry me! Pleeeeease!"

"Angel, you're beautiful!"

They're right about that. She really is beautiful. While I'm five-three and curvy, she's tall, svelte, and elegant. My hair is blond and shoulder-length, hers is long, auburn, and looks like she should be appearing in a shampoo commercial. My eyes are basic blue, hers are a striking green. The only thing I have over her is my boobs. Hers may defy gravity, but mine are real.

I grudgingly admit I understand what Liam sees in her. She's far more in his league than I ever was. Their children will be so genetically blessed they'll probably develop superpowers.

I watch as Liam and Angel continue to sign autographs and pose for pictures. Every action is accompanied by frenzied squeals. I wonder what it must be like to star in something as huge as *Rageheart* and have millions of fans all over the world. Liam's portrayal of the passionate, mostly shirtless demon Zan, who leads a slave uprising and falls in love with the seraph king's daughter, has ignited countless pairs of panties. I think it's safe to say he's the biggest movie star in the world right now.

"Dammit," Josh says. "Does the chiseled Adonis really have to taint my wife-to-be's lips like that? It's gross."

He's referring to Liam's planting of a soft kiss on Angel's mouth as she leans against him. The bunch of paparazzi that were already snapping up a storm go into a frenzy. Nothing sells more magazines or gets more Web site clicks than pictures of Liam and Angel demonstrating their Epic Love. No doubt an explosion of dollar signs just flashed before the paps' eyes.

Marco comes to my other side and peers down. "That 'grossness,' dear Joshua, is what we're banking on. Liam and Angel's rabid fan base will make sure our production is the hottest ticket on Broadway for months. Mark my words."

Josh nods. "Unless, of course, she recognizes her overwhelming attraction to me during rehearsals, and breaks up with him before we open."

Marco looks like a vampire who's been burnt by holy water. "Don't even joke about that. Any rift between these two would mean disaster for our sales, which is why we must handle both of them with kid gloves. Remember, they're used to everyone kissing their backsides, so pucker up, kids."

I sigh. I remember a night when I kissed Liam's backside. And his front side. And all the parts in between. The memories are so vivid, it's as if it happened yesterday.

I seriously consider if it's too late to resign.

Marco puts his arms around me. "Can you feel it, Elissa?"

Yes. Nausea. Anxiety. An overwhelming urge to rush out and buy a one-way ticket to Nepal.

I give him a wan smile. "Oh, I feel it."

"Theatrical greatness, dear girl. We're about to create it. Thank you for being my right-hand woman. I couldn't do this without you."

So, that's a no to Nepal, I guess.

I give him a squeeze and then go back to the production desk. My section is impeccably laid out. Script. Pencils. A rainbow of highlighter pens.

I'm ready.

I'm ready.

I'm ready.

I put my hands on my hips and sigh.

Nope. Not buying it. Screw you, positive thinking. Of all the days to let me down.

When I hear chatter in the hallway, I tense up. Liam's deep voice carries through the walls and vibrates into my body.

"Lissa?" I turn to find Josh looking at me with concern. "You know that not breathing is bad for your health, right? Please chill."

I blow out a breath and nod. "Sure." I roll my neck and it cracks. "I'm good. Bring it on."

"'Atta girl."

As our tiny tall-haired publicist, Mary, sweeps into the room with the stars, I half hide myself behind Josh. Subjecting only part of my body to the full force of Liam's presence seems like the sensible thing to do.

"And this is our production team," Mary says. "Of course, you know our director, Marco. I believe he's spoken to you on the phone."

Marco smiles and shakes their hands. "Delighted to meet you both in person. Welcome."

Mary points to the quivering black girl by the windows. "Over there is our production intern, Denise." Denise melts into the floorboards when Liam smiles at her. I think her crush on him rivals my own.

"And here's our choreographer, Martin."

"It's a pleasure," Martin says, barely sparing Angel a glance before holding on to Liam's hand for several seconds too long for it to be anything but creepy.

"And last but not least, our illustrious stage management team, Joshua Kane and—"

"Elissa Holt." Liam says my name as if I'm some sort of mythical being he never expected to encounter. I try to keep my smile steady as he blinks in surprise. "You're our stage manager?"

I nod. "Yes. Hello, Mr. Quinn. Good to see you again. And it's nice to meet you, Miss Bell." I hold my hand out to Angel. "Please let either me or Josh know if you need anything."

Angel takes my hand and tilts her head at me. "You and Liam know each other?"

Her suspicion is clear. I go into evasive maneuvers. "Not really. Josh and I worked on Mr. Quinn's first Broadway show, many years ago. He just has a good memory."

She relaxes a little and gives me a smile. "He does. Sometimes I envy it. Especially his ability to learn lines."

I glance at Liam to find him staring at me. I can't decipher his expression. Anger? Bewilderment? A bit of both? There's a heat in his gaze that makes me think he's not entirely unhappy to see me, and I fluctuate in deciding whether or not that's a good thing.

Josh steps up beside me. "Hi, Mr. Quinn," he says as he clasps Liam's hand. "Welcome back to New York."

Liam gives him a quick smile. "Josh. Hey. How've you been, man?"

"Not as good as you, Mr. Hollywood. Congrats on all the stardom and adulation, dude."

A wry grin lifts Liam's lips. "Yeah, well, it's not as much fun as it seems. Believe me."

Liam glances at me, and when Josh moves over to talk to Angel, I offer my hand. Liam looks at me for a moment before he grasps it. Then he steps forward and towers over me as his fingers curl around mine, warm and electric. I try to hide the shudder that runs through me. No one needs to know what a single touch from this man can do to me. Especially not him.

I plaster on a smile as the heat of his skin sinks into my bones. "We're thrilled to have you and your fiancée starring in our show, Mr. Quinn. I'm sure it's going to be a huge hit."

"God, Elissa, I . . ." His fingers tighten, and I shiver as he rubs his thumb over my knuckles. He looks down at our hands and then back up to my face. "I'm a bit lost for words here. Seeing you again is . . ."

I wait for him to finish the sentence, but he seems to be struggling to express himself.

By now, my hand is burning, so I pull it back and try to swallow around my too-thick tongue. "It must be nice to be back in New York. I understand you haven't been home for a while."

He fixes me with those incredible aqua eyes. His expression seems way too intimate, considering how long it's been since we've seen each other, not to mention that his fiancée is standing right next to him. He catches himself staring and clears his throat. "Uh . . . no. I haven't been home for a long time. Too long. Every day I've been away, I've missed it."

He looks like he's about to say something else when the rest of the cast starts arriving.

Thank God.

I use the distraction to move away. It's not easy. I feel like a space-ship escaping the inexorable pull of a black hole.

As people fill the room, I go on autopilot. I sign people in, hand out information sheets and rehearsal schedules, and busy myself deal-ing with anyone who isn't Liam.

It doesn't escape my attention that an hour later when we're ready to begin rehearsals, Liam still seems shell-shocked by my presence.

There's an air of excitement in the room as Marco talks the cast through his ideas for the show. Everyone listens and nods, and most people jot notes onto their scripts. Liam, however, isn't holding a script, but leaning forward and frowning in concentration.

He has an energy about him these days that's new. Sort of an aggressive simmer, like there's a dark cloud following him around, drawing down his brows and putting tension in his jaw. I know it's become part of his sex appeal, but I'm intrigued to know what's causing it.

He sits next to Angel without touching her. In fact, when she leans over to whisper something in his ear, a flash of irritation passes over his face before he pulls away. Angel looks around to see if anyone noticed. When she glances in my direction, I diplomatically go back to tapping notes into my laptop.

It's heartening to know they're not always as blissful as they seem in their pictures. It makes them seem more human.

I can't even imagine what it must be like to be engaged to the world's most lusted-after man. It's no secret that Angel regularly receives death threats and abuse on social media from Liam's more rabid ad-mirers. If I were her, I'd be paranoid as hell, but she always seems perky and upbeat. It must be exhausting to stay as positive and put-together as she does. Even when she's caught exiting a spin class, she looks like she's just stepped out of the pages of a glamorous fitness magazine.

Fitness is just one more thing she and Liam have in common. I know they're in the business of looking good, but really, no one needs to exercise as much as they do. It's wrong and unnatural. My idea of working out involves yoga pants without the actual yoga. In fact, my yoga pants should be called "sitting around eating cheese pants." A longer title, sure, but more accurate.

"My final point is this," says Marco. "Even though *Taming of the Shrew* is a play which can easily be seen as chauvinistic, we're aiming to dispel that perception. Angel will portray a Katherine whose bitterness stems from her unwillingness to conform to society's definition of a woman's role, as well as a reaction to her father's blatant favoritism toward her sister. Petruchio will not be her tamer as much as her partner in crime. My goal is to show our audience a couple who brings out the best in each other, who feeds upon each other's unusual sexual desires, and who manages to poke fun at those who are trying to make them something they're not."

He clasps his hands together and smiles. "So, with all that in mind, let's see what we can create together. Let's work through the first scene. Places!"

Over the next few hours, we block out the first three scenes in the first act.

At first, Angel is way too nice as Kate. After Marco asks her to be stronger, she goes too far in the other direction and plays Kate's scenes with her sister and father like a screaming banshee who's likely to hack them to pieces, Lizzie Borden style.

I'm no director, but I think Marco's going to insist on a little more subtlety.

Liam, on the other hand, is excellent right off the bat. His Petruchio is passionate and charismatic, and he has great chemistry with the actors playing his servant and friends.

Being in the rehearsal room with him again reminds me how mesmerizing he is up close. I'm embarrassed to say I've watched the *Rageheart* series too many times to count. But as powerful and intense as Liam is on-screen, he's even more so in the flesh. It's refreshing to see him play a character so different from that brooding and violent demon. His version of Petruchio is a lovable rogue, and I'd almost forgotten how stunning he is when he smiles. He didn't do it much while he was massacring all those sadistic angel overlords.

As I look around, I notice that every single person has their eyes glued to him, and this is why he's a star. Liam is one of those actors who just has *it*. It's part talent, and part confidence, and just enough raw vulnerability to make you want to fuck him and hug him at the same time. At least, that's how he affects most women.

Despite being a six-foot-three wall of rippling muscle who could no doubt beat anyone who messed with him into a bloody pulp, he makes you want to take care of him.

"Did you know he was this talented?" Marco asks when I release the cast for a coffee break.

"He was excellent as Romeo," I say. "I wasn't sure how he'd handle this role, but it fits him like a glove."

Marco nods. "I only wish Angel were as good. I'd hoped she'd bring some level of complexity to Katherine. But she's playing her as a two-dimensional screamer."

"Art imitating life," our production intern, Denise, mumbles beside me.

"Watch how you talk about my woman," Josh says. "Hating her just because she's beautiful and rich is not the least bit cool."

"Oh, please," Denise says. "Even if she ate someone alive, you'd defend her because she gives you a boner, right, Josh?"

Josh opens his mouth to protest but thinks better of it. "I decline to answer."

Denise snorts. "Josh, I love you, but look at you and then look at Liam Quinn. Who do you think she's going to pick to have babies with?"

When Josh sneezes "Fuck you" and flips her the bird, I have to laugh. It's not that he's not attractive, because he totally is, in a hot-geek sort of way. Six foot tall, brown, wavy hair, brown eyes, handsome face. He's broad-shouldered enough to look great in clothes without needing to work out, and girls seem to find his hipster horn-rim glasses sexy. But the harsh reality is, if he and Liam were cast in a movie together, Liam would be the superhero, and Josh would be the sidekick.

"Doubt all you like," Josh says with a shrug. "But that woman is going to be all over me in a few weeks. Mark my words."

"Sure she is." I pat his shoulder and then head out into the hall-way to round up the cast from their break. When I find Liam at the water cooler, I try not to look directly into his eyes. "We're starting again, Mr. Quinn."

He mutters a quiet "Thanks, Liss," and I walk away before he can say anything else.

Once everyone's back, we continue where we left off, and apart from Angel's screeching her lines like a medieval fish merchant, we're all pleased with how things are shaping up by the time lunch rolls around.

As usual, I eat at my desk.

I have a small office down the corridor from the rehearsal room. It's not the Ritz, but it suits me fine. When I'm not rehearsing, I'm usually in here, catching up on paperwork while everyone else is relaxing.

Ah, the glamorous life of a stage manager.

I'm working on adjustments to the rehearsal schedule when Josh rushes in. His cheeks and ears are bright pink. That only happens when he's really angry or really turned on.

"Hey. What's up?"

"Nothing. I need money. Angel needs something else to eat."

We've turned our conference room into a private dining area so Angel and Liam don't have to push through the fans and paps to eat lunch. Some of New York's finest restaurants deliver their meals, but it's Josh and Denise who have the pleasure of being their waiters.

I smile. "Why are you blushing? What did Angel do?"

"Nothing. She's fine." I raise my brow at him and he shoves his hands in his pockets. "She used this sort of flirty, sexy tone to explain she's gluten-free this week, and then, at the end, she stroked my arm and smiled."

"That *bitch*."

"Don't give me shit. Seriously, I'm not in the mood. This woman could flirt me into committing murder, I have no doubt. Now, give me cash. I'll get her a different lunch." He holds out his hand.

I pull out the petty-cash tin and hand him a fifty. Surely that's enough to cover whatever Angel wants. Josh grabs a second fifty and shoves the money in his pocket. "Back soon."

Dammit, our budget is so screwed.

I put the cash tin away, and I'm about to go back to my rehearsal schedule when there's a knock on the door.

"Come in."

The door swings open to reveal Liam. Within seconds, my palms are wet.

I stand to face him. "Mr. Quinn. Do you need something? Is your lunch acceptable? If not, I'd be happy to get you something else."

He lingers in the doorway before moving into the cramped office and closing the door behind him. He looks too big for the small room. His shoulders seem broader than I remember, and traces of ink peek out from the right sleeve of his T-shirt. That's something he didn't have last time I saw him up close and shirtless.

He glances around the room before coming back to my face.

He just stares for a few seconds, and dammit, I can't believe the years haven't diminished his effect on me. Time's supposed to heal everything, right? Well, it hasn't educated my heart to stop wanting a man who doesn't want it back.

I clear my throat. "Mr. Quinn?"

He takes a step forward, and I have a moment of panic because in this enclosed space, my usual tactic to avoid and ignore is impossible.

"Elissa—"

"Mr. Quinn, if there's something you need—"

"Stop calling me that."

"It's your name, sir."

"God, Liss." He sighs and looks me up and down. "I can't believe you're here."

"It's my office. Not that hard to believe."

"I meant on the show."

"Marco asked me to run it."

"I would have thought that as soon as you heard my name, you would have run a million miles."

I don't mention I've considered it. "When I accepted the job, I didn't know you would be the star."

The muscles in his jaw tense. "Of course you didn't. That makes sense." He lets out a bitter laugh and rubs the back of his neck. "If you'd known, you wouldn't have taken it, would you?"

I try to find a nice way of saying it, but there really isn't one. "No."

He nods. I'd say he looks hurt, but why would he? He's been living the Hollywood high life without any contact from me. I doubt he's even spared me two thoughts over the past six years.

"Well, however you got here, I'm grateful." He looks down at his hands. "I've missed you. More than you know."

I almost laugh. *Of course you have. In between making megabuck movies, earning millions of dollars, and banging one of the most desired women on the planet, you've had plenty of time to pine for the short, cheese-obsessed stage manager you once had a thing for. That makes perfect sense.*

He reads something on my face and frowns. "What's that look?"

"Nothing."

"You don't believe me?"

I shrug. "I wouldn't dare question you, Mr. Quinn. That would be very unprofessional."

There's that look again. Hurt or disappointment—I can't decide which. "I guess I haven't given you much reason to have faith in what I say, have I? Just one more thing I regret about us." There's laughter out in the hallway, and he looks over his shoulder before coming back to me. "Speaking of us, does anyone here know about our . . . history?"

"No."

"Not even Josh?"

"He knows we've been . . . intimate. That's it."

"Intimate." He says it like it's funny. "Doesn't really do justice to what we had, does it?"

This conversation is veering off into uncomfortable areas. "Mr. Quinn—"

"Mr. Quinn is my father."

"Your agent requested we address both yourself and Miss Bell in a formal way."

"My agent likes to make people think we're more important than we are. That's his job. Don't listen to him about anything. Especially not about me and Angel."

God, just hearing him say that phrase ties my stomach in knots. "Me and Angel."

"Liss, about Angel—"

"If you're concerned that our past will cause you any discomfort, in either a professional or personal capacity, I'd like to assure you that I'm going to do everything in my power to make this experience as stress-free as possible. For both you and your . . . fiancée."

I nearly choke on the word. Finding out he was engaged didn't snuff out the tiny flame of hope that we'd somehow be together one day. It just stifled it, in the most painful way. "I realize this situation isn't ideal," I continue. "And if you tell me your concerns, I'll be sure to address them."

"Jesus Christ." He rakes his fingers through his hair. "Could you *please* stop talking to me like you're my bank manager? Like we don't even know each other?"

"I don't know you anymore."

"You're the *only one* who's *ever* known me. Fuck, Liss—"

"I'd rather you call me Elissa." He's the only person in the world who calls me Liss, and it feels way too intimate for our current situation.

He walks forward, and I have no room left to retreat. He stands so close, I can smell him. The entire space fills with an intense energy that makes my heart pound erratically against my rib cage.

"Elissa, I'm sorry. That day . . . the last time I saw you. I hurt you, and I hate that."

I can't cope with him being so close, but I clench my jaw and force myself to sound calmer than I feel. "There were faults on both sides. We weren't even in a relationship."

"We both know that's not true. What we shared—"

"Was a long time ago. We were young and stupid. Everything seems epic at that age, and we got carried away. I knew it at the time, and I know it now. I'm over it."

His eyes bore into me. "It?"

I straighten my spine. "You." He blinks a few times, and I ignore his conflicted expression. "Now you're engaged to one of the most beautiful women in the world, and I . . ." *Come on, Elissa, say it. Even if you don't mean it.* "I couldn't be happier for you."

If I were Pinocchio, my nose would be poking his eye out right about now. Well, okay, I'm too short for the eye, but his chest would be getting a bruising. "No matter how it happened, I'm glad you two found each other. It's obvious you love her." I risk looking at his face. "Right?"

As soon as the words leave my mouth, I regret them. Do I seriously expect him to say "no" and take me in his arms? As usual, my unrealistic romantic expectations are way off.

"Yes, I love her," he says quietly. "I'm lucky to be marrying my best friend. Not everyone gets that chance."

A knot of tension coils in my stomach. I really wasn't prepared for how much those words would hurt.

"And what about you?" he asks, his voice quiet. "Are you . . . with anyone?"

It sounds like he's asking if I have a terminal illness. I guess if stubborn singleness were a disease, I could be said to have a chronic case.

What do I tell him? That since our time together, I never go out with a man for more than a couple of weeks? In general, men disappoint me. Yet another thing for which I blame Liam Quinn.

"I've been seeing someone," I say. *Several someones, really. None worth mentioning.*

His stare is intense. Like he's trying to see straight into my soul. "Does he treat you well?"

I almost cave and tell him the truth, but my pride takes over my mouth. "Like a queen."

The tension in him gives way to something else. Relief, perhaps. "Good. You deserve happiness. You deserve . . . everything." When he looks back at me, there's such raw longing there that all the air in the room disappears, and for the first time in my life, I feel claustrophobic. I lean back against the wall, and hope he can't tell.

"Was there anything else before you go, Mr. Quinn?"

"Yes. Stop calling me Mr. Quinn. Everyone else can call me whatever the hell they like, but not you. Please, Elissa."

"Okay, Mr. Qu—" I take a breath. "Sorry. Liam."

The second I say his name, something shifts in the air. My skin prickles and his entire posture changes. In that moment, he's not a movie star, and I'm not his stage manager. We're the same two desperately connected people who fell down a rabbit hole years earlier and climbed out forever changed.

He takes a step forward, and for a moment I think he's going to touch me. But after looming over me for several long seconds, he turns on his heel, opens the door, and strides down the corridor.

When he's out of sight, I collapse into my chair and drop my head onto the desk.

So, yeah.

That went well.

THREE

PAST TENSE

If sitting on the couch eating cheese were a sport, right now I'd be the Olympic champion.

Our first day of rehearsals has left me drained. The thought of enduring another few months of controlling my reaction to Liam has led me to being pantsless in my favorite nightshirt as I inhale a wedge of Jarlsberg.

"Wine?" Josh calls from the kitchen.

"If you have to ask that question after the day we've just had, then we're no longer friends."

I look up to see him in the doorway holding a wineglass so big, it could be seen from space. I suspect it's holding an entire bottle of wine.

"I was being polite, loser. I already knew the answer." He has a six-pack of beer in his other hand. "When we've finished this lot, I vote we move on to the bourbon." He passes me my wine, and then flops next to me as he uncaps a beer. He takes a long drink before letting out the world's most resonant burp.

I groan in disgust. "You're a class act. You know that?"

He holds up a fist. "Word."

"Still pissed about your reaction to Angel?"

"I have no idea what you're talking about."

"Oh, please. You talk a good game when you're trying to get a woman into bed, but as soon as you meet someone you actually feel something for, you get all irritated. You did it last year with Lara, and you're doing it now with Angel."

He leans back and shoves his hand in the waistband of his pants. "Hold that thought while I go get some toilet paper, because what's coming out of your mouth right now is total shit."

"Okay, fine. Live in denial. But you're still going to whack off to pictures of her, right?"

He shrugs. "Probably. Mike's a total slut for leggy redheads." He picks up the remote and starts flipping through channels.

"Remind me again why you named your penis Mike?"

"I didn't. You did."

I frown. "I did not. I don't make a habit of naming penises. Especially not those belonging to my best friend."

"Wrong. You once referred to my dick as 'magic.' Hence, Magic Mike."

I laugh before taking a giant swig of wine. "God, you remember that? I was joking."

"Sure you were."

I smile as I put my feet up on his leg. He halfheartedly gives me a foot rub.

Josh and I have been living together for just over a year, and I never expected to enjoy living with a straight guy so much. After cohabitating with my brother for so long, I was relieved to get away from him. I mean, I love Ethan, but he was pretty high-maintenance. I suspect he'd be more bearable now that he's sorted out his life and gotten back together with his one true love, but still . . .

Josh and I sit on the couch and drown our sorrows for almost an hour before I excuse myself and retreat to my bedroom. My head is all over the place right now, so I figure I should just call it a day and hope tomorrow is better.

After I crawl into bed and close my eyes, thoughts of Liam push back in.

As much as I'd like to think everything that happened is now water under the bridge, it's clear from our little confrontation in my office that there are issues that still need to be sorted out between us.

Feeling nostalgic, I grab my phone and find the picture of us from the first night we met. Liam's hand is on my face, and he's kissing me so deeply, just looking at it gives me tingles. That was the first time I ever laid eyes on him. The first time I ever kissed him. The first time my inner voice ever warned me to stay away from him.

There's a light knock on the door, then Josh says, "Are you decent? Looking at porn? Waxing anything interesting?"

I smile. "None of the above, perv. Come in."

When he opens the door, he gives my room the once-over. "Dammit. Just once I'd like for some underwear to be lying around. Especially those little red ones with the bows on the back."

"Josh, how many times have I asked you to stay out of my underwear drawer?"

"Twenty-three times and counting."

"Well, this makes twenty-four."

"Noted, and ignored."

"Good, then."

He shoos me with his hand. "Make room, woman." When I move to the far side of the bed, he climbs under the covers next to me.

I quickly shut off my phone before he can see the photo.

"So," he says as he turns on his side and props up his head with his hand. "What's up?"

"Nothing. Why?"

"Well, you just watched most of an episode of *Dance Moms* without hurling abuse at the television. That's never happened before."

"I'm just tired, I guess."

"Uh-huh. And perhaps you're preoccupied because of a certain ex-flame."

I pick imaginary fluff off the sheet. "Nah."

"Yeah." He grabs my chin and makes me look at him. "Are you ever going to tell me what went down between you and Quinn? I got the impression you guys were just about the hot animal sex, but you really liked him, didn't you?"

"I didn't want to."

"But you did."

I shrug.

"Lissa, talk to me. You've been keeping your feelings for Quinn on the down-low for years? What the hell?"

I rub my eyes. This is one subject I don't feel comfortable discussing. What I shared with Liam feels like a precious secret, and if I talk about it, the things I remember as bright and shiny will tarnish.

Josh lies on his back and closes his eyes. "Have it your way. I'm just going to rest here for a while. If you want to tell me a story of love and loss, that's cool. If you don't, no problem. I'll just have extra time to refold everything in your underwear drawer."

I smile and push him so hard, he almost falls out of bed.

"Fine," I say as he chuckles and makes himself comfortable again. "Once upon a time on a Friday night, me and my pushy best friend had a date in Times Square."

Six Years Earlier
Times Square
New York City

"Hey, beautiful lady. Where you headed?"

A random drunk dude steps in front of me, and I hit him with a withering gaze. "I'm meeting my karate-expert boyfriend, so step aside or risk him splintering you like a kickboard."

"Oh, sure. You just saying that to get rid of me? Or do you really got a boyfriend?"

I roll my eyes. "Look at me. I'm fine as hell. Of course I have a boyfriend. He's right over there."

I step around him, but I can feel him watching me as I climb the giant red staircase to where Josh is waiting.

"Hi, sweetheart," he says before bending down and planting a soft kiss on my lips. "Can't wait to take you home so we can have all the sex." He says it loud enough for Random Drunk Guy to hear.

"Me, too," I say, just as loudly. "The sex with you is my favorite. Your penis is like magic. And afterward, you can practice your lethal karate moves on people who hit on me."

Random Drunk Guy scowls and turns away, and I sit down and sigh. It's ridiculous how often we have to do that.

"The magic-penis line is new," Josh says as he casually drapes his arm around my shoulders. "I like it. It's good for my ego."

"I'm glad. But you know if you ever say something about my vagina, I'm going to hurt you, right?"

"Yep. I haven't forgotten last time. Neither have my balls."

I smile and lean my head on his shoulder.

Having a boy for a best friend can be both a blessing and a curse. On the one hand, I always have a way to duck unwanted male attention when needed, but on the other hand, guys I *want* to notice me see Josh and assume I'm attached, so they steer clear. It can be frustrating.

I haven't dated anyone seriously since high school, and even though I'm mostly happy about that because men are a distraction I don't need right now, sometimes I have a twinge of longing. A wistful desire for something more.

At least I have Josh. Tonight we're doing one of our fave activities, which is sitting in the middle of Times Square and playing "Fuck, Marry, Kill" with people who pass by.

"Okay, let's do this," Josh says as he points to people loitering in front of us. "Cowboy hat, skinny jeans, and chubby suit."

"Hmmm. Tough one. They're all pretty bad."

"I'm sorry, ma'am, but I'm going to need a decision."

"Fine. Kill Skinny Jeans because then he can't raise sons who will follow in his ridiculous hipster ways, marry Chubby Suit because it's obvious the man has a job and can pay for my cheese addiction, and fuck Mr. Cowboy Hat because he looks like he'd know his way around a filly, if you know what I mean."

Josh frowns. "You'd fuck him because he can walk around a horse? I don't understand."

I elbow him. "Stop it. You know Mr. Literal is my least favorite of your personalities."

"Wow, tough crowd. Okay, your turn."

"Pink faux fur," I say, and point to a girl with three-inch heels and six-inch hair.

Josh screws up his face. "Oh, Jesus. No. Kill."

I point to a girl who I'm guessing has spent the equivalent of a year's worth of wages on plastic surgery. "Fake-boob bobblehead."

Josh tilts his head, and shrugs. "Fuck, but with the lights out."

A girl in fishnets and a bowler hat walks by, handing out flyers to the people in the TKTS line scrambling to get last-minute seats for tonight's shows.

"Liza Minnelli wannabe."

Josh gets a look in his eye I know only too well. Theater girls give him a major boner.

"Marry," he says, and his voice cracks a little. "God, look at her. 'Come to Papa, baby.' She could keep that whole outfit on in the bedroom."

"Nuh-uh. If you marry her, you don't get to bang her."

He turns to me, his brows furrowed. "What? Since when don't married people get to have sexual relations?"

"Uh, since this game was invented."

"Bullshit."

"Josh, how do you not know how this works? You get to fuck some-one once, marry them forever *but* no sex, or kill them dead."

"No way! It's always been fuck them once, marry them so you can fuck them forever, or kill them after you've fucked them because the sex would be horrible."

"Are you kidding me? Out of all the times you've been wrong since I've known you, this is the wrongest."

He scowls. " 'Wrongest' isn't even a word."

"I know, but I had to make something up to fully express how wrong you are right now."

I feel warmth at my back right before a deep voice says, "Your girl-friend's right, man. You've been playing it wrong. You don't get to have sex when you're married. Everyone knows that."

I turn around, and leaning forward from his position on the step behind us is the most attractive man I've ever seen.

Oh, wow.

It's like there was a lottery somewhere on facial perfection, and this guy won the jackpot. Sandy-brown hair, thick and wavy, unbeliev-able blue-green eyes, full lips curled into a wry smile.

Congratulations on your face, sir.

I glance at the thick biceps peeking out of his T-shirt.

And your body. Congrats on it all.

He would be *Fuck*. Most definitely.

Josh must notice my reaction because he quickly says, "Oh, she's not my girlfriend. I mean, we used to date but I couldn't keep up with her in the sack. She was insatiable. All day, every day. I never knew one woman was capable of taking that much dick—"

I squeeze Josh's thigh until he squirms. "Please excuse my friend. He knows I'm going to kill him now, and fear of the afterlife makes him babble."

Mr. Fuck gives me a smile. Well, he gives it to both of us, but I'm claiming it because his gaze lingers on me longer. I'm fairly certain he checks out my boobs. It gives me tingles. I haven't had tingles this powerful for . . . well, ever.

The hottie must approve of what he sees, because his tone is undeniably flirty. "So if your friend is the one getting killed, who are you going to fuck and who are you going to marry?" The way he says it leaves no doubt in my mind which he'd rather be.

He holds his hand out to me. "I'm Liam, by the way. Liam Quinn."

I take his hand and try to keep my expression passive as the feel of his skin lights me up more than all the giant billboards around us. "I'm Elissa. Holt."

"Very nice to meet you, Elissa." He unashamedly stares as he continues to hold my hand.

Oh, he's good. No doubt he uses this technique all the time to turn girls into piles of goo. I'm a little irritated it works on me. I thought I was immune to this type of smug self-awareness.

Liam. Even his name is sexy.

Josh clears his throat. "Okay, so you guys have been shaking hands for a creepy amount of time, and now I'm super-uncomfortable. I'm Josh, by the way. In case you care."

Liam laughs and shakes his hand. "Nice to meet you too, Josh."

Josh gives him a skeptical nod. "Sure it is. Elissa, should we invite our new friend to have dinner with us?"

That snaps me out of my tunnel vision. It's one thing for me to lust after a handsome stranger. It's another to do anything about it.

"Uh . . . I'm sure Liam has better things to do."

Liam shrugs. "Not really. I'm seeing *King Lear* at eight, but considering I've been stood up, I'm at a loose end 'til then."

Josh's scoffs. "*You've* been stood up?"

"Well, 'dumped' would be a more accurate description. By the girl I've been with for a year."

"What the hell?" Josh seems more upset about it than Liam does. "But you look like one of those male-model dudes in the fancy magazines. Fussy woman, was she, your ex?"

Liam shrugs. "She liked me, but hated my bank balance. She's now dating some rich douche from Wall Street."

"Fast rebound."

Liam gives a bitter smile. "Yeah. Not so much a rebound as an overlap, but whatever."

There's a moment of uncomfortable silence before Josh says, "You know, Elissa was dumped as well. What a coincidence, right? Two single, attractive dumpees like yourselves having this random meeting. It's like fate."

Liam gives Josh a smile, then looks at me. "I totally believe in fate."

I look down at my hands. Fate or not, I don't know that I'm ready for the emotions this man is bringing out in me.

Over the past four years, I've had three boyfriends, and all three have thrown me over for other women. To say my confidence with men has taken a hit would be an understatement.

When my last relationship ended in a blaze of abject humiliation, I decided I was done with men, at least for the foreseeable future. I have a very specific five-year plan, and getting destroyed again isn't part of it. Josh keeps hassling me to jump back into the dating pool with both feet, but I'm content to wade in the shallow end. It may be frustrating to never take the plunge, but there's zero chance of drowning.

"So, does the invitation for dinner still stand?" Liam asks as he hits me with those stunning eyes again. "Because I'm starved."

Me, too. I just didn't realize how much before I saw him.

Never one to let an opportunity pass, Josh answers for me. "Absolutely, Liam. Elissa would love for you to come." He smiles over his double entendre.

I grab his sleeve. "Uh, Joshua? May I speak to you for a moment please? Excuse us, Liam."

I pull him down to the bottom of the stairs. "What are you doing?"

"Getting you a date."

"I don't want a date."

"Yes you do. You just won't admit it. I love you, but I've been the only man you've seen naked in months, and that's only because I accidentally sent you dick pics intended for someone else."

How do I tell him that all my alarm bells are going off about Liam? That some part of me thinks he's more than just hot, and therefore, dangerous? I can't even figure out how I'm feeling, let alone find a way to articulate it.

Josh is looking at me with concern. "Hey, I was just following your lead. When your jaw hits the floor over a guy, I play wingman. Is that not what's happening here?"

I run my fingers through my hair. "You're the best, Josh, really. Dick pics aside. I'm just not sure I'm up to this tonight."

Josh glances over at Liam. "Well, let's at least have dinner. Then he'll go to his show and you'll go home, and if you want to jump him in the future, you can give him your number. All good?"

I nod. I guess there's no harm in that.

As we head back over to the stairs, Liam and Josh start up an easy conversation about sports. They look like they've known each other for years.

In some ways, I think that's what's throwing me about Liam. We've just met, but some part of me feels like I've always known him. And that part is freaking the hell out.

Ten minutes later, we're sitting in Gino's on 42nd street, debating which pizza to get.

Liam frowns at the menu. "Uh . . . you guys choose. I'm not fussy. I'll eat anything."

"That's good," says Josh. "Because Elissa is so damn fussy, she'll only be truly happy if they let her in the kitchen to make her own."

I keep my focus down on the menu. "Just because I like things a certain way doesn't mean I'm fussy, Joshua Kane."

"Actually," Josh says. "Liking things a certain way is the definition of fussy. But let's be honest. You take fussy to a whole new level with your food ratios."

"Ratios?" Liam asks, and nudges my foot under the table. "I'm intrigued. Tell me more."

I shake my head. "Nope."

"Aw, come on."

Josh chuckles. "I think she's concerned that if we tell you about her obsession with food proportions, you'll run a mile."

My face heats. *Yes, he probably would.*

"Not likely. I'm too hungry to run anywhere." Liam tries to catch my eye. When I look up at him, he smiles. "Please. I want to know."

I sigh and put my menu down. "When I eat, I like the ratios of all the ingredients to be equal. So, if there are four things on the plate, say, meat and three veggies, I need a little bit of each of them in every mouthful."

"She calls it 'The Theory of Yummability,'" Josh says. "It's fascinating to watch. She carves everything up with surgical precision, then loads the tiny pieces onto her fork. It would be artistic if it wasn't so fucking weird."

Liam shrugs. "I don't find it weird. I think it's cool. I have a similar thing with chips and dips. I need to have exactly the right ratio of dip on the chip, otherwise you can't taste them equally."

"Yes!" I say, and sit forward. "That's my point. It's all about subtle combinations. Why put something in your mouth unless you're really going to enjoy it, right?"

The way Liam's eyes widen makes me realize that statement could be taken a whole other way.

He gives me a slow smile. "I totally agree."

I take a sip of water to cover my sudden blush, and thankfully, Josh swoops in to change the subject.

"So Liam, the question we really need you to answer right now is this: Are you legal?"

Liam moves his attention to Josh. "As in . . . ?"

"Over twenty-one?"

"Uh . . . yeah. Why?"

"Because I need you to order us some beer while I drain the lizard. Pretty sure we all need a drink." He mutters under his breath, "Before we all choke on the sexual tension."

As Josh gets up and heads to the back of the restaurant, Liam looks over at me with concern. "Wait a minute. You guys can't buy beer?"

"In two years we can," I say.

"Two years?!" A nearby couple turns to look at him, and he leans in and whispers, "You're only nineteen?"

"Yes."

He rubs his face. "Oh, God. I'm bad. I'm a bad, bad man."

"Why?"

"I thought you were older."

"How much older?"

"An age that doesn't have 'teen' at the end of it, that's for damn sure. When I saw you tonight, I thought you were . . ." He looks me up and down, and the heat of his gaze makes me fan myself with the menu. "Well, you seemed way more mature than nineteen."

"For your information," I say with an edge of petulance that ironically makes me seem much younger, "I've always been mature for my age. How old are you, then, Father Time?"

He leans back in his chair, and I don't miss the way his T-shirt strains across his impressive chest. "I'm a bona fide adult, kid. Twenty-two. And three quarters."

I feign horror. "Ew, gross! You seemed way younger. I can't believe I've been having impure thoughts about a crusty old man."

He smiles. "Are just saying that to show me how stupid I'm being about our age gap? Or have you actually been fantasizing about me?" He leans forward. "Because I'm really hoping it's the second thing."

I look down at my water glass and smile. "I have a feeling fantasizing about you would lead to nothing good."

"Really?" he asks. I can feel him staring at me. "Because I've never had a single complaint. Well, apart from that one time with my ex-girlfriend, but it was an isolated incident and I'd had way too much to drink."

I laugh and look up at him. He joins in with a low chuckle.

Great. His laugh is just as sexy as the rest of him. Not cool.

We're still smiling at each other when the waitress arrives to take our drink order.

"Three beers," Liam says as he looks at me. "Wait, scrap that. Two beers and a Coke. I need to make sure I'm in top form tonight." When he looks into my eyes, I have that twinge of frustration again that his cockiness actually turns me on.

As the waitress leaves, I take a sip of water and study him. He meets my scrutiny without embarrassment. "You're confident you're going to get lucky tonight, aren't you?"

He shrugs. "I figure you wouldn't have asked me out to dinner if you weren't interested."

"Josh was the one who invited you, and I hate to break it to you, but he's straight."

"Uh-huh, but it was clear he was playing wingman. I saw how you looked at me. I liked it."

I lean back and cock my head. "Haven't you just broken up with someone?"

"Yes. Which is why you should take me to bed and nurse my shattered ego."

That makes me laugh. "I have a feeling your ego is just fine."

"Maybe. But a little extra stroking never hurts."

A shiver of anticipation runs through me. Okay, this isn't good. As a rule, I never sleep with guys on a first date, but Liam is quickly chipping away at my resolve. The trouble is, I have no doubt that having sex with him would lead to a whole mess of emotional stuff I'm not prepared to deal with right now.

When I glance over at him, he's staring at me with a deep frown. I can't figure out if he's concerned or confused.

"You okay?" I ask.

He shakes his head. "Not sure. I have this overwhelming urge to spend more time with you tonight, but I don't want to come across as needy or desperate."

"Hmmm. Dilemma. What are you going to do?"

He reaches into his pocket. "Invite you to come to *King Lear* with me? Thanks to my ex, who'd prefer to bang a guy in a thousand-dollar suit than attend the theater, I have an extra ticket. It'd be a shame for it to go to waste."

He puts the tickets on the table and I study them. "Oh, wow. The Lowbridge Shakespeare Company? My mom has taken my brother and me to their productions since we were kids. I think that's why Ethan and I both chose the careers we did."

"Oh? You guys work in theater?"

"Yeah. We've both applied to The Grove in Westchester."

Liam looks impressed. "Wow. Good school. So you're an actress? I should have known. A woman as gorgeous as you, it makes sense you'd be on the stage."

With talk like that, my blush isn't disappearing anytime soon. "Actually, I prefer backstage. I'm a stage manager."

Liam's expression intensifies. "Okay. Not sure why I find that so much sexier than being an actress, but I do. Weird."

This boy has a silver tongue, that's for sure. I wonder what it would taste like.

"What about you?" I ask. "You're not an actor, are you?"

Liam smiles. "Wow. Don't like actors, huh?"

"Why do you say that?"

"Because it looks like you might laser me to death with your eye-balls if I say yes. Care to explain?"

"Not really. It's a long story." My aversion to actors is strong, but I didn't realize I was so transparent. "I just don't date actors, that's all."

He looks at me for a few seconds, then says, "Well, this isn't strictly a date, is it? So it doesn't matter what I am. However, if you come to the theater with me . . . well, that's a whole other story."

I look down at the tickets. They're fantastic seats, and I really do want to see this production.

Liam notices my hesitation. "To steal a phrase from Josh, I'd love for you to come." He gives me another one of those looks that makes me melt. "Take that any way you like, as long as you say yes."

The sexual innuendo is much more effective coming from him. "Okay. Can I at least give you some money? They're expensive seats."

"No way," he says. "But you can pay for the pizza. Deal?"

"You pay hundreds of dollars for tickets, and I pay twenty bucks for pizza? Hardly seems fair."

"Three hundred dollars for the pleasure of your company, beautiful Elissa? Seems like a bargain, if you ask me."

Jesus. His smoothness is killing me.

As a rule, smugness turns me off, but not tonight. There's a sincerity to his flirting that presses all my buttons.

An hour later, when we all exit the restaurant, laughing like fools, I'm even more conflicted. I never thought I'd meet someone who could match the special dynamic Josh and I share, but Liam does. Easily.

"Okay, guys," Josh says as he glances down the street. "I have a hot date with the girl who's playing Elphaba in *Wicked,* and if I'm lucky, I'll have green face paint in strange and unusual places before midnight." Liam holds out his hand, and Josh shakes it. "Nice to meet you, Liam. Hope we'll be seeing you again. Please keep in mind that, even though you could crush my head with your bare hands, I'm going to have to ask you to treat Elissa with respect, or face the consequences."

"What consequences?"

"Me running into your fist with my head, multiple times. But, be warned. I have a thick skull. Your knuckles will never be the same."

Liam gives him a smile. "Noted. I promise to behave."

"Elissa, I'll call you tomorrow." Josh hugs me and whispers in my ear, "Be good. And if you can't be good, be safe. I snuck a condom into your bag in case you decide to break your golden rule. Don't be afraid to use it."

I squeeze him. "You're the best. And the worst."

After kissing me on the cheek, Josh disappears into the evening crowd, and just like that, my security blanket is gone. Being alone with Liam ramps up the tension between us even more.

We stare at each other for a few seconds before Liam clears his throat. "So, I hear King Lear's a bit of an asshole. We probably shouldn't keep him waiting." He offers me his arm. "Shall we?"

It's so old-fashioned and gallant, I laugh. "I guess we shall." As soon as I link my hand into the crook of his elbow, he sucks in a quick breath. "Are you okay?"

He looks down at my hand on his arm and gives a tight nod. "Yep. Just concerned I may have lied to Josh when I said I'd behave."

We head toward the theater, and I'm acutely aware of how soft his skin is beneath my fingers. "Would it help if I told you I don't sleep with guys I just met?"

"Not really. I don't usually sleep with girls I've just met, either, but you're making me want to murder that rule and melt its body with acid."

I laugh. "Well, we have three hours of Shakespeare about a mad, violent, misogynistic monarch ahead of us. I'm sure by the time we're done, sex will be the last thing on our minds."

He gives me a skeptical shrug. "If you say so."

When we walk out of the theater three hours later, it's clear Liam's skepticism was well-founded. My entire body is buzzing with energy. Not only was the production incredible, but sitting next to him in a darkened theater for all that time was like low-voltage electrocution.

I've never had such a powerful reaction to a man before.

"So," he says. "That was amazing."

"It really was. Thanks for the ticket."

"Thanks for the company."

I hear us making lame small talk, but there's nothing lame about what's passing between us. I've got so much adrenaline going on, I feel like I could Hulk-jump into traffic and flip over a cab.

Liam looks around and bounces on his toes. "I don't know about you, but I'm too buzzed to go home yet."

"Same."

"I was hoping you'd say that. Come on."

As we push through the after-show crowds and head back toward Times Square, Liam puts his hand in the middle of my back so we don't lose each other. It adds another layer of tension to my already overworked adrenal glands.

At this time of night, the atmosphere in the Broadway area is electric. There are thousands of people pouring out of all the theaters, giddy and high in the way only live theater can make someone. Liam and I dodge and weave, but I have no clue where we're going. After a while he gives up trying to steer me from the rear and grabs my hand so he can lead me instead. His fingers are warm and rough, and the shape of them feels so familiar it's bizarre.

"Where are we going?" I ask.

He looks back at me and smiles. "Does it matter?"

I know I should be cautious because I know so little about him, but for some reason, I feel safe. Everything about him is brand-new and familiar at the same time. Like there's been a tune playing in my head for my whole life, and he's finally given it words.

After we pass through the mayhem of the main square, we travel a few blocks down and head toward the river. At last, he stops at a doorway shoehorned between a thrift shop and a dry cleaner.

"This is my building," he says, and brushes his thumb against the back of my hand. "My apartment's old and cramped, but . . . do you want to come up?"

I look at the grimy door. "Do I have to?"

He chuckles. "Of course not. I just . . ." He takes a step forward, and my breath catches. "I don't want to say good night yet. I don't have any alcohol, but I have milk and cookies. And if you play your cards right, I'll show you my roof garden."

"Is that a euphemism?" I'm surprised at how husky my voice sounds.

The way Liam's gaze falls to my mouth, I think he likes it. He leans forward, and I press my back into the door. "It's whatever you say it is." His voice sends shivers across my skin.

"Even if I come upstairs with you, my statement about not having sex tonight stands."

The edges of his mouth twitch, but he doesn't smile. "Okay."

I put my hand on his chest. "I'm serious."

He looks down at my hand, then covers it with his own and presses my palm into his pec. My breathing speeds up. So does his.

"I'm not taking you upstairs to seduce you, Elissa," he says as he lightly strokes my fingers. "Even though I'm pretty sure I could."

"Wow. So arrogant." He gives me a lusty smile, and I narrow my eyes. "You don't think I can resist you?"

He puts his hand on the wall next to my head and moves closer. I put my other hand on his chest. Not to stop him. Just to feel more of his body.

He closes his eyes and exhales before looking at me again. "If you're feeling even half of the attraction I'm feeling toward you, then, no, I don't think you could resist. In fact, I think if I kissed you right now, we'd barely make it through that door before tearing each other's clothes off and fucking like there's no tomorrow. But I promise, if you come upstairs, I'll behave. Maybe you should vow to do the same. The way you're touching me? It makes me think you want to ride me hard and put me away cold. May I remind you that I'm a man, Elissa. Not a sexual plaything."

My lungs tighten as I stare at his mouth. Damn him to hell for conjuring up an image of me riding him.

"Point taken." I reluctantly remove my hands. I'm trying to keep my cool, but his nearness has set my heart to hammering in my chest. "Liam, I swear on the life of my hamster not to use you as a sexual plaything."

He looks crestfallen. "Not even if I beg?"

I smile. "Not even then."

"Just so we're clear," he says as he leans down to whisper in my ear. "If you ever beg to be *my* sexual plaything, I'll make it happen in record time. More than once, if necessary."

"So selfless."

"I really am." He gives me a sexy smile before stepping back to open the door. I follow him inside, and we climb five flights of stairs to get to his apartment. By the time we get there, my desire for him has been joined by a burning in my lungs.

"You okay?" he asks, and gently touches my shoulder.

"Yep. Just trying to disguise my extreme fitness so I don't intimidate you."

"Great job. You have me completely fooled."

"Right? Maybe I should have been an actress after all." I take a deep breath and let it out. Goddamn, I'm unfit.

When we make it inside, I realize how much he wasn't kidding about the size of his apartment. It's a studio with a tiny kitchenette on one side and what seems to be an equally tiny bathroom on the other. In the middle is a space just big enough for a sofa bed.

"So," Liam says, "let me give you the tour." He doesn't move. "Aaaand we're done."

I can tell he's embarrassed, but he needn't be. In New York, there are heaps of micro-apartments just like this. In fact, I've seen worse.

What sets this one apart is that it's spotless. The furniture and appliances are dated, but they're all immaculate. There's not a single thing out of place. The bed is even made.

I narrow my eyes at him. "Were you expecting to bring someone back here tonight?"

"No. Why?"

"It's super-clean. And your bed's made. I have it on good authority from my brother that most men are missing the bed-making gene."

He leans into me, and I feel his warm breath on my ear. "You don't know me well enough yet to have realized I'm not most men. But if it makes you more comfortable, we could unmake the bed. Just say the word."

A shudder of pleasure runs up my spine. "Oh, I wouldn't dream of destroying such perfection. Are those hospital corners?"

"If you find that sexy, then yes."

I let out a soft groan. "Such a turn-on." He chuckles, thinking I'm teasing, but I'm really not. I'm a self-confessed neat freak, and knowing he keeps a tidy house makes me all kinds of hot.

"Well, if you're finished eye-fucking my bed," he says, "I have something else to show you."

"If it's a recently cleaned bathroom, I don't think my body's ready."

He clucks his tongue. "Dammit. I knew I should have scrubbed the tub this morning." He squeezes past me and heads into the kitchen. Within a few seconds, he's grabbed a bag of chocolate chip cookies, two glasses, and a half-empty gallon of milk from the fridge. "Come on. If the apartment gets you hot, then you're going to go nuts over the roof garden."

He leads me out of the apartment and up two more flights of stairs. Goddammit. No wonder he's so ripped. If I had to climb all these stairs every day, I'd be able to bounce the Federal Reserve's entire stash of quarters off my butt.

At the top of the stairs, he flips a switch before opening the door to the roof. When I step out, what I see almost takes my breath away.

It's like a tropical oasis up here. There are dozens of potted palms of various sizes, and in the middle of them is an intricate wooden pergola wrapped in hundreds of tiny lights.

"Wow. That's, just . . . wow." I'm rarely lost for words, but now is one of those times.

"I built the pergola for Mom and Dad's anniversary last year. They just sold their house to move into an apartment, and had nowhere to put it, so they brought it here."

"It's beautiful." The dark wood has been painstakingly carved with vines and flowers. "I bet they loved it."

"Yeah, Mom cried. Dad patted me on the shoulder and went quiet for a while, which is his equivalent of crying."

I smile. "That's a pretty incredible present to give them. Trying to win the award for world's best son?"

He looks down, and I don't miss the subtle change in his posture. "Well, they've had a tough time over the past couple of years. I wanted to do something nice."

I see names carved into the wood at the top of the pergola. "Angus and Eileen. Good Irish names."

"Yeah."

I see another name and squint so I can make it out. "Does that say . . . James?"

Liam blinks a few times. "Yeah. My twin brother."

I just about choke on my tongue. "Twin? As in identical twin?"

Lord, I don't know if I can cope with two men this perfect existing in this world.

Liam takes in a deep breath. "Yeah. We were identical."

"Were?"

"He was . . . he's . . ." He looks at the ground. "He died."

"Oh. Liam . . ."

"Two years ago."

My heart breaks for him. Losing a brother would be bad enough, but I've heard twins share an especially powerful bond. "God, I'm so sorry."

They way he shrugs and waves his hand tells me he doesn't want to talk about it. Before I can say anything else, he urges me forward. "Come on. I didn't bring you up here to watch me wallow. I can do that by myself."

Beneath the pergola are a couple of old couches and a coffee table. We each take a couch, and he lays out our supplies before filling the glasses.

He still seems tense, so I try and lighten the mood. "I love milk, but a beer would have been better."

"Not happening," he says, as his mouth presses into a determined line. "You're underage, young lady, and I refuse to further contribute to the corruption of a minor. Now, drink your milk like a good girl." He gives me a half-smile.

"Yes, Granddad."

We're both quiet for a few moments as we munch on our cookies. When we're done, he stands and gestures for me to follow. "Come on. I haven't shown you the best part." He leads me to the edge of the building and climbs up on the ledge.

"Is that safe?" I ask, trying to peer over. It's at times like this I hate being a short-ass.

He offers me his hand. "Trust me."

Strangely, I do, and when I put my hand in his, he pulls me up with so little effort, it's surreal. For a moment I panic and grip his arms, but then I see that the ledge isn't as narrow as it first seems. Also, there's a fire escape right below us.

"Okay?" he asks, his hands firm on my waist.

"Uh-huh."

"Then look up. The fire escape is cool and everything, but it's not what I wanted you to see."

When I raise my eyes, I see what he means. Across the street is a shiny new apartment complex. The entire lobby is covered in reflective glass, and through some miracle of technology, I can see the visual cacophony that is Times Square blinking up at us.

My mouth drops open. "What am I looking at?"

"Rear projection," Liam says. "Incredible, right? Whoever designed the building realized that one of the huge draws of living in this area is the excitement of Times Square, so they incorporated it into the building's design. It's a live feed of what's happening six blocks away."

I'm floored at how spectacular the projection is. "Have you figured out where the camera is yet?"

"No, but I look for it every now and then. From the angle, I figure it's on a light pole. Look, you can see the stairs where we met tonight."

He's right. The staircase is now teeming with people.

There's an old adage that says no matter where you come from, if you stand in the middle of Times Square for fifteen minutes, you'll see someone you know. I don't know if it's true, but I should try it one day. There's nowhere on the planet quite like Times Square. The ambience, the energy, the connection to all things Broadway. I feel like it's a part of me.

"I could watch this all night."

"Then my evil plan to spend more time with you has succeeded. Excellent." Liam sits on the ledge and urges me to follow. When we're settled, our legs dangle over the edge and our thighs press against each other. It almost distracts me from the view.

Liam leans back on his hands. "This is why I spend so much time on the roof. I can sit up here and people-watch without having to leave my building. Cool, right?"

"Very cool."

I envy Liam for living here, practically in the midst of it all. My parents' brownstone up on Sixty-fourth Street suddenly seems light-years away. And boring as hell.

As if sensing what I'm thinking, Liam asks, "So where do you hail from, Elissa? Manhattan?"

"Yep. Upper East Side. Still living with my parents."

"Of course you are. You're a child." I poke him with my elbow, and he laughs.

"If I get into The Grove, I'll have to move to Westchester. Not gonna lie: I'm looking forward to getting out on my own. Well, I'd have to live with my big brother, but still . . ."

He's silent for a moment, then says, "Westchester, huh? I guess it's not that far away." He says it so quietly, I don't know if he's talking to himself or me. "So your parents are still married?"

"Uh-huh."

"Mine, too. What are the odds? Out of everyone I know, I'm the only person whose parents aren't divorced. Not only that, but my folks are still so in love, it's embarrassing. Gives me hope that true love still exists, you know?"

"That's a romantic sentiment from a man who's just had his heart broken."

He lets out a short laugh. "I'm hardly heartbroken. Don't get me wrong, I liked Leanne, but I didn't love her."

"But, weren't you with her for a year?"

"I was."

"And yet, you didn't love her?"

He shrugs. "We got along well. The sex was fine. That was enough for me." He turns to me, and the lights from the projection across the street sparkle in his eyes. "I figure that when my true love comes along, I'll know. I mean, look at my mom and dad. They met on the subway forty-five years ago. Even though it was love at first sight for both of them, they went their separate ways at the end of the line and didn't see each other again for *six* years. Then, they literally ran into each other in the middle of Central Park. Out of all the people in New York, they ended up finding each other. If that's not fate, I don't know what is."

"Yes, but you said it yourself: Your parents are the exception. It doesn't happen like that for most people."

"Oh, I don't know," he says as he gazes at me. "Look at what happened tonight. Out of all the women in New York, I found you."

I give him a skeptical brow. "Why do I get the feeling I'm not the first woman you've flirted with on those steps?"

"Wrong," he says. "Never done it before. Still not sure why I did it tonight." There's mischief in his eyes, so I have no idea if he's telling the truth or not.

"I see," I say. "So you're saying you fell in love with me at first sight?"

He leans forward. "Maybe. Meet me in the middle of Central Park in six years, and I'll let you know for sure."

We stare at each other for long seconds, and the urge to kiss him is crazy strong.

"You have the most beautiful lips I've ever seen," he whispers. My lips tingle just from his words. I put my hand over them to make them stop. That makes him smile. "And I find it sexy as hell that every time I've said something nice to you tonight, your cheeks have turned bright pink. It makes me wonder why you're so embarrassed to receive compliments. I'm sure men tell you how gorgeous you are all the time."

I press my hand to my rapidly heating face. I'd be lying if I denied receiving compliments regularly, and usually I'm confident enough to take them graciously. But Liam has the power to turn me into a blushing freak, and I find that very uncool.

"Can we please change the subject?" I say. "Blushing isn't my favorite thing to do, and if you keep talking about my lips, it's going to keep happening."

"Fine by me." When I glare at him, he chuckles. "Okay, then, let's talk about why you don't believe in fate. Or love at first sight. Or any of that romantic stuff most girls subscribe to. What's the story?" Subject change or not, he's still staring at my mouth.

"No story. Statistics tell us that true love is a myth, and I haven't seen anything to prove otherwise."

He brings his gaze up to mine, and I can't believe how beautiful his eyes are. Green-blue with a dark navy ring around the outside. I've never seen anything like them.

"Sounds reasonable, but I'm sensing there's more to it. So, you can either level with me voluntarily, or I'll be forced to get the information through less-than-gentlemanly means, and trust me when I say I would *really* enjoy that."

Okay, now he's just flat-out trying to destroy my composure, and I'm horrified it's working.

"It's really not that interesting," I say, looking down at my hands. "Let's just say that if I had a business card, it would read *'Elissa Holt, Preparer of Men for Other Women.'*"

"What does that mean?"

"It means I've had a handful of boyfriends, and they've all dumped me to be with someone else. Every one. It's possible I'm cursed."

I look up to see him watching me thoughtfully. "I see. And where did you meet these mentally incompetent jackasses?"

"In drama club," I say with a laugh. "They were all actors, and they all left me for their leading ladies."

"Ahh, that explains your earlier reaction. So now you think all actors are bastards?"

A ghost of past heartache twinges in my chest. "No. Just the ones I fall in love with. So now, I have a no-actor rule. It's working out great so far."

He's silent for a moment, and then says, "Okay—I get it," before turning to stare across the street.

We're silent for a while, and when his shoulder brushes against mine, I close my eyes and sigh.

Okay, great. He's gorgeous, arrogant, and spends hundreds of dollars on Shakespeare tickets—of course he's an actor. And I've just shut down the possibility of anything happening between us.

I shake my head in frustration over yet again being drawn to exactly the type of man I'm trying to avoid.

Why couldn't he be a policeman? Or a construction worker? Or a cowboy?

Wait, did I just wish for him to be a member of the Village People?

Liam's shoulder brushes mine again. It makes me tingle, and I suspect he's doing it on purpose. I really need to get out of here, because the longer I stay, the more tempted I am to say "screw it" to my sense of self-preservation and just give in to the dozens of horny fantasies currently running through my mind.

Before I can move, he says, "You're leaving, aren't you?"

I turn to him. "How did you know?"

"You've been tensing up for the past few minutes. I figured you were either going to bail or rip off my shirt. Considering my shirt is sadly still in one piece, I guess leaving won out."

I give him a smile, grateful he's not making this harder than it needs to be. "Very perceptive. I have a big day tomorrow. I really should get home and go to bed."

He leans forward a little, and dammit, he's looking at my lips again. "I have a bed downstairs. It would be much faster to go there."

I concentrate on keeping my breathing even as he continues inching toward me. "Yes, but I need to get some rest, and I have a feeling if we go to your bed, there'd be none of that."

He's so close now, he has to turn his head so our noses don't bump. "No. There really wouldn't."

God, he smells good. And I have zero doubt he'd taste good. But more than anything, I know for damn sure he'd feel so good, one kiss would be all it would take for him to have me completely under his spell. Considering I don't have the time or inclination to be in the thrall of a devastatingly attractive actor right now, I lean away from him and order my disgruntled body to stand down.

"And that's why I need to leave," I say, trying to convince myself as well as him. "Plus, you lied when you said you wouldn't try to seduce me."

He frowns. "Is that what was happening? Because I swear it was the other way around."

"All I did was look at you."

"Exactly."

With a resigned sigh, he jumps down from the ledge and holds his arms up for me. I put my hands on his shoulders, then he grips my waist as he slowly lowers me down.

Lord, he's strong. He holds me like I weigh nothing, and though I'm short, I'm also curvy. It's not like I'm a featherweight.

When I'm on my feet, he doesn't let go of my waist; in fact, his fingers tighten and release in an uneven rhythm. And I don't let go of his shoulders. They're beautiful. Hard and round. More muscular than those of any other man I've ever been with.

"There's still time for the shirt-ripping option," Liam says quietly as he stares down at me. "I promise I won't judge you."

I have a moment of weakness and graze my fingers down his arms, over his triceps, elbows, and forearms. His skin is so hot and smooth, I'm tempted to find out what his stomach feels like under his T-shirt. But if I head in that direction, there's no way I'm getting out of here tonight.

As it is, I'm so aroused I'm nearly panting. "Maybe next time."

He clenches his jaw, and I notice that his breathing is a little faster than it was a few minutes ago. "I'll keep you to that."

Our trek downstairs is filled with tension, and when he drops the supplies back in his apartment, I have one last longing look at his perfect body next to his perfect bed before taking him up on his offer to walk me to the subway station.

A few minutes later, we reach the stairwell that leads beneath the street.

I stop on the corner to face him. "Well, here we are." I'm trying to disguise how reluctant I am to go, but there's a good chance I'm failing.

He nods, and I can see tension in his jaw. "I guess so. Tonight was . . . special. Meeting you. Touching you. All of it." He cocks his head. "But I have a terrible feeling you're not going to offer me your number, are you?"

If you weren't an actor, hell yes. But I'm almost sure you are, so I won't.
I shake my head. "But maybe I'll see you around?"

He lets out a short laugh. "In this city? Unlikely."

"Unless fate, right?"

I mean it to be a joke, but his expression turns serious. "Yeah. Fate."

He stares for a few seconds, then shoves his hands into his pockets and gives me a wry smile. "Of course, you know where I live now. So if you ever feel a deep, spiritual need for a booty call, you can drop by anytime. Day or night. Or day *and* night if you're feeling tense. Apart from pristine bed-making, I also specialize in mind-blowing erotic massage."

I suppress a laugh as a ball of warmth blooms in my stomach. "I have no doubt. Sure. I'll drop by."

He shakes his head. "You really are a terrible actress, aren't you. You can't even fake it to spare my ego?"

"I predict your ego will be just fine. Good night, Liam Quinn." I hold out my hand as he goes for a hug. Then we laugh and step back. When he offers his hand, I shake it.

Jesus, most awkward moment ever. It gets even more awkward when we stop smiling and neither one of us lets go. We just continue to stand there and shake hands.

Liam lets out a breath. "Okay, so . . . this is where you walk away."

"Yeah. I'll just . . . go." I take a tentative step away from him, but he doesn't let go of my hand.

My back hits the wall of the building behind me as Liam steps forward. He's so tall and his shoulders are so broad, they block out the light. In the shadows, his expression looks ravenous. I've had men look at me with desire before, but nothing like this. I can feel him holding himself back. Every muscle is tense, yet his fingers are gentle as they caress mine.

"Elissa." He cups my face and leans down. When our noses brush, I can't help but grip the front of his T-shirt. "Maybe you don't have to leave just yet."

My blood pressure is getting higher every second. "I really should." My heart is thundering, roaring blood through my ears.

"Or maybe you can just stand there for a few minutes and let me do this."

I stop breathing as he gently grazes his lips across mine.

Oh. Fuck.

No.

No, no, *no.*

Giant mistake.

My mind seizes. I've never felt lips so soft. He does it again, and my whole body flushes, inside and out.

"Is this okay?" he asks, his voice raspy.

I grip his T-shirt tighter. *Not really.*

I've tried to resist him all night, but now that I've felt his mouth, not wanting more is impossible.

"I've wanted to kiss you from the moment I saw you," he whispers, and grazes my lips again. "You don't even know how beautiful you are."

I lay my hands flat against his chest as he kisses me again, deeper this time. Light suction. Sudden inhale.

Goddammit.

Reality melts away in a lusty haze, and I'm physically incapable of not kissing him back. I suck on his lips as I push up onto my toes. He grunts in response and presses against me, all hard-bodied and strong. When our mouths open and tongues slide, every last shred of resistance frays and snaps. His mouth is heaven, and I want to live there.

"Unbelievable," he mutters before kissing me harder.

I'm gone. Lost in his touch, and smell, and sweet, sweet taste. There's no coming back from this.

I once read an Oscar Wilde quote that said, "A kiss may ruin a human life." It perplexed me, because up until now, I'd always thought kisses were sweet but unimportant. But this kiss? It's ruined me. This is the type of kiss I never knew existed. It's like falling and flying, all in the same moment.

His fingers slide into my hair, and I hook my hands around his shoulders, desperate to get closer. I feel people passing us and even hear a few mutter, "Get a room," but I really don't care.

Liam kisses me like he was born to do it. Like he invented the concept and does it better than any other man on the planet. His mouth moves over mine with instinctual ease, and before long, our hands are grasping and pushing under clothes.

When his hands slide under the back of my T-shirt, a warning bell in my brain reminds me I'm making out on the street. With an actor. A really hot, probably fickle actor.

How much further am I going to let this go before I come to my senses?

Large hands close around my butt, and then he pulls me tight against him. The feel of his erection pressing against my stomach makes me moan.

Okay, then. A little further, apparently.

I'm about half a second away from exploring exactly how hard he is when my common sense screams at me to stop.

Gasping, I hold up a hand and pull back. "Wait a minute." I suck in a few quick lungfuls of air. "I need to ask you a question, and you have to give me a straight answer."

He breathes in shallow pants, his pupils huge. "I know what you're going to ask, and yes, I do have a condom. Also, I'd be more than happy to risk being arrested so I can fuck you against this wall."

"That's not it."

"You sure? That's the vibe I was getting."

"I know you avoided this earlier, but . . . what do you do for a living?"

He flinches. A sick sense of dread settles in my stomach, because I know I'm not going to like the answer.

"So if I said I'm an actor, you'd, what? Walk away from this?"

"I'd have to. You know why."

Please, please, please don't say it. I really like you and want more, but not if you confirm my suspicions.

He sighs. "Okay, fine. I get why you're hesitant. After Leanne, I figure I won't be dating any brunettes from Jersey for a while."

"So now imagine you dated Leanne three times in a row and she dumped you each time. Then another Leanne came along. Wouldn't you feel like a dumb-ass if you went there again? I just can't do it."

I see pity in his expression when he cups my cheek. "I understand. And luckily, I can say without a hint of a lie that I've never set foot on a stage in my life. I work in construction with my dad. Have ever since I left school."

For a moment, I swear I've heard incorrectly. "Wait a minute. You're actually a . . . construction worker?"

"Yes."

I stifle a laugh. "You don't happen to have friends who are policemen, cowboys, and Native Americans, do you?"

His brows furrow. "No. Why?"

"Not important. Why didn't you tell me this earlier? Maybe I would have ripped off your shirt on the roof after all."

He shrugs. "My girlfriend just dumped me for being a broke blue-collar worker. I guess you're not the only one who's afraid of rejection."

I feel myself beaming. "Well, Leanne's an idiot. I couldn't be happier that you're a construction worker. Best job ever."

"Seems to me if you were truly happy about it, you'd kiss me again."

I rise on my toes and capture his mouth. He makes a noise in his throat that vibrates all the way through his body. Then, he presses me back against the wall and takes charge again. Lord, his mouth is talented. And what's more, he tastes incredible. Milk and cookies is now my favorite flavor.

After a few more frantic minutes, I really can't breathe, so I pull back and stroke his chest. "Okay, we could do this all night, but it's almost three a.m., and I wasn't lying about having a big day tomorrow."

He leans his forehead against mine, and his breathing is tight.

"What are you doing tomorrow? And please say it includes seeing me again."

"I can't. I'm stage-managing *Romeo and Juliet* for the Tribeca Shakespeare Festival and our Romeo auditions are tomorrow."

For a few seconds he looks confused. Then he smiles and shakes his head. "That's . . . well, that's great. Romeo auditions. Important job. So . . . uh . . . how are they going to figure out who gets the role?"

"The director's looking for a strong, passionate Romeo. Usually he's played as a whiny boy, but she's wants a man."

He studies me for a few moments. "Sounds reasonable. Can I see you when you're done?"

I pull him down for a soft kiss. "Maybe."

He steps away from me and runs his fingers through his hair. "I'm going to take that as a 'yes.' Now, you should probably leave while I have the strength to let you go. But first, give me your phone."

"What for?"

"Quick selfie to capture the moment."

I reach into my pocket and hand my phone over. He blows out a breath and brings up the camera. "Come here." He puts his arm around me and pulls me into his side. "Ready?"

He holds the phone out, but before I can look up into the lens, he pulls my face around and kisses me, long and slow. Through a surge of dizzying hormones, I'm vaguely aware of the shutter clicking in the background.

When he pulls back, he shows me the picture. I get hot just looking at it. We look amazing together. Like we belong in a million-dollar ad campaign instead of a selfie.

He kisses me once more. "So you don't forget me while we're apart."

As if that's even remotely possible.

He pushes my phone into my back pocket, and not so subtly grazes my butt in the process. "See you soon, Liss."

No one's ever called me Liss before. Lissa, yes, but not Liss. Coming from him, it's perfect.

He turns to leave, but I grab his arm. "Wait, you don't have my number."

"You refused to give it to me, remember?"

"That's when I thought you were an actor. Construction-worker Liam can have my phone number *and* address. Hell, you can have my social security number, too, if you want it."

He smiles and leans down for a final soft kiss. "Don't need it. I'll find you again." He steps back and walks away.

"You seem awfully sure about that," I say to his back.

He turns and gives me a smug smile. "I am. It's fate."

FOUR

AUDITION HELL

I rub my eyes.

It's been a long-ass day. If I never hear another verse of iambic pentameter, it'll be too soon. We've seen thirty-two Romeos today, and most of them had no clue what the hell they were doing. If auditions were people, this one would be Charlie Sheen. It was a disaster.

Beside me, our director, Miriam, is rubbing her temples.

"How?" she says, in a whiny tone. "In this massive city where every second waiter is a goddamn actor, how can we have *zero* serious Romeo candidates? I don't understand."

"Maybe we have to throw our net a little wider. Try some of the students at The Grove?"

"What about your brother?" Miriam asks. "I know he auditioned for Mercutio, but if I can't find someone else to do Romeo, I may need to switch him around."

"Oh, no," I say as I shake my head. "Ethan doesn't have a romantic bone in his body." His track record with relationships is even worse than mine. "Plus, he despises Romeo. I think you'd have a fight on your hands there."

Miriam groans. "Well, unless this final candidate blows me away, it may be a fight I'm willing to have." She picks up the piece of paper in front of her. "Oh, God. This next kid has no agent and no experience. He doesn't even have a headshot, for God's sake."

She slaps the paper back down onto the desk and sighs. "Go bring him in, would you? Might as well get it over with, so I can open a bottle of wine and drown my sorrows."

I pat her on the back as I head toward the door. When I open it and look into the waiting room, there's only one person there, and he's not an actor.

"Liam?" How did he know where to find me?

He takes off his headphones and looks up at me. He's even hotter in the daytime than he was last night. How is that possible?

"Hey, Liss." He stands and walks over to me, and I don't miss the way his gaze travels down the length of my body and back up. "I half expected not to find you today. Last night was so amazing, I started to believe I dreamt it." He studies my face. "I'm glad to see you actually exist. And you're even more beautiful than I remember."

I'm searching for a response when Miriam calls out, "Elissa? Is there a problem?"

"No. Be right there!" I half close the door and lower my voice as I turn back to Liam. "Look, I'm happy you exist, too, but you can't be here. I'm working."

"I know. I'm on the list."

"You're kidding me."

"I'm really not. Check it."

I look down at the clipboard in my hand, and sure enough, over the page and right down at the bottom is "Liam Quinn."

I glare up at him. He gives me a panty-melting smile.

"Elissa, I might not have been entirely honest with you last night, but I swear it was for all the right reasons." He slides past me, pushes open the door, and walks into the room. "Hi, Miriam. I'm Liam Quinn, and I'll be auditioning for the role of Romeo."

As soon as Miriam lays eyes on him, her mouth drops open. It takes her a few seconds before she can form words. I know how she feels.

"Uh, hi, Liam. Great to meet you. Do you need the pages?"

He puts his phone and headphones on a chair and gives her a smile. "No, thanks. I have it memorized."

"Okay, then. Just take your time, and start when you're ready."

I take my seat in a daze as Liam draws in a few deep breaths to prepare.

Next to me, Miriam whispers to herself, "Dear almighty Gods of Theater, I'll never ask you for anything else as long as I live, but please, please, *please* let this man be able to act. I'm begging you."

I'm still too shocked by Liam's presence to even laugh.

He rolls his neck and shakes out his hands, then he closes his eyes for a few seconds. When he opens them, he blows us away by delivering the most incredible interpretation of Romeo I've ever seen.

Bastard.

Miriam is gushing. I've never seen her do that. Most of the time she's terse and straightforward, but right now she's spouting compliments all over Liam.

Can't say I blame her. Not only did he deliver an amazingly intelligent performance, it was also hot as hell. When he was done, Miriam applauded. She asked him to read some more, but he said he hadn't brought his glasses and couldn't see the script without them.

It didn't matter. By then he had the role in the bag.

I'm still reeling that he's here. Wait, reeling isn't the right word. "Furious" is more like it. I'm so angry, I'm shaking.

What breed of asshole lies to someone's face? Oh, that's right, an asshole *actor*. I really do have the worst taste in men.

"Elissa." Miriam comes over to me. "Can you get all of Liam's details and take his measurements? I have to run. Make sure he's back here Monday to read with our Juliets. We'll have to see who has the most chemistry with him."

I have no doubt Liam could have chemistry with a brick wall if he tried.

She pats me on the arm. "See you both soon. Great job today, Liam!"

Liam waves as she leaves, then turns to me. He looks so self-satisfied, I want to smack him.

I walk over with my clipboard and measuring tape. "What the hell was that?"

"According to your director, the perfect mix of romantic passion and masculine power."

"You lied to me last night!"

"No. I told you the truth. I work in construction with my dad and have never set foot onstage. This is my first audition. Technically, I wasn't an actor until just now."

"Oh, what crap. No one is as good as you were the first time at bat."

He holds up his hands. "I swear to God, I'm not lying. I've wanted to act for years, but life got in the way. I saw the audition notice for this a few weeks ago and decided to give it a try."

"So this is just some crazy coincidence? Please."

"No, it's not coincidence. It's fate. I keep telling you that." He takes a step forward, his expression serious. "I know you feel it, too. Or do you not remember how close we came to committing an illegal public act last night?" He winds an arm around my waist. I clench my jaw to stop myself from pressing against him. "We could finish what we started, you know. That table looks pretty sturdy."

Everything slows down as I watch his mouth get closer, but thankfully, my sense of professionalism overpowers my insane attraction, and I find the strength to step away.

"Let's just get these measurements done so we can get out of here," I say in my most no-nonsense tone. I put down my clipboard and unfurl the measuring tape. "Arms up, please."

He raises his arms. Because he's so broad, I have to press against him in order to wrap the tape around his chest. When my nipples harden in response, I huff in frustration.

"Listen, Liss," he says softly. "I'm sorry I bent the truth last night, but if I'd admitted I wanted to be an actor, I'd have missed out on the most incredible kiss of my entire life, and I have zero regrets about that. Let me take you out to dinner to make it up to you."

"I can't." I write down his chest measurement on my clipboard.

"Sure you can."

I look him in the eye. "No, I really can't. Apart from anything else, you're now in a show I'm running, so you're totally off-limits to me." I wrap the tape around his neck. When I graze his throat with my hand, he sucks in a quick breath. *Thank God I'm not alone in being hot and bothered by our proximity.* "And even if I was stupid enough to consider a workplace romance, which I'm not, you're onstage, and I'm backstage. You might as well be a Montague and me a Capulet."

"What, so actors can't date crew?"

I wrap the tape around his waist, then move to his hips. "It's not that they can't, but most don't. A lot of actors consider themselves above the crew and don't date down."

"I don't consider myself above you. No, wait. . . ." He thinks for a second. "Last night there were several times I imagined myself above you. It was hot as hell."

When I hear the smile in his voice, I look up from writing on my clipboard. "This isn't funny."

"It is, a little. I mean, come on."

I squeeze my eyes shut and pray for patience. I don't know if I'm more pissed with him for deceiving me, or with myself for wanting him anyway.

"Liam, this is my first professional gig, and I can't screw it up. Please don't make things hard." I take the outside seam of his legs, then try to keep my cool as I kneel in front of his crotch to take his inseam.

He moves his feet apart, but when my hand grazes his inner thigh, he blows out a tight breath. "I can't make things hard, but you can?

Doesn't seem fair." When I stand and glare, he shoves his hands in his pockets. "FYI, glaring at me also makes things hard. You're sexy as hell when you're angry."

I give up trying to reason with him. "Shoe size?"

"Twelve."

"Head?"

His eyebrows pull down. "Uh . . . are you offering, or—"

I pinch the bridge of my nose. "What's your hat size?"

He shrugs. "Big?"

I scribble "large" on the form, and then hand him a folder of information and his script. He caresses my fingers as he takes the documents, but I step away.

"Elissa, come on. . . ."

"We're done here."

"This is crazy. I like you. You like me. Can't we go somewhere and talk about this?"

"No point. It won't change our situation. I'll see you back here Monday night at six to read with our Juliets. Any questions?"

He stares at me for a few seconds. I stare back as impassively as I can.

"So, this is how it's going to be between us now?"

"Yes. Is there anything else, Mr. Quinn?"

He gives me a bitter smile. "No, ma'am. You've explained everything very clearly." He grabs his gear from the chair, but before I can walk away, he steps in front of me. He's so close, I feel the heat of him in every inch of my skin. "Just so you know, I'm going to respect your work ethic and keep my distance while this show is happening, because I agree that working and romancing aren't the best mix. But in two months, when this production is over, all bets are off, and then . . ." He licks his lips. "Well, by then I'm sure we're both going to have so much sexual frustration, we'll be begging for relief. And I intend to relieve you, Liss. Over and over again. You can trust me on that."

When he strides out and the door closes behind him, I collapse into a chair. I don't know if I'm trembling from disappointment or relief. But I do know Liam Quinn isn't going to give me up without a fight, and that thrills me way more than it should.

FIVE

GETTING CLOSER

Two Weeks Later
Twelfth Night Theater
New York City

The ladder wobbles as I stretch up on my toes to grasp the power cable that hangs from the lighting bar. When I shove the plug into the socket, I breathe a sigh of relief and grip the top of the ladder with both hands. Being a short-ass and rigging lights don't really go hand in hand, but experience has taught me that stage managers on low-budget shows need to be Jacks-of-all-trades. Or Jills, as the case may be. The first week of rehearsals may almost be over, but the hard work for me and my crew has just begun.

I pause when I hear a noise backstage. I listen for a few seconds, and try to ignore the sudden thundering of my heart.

"Hello?"

Silence greets me.

Great. I love being stuck in a dark theater by myself with creepy sounds. Not freaking me out at all.

I'm halfway down the ladder when large hands close around my hips and make me scream.

"Ahhh! Get off me, creeper! I know karate!"

I immediately flail, and kick the ladder over in the process. Strong arms lift me away as the ladder topples noisily onto the stage.

"Hey! Chill, Daniel-san. It's me."

The arms tighten around me, and the familiar smell of all things Liam invades my senses. I grip his hands and exhale as he lowers me to the floor. "You scared the hell out of me! What are you doing?"

When I push away and turn to face him, he looks way too amused for my liking.

"Sorry," he says, not looking at all apologetic. "Didn't mean to freak you out. I thought you heard me behind you."

"Well, I didn't. And if you sneak up on me like that again, I'm going to make you wear a collar and bell." I brush my hair away from my face and try to calm my hammering heart. "Why are you even here? Everyone else went home hours ago."

He wanders over to the ladder and sets it upright. "I think I left my keys in the dressing room. At least, I hope I did, otherwise I'm sleeping on the street tonight. Why are you here? Isn't rigging lights Sean's job?"

"His wife went into labor and we need these specials for tomorrow's rehearsal. Figured I'd just do it before I left."

He stops in front of me, a little too close for comfort. In the low light, the shadows define the hard line of his jaw, as well as the soft curve of his lips. He's so damn attractive, it's frustrating. True to his prediction, being around each other every day and ignoring our insistent attraction is putting us both on edge.

"So, you're here alone?" he asks quietly. "No Josh?"

I shake my head. "It was his gammy's eightieth tonight. Every Kane in the tristate area is at the Four Seasons for her birthday dinner."

"What about you? Have you had dinner? You look . . . hungry." However I'm looking at him right now, it's making his breathing speed up.

"I'm fine," I say, but my voice is breathier than I'd like. "I'll grab something when I'm done."

I force myself to move away from him and head to the lighting desk at the front of the stage. I feel him behind me as I bring up the faders in sequence to check that all the lights are working.

"Let me stay and help you."

"That's not a good idea."

"Why not?"

I grab another light from the cart and walk over to the ladder. "Can't have you dirtying your pristine actor hands doing filthy crew work. How will you sign autographs and wave at all your nubile female fans if you chip a nail?"

He chuckles as I set the light down and reposition the ladder. "You have a point. I guess my hands got too soft lugging around bags of cement and tons of steel when I was constructing buildings for a living. Hanging a few lights is clearly beyond me."

I flinch in surprise when he takes my hands and rubs our palms together. "Hmmm, would you look at that? It seems that of the two of us, the hard-core crew leader is the one with the velvet-soft hands. How did that happen?" He turns my palms over and examines them while trailing his forefinger over the sensitive skin. It shouldn't be unbelievably erotic, but it is. "Liss, you don't have a single callus on these dainty digits. How is that possible?"

A shiver runs through me. "I moisturize." I flip his hands over and carry out a similar examination. As the pad of my finger traces his many calluses, he sucks in a sharp breath.

"Wow," I say. "Looks like you're all out of hand cream. I could grate cheese on these babies." I'm exaggerating. His hands are rough, but not in an unpleasant way. In fact, I love their texture. I remember how they felt when he cupped my face and pushed under my clothes. Not that I should be thinking about that while we're alone together. Nothing good will come of it.

"Liss?"

"Hmmm?" I look up at him. His jaw is tense.

"If you don't stop touching me like that, I'm going to forget I'm supposed to stay away from you and do some very unprofessional things to you right here in the middle of the stage. Now, I'd actually enjoy that, but I'm predicting you wouldn't. So, continue at your own risk."

Reluctantly, I take my hands off him and step back. "It's not that I wouldn't enjoy it. It just can't happen."

He runs his hand through his hair. "I understand. Sort of. I'd better go find my keys. And have a cold shower. Please don't fall off the ladder and kill yourself while I'm gone. That would bum me out."

I try not to smile. "I'll do my best."

He heads backstage to his dressing room. By the time he returns, I've hung the last lamp and have started plotting a few of the light settings we'll be using the next day.

He holds up his keys. "Found them. Also, did you know there's no shower in my dressing room?"

"Yep. There's only one shower in this entire theater, and right now, it's filled with paint cans and half-washed rollers. Welcome to the glamorous world of theater."

He throws his hands up in mock exasperation. "I can't work under these conditions! I'll be in my trailer."

I smile. "Getting a head start on your star attitude, huh? I approve. You are going to be a star, after all."

"Really?" he asks. "I'm doing an okay job?"

I roll my eyes. "Miriam hasn't gushed over your performance enough? You're amazing. We all think so."

He takes a step closer, and suddenly, I have no idea which cue I'm up to anymore. "We? As in, *you* think I'm amazing?"

I pause and give him my most sincere expression. "Eh. You're okay."

He chuckles as I go back to my cue sheet. I can feel his eyes on me as I continue to punch buttons and set light levels.

"Well, I think *you're* amazing," he says, gently. "Is there anything you can't do?"

I smile. "Lots of things. Calculus. Burpees. Nickelback karaoke." He puts his hand over mine, and it makes me suck in a quick breath.

"I mean it, Liss. You're incredible. If you're almost done, we could grab a pizza and head back to my place. Sit on the roof. Watch the lights. Nothing unprofessional. Just . . . friends. Who lust after each other."

He strokes the back of my hand, and I'm tempted. I really am. But being alone with him for an extended period is sure to result in us being naked and handsy. "I can't, Liam. I'm sorry."

He nods. "I figured you'd say that, but I had to ask." He removes his hand and exhales. "Okay, then. I'll let you get back to work. See you in the morning?"

"Yep. See you then."

He smiles and walks away, and when I hear the stage door slam closed behind him, I put my head down on the desk and groan with frustration.

Sometimes having impeccable work ethics sucks giant hairy yak balls.

Most days, I'm the first person to get to the theater. I enjoy it because it means I can take my time and get organized before everyone else arrives.

That's why it's disturbing when I walk in this morning to hear sex noises. They're quiet, but definitely there.

I grab my big metal flashlight and creep backstage, ready to confront horny teenagers who probably snuck in while our security guard, Guido, was off getting his fourth espresso of the day.

As I sneak through the backstage shadows, I realize the noises are coming from Liam's dressing room.

Oh, God. Really?

My heart's in my throat as I approach the door. It's open, and bright light bleeds into the dark corridor.

The soft grunting continues, and I shouldn't find it arousing considering that the thought of finding him with another girl makes me want to throw up.

I close my eyes and take a breath. "Liam? Is that you?"

The grunting stops just long enough for him to say, "Yeah. Come in." Then the noises start up again.

Okay. This could be awkward.

I step into the doorway and freeze. He's not having sex. He's lying on the ground, knees bent, doing sit-ups.

Shirtless.

My sweet giddy Christ.

Pecs, wide and hard. Abs, everywhere. Way too many to be normal. Biceps pop as he presses his hands behind his head.

I'm ashamed to say I've imagined what Liam's naked torso would look like too many times to count, but I've never actually seen it until now. Clearly, I have the imagination skills of a cabbage, because his actual body? In the immortal words of Keanu Reeves: *Whoa.*

"You just going to stand there and watch?" he asks, a little out of breath.

"Yep." The contraction of his abs has me completely mesmerized. I can't look away. "Anyway . . . uh . . . this is about as close to exercise as I like to get. But please, you knock yourself out."

My God, his body is insane.

He chuckles at my slack-jawed expression. "Okay, then. There's a chair if you'd like to make yourself more comfortable."

I lean against the door frame instead. Don't really trust my legs to make it the three steps to the chair right now.

"How many have you done?" I ask, vaguely fascinated.

"About a hundred."

"How many do you have left?"

"Another two hundred."

"Seems excessive."

"Not really, considering Miriam wants me to spend most of the play shirtless. She told me last night. No pressure or anything."

He goes back to grunting every time he sits up. My knees go weak.

"When I heard you," I say, "I thought you . . . um, had a girl in here."

He sits up and rests his elbows on his knees. "What?" I watch as a droplet of sweat runs down his neck and onto his chest.

"I thought you were . . ." I bob my head in the "you know" gesture.

He frowns. "You thought I was having *sex*?" I nod. "In my dressing room?" I nod again. "With someone who isn't *you*?" He screws up his face. "Jesus, lady, go get yourself another cup of coffee, because you're not thinking straight."

He goes back to his sit-ups. "Besides, this sounds nothing like the noises I make when I'm having sex."

"What sort of noises do you make, then?"

"Can't tell you. I want it to be a surprise." He raises an eyebrow, and I can't help but laugh.

"Aaaand on that note, I have to go."

"Really? Wouldn't you rather come?"

I shake my head, and as I grab the door to close it, he starts moaning. "Oh, God, Liss. Yes. Grab that hard door handle. Right there. Fuck, yes. Wrap your hand around it and pull. Ahhhhh!"

I close the door and shake my head as I walk away. I make a mental note that it's not cool in any way to be aroused by exercise grunting or dirty talk about doors. It's a pity my body continues to ignore all logic and reason as far as Liam Quinn is concerned.

I grab the stack of paper off the photocopier, and soon I'm smiling.

Reviews. Lots of them. All of them glowing. Our show is officially a hit, and even though everyone in the cast is excellent, Liam and my brother Ethan, who's playing Mercutio, are getting all the attention.

It doesn't surprise me. Hot actors who are also talented as hell? It's the bedrock on which Broadway was built.

I head backstage and distribute the reviews to the dressing rooms. Actors love reading nice things about themselves. It will put the whole cast in a good mood for the show tonight.

When I get back to my console, side stage, I roll my neck and wince as it cracks. I don't think I've sat down all day, and the dull thud of a potential headache lingers behind my eyeballs.

I jump when large hands curl over my shoulders.

"Relax." Liam's deep voice resonates behind me. "You're so tense you're going to sprain something. Thank you for the reviews; I'm sure my parents are going to wallpaper their living room with them. I appreciate you taking the time to copy them, so I'm here to do something nice for you."

Strong fingers dig into my neck muscles, and I bite back a groan. "Oh, my God."

"Come on now. We're past that sort of formality. You can call me Liam."

I close my eyes as he kneads away the tension in my neck and shoulders. It feels so good, it borders on sexual.

"Liam . . . Oh, wow. Uh . . . you should stop."

"Should I? Why? You seem to be enjoying it, and I'm sure as hell enjoying it."

"The leading man can't be seen massaging the stage manager. It's wrong and unnatural."

"Who can massage you, then?"

"No one. I'm unmassageable."

"Hardly seems fair. You have one of the most stressful jobs here, but aren't allowed a little help to unwind? Fuck that."

He digs his thumbs into the base of my skull and my eyes roll back into my head. "Ohhhh . . . No, really. This is bad. Stage managers are strange creatures. We thrive on stress, caffeine, and lack of sleep. You can't mess with that. Make us too relaxed and we fall apart."

Warm breath and soft lips graze my ear as he whispers, "I'm looking forward to watching you fall apart one day very soon, Liss. Twenty-one days and counting, in fact. I have the closing-night party marked on my calendar."

He pushes his thumbs into the muscles on either side of my spine, all the way down to the waistband of my jeans. When I bite back a groan, he chuckles. "Are you sure you want me to stop?"

"No, but you should."

He sighs. "Fine. But first, stand up and come here. Your back is a mess." I stand and turn to face him. He bends his knees and wraps his arms around me. "This will relieve the pressure on your vertebrae." He lifts me off my feet and tightens his arms, and a rolling series of cracks travels up my spine. Almost instantly, I feel relief.

He sets me down, and I roll my shoulders. "Wow. That's much better. Thank you."

"Are you kidding me? I got to press my chest against your boobs. The pleasure was all mine."

He smiles, and my face flushes. I don't enjoy these involuntary reactions. Despite my best efforts to remain detached, he's like a sexual lightning rod, and all my sparks gravitate toward him. It's exhausting. I try to lean back, but the wall is right behind me.

He's still standing close, staring at my lips. I'm also staring at his. They're beautiful, and every time he kisses Juliet, it drives me insane. Not only because I get hot flashes of jealousy, but the way he holds her face and cradles her in his arms is incredibly passionate and sweet. And then there are those groany sounds he makes in the back of his throat when Romeo and Juliet have sex on their wedding night. Those tiny noises slay me. Every damn time.

I close my eyes and take a breath, and try to pull myself together. "Okay, so . . . I'm about to give the half-hour call."

"I should go get ready."

"Yeah."

"Okay." He reaches over and gently cups my cheek. I don't want to lean into it, but I do. "Here I go," he says as he grazes his thumb over my lips. "Leaving."

I can't deal with the desire in his expression. It makes me so light-headed, I instinctively grip his T-shirt. "Your version of leaving is very . . . stationary."

"Yeah, I'm trying to convince my hand to stop touching you, but it's not listening. And don't even get me started on what my lips are telling me to do." He leans down, and I know I should push him away but I can't. There's not enough willpower in the world to stop this moment. "Did you know I dream about your mouth? How it feels. And tastes. Every time I see you, the urge to kiss you is so damn strong, it hurts to deny it. Tell me you feel the same."

His mouth is right there. All I'd have to do is stand on my toes and I could have it. Put us both out of our misery. "Of course I feel the same, but—"

He cuts me off by grazing his thumb over my lips again. "Less talking. More kissing me."

I'm holding my breath in anticipation of his mouth meeting mine when a burst of laughter makes us both pull back. The actors playing Juliet's parents pass by without a glance in our direction, but the close call reminds me where we are. And who we are.

Liam stares at me for a few more bone-melting moments, then stalks off toward his dressing room without another word.

I slump down onto my stool and pull on my headset. After a few deep breaths to calm myself, I click the button on the microphone in front of me.

"Ladies and gentlemen of the *Romeo and Juliet* company, this is your half-hour call. Thirty minutes until places for Act One. Thank you." It's only when I click off that I realize how stupidly breathy my voice sounded.

At least I don't have a headache anymore. Nope. Now, the ache is a whole lot lower.

"Elissa." I look up to see my brother striding toward me. He's holding up one of his headshots. Someone has defaced it with devil horns and a goatee that looks vaguely like a penis. "Was this you?"

"Ethan, please. Do you honestly think I'd produce such crude work? That penis-beard doesn't even have veins. It was probably Olivia."

Ethan has been pseudo-dating our Juliet, and as usual, he's screwed things up as only Ethan can.

He looks briefly at the photo. "Huh. Olivia did seem pissed when I saw her earlier."

"What did you do this time?"

"Nothing." I shoot him a look, but he holds up his hands. "I mean it. I've barely spoken to her since last week."

I roll my eyes. If my brother were any more clueless about women, he'd be a conservative politician.

I take the photo from him and throw it in the trash. "Did you get the reviews?"

"Yep."

"Some nice things about you."

He shrugs. "I guess. I haven't been ordered to move to L.A. like Quinn, but still . . ." The shock of what he's said must register on my face, because his expression softens. "You haven't heard?"

"Heard what?"

"Last week, some big-shot Hollywood casting agent was in the audience. She cornered Quinn at the stage door and told him if he headed straight out to L.A. when the show closes, she could get him screen tests for some major studio movies. Olivia overhead them."

"And what did Liam say?"

"He said he'd think about it."

I lean back against the wall, shell-shocked. *He might be leaving?* My stomach churns and rolls.

No. He can't.

"Sis?" I turn to Ethan. "You okay?"

"What? Uh . . . yeah. Fine."

"Wait, you two aren't—?"

"No." *But I thought we could be.* "I'm just surprised, that's all. You'd better go get changed. I've given the thirty-minute call."

He stares at me with concern for a few more seconds. "Yeah. Okay. I'll talk to you later."

Once he's gone, I slump onto my stool.

I know I shouldn't be hurt Liam didn't tell me, but I am. The flirting. The touches. The overwhelming connection. I thought we meant something to each other. I've even entertained fantasies about what it would be like to have him as my boyfriend. Wandering the theater district, going to see shows and arguing about which we liked the most. Or walking through Central Park, holding hands. Maybe sitting on a bench and making out in really obnoxious, inappropriate ways.

I squeeze my eyes shut. My headache is back, with a vengeance.

Why didn't he tell me?

I sigh. Even if he did, what would I say? *"Don't go"*?

I couldn't. He has to do it. Of course he does.

But I have a terrible feeling if he goes, it will change both of our lives forever. And not in a good way.

SIX

THE CONSEQUENCE OF WANTING

On the closing night of the show, it's near midnight when Josh and I arrive at the after-party. As soon as we emerge into the uber-trendy warehouse space, our Benvolio, Andy, rushes toward us with a tray of shots. He has the bright-eyed fervor of someone who's already three drinks over the limit.

"Guys! You finally made it. You need to try these."

I pick up the bright blue shot glass. "What is it?"

"I have no idea, but knock it back fast, and try to keep breathing."

I throw back the shot without hesitation. When I swallow, my whole body shudders. "Jesus!"

Andy laughs. "Awesome, right?"

I grab another and knock it back, too. Josh joins me. The impact of the second isn't any less forceful than the first.

"Fuck me." Josh coughs. "It tastes like battery acid mixed with plutonium."

Andy nods. "Yeah, but in a couple of minutes, you won't care. Trust. Oh, and Elissa? Liam's been looking for you. Like, a lot. Just FYI."

He stumbles off to peddle his wares elsewhere, and Josh and I move farther into the party. Behind a gauze curtain, a large group is dancing to the bass-heavy music. I start to feel a little buzzed as I watch them.

"So, you and Quinn going to finally seal the deal tonight?" Josh asks. "Because God knows, if I have to witness one more second of you two panting over each other, I'm going to lock you both in a room until someone comes."

I shake my head. "You know why I can't go there."

"I do. But I also saw the look in his eyes when he left the theater tonight. The man was wired. And determined. He knows you've been avoiding him. And let's be honest. If you were truly serious about not getting involved, you wouldn't have come to this party."

I'd like to be strong enough to stay away from Liam tonight, considering our situation, but I can't deny that the past couple of months have taken their toll. I want him. Desperately. Even if it seems as though I can no longer have him.

Josh stumbles and leans against me. "Whoa. Those drinks were strong. Want me to get us a couple more?"

"Most definitely."

He heads off to find Andy, and I loiter at the edge of the dance floor to avoid seeking out Liam. Everyone's hugging, and kissing, and some are even touching each other in ways that warrant a little more privacy.

My God, theater folk are a horny bunch.

I lean against a post and watch. Whatever was in the drinks is making me feel hot in inconvenient places.

As I look around, I spot Liam across the room. He's surrounded by a group of girls, all trying to get his attention, but it's clear he's not listening to a word they're saying. He scans the crowd and sips a beer. As soon as he spies me, his posture changes, and the sudden intensity in his expression makes every hair on my body stand on end.

Without excusing himself or taking his eyes off me, he passes his beer to one of the girls and crosses the room. All of the women he's abandoning deflate with disappointment.

As he approaches, his expression is so primal I have an urge to flee, but I'm so frustrated and horny, I force myself to stand my ground and see what happens.

When he reaches me, he doesn't say anything. He just takes my hand and leads me to the dance floor.

Several people stop and stare as he wraps his arms around me and pulls me close. After so many weeks of denial, the feel of him pressed up against me makes my head spin. I grasp his shoulders, and he tightens his arms.

"Liam—"

"Don't say it." He gives me a look that shoots sparks straight down to my toes. "Don't you fucking dare. The show's over, so I'm done staying away from you."

He moves his hands over my back, which makes my heart pound and my brain go fuzzy. The alcohol is making me feel like I've done ten shots instead of two, and I'm in no condition to be this close to him, let alone try to deny my feelings.

When he pushes under my T-shirt and grazes the base of my spine, I close my eyes as a shiver runs through me. It feels like my skin is extra-sensitive.

"What the hell was in those shots Andy gave us?" I ask. "They've made us all very—"

"Horny?" The roughness in his voice is crazy sexy.

"I was going to say 'friendly.'"

Fingers trace over my back. Soft and electric. "Right. That's what I'm feeling for you. Intense, throbbing friendship."

"You're making me dizzy."

"There's a treatment for that. Come home with me and I'll show you what it is." His voice is just as distracting as his touch. When he pulls me more firmly against him, I can feel the hardness in his crotch. It awakens a deep ache inside me. "I want to be alone with you, Liss. Naked. Right the fuck now, please."

"I can't leave yet. I just got here."

Without meaning to, I run my hands down his arms, and revel in the flex of firm muscles as he continues to stroke my back. He makes a contented noise in his chest and closes his eyes.

"Put your arms around me," he orders quietly. In a daze, I trail my hands up over his broad shoulders and clasp my hands behind his neck. "Good. Now, loosen up and dance with me."

Loosening up when he's pressing against me like this isn't even a little bit possible. I glance down between us. "Judging from your current condition, you're after more than just a dance."

He keeps stroking my back. "Then we'll start with dancing and see what happens."

"Liam, where, exactly, do you see things going between you and me?"

He moves his hands from my back to my hips, and when his fingers tighten, goose bumps run up my spine. "Well, for starters, back to my place. More specifically, my bed. After that, I have no clue. Maybe the shower? The roof garden? That would be pretty spectacular."

It really would. I close my eyes to banish the mental image of us naked, wrapped around each other beneath the stars. "Spectacular or not, you're leaving on Monday."

His confidence falters and his hands freeze. "Elissa—"

"You weren't even going to tell me? I had to hear people gossiping about it backstage?"

He looks down and sighs. "Telling everyone else was easy. Telling you?" He looks into my eyes. "I couldn't. Just thinking about leaving you . . ." He tightens his arms. "I don't want to."

"Liam . . ." I stroke his face and make him look at me. "Yes, I'm pissed I heard about it from someone else, but this is a once-in-a-lifetime deal. You have to go. If you want proof of fate, then here it is. What are the odds of a talent scout coming to your first show and begging you to let her make you a star? That only happens in movies."

He gives me a wry smile. "You're trying to cheer me up by talking about fate? A concept you don't believe in?"

"Maybe I don't, but you do."

He cups the back of my head. Before I have time to figure out what's going on, he leans forward, and oh-so-gently brushes his lips over mine. Every single molecule of oxygen in my lungs rushes out.

"Yes, I do believe in fate," he says, still so close we're sharing the same air. "And that's why I'm so torn. My head is telling me to go, but my heart wants me to stay. With you."

"But you can't."

His hand is on my cheek, his thumb grazing slowly. "No. I can't." I grip his arms as he rests his forehead on mine. "So us being together is now or never. And since I can't cope with the concept of never, I vote for now."

I draw in a shuddering breath. "But what's the point of us getting in any deeper when we know it has to end?"

"The point is, I'd get to make love to you in all the ways I've been dreaming about since the night I met you." He brings his mouth next to my ear and whispers, "If I only have one more day in New York, I want to spend it with you. Please, Elissa."

He's not allowed to say stuff like that. Not when the only valid response is to drag him into a shadowy corner and mount him.

"Liss?" I look up at him as strong arms tighten around me. "Come home with me. If you don't want to have sex, that's fine. Talk to me. Touch me. Whatever you feel comfortable with. Just be with me. Please. We don't have much time left. And I have the strongest feeling that having part of you is going to be better than having all of anybody else."

I close my eyes and sigh. How can I say no to that?

Without another word, I take his hand and lead him out of the party.

Anticipation is tingling in all of my limbs, making me hot and restless. Liam seems equally tense. His hands are shoved in his pockets, shoulders hunched, eyes darting around nervously before coming back to me, time and again. My face. My breasts. My legs.

All of me.

The sexual tension is making the confines of his apartment stifling, and the boxes of his belongings that are stacked against the wall don't help.

He stares at me for a few, spine-tingling seconds, and then he seems to come to his senses. "I'm being a terrible host. Can I get you anything?" He walks the two steps to the fridge. "I have . . . uh . . ." He opens the door and peers in. "Well, not a lot." I can see that the fridge is practically bare. He shuts it and turns to me. "I spent all my food money on the airline ticket. I've been surviving on crackers and cheese for most of the week."

"Nothing wrong with surviving on cheese. I do it all the time. It's the food of kings."

He gives me a smile. "If I ever become a big star, I'll buy a Hollywood mansion with a dedicated cheese room. You can stay over."

"Just when I thought you couldn't get any sexier, you go and say that." I'm not even joking.

His expression darkens. "Is that right?"

We stare at each other, and I swear to God, the walls inch closer.

Liam takes a step forward. "Elissa . . ." The way he says my name makes me step forward, too. Then his hands are on my face, and he's leaning down, and sweet Jesus, I've never wanted someone to kiss me so much in my entire life. I take a breath and try to keep my eyes open.

"Do you understand how many fantasies I've had about you over the past two months?" he asks, his lips almost touching mine.

"If it's even half the number I've had about you, then yes, and I'm embarrassed for both of us."

"We can compare fantasies later. First, let me do this before I lose my mind."

He brushes his lips across mine, and we both inhale sharply. He pulls back and opens his mouth a little more to capture my lips in his. Light suction spins tiny shock waves down all my limbs.

"These lips have been driving me insane. Also, this neck." Soft kisses trail down my throat. Teeth nibble and tease. "This body. Okay, let's be honest. All of you." He grips my hips and maneuvers me back against the wall. "You're the most arousing woman I've ever met. Will ever meet."

My pulse thunders in my ears as I stare at his mouth. "I doubt that's true."

"Don't. And I don't know how, but . . ." He takes my hands from his chest and pushes them into the wall above my head. Then he traps my wrists in his hands and squeezes. Not enough to cause pain. Just enough to make every neuron overload and scream for more. "I know how to please you, Liss. I've known it from the first time I saw you." He squeezes my wrists again as he grazes over my lips. "I can feel what you need. But I'd still like you to tell me what you want."

I'm not good at saying what I want. I think that's why I've never orgasmed with a man. I boss people around enough in my professional life—I don't want to have to do it in the bedroom. And I definitely don't want to have to draw a man a map to make me orgasm.

"Say it," he says, his voice low and commanding. "I can see you thinking about it. Tell me and I'll make it happen."

He winds his fingers between mine and slides them down the wall until they're beside my head. My breaths are so fast and shallow, I feel like I'm about to hyperventilate.

"Make me come," I say.

His expression intensifies into pure, primal hunger. "Yes, ma'am."

Without another word, he pins me to the wall and kisses me like it's his job.

Oh.

God.

This man. His mouth. The same mouth I've fantasized about every day for the past eight weeks. The same sweet lips. Exactly the right amount of suction to drive me crazy.

When he slides his tongue against mine, I lose control. I kiss him back desperately. His hands roam across my body as we kiss, pushing under my clothes, gripping and squeezing flesh. He's not gentle. That's fine with me. Gentle is boring.

I take the opportunity to touch him in all the ways I've dreamt about. I explore every muscle. Every hard plane and groove.

I grip his forearms as they tense and release, then run my hands up to his biceps. They flex as he cradles my face and covers my mouth with his. When I push under his T-shirt and run my fingers along the waistband of his jeans, he grabs my hands and presses them back into the wall, hard.

"We've just established I have a job to do. Stop trying to distract me."

I kiss him deeper. A low rumble echoes in his chest, dark and animalistic. I've never heard a sexier noise come out of a man. He kisses my neck, then works his way back up to my ear.

"Take your clothes off," he whispers. His warm breath makes me shudder. "I need to see you."

I'm too turned on to even answer, so I nod.

He kisses me once more before he walks over to the bed and sits on the edge.

Nervousness prickles my spine. I like to think I'm confident with my body, but that's when I'm with mere mortals. Liam is the definition of masculine perfection. Being open to his scrutiny is downright intimidating.

"Elissa?" When I look at him, he's leaning forward, elbows on his knees. If possible, his expression is even more intense than before we kissed. His eyes are penetrating. Demanding. "Stop thinking. Start with your shoes."

The roughness of his voice talks straight to the deepest parts of me. Something hot and urgent fires in my belly.

I strip off my boots and socks and await further instructions.

He looks at my feet. I didn't think it was possible for feet to blush, but I swear they do. He brings his gaze back up to my face. "Now the shirt."

I draw up my T-shirt, then pull it over my head and drop it on the floor. I'm only wearing a plain black bra, but his sudden exhale makes me think he likes it. A lot. His gaze lingers on my breasts, making them ache for his hands.

He licks his lips. "Very nice. Jeans next."

I unbutton my black jeans and slide down the zipper. I glance up at him as I push them slowly down my legs. A muscle in his jaw jumps as he sits up straighter. His swollen crotch distracts me for a moment, but then he clears his throat, and my attention goes back to his face.

When I step out of the jeans and straighten up, he lets out a long breath. "Jesus. Okay. So there you are." He breathes for a few moments, then stands, and I watch as he clenches and unfurls his hands. "So much better than the fantasy."

I'm wearing a black thong. Nothing fancy but kind of small. He studies it intently.

"Turn around," he says, his voice rough.

I turn. I hear him swear under his breath, then he's behind me and rough fingers are brushing over my buttocks. He groans and squeezes, then grazes his hands up over my hips, my rib cage. He traces along the line of my bra under my arms before cupping my breasts as he pulls me back against him.

"You," he says as he plants soft kisses on my neck, "are fucking perfect."

Warmth fires in my groin and spreads down all my limbs as I reach behind me to grip the back of his head. This man is too much. Too sexy, too good-looking, too . . . Oh, his mouth. The feel of his mouth on my shoulder, kissing the side of my neck, gently taking the skin between his teeth.

One arm circles my waist, and he grinds against me. Feeling how hard he is makes me ache even more. My whole body feels swollen and desperate. A large hand caresses my breasts. He finds my nipples beneath the fabric, and teases them before moving the other hand down my stomach. When he pushes inside my panties and presses tight circles against me, I suck in a moan and close my eyes.

Oh, this is going to be good. He wasn't kidding when he said he knew how to please me. I may have had only a handful of sexual partners in my nineteen years, but every one of them had been clueless, the type of lazy lovers who claimed that bringing a woman to orgasm was like finding a unicorn, and so they just couldn't be bothered. Clearly, Liam can be bothered. *Hot* and bothered, judging by the way he's breathing against my ear and whispering how good I feel. He seems to be enjoying it almost as much as I am.

He drops his head onto my shoulder as he increases his pace. More pressure. Tighter circles. I anchor my fingers in his hair and hold on for dear life. It helps keep me upright, which is good, because the thick pleasure that's coiling in all my muscles makes standing an impossible concept.

When my knees buckle, he scoops me up and lays me on the bed. I've barely registered our change of location before he's sliding off my underwear and crawling between my legs.

"Just so you know," he says as he pushes my knees apart and kisses the insides of my thighs. "You're getting kind of loud, and these walls are thin. The whole building can hear what I'm doing to you in here."

I'm surprised I'm being loud, considering I can barely speak. "S-sorry."

"Don't be. I love it. I'm sure if I try a little harder, I can make you scream." After a final soft kiss to my inner thigh, he closes his lips over me, and I gasp in surprise as he kisses me down there with just as much passion and hunger as he did my mouth.

Oh, sweet holy . . . fuck!

I throw my head back and moan so loudly, I startle myself. He hums in satisfaction as he continues to work.

Oh.

Ohh.

Ohhhhhh.

If I thought his mouth was a miracle before he went down on me, I now believe the sole purpose of those amazing lips and tongue is to bring me the most debilitating pleasure imaginable. Every time I think I can't feel any more, he proves me wrong.

After an eternity of panting and crying out, every muscle is so tense I'm arching off the bed. He reacts by closing strong hands around my hips and pulling me more firmly onto his face.

Jesus . . . take the wheel.

Thick pulses start, increasing in frequency in time with his tongue, and I can't do anything but hold my breath as all of my wire-tight muscles release. The resulting waves of pleasure are so powerful, I have to bite down on a long, strangled scream.

I squeeze my eyes shut as everything spasms, and when the last shudders move through me, I concentrate on simply breathing. I feel high as Liam kisses his way back up my body. Everything is fuzzy and nothing hurts.

Wow. Okay, so that's what it feels like to have someone else bring you to orgasm. I could get used to this.

Soft lips are on my neck, then my chest. I'm still dazed, but my body reacts. When Liam pulls me on top of him so he can remove my bra, I gasp at how hard he is. He sits up and kisses the swell of my breast, then my nipple. I praise any god who might be listening for Liam Quinn's perfect, talented mouth. I curl my fingers into his hair as he moves to my other breast, and groan as he further demonstrates his divine oral powers. I look down to watch, and frown when I realize he's still completely clothed.

This is not right.

"You intend on stripping soon, right?" I ask. "Because my nakedness is lonely and would like some company."

"If you want me naked, then by all means. . . ." He pulls us both up to standing. "Go right ahead and make it happen."

He holds me tight for a moment while the strength returns to my legs, then lets me go and stands back. I can feel his hot-blooded stare all over me as I bend down to remove his shoes and socks. When they're off, I stand and look him in the eyes.

"Your shirt," I say. "Off. Now."

He suppresses a smile, then reaches over his shoulder to pull off his T-shirt. "Have I told you how hot it is when you boss me around?"

"Not half as hot as when you do it to me." My voice wavers as I take in his beautiful body. Broad shoulders. Wide, hard pecs. Ridiculously defined abs that lead down to crazy-sexy hip muscles and a smattering of light hair.

He drops the shirt on the floor. "You like it when I tell you what to do?" I swallow my excess saliva and nod. "In that case, get on your knees, Miss Holt."

The air of dominance in his voice sends a shiver up my spine. I've never had a man be so commanding in the bedroom. I like it.

I keep eye contact as I drop to my knees. From this angle, he looks even more magnificent. Smooth, lightly tanned skin. Rippling muscles. An expression that screams of being so turned on, it hurts.

"Unbuckle my belt." His voice has dropped to a dark whisper. My hands tremble as I grab the belt and release it. "Now, the jeans." I pop the button and pull down the zipper, then breathe shallowly and stare at the waistband of his boxer briefs as I wait for his next order.

He grips my chin and urges me to look up at him. "Whatever you want to do to me, I'm going to enjoy. Trust me on that."

I smile. "I know. I was just waiting for permission to blow your mind."

At that, he clenches his jaw, and the fingers holding my face tighten a little before releasing. "Do it."

I hold his gaze for a second longer before moving my attention lower. With restrained impatience, I work his jeans and underwear down and off, and then there he is in all his glory.

Good Lord. That's . . . well, that's a whole lot of man.

I try to keep my breathing steady as I take in his impressive erection, jutting stiff and proud from his body.

I touch him, gently at first, getting to know the size and weight of him. He takes a ragged breath as he winds his fingers through my hair and pulls it away from my face.

"Fuck. Liss." His voice cracks, and I move with more confidence. Well, as much confidence as is possible when one is faced with something of this size. None of my previous lovers was this big. Just more proof I've been sleeping with boys up until now, and that Liam is a full-fledged man.

When I put my mouth on him, he groans, loud and long. I glance up to see his head thrown back, eyes closed. His fingers clench and release sporadically in my hair, and it only spurs me on to please him further. I continue kissing and sucking, and take special note of what I'm doing whenever I make him curse or grunt. When I start using my hand in tandem with my mouth, he lets out a low growl before he steps back and pulls me to my feet.

"Fuck, woman." He picks me up and all but throws me onto the mattress, then climbs over and kneels between my legs. I have a moment to appreciate how supremely sexy he is as he reaches into the nightstand, tears open a condom package, and rolls it on with sure fingers. When he's done, he looks down at me.

"You are . . ." He shakes his head. "I've never ached for a woman as much as I ache for you." He settles between my legs and braces on one arm. "I feel like I can't get enough of you, no matter how hard I try."

He drops his pelvis down and then kisses me. I wrap around him, and kiss him back. I know exactly what he means. It's like feeding my hunger for him just makes me more insatiable.

I close my eyes as he uses his mouth all over my chest, and when his hips push forward, the pressure of him makes me gasp.

Oh, *God.*

He kisses me and moans at the same time, all the while moving forward, then back. Small movements that bring him a little deeper each time.

Sweet mother, the feel of him. I'm not a big woman, but he's a big man, in every sense of the word. I suddenly experience a real concern about our size difference.

"Relax," he says between kisses, picking up on my tension. "There's nothing to worry about. It will feel good soon, I promise."

He keeps kissing and touching, trying to soothe me as he pushes and retreats. I breathe through the pressure and run my hands over all of him. His amazing back. His magnificent chest. His abs that tremble with every deepening thrust.

"You feel so . . ." He groans into my neck. "God . . . Liss."

As his thrusts become more confident, I realize he was right: He fills me so completely, it feels amazing. He slides one hand beneath my butt and lifts my pelvis, and . . . *Sweet Jesus!*

I grip his shoulders and moan. He's hitting a place inside me I never knew existed. Every time he thrusts, I gasp, and each subsequent gasp gets louder and more desperate.

"There?" he asks, panting as he watches my face.

"God, yes. Right there. Don't stop. Please . . ."

He thrusts harder. I can't even cope with how good it feels.

"Touch yourself," he says as he gains speed. "I want to feel you come while I'm inside you."

I reach down and circle my fingers.

Oh.

Sweet.

Holy.

Mother.

My orgasm builds so quickly, I'm not even remotely prepared for it. Liam's powerful thrusts, in conjunction with my hand, bring me to a place I've never been before. I gasp as I feel the first sparks of my orgasm begin to fire.

Liam groans, and when I look up at him, it's clear he's struggling to hold on.

"Please, Liss. God . . . I can't—"

I move my hand faster, and it's only a few more seconds before I'm coming so hard, I'm arching off the bed and groaning his name.

Everything explodes. My mind. My body. The sensation is indescribable. I hear a keening noise and realize it's me.

I'm still reeling when Liam moans into the side of my neck. Every muscle in his back tightens as he presses in as far as possible, and I grip him and stroke his back as he trembles with the force of his orgasm. After tense seconds and a final muttered curse word, he relaxes and collapses on the bed beside me. We both lie there for a while, panting and blinking. Wondering what the hell just happened.

My body is still in shock.

"What was that?" Liam asks, still out of breath.

"Sex?"

"No way. I've had sex before, and it was nothing like that. Tell me you felt it, too."

"Are you kidding me? I'm still feeling it." I'm not exaggerating. Little ripples of pleasure are still spasming inside me. For a moment, I wonder if his size made the difference, but I have a feeling that he could have had the most average-sized penis in the world and still shattered me into a million quivering pieces.

"After that," he says, "are you still going to deny that we're fated? Because let me tell you, sex like that doesn't happen every day. Or every year, for that matter. Or in my case, even every twenty-two and three-quarter years. You need to finally accept that this"—he turns to me and points between us—"is freaking extraordinary. Because

I'm not above spanking you into submission if you continue to delude yourself that's it's not."

Part of me wants to deny it just to find out what it would be like to be spanked by him. Those big, rough hands, one holding me in place while the other one—

I close my eyes and push away the urge.

"Elissa?"

"I'm pleading the Fifth."

"That's as good as admitting I'm right."

"No, I'm just not saying you're wrong."

"Hmmm. Not sure whether or not that earns a spanking. I'll think it over."

"You do that. My butt awaits your verdict."

He chuckles, and I feel the mattress move as he gets up to dispose of the condom. When he climbs back into bed, I turn to look at him.

His face is flushed, his lips are swollen, and his hair is insane, but I've never seen a more attractive man in my life. He studies my face, then brushes a damp piece of hair away from my forehead.

"Stay the night," he says quietly. "I want to see how many more times I can make you scream before morning."

Before I can turn him down, he pulls me over and kisses me, his hand gentle on my cheek. It's unexpectedly sweet and makes me forget all about the excuse that was on the tip of my tongue. He pulls back and nuzzles my neck. "Plus, I'm an excellent snuggler. Stay."

A tiny voice warns me it's a bad idea. That getting any closer will only make things harder when he leaves. I tell that voice to shut its mouth. After what I just experienced, I need more of Liam Quinn. Much more. Consequences be damned.

"Okay."

SEVEN

BITTERSWEET

How long does it take to fall in love?

A second? A week? A year?

It's like asking how long it takes to fall asleep. Some people are gone as soon as their head hits the pillow. Others lie awake for hours, and it's only when their brain stops churning for a while that sleep sneaks in and drags them under.

That's how I visualize people falling in love. Some people fall so easily, they seem reckless. They love freely and unashamed.

Those people are idiots.

Or at least I used to think so. Until now.

I tried to stay as detached as possible with Liam last night, but every time I thought I'd pushed out any real emotion, he'd kiss me, or whisper something sweet that made it come crashing back in again. In the end, I just went with it. I knew it was dumb, considering our situation, but I couldn't help it.

And now, he's behind me, wrapped around me like he never wants to let go. His breath is warm and steady on the back of my neck as he sleeps, blissfully unaware I'm getting more uptight by the second.

In our current position, every inch of my naked back is pressed against every inch of his naked front, and my head is resting on a plump bicep while his other arm is wrapped around my waist.

I sigh and squeeze my eyes shut. It shouldn't feel this good to be enveloped in a man, especially one I can't have.

I try to pull his arm away from my waist, but it won't budge. Damn. Stupid giant muscles.

"What are you doing?" he mutters, voice dark with sleep.

"I have to go."

"No you don't."

"Yes I do. I have things I need to take care of."

"Me too. All of them involve being inside you. Leaving isn't an option."

I pull at his arm again. It's like iron. "Don't you have to pack?"

"All done. I'm having dinner with Mom and Dad tonight and then they're taking me to the airport in the morning. Other than that, I'm free." He loosens his grip and pushes me onto my back, then leans over for a lingering kiss. "Is this convincing you to stay?"

"Hmmm. I'm not sure. Maybe you should try harder."

He presses his very obvious erection against my hip. "This hard enough?"

My whole body reacts. "Ah, yes. That'll do."

"Man, you're easy. Thank God."

I squeal as he pins me to the bed.

Forty minutes and two orgasms later, I'm boneless. I drift in and out of consciousness, and when I open my eyes, Liam's there, head cradled in his hand, staring down at me.

"I'm confused," he says with a frown.

"About what?"

"You say you've had boyfriends who've left you for other women."

"Yes. Three of them, to be precise."

"Did you exclusively date blind men? Or were they just total idiots? Because honestly, apart from those options, I don't see how it's possible."

I smile. "I told you the reason already. They were actors."

"That explains nothing."

"Doesn't it?" I turn on my side to look at him. "Tell me about how you feel about Olivia."

He frowns. "Olivia? As in Juliet-Olivia?"

"Yes."

He looks at me dubiously. "Is this one of those tricky female questions I shouldn't answer for fear of being smacked?"

"No. Just be honest."

He doesn't seem convinced. "Okay. I . . . like her?"

"As a friend?"

"Yes. Just a friend. Definitely nothing more." He still looks nervous, so I stroke his chest to calm him. Also, because his chest is beautiful and I want to touch it.

"So now explain how your love scenes in *Romeo and Juliet* were as hot as hell."

"They were?"

"God, yes! Did you not notice me subtly fanning myself every time you guys made out?"

"I just figured you were warm."

"I was. In my pants." He laughs and lies back on the bed. When he puts his hands under his head, I don't miss the way his biceps pop. I run my forefinger over one.

"I had no clue you were turned on," he says. "I was trying so hard to stay away from you, I avoided looking at you most of the time."

"So, how did you do it?"

"Stay away from you? It wasn't easy. Cold showers and heavy drinking helped."

I pinch his bicep, and he squirms. "I mean, how did you appear so in love with Olivia when you only liked her as a friend?"

He pauses. "I don't know. I just used my imagination, I guess. As Romeo, when I looked at Juliet, I made my body feel things for her. My adrenal system is pretty gullible."

A tinge of jealousy squirms inside me. "So you just *made yourself* feel love for her, and then expect me to believe those feelings don't bleed over into real life?"

He turns to me and props himself up on one arm. "It's not that simple. Onstage, Romeo was completely in love with Juliet, but offstage . . . I don't know. Olivia was a different person. So was I."

"But she's not. And you're not. You're the same people with the same faces and bodies. How is it possible for actors to make love to someone every night onstage and stay faithful to their wives and girl-friends offstage?"

"Lots of actors do it."

"And lots don't, and it seems I have a talent for choosing the ones who can't separate fantasy from reality. That's why I didn't want to get close to you. I couldn't cope with being collateral damage again."

He sits up and frowns at me. "So what you're saying is that if we were in a relationship, I'd naturally develop feelings for my leading lady and dump you?"

"History would suggest yes."

"My unbelievable attraction to you would suggest no fucking way."

"Attraction fades."

"Wrong. *Lust* fades. Attraction keeps people together long after lust is just a distant memory."

"And what makes you think that what you feel for me isn't just lust?"

He cups my cheek. "Because I've lusted after a lot of girls in my life, and let me tell you, not *once* did it feel like this."

He leans down and kisses me gently, and I know he's right. A simple brush of his lips may be enough to set my whole body on fire, but beneath that simmer is something else. A feeling of *rightness*. Hell, I'd even go so far as to entertain his romantic concept of fate if I wasn't so stubborn. But how can fate call him to Hollywood as well as make it feel like he's mine? That's not even a little fair.

I pull back, and he sighs. "If I wasn't leaving I could prove to you that not all actors are abandoning assholes."

"And yet, you're about to abandon me."

"Totally different."

"I know. But it still sucks." Thinking about it makes an unexpected lump form in my throat.

"Yeah, it does." He's quiet for a moment, then asks, "Will you miss me?"

I want to say no, because admitting how much I'm going to miss him is crazy. Instead, I force a smile. "I'm sure we'll both be so busy we won't have time to dwell on it."

He nods. "Yeah. Sure. Dwelling would be bad." He crosses his arms over his chest and stares at the wall, a deep frown furrowing his brows. The openness from earlier has vanished. "Maybe I'll bomb in Hollywood and be back here before you know it."

I'm an asshole for wishing that would happen, but I know very well it won't. "Liam, Hollywood is going to lose its mind as soon as you arrive. I have no doubt. And when you're a big star, I'll be able to say I knew you when."

He doesn't answer, but his frown deepens. When I climb out of bed to gather my clothes, he doesn't try to stop me. I quickly retreat into the bathroom.

Okay, Elissa, get it together.

You're fine. He's fine. Everything's fine.

He'll leave, and you'll forget about him, and everything will go back to normal. Stop freaking out.

After a warm shower, I exit to find him sitting on the bed with his head in his hands, wearing only his jeans. When he sees me, the look in his eyes almost makes everything not-fine.

"Elissa, listen—" But I'm sure if I do that, I won't get out of here in one piece.

"Liam, I really do have to go. Thanks for . . . everything." *All the orgasms, and kisses, and deep, longing gazes. Thanks for screwing with my mind and heart as much as with my body.*

I finish pulling on my socks and boots and grab my messenger bag.

When I stand, he walks over and puts his arms around me. Such a simple gesture, but the affection with which he does it makes me sigh.

He drops his head onto my shoulder and squeezes me in a tight hug. "I don't want this to be the end for us."

I grip his arms, and try to bring him closer. "I don't either, but we're going to be on opposite sides of the country. I don't know about you, but I couldn't cope with that if you were my boyfriend. It would be torture."

He pulls back and gazes down at me. "True. If I were your boyfriend I'd definitely need to not be away from you. Ever." He cups my face and slowly leans down. "I'd need to be close enough to do this, every . . . single . . . day."

He kisses me, soft and slow, and I've never wanted to live in a moment more than I want to live in this one.

"Liss, tell me not to leave. Please. I'd stay if you asked me to."

"You know you can't. And if you gave up this opportunity for me, I'd never forgive myself." Fingers graze over my arms, and I shiver. "Anyway, there are thousands of beautiful women in L.A. I'm sure you'll forget about me in no time."

"Not going to happen. Ever. Trust me on that." He kisses me again, but this time, it's hard and desperate.

After a few more frantic minutes, we pull back, and we're both breathing heavily. It would be so easy to let things get out of control, but we both know there's no point in taking this further. The kiss, or the relationship.

Standing on my toes, I give him one final hug before pulling away. I hate how the distance between us suddenly makes everything feel cold.

I walk to the door and open it, then turn back to him. He looks at me with a conflicted expression, and I know exactly how he feels.

"I'm not saying good-bye," he says as he shoves his hands into his pockets. "Because this isn't over. One day, fate's going to fix this. Bring us back together. I believe that."

I smile. "Yeah. One day." My smile is too fake, and my heart is too sore, and I can't begin to cope with how he's looking at me.

"See you soon, Liss."

I nod. "Bye, Liam. Travel safe."

I clench my jaw against the tears that threaten as I close the door behind me.

EIGHT

NO EXCUSES

Eight Months Later
Central Park
New York City

I used to think missing someone was a choice, but that was before Liam. Now I realize all you can do is choose to *ignore* missing someone. The actual longing never goes away. It stays in your body like a toothache, deep in your bones, and every time you forget to deny it, the hum of it builds into a roar that's so loud, it's the only thing you can hear.

He's been gone eight months now, and I still have to concentrate to stop thinking about him every day.

It doesn't help that Josh is also gone. He got his acceptance letter to The Grove the same time I did, but decided to accept an offer from the UCLA School of Theater, Film and Television instead. For years he'd fantasized about living in L.A., and even though I suspected his decision was fueled by his obsession with all things young, hot, and actressy, I tried to be as supportive as possible.

The result is that the two people I want to be with most are both thousands of miles away. This has worked out well.

I sigh as I cross the road and head into Central Park. Stupid Liam.

Making me feel things. Forcing me to miss him. If I didn't love him so much, I'd hate him.

As I head toward the lake, "I'm Too Sexy" blares out of my phone, and even before I answer it I'm smiling.

"Madam Elissa's House of Snark. How may I help you?"

"Move to L.A. Right the fuck now," Josh says.

"Certainly, sir. I'll be on the next plane."

"Don't mess with me, woman. I'm homesick, and haven't been laid in over a week. I'm in a very vulnerable place right now. What are you doing?"

"Walking through Central Park. Heading to my reading tree."

"You back home for the weekend?"

"Yeah. I had a few days off in between Grove shows, so I've come home to recharge." I reach my reading tree near the lake and drop my bag on the grass before sitting. "What's up?"

"Nothing. Just wanted to talk to my bestie. How's your love life? Found anyone interesting at The Grove?"

I lean back against the tree and stretch my legs out in front of me. "Nope."

"Aw, come on. It's an arts college. There has to be a decent quotient of hot men."

I pick at the grass. "Oh, there are lots of hot men, but it's a drama school. It's full of damn actors."

"Okay, then branch out. There are also musicians and artists, right? Find a hot rock god. Or a sensitive painter. I know for damn sure you could get a date with anyone you liked if you just tried. At least have some meaningless sex. You're wasting your college experience."

The thing is, as much as I'd like to use sex to blow off steam, I'm just not interested in any of the guys at The Grove. I'm only interested in the man who's closer to Josh than he is to me.

Josh clears his throat. "Aaaand we've reached the part of our conversation where I mention sex, and you go quiet so you can daydream about Liam Quinn."

God, am I that predictable? "Sorry, Josh."

"Don't be. It's just crappy he's here instead of there. Did you see him in the latest Coke ad?"

"Yeah. It's hard not to see him." Shirt off, body glistening with water. A perfect-boobed blonde hanging off his arm as he smiles and embodies a man loving his life.

It makes me so jealous, I have to change the channel whenever it comes on.

"At least he's getting work out here," Josh says.

"Of course he is. He's a casting agent's wet dream."

Josh pauses for a few seconds, then says, "You know, if you came out here to visit me, you could also see Quinn. I hate saying that because the risk is you'd fall into bed with him and not have time for me, but still. It's a thought. I predict that if you and him were in the same city, your no-sex embargo would vanish in a puff of very horny smoke. Might do you some good."

The hairs on the back of my neck stand on end. God, what a thought. Seeing Liam in the flesh. Touching him. Kissing him. It would be amazing.

I squeeze my eyes shut.

Godammit. Just thinking about him is making me miss him even more. My chest actually aches.

I lean back against the tree. "Can we not talk about this anymore? Don't you have to go to class?"

"Only if I want to graduate. So, yeah. Call me tomorrow?"

"You bet."

"And, Lissa?"

"Hmmm?"

"Just think about what I said, okay?"

"I will. Love you, Josh."

"Love you, too."

I hang up and sigh. Thoughts of seeing Liam wind around in my brain. It's tempting. Very tempting.

I go to my contacts and pull up his number. Next to it is the picture he took the night we met. The one where he's kissing me so deeply, I felt it in my toes.

When he first left, I sent him text messages now and then, just to check if he was okay. I tried to keep them casual and friendly, but it somehow made me feel closer to him.

He'd never reply. Not with texts, anyway. The first time he called me, I panicked and let it go to voice mail. He left a message. Just listening to his voice made missing him both easier and harder.

I punch in the number for my voice mail. I'm embarrassed at how often I play these messages. When I hear them, I can almost imagine he's with me.

"Hey, Elissa. How's it going? Got your texts. I'm not great at replying to those things, so thought I'd call you instead. I made it to L.A. safely. Although after nearly six hours on a plane, I wanted to murder someone. Preferably the dude who made sure anyone over six feet tall would have to bend themselves like a pretzel to fit into those stupid economy seats. I suspect the asshole was a sadist. It's the only logical explanation. Anyway, I'm going apartment hunting tomorrow. On my budget, I'll be lucky to get something with running water and electricity, but I'll do my best. Are you at The Grove yet? Surviving living with your brother? Okay, better go. Hope you're well. Give me a call sometime, okay? I'd love to hear from you."

A week later, I called him back. He didn't pick up either, so I left him a voice mail. I told him about my course, the torture of living with Ethan. Everything and nothing.

After that, we fell into a cycle. Phone messages became our way of staying in touch without the pressure of an actual conversation. It worked for us. It took away the temptation of saying things in real time that would make our separation even more painful.

Or at least, that's how it started.

"Hey, Liss. Sitting here, thinking about you. Thought I'd give you a quick call. I have my first screen test today. I'm nervous as hell. Please tell me it gets easier. Hope you're well."

"Liss! I got a national ad for Coke! It's not Shakespeare but it's a start. Now I can finally buy real food and pay my rent on time. Winning!" There's a pause and a change of tone. *"If you were here, I'd take you out to celebrate. Hope you're well."*

See? Casual. Easy. Nice. I always replied.

But one day, the tone of Liam's messages started to change.

"Hey, Liss. I kind of want you to pick up one day so we can have a proper conversation, but I know it would make me want to jump on the first plane home. I miss you. And New York. L.A. is driving me crazy, and Hollywood is . . . challenging." He pauses. *"The one thing that keeps me going is knowing we'll be together again one day. I have no doubt about that. Leave me a message when you get a chance. I miss your voice. Well, I miss all of you, but hearing your voice makes me miss you a little less. Hope you're well. Bye."*

From that day, my messages also got more plaintive. I kept the content the same—life at The Grove, my brother and his tragic love life, shows I was working on, and so on. But I also let him know I missed him. And putting that into words made the distance between us even more painful.

Then, a couple of months ago, I received this:

"Hey, my beautiful Liss. My bliss. See what I did there?" His voice is low and makes me tingle. *"I've had a few beers, but I'm not drunk. I'm just . . . missing you. I keep hoping being away from you will get easier, but it doesn't. If anything, it's getting harder. I can't stop thinking about our final night together. How good it felt when I put my hands on you. Even better when you put your hands on me. Do you remember? I can't get it out of my mind. The feel of you. The sounds you made. God, just thinking about it does very horny things to me."*

I hear a low groan and squeeze my eyes shut. *"I love listening to your messages. Your voice. I love hearing you say my name. I replay that part over and over again. Pathetic, right?"* He lets out a low chuckle. *"Yeah. Pathetic. Anyway, some big things are happening here right now, but I don't want to jinx it and tell you before it's all set in stone. Hopefully I'll have good news next time we speak."*

There's a beat, but I can hear him breathing. *"Okay, well . . . that's all I wanted to say, I guess. Oh, and one more thing. I'm in love with you. I have been for a long time. No big deal."* He pauses again and sighs. *"Shit. I promised myself I wouldn't say that until I saw you in person, but I guess I'm impatient, and dammit . . . I want you to know. I'm not stupid. I'm sure there are men falling over themselves to date you at The Grove, and the thought of anyone but me making love to you drives me insane. I don't want you to date other men. I want you to date me. Unfortunately, geography has other ideas, so I guess I'm screwed."*

I hear him take a sip of his drink and swallow. *"Okay, well, now that I've spilled my guts way more than I intended, I'd better go. I don't want you to think I'm trying to claim something I can't have by saying the L word. I really don't. And I certainly don't expect you to say it back. In fact, please don't. Saying those words just because someone else does is hollow. If and when you say it to me, I want to look into your eyes and know that you mean it. Because I mean it. You don't even understand how much. Hope you're well. And missing me. Love you. Bye."*

Every time I hear him say that, it makes me just as giddy as the first time. Of course, I called him straight back to tell him I felt the same, but when the message tone sounded, I couldn't go through with saying it to a machine. Instead, I asked him to call me back ASAP so we could talk properly. He didn't. In fact, my next three messages asking him to call also went unanswered.

Now, I have no idea where I stand. Is he embarrassed about saying he loved me? Or did he realize it was the booze and nostalgia talking rather than him?

Either way, I feel like I'm in limbo. And until I speak to him—the real-live him—I don't see that changing.

I take a deep breath as my finger hovers over his number. Screw it. I'm going to keep calling until he answers. One way or another, we're going to have a conversation today.

Adrenaline surges through me as I make the decision. I stand, sling my bag over my shoulder, and start walking. I try to expel nervous energy as I hit his number.

I tap my thigh as the call connects and starts to ring, once . . . twice . . . three times. After the sixth ring, it goes to voice mail. I hang up and redial.

Three more times it connects to voice mail, but on the fourth try, he answers.

"Liss? What's going on? Are you okay?"

The relief I feel at the sound of his voice is so intense, my knees go weak. "Liam. Hey. Hi. I'm fine. I just needed to talk to you. The real you. And . . . wow. I am."

I hear him exhale. "I . . . God, Liss. It's good to hear your voice."

"You, too. Your voice, I mean. I . . . uh . . . I can't believe I'm speaking to you." I'm so nervous, my saliva has dried up. "How are you?"

"Good. You?"

"Good." I shake my head as I reach the stairs leading down to the fountain. I've never felt awkward with him before. Why am I starting now? "How's everything going? I haven't heard from you in a while. I mean, I've tried a few times. I wanted you to know how much I loved your last message. I *loved* it. Really. Why didn't you call me back?"

There's a pause. "Yeah, sorry about that. I've been crazy busy. Actually, I've been meaning to call. I . . . uh, got a movie. Well, a movie franchise, actually."

My heart skips a beat. "What?! Seriously? Tell me everything."

"I auditioned for it when I first got here. They've made me do about twenty screen tests since, but a couple of months ago, they told me I got it. Have you heard of *Rageheart?*"

I stop dead in my tracks. "Are you kidding me? I read the script when it was leaked online. Please tell me you're playing Zan. Oh, God, on second thought, no. He's already too sexy. If you were playing him it would be disastrous for women everywhere, and me in particular. Okay, wait." I take a deep breath. "Break it to me gently."

He chuckles. "I'm playing Zan."

I actually squeal and do a little jump. I don't think I've ever done that before, but this is news worth squealing about. "Liam, that's incredible! I'm so happy for you! This is it. Your big break to megastardom."

As I come down the stairs, I pause to watch a group of people milling around near the fountain and wonder what's going on. Knowing New York, someone's filming here. It's a daily occurrence.

Down the phone, I hear Liam sigh. "The whole thing has happened so fast my head is spinning. We're already rehearsing and doing press."

"Who's playing Areal?"

He pauses. "Uh . . . Angel Bell."

I frown. "Really? I didn't know she was an actress. I just thought she was a professional famous person."

"She's done a few small movies recently, and I guess someone thinks she's ready for the big leagues."

"Well, that makes two of you. You'll look incredible together. People are going to lose their minds."

He pauses. "Listen, Liss, there's something I want to talk to you about."

"I have something to talk to you about, too. That's why I called."

"Okay."

"Since I got your last message, I've been wanting to tell you . . . Well, I need you to know that . . ." As I get closer to the fountain I see a group of people setting up for a photo shoot. Over to the side I spy the back of a particularly gorgeous male model. My whole body flushes at the sight of him.

Helloooo, handsome.

I frown. That back is awfully familiar.

"Wait, Liam. Where are you?"

"Uh . . . talking to you on the phone."

"Yes, but where? In L.A.?"

"Actually, no. I'm back in New York for the weekend. I have a photo shoot for some entertainment magazine. So strange."

"You're shooting in Central Park?"

He pauses. "Yes. How did you know that?"

I smile. "Turn around and look halfway up the stairs."

He turns and scans the crowd behind him. When he sees me, his face goes through such a range of emotions, I have trouble deciphering them all. Finally, he gives me the most dazzling smile I've ever seen. He strides toward me, and I head toward him, and when I reach the bottom of the stairs, I launch myself into his arms. I swear we both stop breathing as we wrap around each other in the world's tightest hug.

"Liss." It not even a word. Just a sigh.

"Hey, you." I'm so happy I could cry. He feels just as good as I remember. Smells even better.

I dig my fingers into his back as he breathes against my neck, "God, I've missed you. A lot. More than I should."

"Likewise. I can't believe you're here. And I'm here."

He pulls back and shakes his head without looking at me. "Finding each other randomly in the middle of Central Park? Yeah. That sounds about right for us." He glances over his shoulder, then back at me. "Listen, we're about to start shooting, but I . . . I really need to talk to you. Can you meet me somewhere? After?"

"Of course. Call me when you're done. I'll be around."

"Okay. Sure." He shuffles his feet, and it's clear he doesn't want to go. I don't want him to go, either. After our being apart for so long, having him close is intoxicating. He studies my face, like he's trying to figure out what to do. I really want him to kiss me, but I understand that he's working. It can wait until we're alone.

"Mr. Quinn?" We turn to see a scrawny kid in skinny jeans and Chucks hovering nearby. "We're almost ready for you."

"Thanks. Be right there." The boy disappears, and when Liam turns back to me, his face is drawn.

"Mr. Quinn, huh?"

He gives me a wry smile. "Yep. I hate it."

"Well, get used to it. It won't be long before we're all calling you that."

I expect him to smile, but he doesn't. Instead, he takes my hands and mutters, "I'd better go."

"Liam, wait. I just need to—" I take a step forward and look up at him. "We can talk about this more when you're done, but I just want you to know . . ." This would have been so much easier on the phone. I get all turned around when I'm this close to him and he's staring at me with those incredible eyes. I glance down at his fingers wrapped around mine, and I'm hit with the same sense of rightness I always feel when we touch. Our hands look perfect together. They *feel* perfect. Seeing that helps me find my words. "I know we said we wouldn't do the long-distance thing, but . . . I can't stop thinking about your last message, and you need to know that I—"

"Liss, you don't have to—"

"Wait a sec, just let me say this before I lose my nerve, okay?" I take a breath and look up at him. "I've never met anyone like you, and I doubt I ever will. Recently I've come to the conclusion that life's too short not to spend it with the people we love and . . . I love you." I laugh and shake my head. "Wow, it feels weird to say that out loud. But I'm not saying it just because you said it. I promise. I'm saying it because I mean it, and I've been dying to tell you. I know that making things work when we're so far away from each other will be tough, but . . . I want to try. If you do."

His jaw tightens, and if I didn't know better, I'd think he was on the verge of tears. His hands clench and release around mine, and I search his face as he swallows heavily.

"Liam?"

"Liss, I—"

The production assistant appears again, more nervous than before. "Mr. Quinn. We really need you to come now. Please, sir."

Liam turns to glare at him. "I'll be there in a second." His expression makes the boy scurry away.

When he turns back to me, his face is still hard. "Sorry, I have to go. We'll talk more later, okay?"

"Okay." My heart is hammering in my chest. This isn't how I saw my first declaration of love ending. I thought for sure Liam would say it back and then we'd have mind-blowing sex, or at least a toe-curling kiss. This is . . . not that.

Liam bends down and gently brushes his lips across my cheek. I close my eyes and shiver.

"I'll call you later," he whispers.

I nod, and then he leaves me and heads back over to the fountain. When he gets there, the photographer calls him over, and a beautiful redhead appears on the other side of him. *Ah. Angel Bell.* Holy wow, she looks like a goddess.

Something unpleasant fires in my stomach. It intensifies when she and Liam take up their positions, and she grabs his arm possessively.

The photographer shoots and calls out instructions, and Liam and Angel move through various intimate poses. When the photographer walks over and talks to them, the poses get a whole lot sexier. Liam's shirt is unbuttoned. Angel's hands are on his chest and abs. He gazes at her like he wants to eat her.

"You know him?"

I turn to see a man with greasy hair and a goatee standing next to me. He's holding one of the biggest cameras I've ever seen.

Geez, dude. Overcompensating, much?

"I'm sorry, what?"

"Liam Quinn. I saw him talking to you. You friends? Family?"

I turn back to watch Liam grab Angel and pull her against him.

"Friends." *For the moment. Very soon, I'm hoping we'll be a whole lot more.*

The man brings up his giant camera and squeezes off a few shots. "Anything you can tell me about him and his costar? When did they start dating? Did they know each other before they got the movie?"

I look at him sharply. "You a reporter?"

He shrugs. "Sort of."

"Then you're misinformed. They're not dating."

He laughs. It's not a pleasant sound. "Haven't seen your friend for a while, have you? They're dating, all right. Well, 'fucking' would be a better word for it. Pardon the language."

My stomach clenches. "Why the hell would you think that? They're working together. That's it."

He smiles, showing nicotine-stained teeth, then glances around, as if to check that no one's looking. "I shouldn't be showing you this, but what the hell? Come tomorrow morning everyone's going to know anyway. I've sold these babies to four national mags and three Web sites. There's nothing like hot actors screwing each other's brains out to boost audience pull." He fiddles with the controls of his camera. "Friend of mine tipped me off that Quinn was going to be the next big thing in Hollywood, so I started following him a few weeks ago. Seems like he and his costar have been busy getting to know each other."

He turns the camera around so I can see the screen, then he scrolls through photos. My face flushes with heat. I feel sick.

There are dozens of pictures of Liam and Angel together. Gazing at each other lovingly. Kissing across a table at lunch. Making out in the doorway of his apartment after obviously spending the night together.

My head pounds as nausea rolls through me. I look away. The man chuckles and hands me his card. "So, yeah. The story's about to break about these two, big-time. If you ever have dirt on him you want to sell, I'll make it worth your while. He'd never have to know it came from you."

As he presses the card into my hand, humiliation sinks into my bones.

He said he loved me. That he missed me. That some actors might fall for their leading ladies, but he never would. And I believed him.

I bought every single line he fed me and begged for more. I really am a special breed of idiot.

Part of me is blindsided, but another part is completely unsurprised it's happened again. Of course it has.

I look back at Liam and Angel, still groping each other for the camera. Liam's eyes flicker to me, and I see it—the exact moment he realizes I know. His face drops and clouds with guilt, and then a look of indescribable sadness settles on his features. The photographer barks something at him and Liam glances at him briefly before turning back to me.

As I stare at him, my eyes prickle with hot tears, but I refuse to let them fall. I'm filled with so much rage, I'm shaking. More than anything, I'm angry with myself. I knew the risks of falling for him, and I let it happen anyway.

I *deserve* this. It's as much my fault as it is his.

When I can't bear to look at him anymore, I turn and walk away. I hear him yell my name, but I don't stop. What would be the point?

Everything hurts as I walk, and I curse myself for wanting to run back and beg him to change his mind.

What the hell is wrong with me? Am I really that unlovable?

Tears well up again, and I tense every muscle to stop the emotion from overwhelming me.

Maybe I'm just supposed to live out my days with Josh and have casual sex with others. Maybe there isn't a man out there who loves me enough to want my body *and* heart.

I want to deny that I love Liam so it won't hurt so much, but I can't. I don't think I really loved the other guys who dumped me, but him . . . For all my ranting about fate, it felt like he was meant for me. Why couldn't the only one I *really wanted* want me back?

I wipe my eyes in frustration. My face is hot with shame and embarrassment, and I'm so weary all I want to do is curl into a ball and close my eyes.

I'm almost to the subway station when my phone buzzes with a message. I stop dead when I see it's from Liam. I stare at it for a long time.

I expected him to roll out the usual shtick: "It's not you, it's me." Or, "We want different things." Or my personal favorite: "I think we're better as friends."

The message I'm staring at is none of those things. It simply says, "I'm sorry."

No denial. No excuses.

I don't know why those two words crack my self-control, but they do. I break down in the middle of the pavement and cry in a way I've never cried before. It's ugly, and every sob shoots pain through my chest. And even though I know people are staring, I can't stop.

Years ago I saw a magazine article that claimed everyone should have their heart broken at least once in order to become a better person. It said that the pain of losing someone you love will teach you about yourself. Develop your strength and resilience.

Whoever wrote that article can go fuck themselves.

Heartache doesn't teach you to be resilient. It teaches you to protect your fragility. It teaches you to fear love. And it draws a bright red circle around all the ways you've failed as a person and laughs while you cry.

I don't know how long I stand there and sob, but after a while, all my tears are gone, and I collapse onto a nearby bench as I try to pull myself together. There's a deep, angry pain in my chest, and I wonder how long I'll have to live with it.

When the shadows start to lengthen and the streetlights flicker on, I stand and slowly head toward home.

At least having my heart broken by Liam Quinn taught me one thing. It's taught me that I never want to feel this way about a man ever again.

NINE

PRESENT TENSE

Present Day
Pier 23 Rehearsal Rooms
New York City

The morning after I spill the beans about Liam to Josh, I feel better. Until then, I'd never let myself mourn losing Liam, and maybe that's why I couldn't let him go. Perhaps Josh was right. I should have confided in him about all of this years ago. He remains dubious about my ability to keep my personal and professional lives separate, but I reassure him I've been subjected to countless pictures of Liam and Angel over the years. I'm practically desensitized to their coupledom by now.

I'm still setting up the rehearsal room when noise from the fans downstairs escalates. Just like yesterday, the golden couple's arrival is heralded by a cavalcade of earsplitting screams. The difference is that when they stride into the room today, they're accompanied by a whole slew of extra people. Two camera crews, a sound guy, a pimply production runner, and a hassled female producer who looks like she hasn't slept in three days trail after them. They circle the stars like anxious human planets. Marco hurries over to the production desk, followed closely by our publicist, Mary. The tiny Botoxed woman looks like the cat who swallowed the canary, while Marco looks like a serial killer who's about to flay people alive.

"Great news, team!" Mary says with her trademark enthusiasm. "As previously discussed, from today until the show opens, Liam and Angel will be filming their upcoming reality show, *Angeliam: A Fairy Tale Romance.*"

I cringe over the hideous moniker the pulp media have named them. *Angeliam?* Is that necessary? It sounds like an antifungal cream: *"My crotch rot used to get super-itchy, but now, with a generous application of Angeliam, I barely notice it."*

Mary turns to me. "Elissa, can you make sure you stay on top of their filming schedule? You have the list of the setups they need, right?"

"Yes. All fine."

"Marco will rely on you and Josh to ensure rehearsal disruption is kept to a minimum."

"I'll take care of it."

We've known for a couple of weeks this reality show would intersect with our rehearsals, and even though Marco hates the idea, he's grudgingly agreed it's great publicity. Unlike most reality shows, which are produced months in advance, this one is televised the weekend after it's shot. I suspect that's why the producer looks so frazzled. Piecing together dozens of hours of footage into some sort of interesting narrative must be a nightmare.

Amidst all the mayhem, Liam and Angel chat quietly in the corner, arms around each other. How they can look so natural and unaffected when there are cameras two feet away, I'll never know.

I hear Angel say, "I love you, baby, and I can't wait to finally be Mrs. Quinn." Liam gives her an adoring smile, then kisses her gently. The part of me that still loves him swoons. I remember what it was like to be kissed like that.

"Elissa?" Mary says.

"Hmmm?"

"I also need you to make sure everyone in the rehearsal room has signed the release forms. That includes you guys."

Beside me, Marco groans. As flamboyant as he is, he has no desire to be on TV. I know how he feels. Josh, on the other hand, can't wait. He believes his natural charisma and winning personality (his words) are going to make him a fan favorite. Knowing Josh, he's probably right.

As soon as everyone has signed in, I round up the cast so Marco can start. For the most part, the TV crew stays out of the way, but whenever we have breaks, they follow Angel and Liam around like shadows.

At lunchtime, I'm pinning the shooting schedule to the notice board when I feel a presence behind me. I turn to see Angel there, smiling sweetly. A film crew hovers beside her.

"Hey, Elissa."

I glance at the camera. God, this feels weird. We've all been told to ignore the camera and act natural, but that's easier said than done. "Uh . . . yes, Miss Bell. Can I help you?"

She glances over her shoulder. "Sorry about the tagalong. You get used to it after a while."

"I'm going to take your word on that. What can I do for you?"

"Oh, nothing, really. I just came over to say hi. Yesterday was such a blur, I didn't get to talk to anyone. But I figure we're all in this together for the next few months, so we should at least try to get to know each other."

Out of the corner of my eye, I see Liam standing near the water cooler. He looks concerned. I've already reassured him I'm not going to tell her about us. What does he have to be worried about?

I plaster on a smile. "Of course. Feel free to ask me anything, Miss Bell."

"Oh, please. It's Angel. Well, it's Angela, but only my father calls me that. So tell me, what exactly does a stage manager do?"

"She runs the whole show," Liam says as he walks over to us with his own camera crew in tow. "Every single stage direction, costume change, set piece, prop, lighting cue, sound cue—all of it is overseen by the stage manager. After Marco finishes directing the show, it's going to be up to Elissa to make it happen every night."

Angel links her arm through Liam's but keeps her eyes on me. "Wow, sounds like a lot of responsibility. You must have to work under a lot of pressure."

I nod. "I don't mind pressure."

"Don't be modest," Liam says. "Elissa thrives under pressure. I've never seen someone become so focused while everyone else loses their minds."

Angel puts a hand on his bicep. "Sweetie, we should take Elissa out for dinner one night, yes? You two probably have some amazing stories from the show you did together. I'd love to hear about your early days. You never talk about them."

Before Liam can say anything, Angel turns to me. "What do you say, Elissa? It'd be fun, right? Plus, any friend of Liam's is a friend of mine."

I open my mouth to say that Liam and I have never been friends, but the look on his face stops me. Instead I say, "Sure. That would be great."

Considering Marco's directive to keep our leads happy no matter what, I figure I have no choice but to agree.

"Mr. Quinn?" Josh steps beside me. "Marco is ready for you." His tone is less friendly than usual, but if Liam notices, he doesn't let it show. Josh turns to Angel. "Miss Bell, I'll be back to collect you in a few minutes."

Angel beams at him. "Thanks, Josh."

Josh's ears turn pink. I wonder if that's going to happen every time he talks to her.

Liam starts to leave, but before he can, Angel grabs his arm and pulls him over. "See you soon, honey." She stands on her toes to give him a light kiss. The camera crews jostle to get the best shot of the lip-lock.

When Liam pulls back, he looks over at me for a millisecond before returning his attention to her. "See you soon."

Josh escorts Liam and his entourage into the rehearsal room, leaving me and Angel alone. "So, Elissa, how long have you and Josh been together?"

"Ten years."

Her mouth drops open. "Whoa. Did you start dating when you were toddlers?"

I laugh. "We've been best friends since high school. We're not romantically involved."

"Really? But Denise said you live together."

"We do. But we don't sleep together."

"Oh. Sorry. I just assumed . . ." She waves her hand. "Never mind. It's great you two are able to work and live together. Having someone who can sympathize with the stress of your job is invaluable, right? I'd be a total basket case if I didn't have Liam to keep me grounded. When the crazy train gets to be too much, he knows just how to talk me down."

Of course he does. He's that kind of man.

"I can imagine your world would be pretty insane at times. I'm sure you help him just as much as he helps you. It's great you have each other." I almost get through the entire sentence without choking on my jealousy.

Angel smiles at me, and when I smile back, she surprises me by wrapping her arms around me and giving me a tight hug. "You're the sweetest. Thank you." She gives me a final squeeze, then Josh is there to take her back into rehearsals.

Once she's gone, I run my hands through my hair.

Well, that was surreal.

As much as I'd love to hate Angel Bell, there's something appealing about her. She's warm, friendly, and looks at me in a way that makes me believe she's interested in what I have to say.

As if this situation with Liam wasn't already weird, liking his fiancée has taken it to the next level.

"So, then," Angel says, and leans forward in the chair beside my desk. "As we're leaving the club, this idiot starts harassing Liam. I mean, the guy only came up to the middle of Liam's chest and would blow away in a strong wind, but he was drunk, so I guess he thought talking smack to someone twice his size was a good idea." I'm supposed to be working, but Angel's made a habit of sitting in my office every lunch hour and distracting me with stories. I both hate and love these little insights into her life with Liam. My life seems completely boring in comparison.

"What did Liam do?" I ask.

"Well, he tried to walk away, but the little shit just kept getting in his face, and by now, he's just hurling abuse about how much *Rageheart* sucks and what a pussy Liam is. Now, Liam's a pretty patient guy most of the time, but I could see him simmering. Then the guy starts insulting me, calling me a talentless bimbo and whatever, and going on about my fake boobs, and that's when Liam snaps. He picks up the dude by his shirtfront and gets this murderous look on his face. Then he pulls the guy right up to his face and whispers, 'Feel free to ignore this, considering I'm such a pussy, but if you say one more word about Angel, I'm going to tear off your arms. Understand?'" She laughs and leans back in her chair. "The guy went white as a sheet, and when Liam lowered him to his feet, he almost fell over. Liam helped him regain his balance, then gave him a wad of cash and apologized for ruining his shirt. Dude just stood there with his mouth hanging open before he burst into tears."

"Oh my God."

"Yep. And I'd like to say that was a weird night for us, but it really wasn't. Seems like a whole lot of folks either love us or hate us. Or hate to love us, and love to hate us. It's a thing. We're used to it."

I shake my head. "I don't know how you cope."

She shrugs. "Practice. And hard drugs." When she sees my face drop, she laughs. "Kidding." I sigh in relief before she adds, "I've been off the crack for ninety days now. It's all good. Barely miss it anymore."

The sincerity with which she says it makes me laugh. I'm surprised how often I do that around her. I really do enjoy her company. I've been best friends with Josh for so long, I've forgotten what it's like to have a female friend.

She crosses her legs and cocks her head. "So, I was thinking . . ."

I flash her a look of concern. "Should I be worried?"

"You're hilarious." She rolls her eyes. "I was thinking we should have dinner together. Tonight."

"Ah, Angel . . ." I cringe. "I don't think—"

"Come on, Elissa, please. I've arranged a private table for us at Lumiere, and considering that place usually requires bookings months in advance with proof of your bank balance, it wasn't easy to achieve. We really want you to come."

"We?"

"Me and Liam." Clearly, she's failed to notice her man avoiding me all week.

"Liam agreed to this?"

"Of course. Oh, and bring your boyfriend." I make a surprised sound. "Liam said you were dating someone. Bring him. Please. Liam and I are sick of each other's company. We'll go insane if we don't interact with real people for a change."

"So you usually hang out with imaginary friends?"

She shakes her head. "Real, as in *normal*. Not actors, or ass-kissers, or Hollywood fakers."

I'm about to try to come up with a believable excuse when there's a knock at the door. "Come in."

Liam steps into the room, and does a double take when he sees Angel.

"Uh . . . hey. I thought I heard your voice."

She gives him a formal nod. "Love of my life. Hello."

He looks at me, then back to her. "What are you doing in here?"

"Chatting. Bragging about you. Torturing Elissa. You know, the usual. I'm trying to convince her to have dinner with us." She stands and goes over to him. "Please tell her there's no use resisting. She seems to think she has a choice in the matter."

Before he can say anything, Angel's phone rings. She looks at it, then at me. "I have to take this. Be right back. Liam, give her your puppy-dog eyes and tell her she needs to join us." She swipes her phone. "Daddy! How are you?"

She takes the call out into the hallway, leaving Liam and me staring awkwardly at each other. He glances away and shoves his hands in his pockets. This is how he's been all week. He avoids looking at me whenever possible, and goes through Josh for questions and notes to avoid addressing me directly. Probably for the best. I seem to have a *Best of Liam Quinn* pornographic show reel on standby in my brain, and whenever we're alone together, it starts playing.

"Insistent little thing, isn't she?" I say, and smooth back the wisps of hair that have escaped my ponytail. True to form, images of him and me making love flash through my brain. I try to keep my expression neutral as my body tingles with the phantom graze of his hands.

As for Liam, I have no idea what's going through his mind, but the way he's looking at me isn't helping. After a few seconds, he breaks eye contact to stare at the floor.

"Angel likes you. So you should just agree to come to dinner and be done with it. Lord knows, I haven't yet found a way to win an argument with her."

I look down and shuffle some papers in front of me. "Angel and I can just go by ourselves. You don't have to come."

Out of the corner of my eye, I see him focus on me again. "What if I want to come?"

"You don't have to feel obligated to spend time with me just because your fiancée likes my company." I chance a look at his face. He's frowning. "Things between you and me haven't been exactly friendly for the past week."

"I hadn't meant to avoid you, but—" He exhales. "Being around you again is . . . complicated. Plus, I know you aren't exactly thrilled to have me on the show. I was trying to give you space."

"I'm your stage manager. It's not like you can get away from me."

"I don't want to get away from you. That's the problem."

I stiffen. "What does that mean?"

He stares at me for a few seconds before taking a step forward. "It means having you and Angel in the same room is all kinds of fucked up, but I don't want it to be. I'd like to be able to spend time with you without all this weirdness."

He's so close now, I have to tilt my head to see his face. Images of him with his hand in my panties loops through my brain. "So, what? After all this time, you want to be *friends*?"

He blinks a few times. "Yeah. Sure. Friends. Dinner might be a step in the right direction."

"Friends" is one of those terms that seems benign but has a whole host of barbed-wire boundaries. Once you've made love to someone with so much passion that his name is branded on all your cells, is it possible to ever think of him as just a friend? Or is the heat of an old flame always going to lie dormant, just waiting to consume you again?

"Elissa?" When I look up, he gives me a pleading look. "To borrow a phrase from the night we met, I'd love for you to come. Please, don't make me beg."

I shake my head and sigh. There's no way we'll ever be friends. I think he knows it as well as I do. But for Angel's sake, it looks like we're both willing to try.

"Fine. I can't guarantee it won't be weird, but sure. Why not?"

"Thank you." He pauses for a moment, as if unsure of what to say next. "Liss . . ." When I look up at him, his expression fades into an echo of what I used to see when he looked at me. A quiet desperation. His gaze rakes over me with the sort of raw need that makes me feel like the most beautiful woman he's ever seen, which is ridiculous considering whom he's marrying. "You have to know that . . ."

"What?"

Just when I think the intensity in his expression is going to make me combust, Angel strides back into the room. "So, did you seal the deal? Is she coming?"

Not yet, but if your boyfriend keeps looking at me like that, it's a real possibility.

"I'll be there," I say, and step back to tidy my already neat files.

"Yes!" Angel says, and beams. "Eight o'clock. Dress up and wear sexy shoes. There's a dance floor."

She grabs Liam's arm before waving good-bye. I can see tension in Liam's shoulders as they exit my office and disappear down the hallway.

I sit and lean back in my chair.

Not only do I have to get through dinner with Mr. and Mrs. Perfect, I have to put on makeup and be expected to dance. Oh, and show up with the boyfriend I don't have. This has disaster written all over it.

As we walk into the elevator that leads up to Lumiere, I slap Josh's hand away from his tie. "You look great. Stop fiddling."

He slides a finger into his collar and pulls. "Remind me why I'm here again?"

"Because I was invited to bring my imaginary boyfriend, and considering we had a nasty imaginary breakup yesterday, he was unavailable."

"Got it. You look amazing, by the way."

I smooth down my plain black dress and run my hand over my sleek hair. "Really?" It's strange to deviate from my usual uniform of ponytail and jeans, but I figure I should look like I at least made an effort. Anyway, this skintight black number is the only dress I own, so it wasn't like I had a lot of choices.

"Quinn's eyes are going to bug out of his head."

"Oh, please. He's sleeping with one of the most beautiful women on the planet."

"True. But you're also an inferno of white-hot womanhood, and no matter how much he loves his fiancée, he'll still have a boner over you in that outfit."

"Josh, no."

"Lissa, yes." The elevator opens and he puts his hand on the small of my back as we exit. "You two had phenomenal sex in the past. A man doesn't forget about that, no matter if he's single, married, or pledged to the Flying Spaghetti Monster. When he's in your presence, his dick will react. Trust me on that."

I stop just before we reach the doors and face Josh. "Please tell me you're going to behave yourself in there."

"Why wouldn't I?"

"Because you've been kind of cold to Liam since I told you what happened with us."

"That's because what he did was a dick move, and unlike you, I don't like dicks."

"I don't disagree, but if I can be nice to him, so can you."

He huffs. "Fine. I'll behave. Besides, Angel will be there, annoying me with her perfection. I doubt I'll even register Quinn's existence."

We head into the restaurant. When we give Angel's name to the hostess, her eyes light up for a second before she regains her composure. With a flip of her perfectly coifed hair, she leads us toward the back of the packed restaurant.

"This place is huge," Josh whispers. He's not wrong. On the far wall is a stage complete with a dinner band, and there's a dance floor in front of the stage, around which tables are set. On the outer walls are several curtained-off VIP areas. Our hostess leads us to the most private of these, in the far-back corner of the restaurant. Angel and Liam are already there. They stand when they see us approach.

"Elissa!" Angel envelops me in a hug. "I'm so happy you guys came." She looks incredible, as usual. I feel like an ugly stepsister in comparison.

She turns to Josh and hugs him. "Josh. Hi. What an unexpected surprise." I swear I hear Josh moan as she wraps her arms around him.

I look over at Liam, who's watching me nervously. "Hey." I feel lame, but I have no idea of the proper etiquette in greeting an ex-lover one is still in love with.

"Hey." Liam must also be clueless, because he takes a breath before leaning over and giving me an awkward one-armed hug. I return it as best I can, grateful I'm not being subjected to the full pressure of his body against mine.

When we pull back, Liam clears his throat, and I swear he's blushing. "You look . . . great."

I doubt it. My face feels like it's on fire. "Thanks. You, too." He really does look amazing. Sharp gray suit. Crisp white shirt with no tie. If he wasn't an actor, he could rule the world as a model.

"Shall we sit?" Angel asks, oblivious to our discomfort.

Liam pulls out Angel's chair, and Josh quickly follows suit for me. Then Josh sits opposite Angel and I find myself staring at Liam.

Wonderful. So this blush is here to stay, then.

I'm grateful when a waitress appears with ice water, and wonder how uncool it would be for me to hold the glass against my cheeks.

"So your boyfriend couldn't make it?" Angel asks.

The question catches me off guard. "Huh? Uh . . . no. He couldn't. Sorry."

"Come on, Lissa," Josh says. "We're all friends here. You can tell them the truth." I flash daggers at Josh, but he simply smiles. "She doesn't want you to know she had to break up with him. He was getting obsessed with her. Constant flowers and presents. Love poetry. Serenading her in the street. The boy had it bad."

Liam looks over at me, his brows furrowed.

"Sounds a bit stalkerish," Angel says. "And I should know. I'm the Pied Piper of whack jobs."

Liam's still staring. "How did he take the breakup? Because Angel's right. With guys like that, rejection can set them off. You need to be careful."

His concern is appealing, but I'm embarrassed by the attention. "It's totally fine. Josh is exaggerating."

Josh puts his hand on the back of my chair. "Not by much. I don't think he'll cause trouble, but he was pretty devastated when she broke it off. He really loved her. And who can blame him? She's spectacular."

I grab Josh's leg under the table, but he ignores it.

"I'm with you, Josh," Angel says. "I've only known her for a week and I'm in love with her. Is this a common issue, Elissa? People falling for you?"

I almost spit out my water. "Uh . . . no. Not really."

"Yeah, I'm not buying that. You're beautiful, smart, amazing at your job. I bet you have men lining up around the block. Josh, back me up on this."

Liam's gaze intensifies as Josh says, "She gets lots of attention, yes."

Angel looks at Josh quizzically. "Then why hasn't she found Mr. Right yet?"

I grab a menu. "I'm sitting right here, you know? In case you'd forgotten."

"There was one guy," Josh says, like I haven't spoken. He gives Liam a sideways glance. "Years ago. I thought he might have been the one."

Angel leans forward. "Ooh! What happened?"

"He turned out to be an asshole. Dumped her for someone else."

The menu slips from my fingers and hits the table with a thud. I look over at Liam. He's staring down at his hands.

"Okay," I say, and pick up the menu. "Let's stop talking about me now, please. I'm starving. We should order."

Angel flashes me a sympathetic smile. "Aw, honey. Don't be ashamed about being dumped. We've all been there, done that. God knows, I have the therapist's bills to prove it." She studies her menu. "The one thing I've learned is to not take the blame for things beyond your control. None of us can help who we fall in love with. Or out of love with, for that matter. My therapist says love is like a lion in captivity—it can be embraced, but never tamed. Deep, right?"

She doesn't notice that Liam and Josh are now having a glaring match. I dig my fingers into Josh's thigh. He squirms and finally breaks eye contact to look at his menu.

Liam looks at me briefly before taking a sip of water and gazing across the room.

Okay, so this is going well.

The only person who seems oblivious to the tension is Angel.

"God, this food looks amazing," she says. "My taste buds just squirted all over the place. I've heard the duck here is to die for."

"Why aren't there any prices?" Josh whispers to me.

I lean over to him. "Because if you have to ask, you can't afford it."

Angel waves her hand. "Order whatever you like. My treat. I just want us all to have a good time, okay?"

I feel bad about letting Angel pay, but I'm realistic enough to know Josh and I could never afford to eat here on our wages.

We spend the next few minutes looking through our menus and making small talk. All but Liam. He leans close to Angel as she reads him the menu. When she sees me watching, she says, "He never brings his reading glasses, and he's useless without them. I don't think he even knows where they are these days."

"They give me a headache," he says. "If I can get away with not wearing them, I will."

"You near-sighted?" Josh asks. Liam nods. "Yeah, that sucks. Taking them on and off all the time would drive me nuts. I don't blame you for ditching them."

Liam smiles, and for some reason, that small exchange makes the whole mood lift. We order our food, Angel chooses the wine, and we fall into the kind of easy dinner conversation I wouldn't have expected with this group of people. There's still tension, especially between Liam and me, but not so much that I can't enjoy myself. Of course, the wine also helps.

By the time we're on our third bottle, we're getting kind of loud. Liam and Josh have had a hardy debate about football versus baseball, Angel and I have discussed our families and current events, and Josh and Angel have fallen into a friendly but passionate argument about the various incarnations of *Star Trek*.

"You take that back," Josh says as he narrows his eyes at her.

Angel lifts her chin. "Not going to happen. Picard is sexier than Kirk. It's a fact."

"Not in this universe, it fucking isn't. Kirk is king, lady. Deal with it."

Liam looks over at me and smiles. "We may have to step in soon. Or take away their cutlery."

"Angel just dissed Josh's hero and role model. I'm surprised he hasn't flipped over the table in disgust and walked out."

He links his fingers together in front of him. "I was always more of a Spock fan, myself."

"Really? Why?"

He gives a small shrug. "He was always the voice of reason. Sometimes he had to use logic to make the hard decisions. That's not easy to do."

I smile. "'The needs of the many outweigh the needs of the few.'" It's one of my favorite movie lines.

He stares at me with a strange expression before finishing the quote. "Or the one. Exactly."

We're quiet for a few seconds, and Liam startles a little when Angel puts her hand on his arm.

"Well," she says, "as much as I'd like to continue kicking Josh's ass about Starfleet captains, I think we should dance. This band is one of the main reasons I wanted to come here, and right now, they're going to waste."

Josh glances over at the dance floor. "I'd rather continue to have my ass kicked, thank you."

Liam holds up his hand. "Me, too."

"Tough," Angel says, smiling as she drags Liam to his feet. "I've spent thousands of dollars on dance classes for Liam and me for the wedding, and I aim to get my money's worth. So, everyone up."

I grab Josh's hand. "Our mistress has spoken."

He grunts in frustration. "Fine, but if I break out my white-hot robot moves, you can't be embarrassed."

"It's ballroom-dancing music, Josh."

"And your point is . . . ?"

We all head to the dance floor. Liam wraps his arms around Angel, and I put my arms around Josh's neck. Within a few minutes, we're all swaying sort of in time to the music.

"Sorry about earlier with Quinn," Josh says, looking over at Liam and Angel a short distance away. "I should have kept my mouth shut, but . . . I don't know. Every time I think about him hurting you, it pisses me off."

I brush some lint off his shoulder. "I've learned there's no point being bitter about it. It won't change anything. They're getting married, whether I like it or not."

Josh looks down at me. "Not necessarily. Have you not noticed the major heat between Angel and me tonight? I'm still predicting she'll dump Quinn's moody ass and come over to Team Josh."

I laugh and hug him. "Your unwavering optimism is one of the many reasons I love you."

After we dance to a couple of songs, Angel comes over and taps me on the shoulder. "Okay, time for a swap. Despite lessons, Liam's already trodden on my toes three times. I'm hoping Josh is more graceful."

As Angel takes Josh's hand and leads him away, he raises an eyebrow at me and mouths, *"See? She wants me."*

I laugh. When I turn around, Liam is there, waiting. He holds out his hands. "Shall we?"

I give him a skeptical look. "I don't know. Angel tells me you're dangerous."

"I promise, I'll be gentle," he says as he takes my hands. "Right up until you beg me to be rough." His mischievous smile does nothing to diminish how my body reacts to that statement. I put one hand on his shoulder as he winds an arm around my waist, and when our palms press together, I can't help an audible intake of breath. He freezes as well.

"Is this okay?" he asks quietly.

I nod. "Yeah. If it's okay with you."

He pulls me a little closer, but makes sure to keep distance between our bodies. "So far, so good. But it's been a while since I danced with you, so anything could happen. You're a little taller than I remember."

"Yes, high heels are a wonderful thing. Unless you try to walk in them. Or dance. Last chance to sit this one out and save yourself."

He smiles down at me. "Not happening. They'll have to pry you from my cold, dead hands. Let's do this."

We begin to sway. It's awkward at first, but as we get used to touching each other again, we begin to relax.

"See?" he says, a little breathless. "Nothing to worry about." He glances over at Angel and Josh. Angel's laughing and Josh is glaring. Surely they're not still talking *Star Trek*. "So, I take it Josh now knows the full story about us?"

"What gave it away? Him calling you an asshole?"

He shrugs. "It was subtle, but I picked up on it."

"Yeah, sorry about that."

"Don't be. I deserved it. To be honest, I expected something like that way before now."

He adjusts his hand around mine, and I notice how much softer his fingers are these days. No construction work to create calluses, I guess.

"Just so you know," I say, "those were Josh's words. Not mine."

"You don't think I'm an asshole?"

"No. Like Angel said earlier, you can't help who you fall in love with. And she's an amazing woman. I can see why you'd choose her."

For a second, his fingers tighten around my hand, then they release. "That's a pretty mature attitude. Can't say I'd be as understanding if I were in your position."

"Sure you would."

His expression turns dark. "I really wouldn't. Trust me. I'm still recovering from you having a boyfriend. Well, ex."

Before I have time to ask what that means, he sighs and gives me a smile. "Anyway, let's see how you cope with me taking this dancing thing up a notch. I have moves that will blow your mind. Brace yourself."

He takes a step back and spins me under his arm. I clumsily follow his lead, all the while cringing at my complete lack of grace.

"Not bad," he says as he wraps his arms around me from behind. "I give you points for effort." He grabs my hand and pushes on my waist, and I spin out before he pulls me back in again. Then, as I'm busy trying to regain my balance, he dips me. The action is so unexpected, I squeal and lose my footing. Just when I'm sure I'm going to face-plant into the dance floor, his arm tightens around me to stop my descent. "It's okay. I've got you." He smiles as he holds me nearly horizontal to the floor. "And what's more, I've finally found it."

"What?" Still nervous about being dropped, I grasp his arms as he leans over me.

"The one thing you suck at. And I thought *I* was a terrible dancer. I'm freaking Nureyev compared to you."

I slap his arm. "Hey."

His eyes sparkle in the low light. "Just keeping it real, Liss."

He pulls me up into a standing position, and I grip his biceps until I regain my balance on my heels. Once I'm steady, he loosens his grip. "Okay, well. Clearly that needs some practice. Want to try it again?"

"I don't know. Are you going to insult my technique again?"

"That depends on whether or not you continue to suck. So try not to, okay?"

I can hear Josh and Angel laughing as Liam guides me through the sequence again. Soon, I'm laughing, too.

Okay, fine. I'm a terrible dancer. So sue me. Yet another reason I'm backstage, not onstage.

We swap partners again, and dance for a bit longer, but the wine and the exertion soon take their toll. Angel starts yawning, and it's not long before we all join in. It's been a big week for all of us.

After we agree to call it a night, Angel texts her driver, pays the bill, and we head down to the street. We've barely stepped out the door when a barrage of flashbulbs hits us.

"Dammit," Liam mutters. "Everybody, run for the car." He pushes through the throng of photographers, then holds the car door open and ushers Angel and Josh inside. My short legs and high heels make sure I get there last. I'm about to climb inside when I'm shoved hard in the shoulder by a burly man who's jostling to get shots of Liam.

"Elissa!" Liam reaches for me as I stumble back on my heels, but it's too late. I trip over the curb and make a grunting sound as I fall heavily onto my hip.

Dammit. That's going to leave a mark.

I'm awkwardly trying to navigate around my tight skirt to get myself upright when I'm nearly blinded by machine-gun flashes, right in my face.

"Back the hell off," Liam growls before the owner of the flash is hauled backward. A young photographer in a baseball cap hits the wall with a thud, and I scramble to my feet to see Liam tear the camera out of his hands.

"Hey! Give that back!" The pap reaches for his equipment, but Liam yanks out the memory card and pockets it before throwing the camera to the ground. The pap howls in dismay. "That's a three-thousand-dollar camera, asshole!"

"Bill me," Liam mutters. He shoves more bodies out of the way to get to me. "Get the hell away from her!"

He leans down and searches my face. "You okay?"

"Yeah. Embarrassed more than anything."

The photographers yell at him to look in their direction, but Liam ignores them all as he wraps his arm around me and guides me toward the car. I limp around the pain in my hip.

When we're safely inside, Liam yanks the door shut so hard, the whole car shakes. Flashes continue to light up the interior as the paps press their lenses against the window.

"Get us out of here," Liam says to the driver. The engine revs as we pull out into the relentless New York traffic.

I lean back in my seat and exhale. "Well, that was a bracing way to end the evening."

"Are you okay?" Angel touches my shoulder.

"Fine. No permanent damage."

"Fucking animals," Liam says as he examines my arms for scrapes. "They behave like that and then wonder why we get pissed."

Angel gives him a disapproving look. "Still, you shouldn't have broken his camera. You know that sort of reaction is gold to them. You're going to be splashed all over TMZ within the hour."

"The bastard was taking photos up Elissa's dress," Liam says with disgust. "He's lucky I only broke his camera." He pulls the memory card from his pocket and snaps it in half. "At least those pictures won't show up on some sleazy Web site."

Angel nods. "He'll come after you for damages."

"Let him. He won't be the first. Or the last." He sits back and stares out the window, and I can still feel the anger coming off him in waves.

"How did they know you were at Bella Vita?" Josh asks.

Angel turns to him. "One of the staff probably tipped them off. It happens all the time. Paps pay good money to people who call in celebrity sightings. Before you know it, one pap turns into two, and two into three. Then there's a whole swarm of them. They're like piranhas. The merest smell of a famous face and they go into a frenzy."

Josh studies her. "Unlike Quinn, you seem pretty calm about the whole thing."

She shrugs. "I'm a senator's daughter and my sister is America's favorite journalist; I've been getting papped for most of my life. I've developed a more philosophic approach than Liam. I see the paps as a necessary evil. Like it or not, they help keep our profile high, which makes us more valuable commodities. They're sort of like a barometer for our popularity. The day they stop foaming at the mouth to get our picture, I know our fairy-tale ride in Hollywood is over."

Liam looks over at her. "Sometimes, don't you wish for it to be over so we can live normal lives? Or is that just me?"

Angel stares at him for a second, and I feel like I'm intruding on a private moment between them. A wistful expression passes over her face, and Liam gives her the smallest of smiles.

Angel glances briefly at me and Josh, then looks out the window. "Sometimes."

Liam's quiet for a moment, then he turns to me and gestures to my hip. "Does it hurt?"

"A little." When he presses his fingers against it, I wince.

"You'll need to ice it. It'll probably be stiff and sore for a few days."

I nod. "So this is just a normal night for you guys, huh?"

Liam nods. "Unfortunately. We're like exhibits in a zoo."

"Yet another reason I'm glad I'm in theater and not movies. All that attention on a regular basis would freak me out."

Liam doesn't say anything to that, but he frowns and crosses his arms over his chest. He stays like that until we pull up outside my apartment building.

"I'm going to help Elissa upstairs, okay?" he says to Angel as he opens the door. "I'll be right back."

"Of course. Take your time." Angel leans over and hugs me. "Take care of yourself, honey. I'll see you on Monday. If you need anything, let me know."

She says good-bye to Josh with a quick kiss on the cheek. He blushes and mumbles "Good night" as Liam helps me out of the car.

Liam holds my arm, and after some minor hobbling, I make it to the sidewalk.

Josh watches with concern. "Liam, I can help her upstairs if you want to go."

Liam waves him away. "I got it."

Without any more discussion, he scoops me into his arms and follows Josh into the building. Our apartment might only be on the third floor, but I still marvel at how Liam can carry me up all those stairs without breaking a sweat. It's not normal.

"This really isn't necessary," I say, uncomfortable at how right it feels to be in his arms again.

"It is necessary. It's my fault you got hurt."

"Actually, the guy who pushed me over looked nothing like you, so—"

"I should have known they'd be there. Taken you out a different way. Protected you." He shakes his head, angry with himself.

"Liam, it's okay."

"No, it's not."

"I've never seen you angry like that."

He looks down at me, and his expression relaxes a little. "Those assholes have no right going after you. I signed up for this life. You didn't. I never wanted you to be a part of it."

We reach the door and Josh unlocks it, then holds it open for us. "You can put her on the couch. I'll get an ice pack."

Liam walks over and lays me gently on the couch, then sits beside me. When Josh hands him the ice pack, he presses it against my hip.

I lie back and watch as he frowns in concentration. "You know, I can do this myself."

"Quiet. The doctor is working."

"It takes a medical degree to apply an ice pack, does it?"

He raises an eyebrow. "If you want to do it right."

"Are you guys okay for a second?" Josh asks as he tugs at his tie. "Because if I don't get out of this monkey suit, stat, I'm going to lose it."

I give him a smile. "Go. 'Doctor Quinn, Medicine Woman' seems to have things under control."

Liam nods at Josh. "Damn straight."

Josh shakes his head and disappears into his room.

Once he's gone, Liam turns back to me. "You should also elevate this."

"It's on my hip. How do you suggest I do that?"

He grabs a pillow from the end of the couch and then pushes a hand beneath my butt. I make a noise as he lifts up my pelvis with one hand and shoves the pillow under it with the other. "Like that."

"Well, this is elegant," I say, my chin pressing into my chest while my knees point to the ceiling.

He looks at me for a moment. "You're making it work. But then again, you'd look good in full traction, so . . ." He smiles at me, and I smile back, and it makes me crazy that I can miss him so painfully even when he's sitting right beside me.

After a few seconds, his smile fades and he glances at the door. "Well, I'd better get going. Angel is waiting."

"Yeah." I want to take his hand, but that's not how we are now. Instead, I give him a smile. "Thanks for the lift. Both up the stairs and with the pillow."

"No problem. Next time we go to dinner, I'll try to make sure my lifestyle doesn't damage you." He gives me a final smile, then gets up and heads to the door.

I struggle to stand, and follow him. When he notices, he holds out his hand. "Hey, stop. I can see myself out. Back onto the couch, lady."

I wave him off. "I'm going to bed. If I have to have my ass in the air, I'm at least going to be in the appropriate setting."

Oh.

Shit.

Liam's eyebrows just about disappear into his hairline. "And on that note—"

"Okay. So, ignore that. Wow."

I put my hand over my face, but he gently takes my wrist and pulls it away. "I love it when you blush around me. Always have. Always will." I look up at him, and his thumb brushes over my pulse. "You sure you'll be okay?"

I nod. "I've had worse. Once a twenty-pound light fell on my head. I ended up calling the show with a concussion. I'm a tough nut. You should know that."

"Yeah. I should." I open the door for him and he steps onto the landing before turning back to me. "You know, apart from the last part, I really enjoyed tonight."

I lean on the door. "Me, too. I think for our first venture as sort-of friends, it went well."

"It did. Except for your dancing. That sucked." He smiles and moves a bit closer. "See you at rehearsal Monday."

He touches my shoulder and runs his hand down to my wrist. I try to keep my expression neutral, but I think my eyelids flutter. "See you then."

On a whim, I move forward and hug him. He freezes for a moment, then tightens his arms and sighs. When our bodies press fully against each other, the contact makes me gasp.

Liam's hard.

Very hard.

He must realize I notice, because he quickly pulls back. "Shit. Sorry. My . . . uh . . . body hasn't gotten the memo about us being friends yet. Mind you, you're not helping matters by wearing that dress. Give a guy a break, Liss." He runs his hands through his hair and exhales. "Okay. Now *I'm* blushing. Good night."

After he disappears down the stairs, I close the door behind him and lean back on it. Josh comes out of his bedroom and heads into the kitchen. He's wearing his favorite Captain Kirk pajamas. He grabs a bag of frozen peas from the fridge and comes over to swap them for the barely cold ice pack in my hands.

He gives me a smug look. "You gave him a boner, didn't you?"

I press the peas to my hip and hobble toward my room. "Good night, Joshua."

"Okay, fine. My 'told you so' can wait until morning. Oops. Look at that. Seems it can't."

I smile as I shut my bedroom door and flop onto the bed. My hip may be aching, but I'm kind of thrilled I can still make Liam Quinn's body dance to my short, curvy-girl tune.

TEN

A VERY BAD PLAN

Monday morning, I have a killer bruise on my hip and a slight limp, but other than that, I have no lasting damage from Saturday night. Well, apart from the memory of Liam's erection pressing into my stomach.

"Morning, sweet friend," Angel says, as she comes over and hugs me. "Present for you." She lays a copy of *Dancing for Dummies* wrapped in a big red bow on the production desk.

I give her a deadpan look. "I hate you."

"Impossible. I'm adorable." She laughs and heads off to prepare for rehearsal.

Beside me, Josh sighs in frustration. "Screw her and her perfect sense of humor." He points to his computer. "By the way, have you seen this?"

I lean down and examine the screen. It's a gossip site, and they have dozens of pictures of all of us leaving the restaurant Saturday night. Of course, the main focus is the series of shots of Liam shoving people aside, his face contorted and angry. I roll my eyes at the headline—DOES THIS *RAGEHEART* STAR NEED ANGER MANAGEMENT?—and the accompanying article: "Tough guy Liam Quinn allegedly assaulted innocent bystanders while out and about with friends on Saturday night. At this stage, it's not certain if charges will be brought."

Just then Liam enters the room. When he sees me, he gives me a quick wave, then goes and sits down. He seems on edge as he pulls out his script and bends over it in concentration. When the camera crew comes over to film him, he shoos them away, then goes back to squinting at the page in front of him.

Huh. I've never seen him with his script before. He tugs on his hair in agitation, and I wonder if it's because his picture is splashed all over the Internet. Or maybe he's still embarrassed about our exchange at the door on Saturday night. Perhaps both?

When we start rehearsal, it becomes even clearer he's distracted. Angel enters for their first exchange, and he messes up nearly every line. After a few failed attempts, he sighs in frustration. "Shit. Sorry, Marco."

"It's all right, Mr. Quinn," Marco says. "Elissa, please remind Liam of his next speech."

I read Petruchio's lines from my script. "You lie, in faith for you are call'd plain Kate. And bonny Kate and sometimes Kate the curst. But Kate, the prettiest Kate in Christendom. Kate of Kate Hall, my super-dainty Kate. For dainties are all Kates—"

"Stop," Liam says, and holds up his hand. "Just slow down for a second. What comes after, 'And bonny Kate'?"

I reread the line. He shakes his head and sighs. "Again."

I repeat it. He says it back.

When we restart the scene, he nails it, but everything grinds to a halt again after Angel gives him his next cue.

She walks over and cradles his face. "You okay? You look flushed."

Liam's takes her hands and squeezes them. "Just having a bad day, that's all. I'll be right back."

He pulls away from her and takes off his mic pack. Then he points to the camera crew and says, "Stay," before he strides out of the room.

Okay, what the hell is going on? I've never seen Liam so unprepared.

"Damage control, please, Elissa," Marco whispers. "I'll stay here and work with Angel. Find out what's going on and fix it. The last thing we need right now is to fall behind schedule. Our backers are coming next week, and I want them to feel confident our stars are worth their exorbitant fees."

"On it." I head off to find Liam. I check the conference room first, but it's empty. When I hear banging coming from the men's bathroom, I open the door to find Liam standing over a destroyed trash can.

"So, did it attack you first and you were just acting in self-defense, or—"

"Sorry. I'll replace it."

"No need. That trash can's an asshole. We're all better off without it."

He runs his hand through his hair. I can tell he's trying to calm himself down, but right now, he looks as though he'd like nothing more than to beat the crap out of another inanimate object. Everything in his posture screams of tension and barely controlled aggression.

"Liam, what's going on?"

"Nothing."

"We both know that's not true. You're blowing lines right and left, and that's not like you."

He leans back against the wall and drops his head back. "I didn't get as much time to prepare for this week's rehearsals as I would have liked. I don't know the lines."

I step into the bathroom and close the door behind me. "Well, you should have said something. I'm sure Marco will let you hold your script."

"I can't use the script." I don't miss how his hands are curled into fists.

"Are you really that averse to using your glasses? It would only be for a few days."

"No, Elissa. It's not about glasses. I can't—" He pushes away from the wall and shakes his head. "I can't believe I have to tell you this."

A shiver runs up my spine. "Liam, you're . . . You don't need glasses, do you?"

He pulls in a shaky breath. "I'm dyslexic. Severely. I can make out a few words here and there, but it takes forever. All the words swim and blur in front of my eyes."

I take a moment to process it. "Why didn't you ever tell me?"

"Like I wanted you to know I'm a dumb-ass."

"Oh, please. You're one of the most intelligent men I know."

"And yet, I can't read a menu at a restaurant without hurting my brain." I can see how much he hates admitting it. "Outside of my family, only my agent and my assistant know. And now you."

"Angel doesn't know?" He shakes his head. "Liam, she's going to be your wife. She loves you. Telling her isn't going to change that."

"She'll treat me differently. Everyone who knows does. They don't mean to, but they do."

"I won't."

"You say that now, but give it time."

"How have you managed to hide it all these years?"

"The glasses excuse is gold; usually, no one thinks to question it. When I first started acting, Mom would run lines with me. Or record them so I could learn them in my own time. When Anthony Kent signed me, I figured he should know. He immediately lined me up with David, my assistant. He's been with me on all the movies."

"How on earth do you learn a whole movie's worth of words?"

"Easy. On a movie set, we only ever get a few pages of dialogue each day. But in theater . . ." He leans against the vanity. "You guys expected me to have the whole play learned by the time I got here. Do you know how many freaking lines Petruchio has? And Shakespeare isn't exactly the easiest stuff to remember. I thought I was doing pretty well staying ahead of the schedule. Then on the weekend, David's dad had a heart attack back in England."

"Oh, no . . ."

"His dad survived, but he's in the hospital. Of course, I put David on the first plane home. I've been trying to learn today's scenes by myself, but . . ." He kicks the remnants of the trash can, which flies across the room and slams into the wall. "I have to reread everything five times, and even then, I don't know if I have it right."

"It's okay. We'll figure this out."

He sighs. "You can't tell anyone. Please."

"Liam, having dyslexia is nothing to be ashamed of."

He stares at a spot on the wall, and I hate how down on himself he seems. "You don't understand what it's like to not be able to do something most six-year-olds can. How stupid it makes me feel. This is why I took so long to try my hand at acting. I knew it would be a major obstacle."

"Well, Tom Cruise has done okay over the years, and he's hugely dyslexic."

That gets me an eye roll. "Yeah, but he also believes people are inhabited by the souls of dead aliens. Please don't hold him up as a role model."

My mind races. In all my years of professional theater, I've never come up against something like this. Still, I'm all about finding solutions, so that's what I'll do.

"Okay, tell me how I can help you."

He rubs his forehead. "I don't know. Go over the lines with me, maybe. We're only doing one page of that scene, and then we're going to go over some scenes from last week. If I can make it through this morning I'll be okay, for today at least."

I look at my watch. "How long will it take you to learn the lines?"

"A whole page? Maybe fifteen minutes."

"Be right back."

I race to the rehearsal room and grab my script from the production desk. Josh is there making notes on the scene Marco is running with Angel.

"Hey, what's up? Is Liam okay?"

"He just needs to run some lines. Tell Marco we'll be back soon."

I rush down the corridor to the men's room and find Liam waiting. "Okay," I say. "Let's do this."

Exactly twelve minutes later, Liam and I walk back into the rehearsal room, and even though Marco raises an eyebrow at me, he doesn't ask what's going on.

I help Liam reattach his mic pack. Within seconds his camera crew is hovering.

Angel walks over and puts a hand on Liam's arm. "Everything okay?"

He gives her a warm smile. "Fine. Not enough sleep. Just needed a little refresher on the lines."

"That's not like you."

"I know. It's fine. Elissa helped me out."

"Okay, then," Marco says, "let's try it from the top of this scene."

Liam shoots me a nervous look. I hope he can pull this off. He learned the lines in record time, but I worry about his retention. Twelve minutes to learn a page of Shakespearean prose is no easy task.

Marco calls for quiet, then says, "Begin when you're ready."

They start the scene, and I'm relieved to see it's a huge improvement over their earlier attempt. Not only is Liam on point with his lines, but Angel's time with Marco has also yielded results. She's learning how to imbue Kate with enough vulnerability to match her bitterness, and the chemistry she and Liam create is palpable.

It's the first meeting between Kate and Petruchio, and the way Marco has directed it makes all of the verbal barbs and insults seem like wordy foreplay.

"If I be waspish, best beware my sting," Angel says, assessing Liam like he's something to eat.

Liam moves toward her, slow and seductive. "My remedy is then to pluck it out."

"Ay, if the fool could find it where it lies." Angel's voice becomes breathy.

"Who knows not where a wasp does wear his sting? In his tail." He winds his arms around Angel and unapologetically strokes her butt.

Angel looks like she's about to orgasm. "In his *tongue*."

"Whose tongue?" The way he's looking at her is making me hot. In my pants.

Angel looks like she's feeling the same. "Yours, if you talk of tails. And so farewell."

She attempts to break away, but Liam traps her hands behind her back. Angel lets out a quiet moan.

Liam smiles at how he affects her. "What, with my tongue in your tail? Nay, come again, Good Kate. I am a gentleman."

My tongue in your tail? My God, Shakespeare was a perv.

Liam leans down and holds his mouth just above Angel's. Everyone in the room holds their breath.

Angel battles with her composure for a few more seconds before she stands on her toes to kiss him. Liam moans and releases her hands as he kisses her back.

My face flames when they move against each other, kissing and grasping. My feelings vacillate between extreme arousal and violent jealousy. It's not pleasant.

Then Angel breaks away and slaps Liam, hard. "*That* I'll try."

He smiles in triumph. She goes to hit him again but he grabs her arms roughly. "I swear I'll cuff you, if you strike again." His tone is dark but promises more pleasure than pain. Angel looks even more turned on than he does.

"Yes, good, Liam," Marco says beside me. "Now, cross downstage left, and take her with you. Don't be gentle. Remember, the more forceful you are with her, the more it arouses her. She likes to be dominated."

Liam glances at me, and I avert my gaze to my script. I take in a shaky breath and write down the stage directions.

When Liam ends the scene by throwing Angel over his shoulder and soundly smacking her butt, Marco says, "Okay, stop there. Excellent work! That's coming along nicely. This scene needs just the right balance of lust and violence to set up the first BDSM interpretation this show has ever received. I can't believe no one has ever explored the possibility that the reason Kate provokes *Petruchio* so much is that she's desperate for a good spanking. Or that *Petruchio* morphs from a jovial hood into an alpha male because he's at last met someone who wants to be dominated by him. It seems so obvious."

Now I really need to fan myself.

I'm concerned that Liam playing a dom may make my body spontaneously combust.

The camera crews have left, and the cast is packing up at the end of the day when I notice Liam throwing me nervous glances. Angel is chatting to Marco about her costumes, so when Liam gives me a pointed look before he heads out the door, I wait a minute, then follow.

On a hunch, I find him in the conference room.

"Thanks for saving my ass today," he whispers. "I never want to be in that situation again."

"Ditto. Although I can't take the credit for anything. You're the one with the super-fast memorization skills."

"Yeah, well, that happens when scripts are useless." He looks at the door, then down to his hands. "Listen, I know it's a lot to ask, but could you . . . I mean, could I ask you to help me learn my scenes, just until David gets back?"

"I . . ." A big part of me is dying to say yes, because it means I'd get to spend more time with him, but the logical part knows spending more time with him is the worst idea ever. "Liam . . . I just—"

"Look, I know you have a lot on your plate, but I don't trust anyone else. You'd just need to run lines with me for an hour or so each night until I get the scenes down for the next day. David should be back by next week. Please. I can't do this without you."

"Where would we go?"

"My apartment is right around the corner."

"Won't Angel get wise that something's up if we're running lines in front of her?"

He blinks a few times. "Uh . . . well, we aren't sharing an apartment while we're in New York. She has her own place."

I frown. "Isn't that weird? You guys are engaged. I kind of thought living together came with the territory."

"Not for us," he says. "Working and living together is stressful. Plus, she drives me insane with her messiness, and she hates my compulsive cleaning. It's just easier if we have our own space. She's just one floor down, though, so we're still close."

From all my cyber-stalking, I thought I knew the ins and outs of their relationship, but apparently not.

"Do you not hang out after rehearsals?"

"Sometimes, but most nights she locks herself away to work on her lines. Another reason I don't want her involved in this. She has enough pressure without me adding to it."

"Okay, fine. Your place. I'll get there as soon as I can after I finish up here."

"Great," he says, and gives me a knee-buckling smile. "You're amazing. Thank you."

"*Liam?*" Angel calls. "*Where are you?*"

Liam pushes me behind the door and holds a finger to my lips. When the door swings open, he catches it right before it smashes into my nose.

"Hey," he says to Angel.

"What are you doing?"

"Just grabbing some water for the ride home. Ready to go?"

"God, yes. There's a bottle of low-carb wine at home with my name on it. Want to come over for a drink?"

"Ah, not tonight. I have to learn some lines."

"Me, too. It's never-ending. My brain hurts."

"So just a small ache, then?"

She groans. "You're not funny."

"Yeah, I am."

After they leave, I head back into the rehearsal room and clean the production desk in a semi-haze.

I'm finishing up when Josh and Denise come over. "Drinks at Lacey's?" Josh asks.

Denise immediately says, "Hell, yes!"

"Can't," I say. "Got stuff to do."

"What stuff?" Josh asks.

I hate not telling him, but I know I can't. "Just work stuff, but it has to be done before tomorrow. I'll see you at home later, okay? You guys go and have a good time."

Josh hugs me good-bye, but I can feel he's suspicious.

After he and Denise have left, I take some deep breaths and tell myself it's possible to be alone with Liam and not let him know how hung up on him I still am. Power of positive thinking and all that.

When I finish the tenth affirmation and still don't feel prepared, I mutter, "Screw it," and head to the exit.

Liam opens the door shirtless.

I nearly pass out.

"Hey," he says, out of breath. "You got here fast. I was trying to get in a quick workout."

I'm gaping at the thin sheen of sweat making all of his muscles glisten when he selfishly puts on a T-shirt. I inwardly curse that I didn't even get to examine his new ink.

I shake my head to clear it. "So, let me get this straight. You rehearse for eight hours, then have the energy for a workout? You're such a freak."

He checks the fitness tracker on his wrist. "You say the nicest things. Did it occur to you that the reason I have the energy to rehearse for eight hours is *because* I work out?"

"I'm going to have to take your word for that."

"Still not a fan of exercise, I take it."

I whisper, "Not a lot of people know this, but I'm in the fitness protection program."

He tries not to smile. "Is that right?"

"Yep. Every new year I'm hunted by gym memberships, but they haven't found me yet."

He laughs, and man, I love that sound. "Wow. Badass."

"I know, right?" I look down the hallway. "So, are we planning to rehearse out here? Or are you going to invite me in?"

"Oh, shit. Of course." He holds the door open for me. "Come in."

I walk past him, making sure to stay as far away from his rippling body as possible. The T-shirt and workout shorts are really doing nothing to hide his hotness.

When I see the full extent of his apartment, it hits me just how far he's come from the man I knew six years ago. A far cry from his old Broadway apartment, it's a penthouse in one of the new kazillion-dollar complexes that are springing up more and more in the theater district. Everything is sleek and glass—high-tech and luxe beyond what most normal people could comprehend. Of course, it's spotless. There's not one fingerprint on the high-gloss kitchen cabinets. Impressive.

"Wow," I say. "You own this?"

He shrugs. "I was told it was a good investment, but I'm hardly ever here."

I can feel him watching me as I take in the open space and million-dollar views. It's weird how awkward I feel in this environment. It's hard to process this version of him. The millionaire. The movie star. Yet in a lot of ways, he still feels exactly like he used to, just with more money and nicer stuff.

"I don't think I'd know what to do with myself in a place this pretty," I say. "I'm used to noisy radiators, mismatched dishes, and nonexistent water pressure. I'll bet this palace has none of those things."

"Not true," he says, and pulls open one of the kitchen cabinets. "Observe."

There are four plates in the cupboard, and two of them have cartoon characters on them.

I smile. "You eat off *Captain America* plates?"

"Not anymore. But these guys are hangovers from my old place. Back then, I only had two plates, and two glasses that used to be jam jars."

"I remember those. You served me milk in one the night we met."

He smiles and rubs the back of his neck. "Yeah, and because I was trying to impress you, I gave you the one without the chip in it. Plus I would never have forgiven myself if you'd cut your lips."

I remember how he kept staring at my lips that night. It's similar to how he's staring at them now.

He blinks, then takes a breath and closes the cabinet. "Anyway, can I get you something to drink?" He walks over to the gleaming fridge. "I promise, I have proper glasses these days."

"Please tell me you have alcohol."

"One thing I definitely have is alcohol." He opens the door to reveal shelf upon shelf of fresh food, as well as a plethora of wine and boutique beer. And cheese. Lots and lots of cheese.

"Did you stock up for me?" I ask, and point to the cheese. "Or do you usually have a fridgeful of potential mouthgasms?"

He smiles. "The cheese cabinet at a deli would be like a porn shop to you, right?"

"Pretty much."

He grabs a wheel of something covered in wax and expensive-looking and slides it across the island to me. "As much as I'd like to say I stocked up for you, I didn't. The irony of being so rich you can afford anything is that people insist on giving you free stuff. When you're broke, people wouldn't piss on you if you were on fire, but rich and famous? 'Here: Take everything!' "

I grab the cheese and bring it up to my nose. "Oh my God. Italian. Aged. Smells amazing."

He raises an eyebrow. "Would you like to be alone with it?"

I put the cheese on the counter and stroke it, lovingly. "No. As much as I want him, he isn't mine. I'll just pine for him from afar." Funny how that seems to be a recurring theme in my life.

Liam grabs a carry bag from the cupboard. "Unacceptable. True love should never be denied." He places the cheese inside, then holds it out to me. "I hope you two are very happy together."

I put my hand over my heart. "Wow, this is a defining moment in our relationship. Only a true friend would give me cheese."

When I take the bag from him, our fingers brush. In that second, all the buoyancy in the air turns to lead. We lock eyes, and for a few hideous moments, I think I'm going to launch myself at him.

He breaks eye contact and clears his throat. "So, beer?"

"God, yes."

He heads back to the fridge to retrieve two beers, then pops the caps before holding one out to me. "Try this. It's my favorite."

I take a mouthful and swallow. "Wow. Expensive beer actually tastes like it's been fermented with money. That's delicious."

"Glad you like it." He walks over to the couch and invites me to take a seat next to him. I drop my bag on the floor and sink into the soft leather.

Oh, God. I'm never getting up. This is amazing. It's like being hugged by a leather jacket.

I sit back and close my eyes. It's possible I moan.

When I feel heat on my face, I turn to see Liam staring at me, eyes hooded and dark. "Comfortable?"

"Very." I shouldn't like his eyes on me as much as I do. It's wrong. And stupid.

"Good. I want you to feel at home here."

I'm tempted to say I feel at home wherever he is, but even for me, that's too cheesy. Still, that doesn't make it not true.

"Was it strange?" I ask. "Getting used to all this?"

He looks around. "This apartment?"

"This life. The money. Fame."

He looks down at his beer. "What makes you think I'm used to any of it? Every paparazzo on the West Coast will tell you how well I *don't* deal with it. Hell, you saw it firsthand the other night. I don't think I'll ever get used to being treated like a commodity instead of a person."

"I guess to Hollywood, it makes sense to treat you like a commodity. I mean, think about it like this—if Hollywood is an Italian restaurant, then you're Parmigiano Reggiano and Angel is black truffle."

"Wait, why does Angel get to be one of the most expensive foods ever, and I'm stinky cheese?"

I smack his arm. "Who the hell are you calling stinky, buddy? I'm talking about one of the most delicious and exclusive cheeses in the world."

He thinks for a moment. "You're right. I apologize. Knowing how much you love cheese, I should have realized that's the highest compliment you could have paid me. My ego is satisfied. Continue."

I smile, happy to see that his adorable arrogance is still intact. "Okay, so, the chef knows that if he uses the cheese and truffles, everyone is going to love that dish before they've even tasted it. It's a surefire hit. Same with you and Angel. Put you two in a movie together, and even if the rest of the ingredients are crappy, you'll make it a hit."

He takes a sip of beer. "Okay, I see your point, but I still think it's unfair to stalk and harass truffle and Parmesan until they have zero life. It's bad enough that they can't go anywhere, but it's even worse that no one seems to want one without the other. I mean, what if the cheese just wants to be in a dish by himself? Are you telling me that dish will only be half as good without the truffle?"

"Not at all. But do the math. Parmesan has passionate fans. Truffle has passionate fans. Put them together and twice as many people are going to order the dish."

He frowns. "I think you're talking about ticket sales now, but this metaphor is making me so hungry, I'm having trouble concentrating. You want some food?"

"Uh . . ." Before I can refuse, he's up and striding into the kitchen.

"I don't have truffles, but I'm sure I can whip up some decent pasta." He pulls open the fridge and starts placing ingredients on the bench. "Hey, look at that." He holds up a wedge of cheese. "Parmigiano Reggiano."

He gives me a smile, and for a single glorious second, I pretend that we're in a different reality, one where he's allowed to smile at me like that, and I'm allowed to get butterflies in my tummy because he's so damn beautiful.

"Liss?"

I blink at him. "Hmmm?"

He gets out a cutting board and grabs a knife. "Come and sit by me while I cook. You're too far away."

I push up off of the sofa and sit on one of the stools at the island. He quickly puts on a pot of water before dicing an onion and some garlic and throwing them into a sizzling fry pan. Then he chops some bacon and throws it in as well. A blast of mouthwatering aroma hits me.

"God, that smells good."

He flashes me a smile and keeps going. He looks so sure of himself in the kitchen, it's just adding to my attraction to him—the last thing I need.

"Your mom teach you how to cook?" I ask.

He nods. "She started teaching me and my brother when we were little. The first thing we learned was scrambled eggs. Mom showed us how to gently crack the eggs, but Jamie and I were only about five so we didn't know the meaning of the word 'gentle.'" He laughs and shakes his head. "There was so much eggshell in that first batch, it was crunchy as hell. But Mom smiled and ate it anyway. Said it was the best eggs she ever had."

For a moment, sadness crosses his features. Then, it's gone, and he puts some diced tomatoes into the fry pan before adding all sorts of herbs. "What about you? Do you cook?"

I nod. "My mom passed along her love for cooking to Ethan and me. From the age of ten, we each had to cook one family meal a week. Of course, the first thing I learned to make was mac and cheese."

He looks up from the fry pan. "Of course. Not normal cheese, though, right?"

I scoff. "As if. My first attempt included Castello White and buffalo mozzarella. It was heaven, even if I do say so myself."

"I love mac and cheese. Promise you'll make it for me one night?"

I want to remind him that making each other dinner is stepping over all sorts of lines, but his face is so hopeful, I knock it back to a simple "Maybe."

He throws some pasta into the boiling pot along with a decent pinch of salt. "Angel can't cook at all. She loves gourmet food, but has no idea how it's made. I guess that's what happens when you grow up in a house with a nanny, a chef, and a housekeeper."

At Angel's name, I tense up. With everything falling back into such a comfortable routine with Liam, it's easy to forget we now live in completely different worlds.

If he notices, it doesn't show. He nods toward the cheese on the bench. "Want to grate some of that for me? Grater's in the drawer, bowl is in the cabinet behind me."

I hop up and do as I'm asked. When I've grated a decent amount,

I place it next to him and glance over his shoulder into the simmering pan. "The sauce looks amazing."

He stirs it once more before scooping up a little with the wooden spoon and blowing on it. "Here. Taste." He holds his hand under it and moves it toward my mouth. Without even thinking about the intimacy of the action, I close my mouth around the spoon. I immediately freeze, and when I look up, Liam's staring.

I lick my lips and swallow, feeling more than a little self-conscious. "Delicious."

His gaze travels up to my eyes and then back down to my mouth. "Uh-huh. Is there . . . uh . . . enough salt?"

"Yep. Perfect." After a couple more seconds of pinning me in place with his gaze, he turns back to the sauce. I sigh in relief and head back to the safety zone on the other side of the island. My entire body is buzzing. I wonder if he affects all women the same way. Does Angel feel like this? Like he's a bolt of lightning in human form, charging the air around him?

I sip my beer, and we lapse into silence as he finishes the dish. When he places a steaming bowl in front of me, topped with a generous serving of Parmesan, my mouth waters like crazy.

"Thank you."

"As usual with you, Elissa Holt," he says with a mischievous smile, "the pleasure is all mine. Bon appetit."

He sits next to me as we eat. It's both comfortable and tense, and I'm realizing that's kind of normal for us.

"So," I say. "You seeing your mom and dad while you're in town?"

He shakes his head. "I bought them a round-the-world trip ages ago, and didn't realize it coincided with my stay. They're traveling for the next two months. Hopefully I'll get to see them before I head back to L.A. If the show lasts that long."

I finish my last bite and wipe my mouth with a napkin. "Oh, it'll last. Don't worry. Parmesan and truffle onstage every night? Audiences will eat it up."

He laughs, then takes our empty bowls over to the sink. "Well, that's encouraging." He grabs two more beers out of the fridge and passes me one. When we head back over to the couch, I wince as I sit.

He looks at me with concern. "Hip still sore?"

"Only a little. My bruise, however, could win awards. It's kind of cool, in a gross, blood-filled way."

He lays his arm along the back of the couch. "Can I see?"

"My bruise?"

He nods. "Purely for medical purposes. Sometimes a severe contusion can cause vascular issues. Better let me run my expert eyes over it, just to be sure."

I blink. "Are you serious?"

"As a heart attack. Come here."

He puts his beer down on the coffee table as I push up out of the couch. When I stand in front of him, he lifts up my T-shirt and examines the dark purple crescent that peeks over the edge of my low-rise jeans.

He looks up at me, and just having him this close makes me dizzy. "Can I see the rest?" His voice is dark, and way too sexy.

"Do you really need to?" I know my limits, and every one of them is fast approaching.

"I'd like to. Just to check it. I still feel responsible for you getting hurt."

I bite the inside of my cheek as I release the button on my jeans and pull down the zipper. Everything feels very heavy. Liam is watching my hands, and I focus on his lashes as he blinks slowly.

I push the side of my jeans down, revealing the full extent of the bruise, along with the strap of my black thong.

Liam exhales and just stares for a few seconds. I see his Adam's apple bob twice before he speaks. "Well, yeah. Medically speaking, that's one hell of a bruise."

The skin is dark purple with angry yellow highlights over my hip bone. He grazes his fingers over it, and I have to close my eyes and clench my teeth to stop myself from making a very aroused sound.

"It's warm. Does the joint hurt?"

Nothing hurts right now. "No. Just my thigh muscle."

"Uh-huh." I open my eyes. He moves his thumb down to the top of my thigh. "Here?"

He presses gently, and I suck in a breath. "Yes." The pain isn't severe, but coupled with how light-headed he's making me, I have to put my hands on his shoulders to keep my balance.

He grips my hips to help steady me. "Sorry. You okay?"

"Yeah. Fine."

Except I'm not fine. He's looking up at me with a sense of need that threatens to ruin me, and his hands are warm and firm, and I want to feel more of them. I want him to push my jeans down and rip off my panties, and put that magic mouth of his right where I'm aching most. I want him to realize he made a mistake by leaving me, and dump his amazing fiancée, and break his fans' hearts just to satisfy my selfish craving. And I hate myself for wanting all of those things because any one of them would hurt a lot of people, and part of me is absolutely okay with that.

"Liss." He's gazing at me, eyes blazing, jaw tight. I become aware of his hands, gripping and releasing my hips in an erratic rhythm. Everywhere he's touching me sparks and warms. "You can't look at me like that and expect me to respect our friends pact. You really can't."

My breath catches. "How am I looking at you?"

"Like you want to straddle my face." My fingers dig into his shoulders, and he hisses. "You need to stop, or I swear to God, I'm about three seconds away from making it happen." He squeezes his eyes shut. "I vowed I'd keep my cool around you, but every time you're close, that becomes more and more impossible."

Without thinking, I stroke the hair away from his face. "Liam . . ."

He sighs and leans into my touch. "You can't say my name like that." He drops his head. "Seriously. I'm hanging on by a thread here." My stomach flips when he pulls me forward between his legs so that his forehead is resting on my stomach. His warm breath makes me shiver, and when he wraps his arms around me, I can't stop myself from hugging him back.

"I've missed you, Liss. It hurt not seeing you for all of those years, but this? You being right here and me not being able to have you? Hurts so much more."

He pushes his hands under my T-shirt and grips my back, fingers splayed. Like he's sure I'll disappear if he's not touching my skin.

I try to enjoy the moment, but I get a flash of what would happen if Angel walked through the door right now. How she would feel seeing me, jeans hanging open, Liam clutching me and breathing heavily against my skin.

It would devastate her.

As much as I acknowledge my own selfishness, I also know I could never hurt her like that.

I put my hands on his shoulders and push him back. "Liam—"

"I know." He falls against the couch and pushes the heels of his hands into his eyes. "I know I have to resist, but whenever you're near I just . . . can't think straight."

I exhale and refasten my jeans. "I'm to blame, too. Clearly, there's still an attraction between us, and hugging isn't the best way to deal with that."

"It's not the hugging," he says. "It's just being together. It's always been this way. Look."

He leans forward and takes my hand. I'm about to tell him to stop when he slowly pushes his fingers between mine. Skin slides against skin, soft and sensitive.

Ohhhhh, God.

Such a simple, innocent gesture, but I feel it everywhere.

"See? I can't even hold your hand." He gently pulls his fingers back, then pushes them in again. My eyelids flutter as I try to keep breathing.

He keeps staring into my eyes, and I have no choice but to stare back. He continues to caress my fingers, but doesn't touch me anywhere else. He doesn't have to. I feel it so strongly in every part of my body, he might as well be grazing my breasts, or my thighs, or have his hand in my pants.

Judging from how dilated his pupils are, he's just as turned on as I am.

"See? This is the problem." His voice is low and husky. "I've spent years trying to block out how you look. And sound. And feel. And before this show, I'd gotten pretty good at it. But now, here you are, in front of me every day, and it blows my mind that a single touch from you still has the power to ruin me. And whenever it happens, I forget about the choices I've made, and the circus my life's become, and I *want you*. Consequences be damned."

"Liam, you're engaged. To an amazing woman."

"I know." He looks down at our hands for a few seconds, then shakes his head. "Believe me, I know." He brushes his thumb across the back of my hand. "And dragging you into the shitstorm of my life wouldn't be fair, to you or to Angel. I knew what I'd be sacrificing when I made a commitment to her, and I refuse to be one of those assholes who thinks he can have it all, because I know very well I can't."

So there it is. He didn't come out and say, *"No matter how much I feel for you, I'm still going to marry Angel,"* but that's what I heard.

After a few more seconds, he slowly pulls his fingers free from mine and lets out a ragged breath. "So, yeah. I can't touch you. I have to think of you as my friend, and nothing more."

I put my hands on my hips and exhale. "Maybe being alone together is a bad idea."

"No, we can do this. Please." He goes to take my hand again, but catches himself. "I need you—as my stage manager, if nothing else.

But, if you could also find a way to stop being so insanely attractive, I'd appreciate it."

I almost laugh. "Uh-huh. I'll get right on that."

His expression turns serious. "Don't do that."

"What?"

"Act like I'm saying that out of obligation or pity. I'm not."

"Well, Liam, come on. Look who you're engaged to and then look at me. There's no comparison."

He stands and looks down at me, and his athletic shorts aren't doing a thing to disguise how aroused he is right now. "You're right. And if you had any clue of what you do to me—what you've always done to me—you'd know that."

I can't help but glance down. "Well, I guess even if I doubted you, I can't doubt him."

He looks down, then rubs his forehead and sighs. "Okay, so, standing up wasn't a great idea. Just ignore it. It'll go away eventually."

"Uh-huh."

He sits on the couch, and I sit next to him.

"Okay, then," I say, in my most authoritative voice. "Here's how it's going to work: We're going to run lines and discuss the show when necessary. There will be no touching. No reminiscing. No unprofessional behavior of any kind. If either of us fails to adhere to these rules, this arrangement is terminated and I'll find someone else to run your lines. Agreed?"

"Agreed." He stares at me for a few seconds, then grabs his beer and takes a long drink. When he turns back to me, he's frowning. "I'm tempted to tell you how incredibly hot I found that entire rant, but that would be highly unprofessional, so I'll keep it to myself."

A nervous laugh bursts out of me. "Liam?"

"Yeah?"

"Just for the record, I've missed you, too." *Way more than you'll ever know.*

He gives me a warm smile. "Thank you, Liss."

I open my script, and don't bother reminding him I've requested he call me Elissa. Liss is the girl who still goes weak at the knees for him, and right now, I need to be slick, professional Elissa more than ever.

For the next hour and a half we run lines. No personal anecdotes. No lingering gazes. Just business.

When he seems satisfied and comfortable, I bid him a quick good night and head to the subway station. I'd congratulate myself on my self-control if I didn't still feel a little high from having had his hands on me.

ELEVEN

DRESSES AND DIVAS

The rest of the second week of rehearsals flies by. Days are spent blocking the show. Nights are spent running lines with Liam.

For the most part, we're successful in keeping things professional. Every now and then, I catch myself staring and turn away before he can see. At other times, he tries to draw me into conversation at the end of the night, but I'm careful to shut him down. I get in, run the lines, and get out. Quick and unemotional. It's the only way things between us can work.

In the rehearsal room, it's harder to stay detached.

Even though I thought I'd gotten used to seeing Liam and Angel's regular displays of affection over the years, now that I know he still has feelings for me, every time he touches or kisses her, I feel a stab of jealousy. I try not to let it affect my friendship with Angel, but it's tough. I find myself making excuses to not talk to her during lunch, and whenever I need to discuss show-related matters, I send Josh to do my dirty work.

I feel bad, because none of this is her fault, but the human heart has a flawed logic all its own, and no amount of reasoning will convince it to stop making people like me behave like assholes.

For her part, Angel seems oblivious. She continues to be friendly, easygoing, and hardworking, and for some reason, that makes things worse. If she was a total bitch, I wouldn't feel so bad about my negative feelings for her. But she isn't, so I do.

I'm packing up on Friday evening when I see her approaching with an expression of suppressed excitement. Right away, I'm nervous.

"Hey, you," she says, and takes both of my hands. "What are you up to tonight?"

"I was going to finish up some work, then head home. Why?"

She looks like she's about to burst out of her skin. "Well, there's a super-exclusive bridal boutique in the garment district I've been dying to visit, and they've offered to give me private access tonight to try on some gowns. Since we haven't been able to spend much time together this week, I thought you might like to come. You know, girls' night out. There'll be champagne."

"Well, uh . . . who else is going?"

"Just the camera crew. The producers are dying to get shots of me in wedding dresses. You know how it is." She squeezes my hands and bounces on her toes. "Please come. I don't have any other female friends in New York. You'd save me from being a total loser trying on dresses by myself. Pleeeease?"

She bats her eyelashes, and I can't help but laugh. Even though the absolute last thing I want to do in my spare time is help Angel become the world's most gorgeous bride, the guilt I feel for avoiding her all week wells up, and I can't seem to refuse. "Okay, sure. I'd love to come."

"Oh, yay!" She does a little jumpy clap. It's so adorable, I hate her. And then I hate myself for being a bitch.

"I'm just going to freshen up," she says. "I'll meet you downstairs in ten minutes, okay?"

"Great."

As I'm packing up the rest of the production table, Josh appears beside me.

"Sounds like you're in for a fun evening. Leave this. I'll finish packing up for you." He gives me a sympathetic smile and slings my bag over my shoulder before grabbing my phone off the table. "Want me to text Quinn and tell him you'll be late for line practice?"

"Yes, please." Josh is the one person who knows about my nightly visits to Liam's apartment, and even though I haven't said anything about dyslexia, I know he suspects something like that.

"Should I tell him the reason you'll be late?"

I frown. "Yes. Why?"

He gives a one-shoulder shrug. "Just not sure how he'd feel about his ex picking out wedding dresses for his woman."

"I'm barely his ex. Anyway, he was the one who told me it's impossible to say no to Angel. It is, by the way."

He chuckles. "Oh, believe me, I know. She asked me to sing for her the other day, and I did."

"What? But you never sing. I mean, I've heard you in the shower, but that's it."

"I told you, the woman has me wrapped around her finger. It's both hot and annoying." He taps on the phone. "Okay, so 'Gone wedding-dress shopping with Angel. Be over later.' Want me to include anything provocative? Broken-heart emoticon, perhaps? Jealous green-face?" He gives me an innocent look, and I give him my best glare. He looks back down at the phone. "Hmmm, not sure there's a shriveled-balls emoticon, but I'll do my best."

I smile. "Just send the message, Josh."

He finishes and presses "send" before handing the phone back to me. "So, you told me not to be worried when you started running lines with Quinn every night, even though I think you're playing with fire. Are you also going to tell me not to worry about going wedding-dress shopping with your arch nemesis? Because honestly, my Spidey sense is tingling, and not in a good way."

I look up at him. "What's the worst that could happen?"

"Oh, I don't know. You crumble into an emotional heap and confess your undying love for her future husband?"

"Hmmm. I *was* planning on doing that, but now that you've said

it out loud, it doesn't seem like such a good idea. Maybe I'll rethink."
I kiss him on the cheek. "See you later."

"Yes, you will." He gives me a tentative thumbs-up.

I give him my "I seriously need to get drunk" signal, and head downstairs to meet Angel.

This should be fun. And when I say "fun," I mean incredibly uncomfortable, with just a touch of impending doom.

Angel twirls in what must be her twelfth dress. They all look amazing
on her; it's annoying as hell. I've given up trying to pick a favorite. The
camera crews shoot her from all angles and sometimes the producer
gets her to do specific poses. I don't know much about television production, but I smell a montage.

I refill my champagnes glass and sigh. This is so screwed up on so
many levels, it's making my head pound. Helping Angel pick out the
dress she's going to wear to marry the man of my dreams is messing
with me, big-time. And yet, because she's such a lovely person, I'm
torn between hating her guts and loving her like the sister I never had.

Is it any wonder I'm well on my way to being stinking drunk?

"I think I like this one the best," Angel says as she studies herself in the mirror and sways in blush-colored chiffon. She's a little
drunk, too.

"That's what you've said about the last ten dresses, princess."

"And it's been true every time." She turns to the sales assistant.
"How much is this one?"

The dark-haired woman gives her an almost-warm smile. "It's
a little more than the others you've been looking at. This one's a
hundred thousand, Miss Bell."

"The *fuck*?" Everyone looks at me, and I'm a little surprised to have
said that out loud. I wave my hand and laugh. "Sorry. Just . . . wow.
Lotta money. I could buy a whole lotta cheese with that. Hell, an entire cheese factory."

"We don't pretend our gowns are cheap," the snooty assistant says. "But the women who shop here want something extraordinary for their big day, and they're willing to pay for it. I'm sure when you get to this point, you might view it as a worthwhile investment."

I take another mouthful of champagne. I'm betting I'm never going to think a hundred grand for a dress you wear once is a worthwhile investment. Besides, at this point, I doubt I'll ever need a gown. I'm twenty-five and single with zero prospects on the horizon. Oh, and did I mention that the love of my life is marrying someone else?

Weddings in general can bite me. This wedding in particular can die in a fire.

I down the rest of my champagne in two mouthfuls and stagger over to the racks of dresses. There's got to be something that Angel looks terrible in, and goddammit, I aim to find it.

"I'm filling up your glass, okay?" Angel says, and her words are starting to slur. When I glance over at her, she's drinking straight from the bottle and trying to hide it from the disapproving sales assistant. It makes me giggle. Why can't she be a bitch so I can hate her? Stupid likable woman.

I push through the dresses, and to my dismay, they're all gorgeous. I'm about to give up when a flash of pale green catches my eye. I pull out the dress to get a better look.

Oh, my God.

It's one of the most hideous dresses I've ever seen. The color is the least of its problems. The green by itself wouldn't look too bad, but the designer has clearly tried to make this dress into a couture version of *The Secret Garden*. There are flowers of all colors and styles stitched onto the bodice, and farther down on the skirt, there are even butterflies, bees, and dragonflies.

What the hell were they thinking? Any bride who wore this would be a laughingstock.

"Oh, Angeeel!"

She totters over. "You have something for me to try?"

I hold the dress out to her. "What do you think?"

She looks it over, then squints at something on the skirt. "Wait, is that . . . is that a frog?"

I look down. "Oh, wow. It so is. This dress is *perfect*!"

Angel shrugs and takes it from me. "If you like it, I'll try it. The color's really pretty."

She disappears with the assistant into the dressing room, so I take my seat again and grab my champagne. If I just keep drinking, I can ignore my growing sense of guilt. One of the cameras hovers around me as if to say, *"I see what you're doing. Every petty, bitchy move."*

I want to swat it like a fly.

Angel emerges in the nightmare dress, and I almost cry with relief that finally, she looks bad in something. Well, that's not true. She still looks perfect, but that dress is diabolical.

She tilts her head and studies it. "Hmmm. I don't know. Do you think it's too much?"

"No way," I say. "It's unbelievable! Just so . . . *unique*. No one has ever had a dress like this. People will be talking about it for months."

That's true. That dress will hit every single worst-dressed list known to man. Possibly more.

Angel twirls and giggles. The camera follows her.

I pour myself more champagne and drink away my feelings.

"Miss Bell?" the sales assistant says as she goes over to Angel. "Would you like to try something else? Or have you made your decision?"

"Just give me a minute," Angel says, and stumbles over to me. "I'm thinking." She flops down next to me on the white leather chaise, and we're both enveloped in acres of silk and flowers. "So? Verdict? You like this one? It's sooooo twirly."

"You looked amazing in all of them, but this one? It has a frog, Angel. A *frog*. None of the others had a frog."

She beams. "Right? There aren't enough frogs at weddings. I should totally wear this dress. See? I knew you'd help find me the perfect

one. You're the best." She lies down and puts her head into my lap.
"This dress is the bomb."

Could I actually do it? Let her wear this abomination as punishment
for marrying the man who should be mine?

Angel sighs and looks up at the ceiling. "I can't wait to marry Liam.
He's going to look so incredible in his tux. Everyone who's anyone in
Hollywood will be there. It will be the wedding I've always dreamed
about. He'll be my Prince Charming and I'll be his princess, and for
once, Daddy will be proud of me instead of my dumb, perfect sister."
She looks up at me. "Tell me about your dream wedding."

I stroke her hair away from her face. "I don't have one."

"Aw, come on. Every little girl has a wedding fantasy."

"Not me. I guess I'm just not the romantic type."

Her face softens. "Elissa." She looks at me like I've just told her
I'm dying. "Have you never looked at a man and just thought, *Yeah,
I'd like to wake up with you for the rest of my life?*"

I look down at the bubbles in my glass. "Once."

"Is this the man Josh mentioned the other night at dinner? The
one who got away?" I squirm, really uncomfortable with this line of
questioning. "Are you sure there's no chance you two will get back
together?"

I laugh. It sounds high-pitched and wrong. Tinged with hysteria.
"I'm sure. He's with someone else. And she's . . ." I take a breath. "She's
beautiful, and loving, and funny . . . and I should be happy he's found
someone so incredible, but I'm not. I'm selfish and still wish he was
mine." I take a mouthful of champagne, but swallowing it requires
effort.

Angel sits up and puts her arms around me. "Elissa, I'm so
sorry."

I clench my jaw and refuse to cry. "It's fine."

"No, it's not. I don't care how beautiful and loving his new woman
is, that guy was an idiot for letting you go."

I laugh again. It sounds more like a sob. I hug Angel and push the sadness down. No matter what happened in the past, she's about to have her dream wedding, and she deserves my support.

I pull back and give her a smile. "Maybe you shouldn't wear the frog dress. I don't think the world is ready for that much awesome."

"No?"

"No. Go with the blush-colored one. You looked stunning in that. Liam isn't going to know what to do with himself when he sees you walking down the aisle in it."

She closes her eyes and sighs. "I loved that one, too. It's perfect." She's quiet for a few moments, then says, "Speaking of Liam, what do you think of him?"

"Uh . . . what do you mean?"

"I mean, you guys have known each other for a while. What do you think about him? As a man?" The alcohol is really taking its toll on her now. Me, too. I have to be careful about what's about to come out of my mouth.

"Well, I . . . I think Liam is talented. Committed. Professional." *Most of the time.*

"Oh, screw 'professional.' Do you think he's hot?" She giggles, and a fierce blush starts in my cheeks and crawls down my neck.

"I really don't think it's appropriate for me to comment."

"Aw, come on, Elissa." She pours more champagne. "He's gorgeous, right? I mean, annoyingly beautiful. Whatever angle you look at him from, he's perfect. Just admit it—I won't be mad. I like it when other women find him hot. Is that weird?"

She's so drunk, her honesty makes me laugh. "Yeah, that's a little weird. Most women don't like it when their men are lusted after."

"But you don't understand," she says, and the last word comes out "unnerstan." She continues, "I have something everyone wants, and that makes me powerful. Even my dad thinks so, and he never used to take any notice of me before I hooked up with Liam. Now, I'm the apple of his eye because Angeliam is a hot commodity, and my sister hasn't even got a boyfriend. Get it?"

"Not really."

She waves her hand. "Doesn't matter. Just say you think he's hot. Do it for me."

I sigh as she refills my glass with more champagne. "Okay, fine. He's very handsome."

She pokes her finger at me. "Not handsome. *Hot*."

"Yes, he's hot."

"Fucking hot. Like, molten-lava hot."

She's so serious, it makes me laugh. "Oh, my God, fine. Yes, Angel, your fiancé is the hottest man I've ever laid eyes on."

"Good!"

"He's a perfect specimen of manhood."

"Keep going!"

"If he wasn't engaged to you, I would ride him like the sexy love stallion he is."

"Yeah, ya would!"

"I would fuck him ten ways from Sunday."

"And he'd love it!"

"I would climb him like a tree and bang him like a screen door in a hurricane!"

Her face drops in an instant, and she looks at me with a hurt expression. "Okay, that's too far."

My smile fades. "Oh, God, Angel—"

Her lips tremble, and my chest aches when her eyes fill with tears. "Why would you say that? I thought you were my friend. Bang him like a screen door in a hurricane? That's disgusting, Elissa!"

"But you asked me to say—"

A huge snort of laughter rips out of her before she bends over in a fit of giggles. "Oh my God, your face!"

"What? You . . . Oh, you—" I struggle to react to her hyena laugh. "Goddamn actors!" She's in hysterics now, and despite my near heart attack, I smile. "You will pay for that." She laughs harder. "One day, when you least expect it, I'm taking you down, lady. That was mean!

America's sweetheart, my ass! I should fuck your man just to spite you."

That's when I remember the cameras are there. I clap my hand over my mouth. "Oh, no. You guys can't use any of that."

The producer smiles. "Sure. We'll cut that out."

"No, seriously," I say. "It was a joke. I was joking. You can't put that in the show." What would everyone think? God, what would *Liam* think?

I go over to the producer. "Please. I'll pay you. How much to burn that footage?"

She smiles again, and I swear to god, she looks like a barracuda in lipstick. "Good television is priceless."

Angel comes over and pats my arm. "It's fine. Don't worry. I say stupid things all the time. They'll definitely edit that out. Right, Ava?"

Ava nods. "Of course, Miss Bell." She has all the sincerity of a snake oil salesman.

"See?" Angel says. "All good. Now, come with me." She grabs my hand and leads me into the dressing room. "You need to try on one of these dresses. You say you don't have a wedding fantasy, but you will by the time I'm done with you."

I try to pull away, but dammit, the girl is stronger than she looks. "Angel, no. I don't think they let random chicks who aren't getting married into their super-expensive gowns."

She waves away my concern. "If I'm going to be dropping a hundred grand in their store, they'll let me dress up my friend for a few minutes. Right, Bianca?"

The sales assistant plasters on her most patient smile. "Of course, Miss Bell. Let me help you."

I try to resist, but as usual, Angel won't be denied. She pulls off my clothes, then she and Bianca help me wiggle into a jewel-encrusted, low-cut sheath that hugs all of my curves a little too tightly.

"Oh my God," Angel says as she pulls back. "You . . . look . . . incredible!"

Bianca steps in to fuss with my hair and a veil, then hands me a bouquet. When she's done, Angel drags me out to stand on the little podium in front of the giant mirror.

"Look how beautiful you are!"

For a second, I have no idea who I'm looking at, because it sure isn't me.

"Oh. Wow."

Angel gestures for the cameras to get shots of me. "Now this is footage you can use. You're stunning, Elissa. You're going to make some man very happy one day."

I look at the woman in the mirror. Blond hair up in an elegant chignon, veil draped over my bare shoulders, my body seeming long and svelte in the tight, thick fabric. The beading sparkles in the mirror, and I've never seen myself like this before. Beautiful. A bride. A wife-to-be.

Emotion coils in my throat, because for the first time in my life, I can imagine getting married. I can picture myself walking down the aisle to Liam, him all gorgeous and tall in his sleek tux. Love is written all over his face as he watches me make my way toward him. The mental image is so vivid, it takes my breath away.

And then I'm hit by a wave of indescribable sadness, because what I'm seeing is Angel's future, not mine.

Suddenly, the dress is too tight, and my heart is beating too fast, and I have to get out of here before the panic simmering beneath my skin boils over.

"I have to go."

"What, why?"

I step off the podium, but when I turn to head into the dressing room, I trip on the train and tumble to the ground. Of course, I fall on my sore hip. "Goddammit!"

I scramble to my feet, but I've had so much to drink, it makes balancing difficult. Angel tries to help. I wave her away, then hurry back to the dressing room. The stuffy sales assistant is more than happy to remove my peasant flesh from her couture gown in record time.

When I'm dressed, I go and hug Angel. She's frowning. "Why are you leaving? I thought we were having a good time."

"We were, but I've got heaps of work to finish up before tomorrow's rehearsal. See you in the morning, okay?"

The ever-present cameras move closer as she grabs my arm to stop me. "Wait. Elissa. I know I haven't asked you officially, but . . . you're going to come to my wedding, right?"

A lump forms in my throat. "Angel, you barely know me."

"And I love you like a sister. If I hadn't already locked in my bridesmaids, I'd be hitting you up to be in the bridal party. But I really want you there. You and Josh. Say you'll come."

She looks at me with such hope, I have to look away. "Of course I'll come." I'd rather stab myself in both eyes than watch another woman marry Liam, but I can't tell her that. "I wouldn't miss it for the world."

I hurry out of the salon and down the stairs to the street. When the cool night air hits my cheeks, I take a deep breath and close my eyes.

Okay, just chill. Seriously, this is silly. It was a fantasy, nothing more. Come back to reality and calm the hell down.

The champagne is making me shaky and emotional. Or maybe it's the situation.

If I were a better person, I'd be happy that someone as sweet as Angel is getting her happy-ever-after with Liam, even if I'm not.

But I'm not a good person. And selfish me hates the idea.

TWELVE

TACTICAL RETREAT

When Liam opens the door, he takes one look at me and frowns.

"What's wrong?"

"Nothing. I'm fine." I walk unsteadily past him, and dump my bag on the couch. I thought the walk over here would sober me up, but I actually feel more drunk. "Ready to work?"

"Liss, have you been drinking?"

I flip through the script and frown when nothing makes sense. Then I realize I'm holding it upside down. "A bit. There was champagne. It forced itself on me." I'm trying not to slur but my tongue isn't cooperating. The room spins, and I lean against the couch for support. "Why is your apartment moving?"

He grabs a bottle of water from the fridge, then comes back, takes my hand, and leads me to the couch. I don't want to sit, but he eases me down. When I try to close my eyes, he touches my face and makes me look at him instead. "What happened with Angel?"

Even out of focus he's handsome. "I love your face," I say, and touch my fingers clumsily to his lips. "I shouldn't, but I do. So beautiful."

He grabs my hand and holds it in both of his. "You're beautiful, too. But right now, I want to hear about you and Angel."

I shrug. "Angel was fantastic. You're engaged to a sweetheart, Liam.

You're going to lose it when you see her in her dress. I picked a good one."

"*You* picked her wedding dress?"

I nod. "I was gonna make her wear the frog, because I'm a bitch. But I couldn't. She's so nice. And she trusts me. But she shouldn't, because I'm not a good person. God, the Secret Garden was hideous. Oh, and also? There's no way in hell I'm going to your wedding. No matter how much she wants me there."

"Liss, what are you talking about?"

"Did you know she likes it when other women lust after you? It's true. She wanted me to admit I thought you were hot, and I didn't want to, but she made me. And then when I started, I couldn't stop. I said all these things. Really wrong things. True things, but stuff I shouldn't say out loud. And then I started yelling about how much I want to fuck you, and they recorded it all. Everything. All my dumb words. I'm such an idiot."

"Wait, what?"

"And then, just when I thought everything was okay, Angel made me try on a dress. And it was *beautiful,* and I looked beautiful in it, and . . . and then nothing was okay." I close my eyes. The memory of it makes my throat tighten and my chest hurt. I feel sick.

He gently grabs my arms and turns me to face him. I open my eyes to his handsome, concerned face. "Liss, *what happened*?"

I shake my head, and take in a shallow breath. "I'd never thought about it before, you know? Not the dress or the ever after, or any of it. Never had reason to. But then tonight . . ."

"Tonight?"

I look up at him, and I know he sees how wet my eyes are, but I can't help it. "Tonight, I saw myself in that dress, and it hit me. You're getting married. *You.* To someone else." I swallow and look at his chest. "I mean, I knew you were, but I didn't *know*, you know? And now I do, and it *sucks*."

"Liss . . ."

I shake my head as tears slide down my cheeks. "And I feel so *stupid* because there's no reason for me to get so upset about this. I have no right. You're not mine. You've *never* been mine. We had one night together a million years ago, and I should be over it by now."

"Liss, come on. We were never just about one night. You know that."

"No, I don't. Because I only got you for that tiny amount of time and now she gets you forever. And there's no way that's fair. It's just not."

"Jesus, sweetheart." Then his hands are on me. Pulling me. Wrapping around me. And I'm pressed into his chest and surrounded by his smell, and I beg the tears to stop but they don't listen.

Goddammit.

I *hate* this.

Love.

Longing.

Attraction.

Need.

Everything he brings out in me.

I'm so tired of wanting what I can't have. *Wanting him.* I can't do it anymore.

I can't.

I fist his shirt and close my eyes. His hands stroke my back. His lips press against my forehead. Warmth and comfort surround me, and even though I know they're not mine to keep, maybe for tonight, I can pretend they are.

My head is pounding. I try to ignore it because I'm warm and comfortable, but it beats a sick, insistent rhythm behind my eyes.

Ugh. Stoppit. I'm awake already.

I rub my hand over my forehead and groan. I haven't had a hangover this bad in years. Curse you, Champagne, and your evil, delicious bubbles.

I crack open my eyes and frown. *Where the hell am I?*

Warm, muscled arms tighten around me, and I stop breathing.

Liam? Why the hell am I in bed with Liam?

I squeeze my eyes shut and try to think. *Wedding dresses. Champagne. Liam answering the door. Tears.*

I take long, measured breaths. The details are fuzzy, but the squirming in my stomach reminds me how far I went. How I broke down and blurted out all my messy, unrequited feelings. After the tears, however, I'm at a loss as to what happened.

Please God, tell me we didn't have sex. If there was one way to make this entire situation exponentially worse, that would be it.

When I look down, I breathe a sigh of relief: I'm in my underwear. A glance over my shoulder, however, reveals Liam's naked chest and shoulders.

Please, no.

I lift the duvet and look down. He's wearing boxers. They're doing nothing to disguise his morning wood.

Okay, so I'm assuming we didn't have sex. Also, if Liam had been inside me, there's no way I wouldn't be feeling it this morning. He's kind of huge.

Reluctantly, I ease myself out of Liam's arms. When he moans my name, I freeze and hold my breath, but after a few seconds he turns over and goes still again. Moving as quietly as possible, I climb out of bed and look around.

Even in the early morning gloom I can tell his bedroom is bigger than my entire apartment.

I tiptoe around until I find my clothes folded neatly on a leather chair, then quickly pull them on, along with my shoes and socks. My pounding head reminds me I need pain relief, so I make my way into the giant *ensuite* and gently close the door before flicking on the light.

"Jesus, fuck!" I whisper, and squeeze my eyes shut as the world's brightest bathroom lights pierce my brain. "Dammit, Liam. Do you perform surgery in here? Who the hell needs lights this bright?"

I fumble with the dimmer until they reach a less blinding level, then carefully open the mirrored cabinet in the hope of scoring some Tylenol.

I scan the shelves. *Shaving cream. Razor. Aftershave.* I pick up the bottle and sniff it.

God. Yes. Liam scent.

The shudder that runs through me makes me curse at myself. One thing I remember about last night is swearing to be done with Liam. Pretty sure sniffing his cologne like a creeper is several hundred steps in the wrong direction.

After replacing the aftershave, I spy some Tylenol on the top shelf and down two with water from the tap. *Thank you, Jesus.*

I take a deep breath as I assess myself in the mirror. I make a plan to sneak out, grab a few hours of sleep at home, and face him later when I'm in better shape to have the conversation I know we need to have.

Okay. Let's go. Stay quiet. Avoid head exploding.

I turn out the light and crack the door open, and that's when I freeze. There's a shadowy figure crossing the bedroom, and it's not Liam-shaped. I'm about to scream blue murder when I hear Angel say, "Hey, sleepyhead. Good morning." She's wearing workout gear and trainers. When she sits on the bed next to Liam, he moans and wraps his arms around her. She laughs and whispers, "Okay, steady, tiger. Come work out with me. I drank a crapload of champagne last night and have a severe case of the bloats. Not to mention a killer headache. I need some endorphins to clear the fog."

"What are you talking about?" Liam mumbles as he grabs for her again. "You hate exercise, remember? Fitness protection program. Stay here. Snuggle."

Angel frowns. "Liam? Are you even awake right now?" She shakes him. "Come into the real world, please. You're not making sense."

Liam sits up with a start. "Angel?"

"Uh, yeah. Expecting someone else in your bedroom, stud?"

I hold my breath behind the door as Liam looks around the room. "What? No. Just—" He looks around again, then runs his fingers through his hair. "Sorry. Just a dream."

"Okaaay," Angel says, dubiously. "So, I have about a thousand alcohol calories that need shifting. Are you coming to work out with me or not?"

Liam pulls the sheet up. "Uh, not. Sorry. Didn't sleep well."

Angel climbs off the bed and sighs. "Fine. Abandon me in my hour of need. See if I care. But if I don't fit into the kick-ass wedding dress Elissa helped me choose last night, I'm blaming you."

"Uh-huh."

Angel puts her hands on her hips. "You're not even going to ask me about the dress? This is your wedding, too, you know."

Liam scrubs his hand over his face. "God, sorry. Not really awake yet. You found something you liked?"

"Heaps, but Elissa helped me narrow it down to the perfect choice. God, that chick is amazing. I swear, I'm going to kidnap her when we leave New York. You'd be cool with her living with us when we're hitched, right? We could be the first out and proud polyamorous trio in Hollywood." Liam looks like he's about to have a heart attack. Angel bursts into laughter. "Kidding! Sort of. But if I was into chicks, I'd definitely make a move. She shouldn't be single. Don't you know any hot actor friends you can set her up with?"

"Uh . . . no. Anyway, she doesn't date actors."

"How do you know that?"

He rubs the back of his neck. "She . . . uh . . . told me years ago. Every bad relationship she's had has been with an actor."

Angel shakes her head. "Yeah, well, no wonder. We're a bunch of assholes. Still, I'm sure I can find some hottie for her if I really try. You try to think of people, too. That girl deserves some man to worship her, and I aim to make it happen." She bends down and kisses his cheek. "Okay, I'm outta here, fatty. See you at rehearsals later."

"Yep. See you, then."

Angel leaves, and when Liam hears the apartment door close behind her, he releases a sigh of relief and flops back on the bed. "Jesus Christ."

I pull open the bathroom door and step out. As soon as he sees me, he leaps out of bed and comes over.

"Liss. Hey." He blinks at me. "I thought you'd left."

"Hey," I say, my heart still pounding from our close encounter of the Angel kind. Also, dealing with him in just his boxers isn't easy, especially in my current state. "So, Angel has a key to your apartment, huh?"

He looks at the front door, then back to me. "Uh, yeah. But she never uses it. She must have knocked, and only come in when I didn't answer. You okay? You get some painkillers?"

"Yep. Thanks." I tuck my hair behind my ears. "Sorry about the whole . . . well, everything, last night. I didn't mean to crash."

"Don't worry about it. I'm happy you passed out here rather than on the subway."

I nod. "So, you undressed me?"

He stands up straight. "Uh . . . yeah. I thought you'd be more comfortable. I was going to sleep on the couch, but you grabbed me and wouldn't let go. I meant to just stay until you were unconscious, but I guess I fell asleep." He puts his hands on his hips and assesses me. "You feel up to some breakfast? I have bacon and eggs in the fridge. Might settle your stomach."

After what just happened, the thought of food makes me shudder. "No, thanks. I'd better get going."

I squeeze past him and head out into the living room to find my bag. It's under the coffee table, and I thank God Angel didn't spot it.

"Hey, wait a second." He catches up to me and grabs my arm. "You don't have to leave so soon."

I turn to face him. "I really do." I take a deep breath. I didn't want to do this now, but I guess I have no choice. "Liam, I can't come here anymore. From now on, Josh will run your lines with you. You can trust him with your secret. He'll be very discreet."

It takes Liam a few moments to process what I've just said, but when he does, his whole face drops. "Wait. What?"

"I'm sorry."

"I don't understand. Is this about last night? Are you embarrassed about what you said?"

"It's not about last night. It's about the past six years. And it's also about the fact that your fiancée very nearly walked in and found us in bed together."

"Liss—"

"No, Liam. This isn't fair to her. Also, if Marco and Ava were to find out I'm visiting your apartment every night in secret, my career would be over. They'd fire me on the spot."

"They couldn't. You're here in a professional capacity."

"No, I'm not. That's the problem. Sobbing into your arms about my pathetic infatuation with you isn't professional. And you being aroused by me isn't, either. And for the record—me waking up half-naked in bed with you? Absolutely not professional."

He runs his hand through his hair. "Nothing happened. You know I'd never take advantage of you like that."

"It doesn't matter whether or not something happened. You're an engaged man. I shouldn't be alone in your apartment, let alone in your bed. Can you imagine if the press got a hold of this? Former lovers spending every night together right under the nose of America's sweetheart? They'd have a field day, and Angel would be devastated. She considers me her friend."

He rubs his forehead, and his voice is tinged with frustration. "Christ, Liss, we haven't done anything wrong. We've been running lines. That's it. I'm not fucking you. I haven't even kissed you. In fact, I've done *everything* in my power to make sure I didn't cross the line, even though every time you walk through that door, all I can think about is dragging you into my bedroom and making love to you until you can't see straight."

As soon as he says it, the air snaps with tension. Part of me is thrilled by the declaration, but there's another, bigger part that wants to scream at him that if he'd chosen me in the first place, he could have had all that and more. My love. My body. All of it. Instead of denying this clawing, desperate need we both feel, we could have spent the last six years being slaves to it.

I almost laugh. *What am I saying? I have been a slave to it. I still am.* This man has completely owned me from the moment we met, and it can't continue.

Liam reads my face. Whatever he sees there makes his expression drop. "I'm sorry. That was a stupid thing to say."

"No, it was honest. And that's why I have to go. I don't know if this reaction to me is just your version of cold feet with all this wedding talk, but you need to concentrate on your fiancée, and the show. That's it. And I need to stop wanting a man I know very well I'll never have."

I pick up my bag and sling it over my shoulder. When I get to the door, I turn to him. His hands are on his head. Shoulders slumped.

"Liam?" He looks up at me, and I hate the fragile hope in his expression. He thinks I've changed my mind. "I need you to do something for me."

"Anything." He walks forward, but I stop him with my hand.

"Last night, I said some really . . . inappropriate things about you while I was with Angel. Is there any way you could make sure that footage disappears? If anyone sees it, my professional reputation will be ruined. I know it's a lot to ask, but—"

"I'll take care of it." His words are clipped. Eyes downcast.

"Thank you." I take a breath and adjust my bag. "And Liam?" He looks up at me. "I still want us to be friends, if that's possible. I mean, we still have to do this show together, and I don't want things to be uncomfortable. We just can't see each other after hours, okay?"

He gives me a resigned smile. "Sure. I understand. Friendly. Nothing more. No problem."

"I'll see you later at rehearsals, okay?"

"Yep. See you then."

I let myself out, and close the door gently behind me. As soon as it clicks, I exhale and lean back against it as adrenaline pounds through every vein. It takes me a few long breaths before I find my legs again, and as I walk away, I'm sure I hear Liam swear before something shatters against the wood.

THIRTEEN

DESPERATE TIMES

Josh stands in front of the door to our apartment, barring my way. I don't think I've ever seen him so adamant before.

"Lissa, I know this thing with Quinn has you all messed up, but this isn't the answer."

"Move, Josh. I'm doing it."

"Think about this for a second. Think about who you are. Your core values. This isn't you."

"Yeah, well, being me has gotten me exactly diddly, so maybe it's time for a change. And God knows, I could use the distraction."

He shakes his head. "If you do this, I won't be held accountable for your actions. Don't come crying to me when it all goes to hell."

"Noted. Now step aside."

He sighs and opens the door for me. Before I can get past him, he grabs my hand. "Lissa, wait. Just promise me one thing." I look up at him. "Stretch before you start. Your fitness levels are appalling. You could legit pull something. Jogging isn't a game. It's serious business."

I give him a somber nod. "I understand. And I promise I'll be careful, Dad."

I head down the stairs as he calls after me, "And for God's sake, stay hydrated. And don't talk to strangers."

I smile as I push through the door to the street and then do a few basic stretches. I feel exposed in my new spandex jogging outfit, but I figure I might as well look the part, even if I don't know what I'm doing.

I take off at a slow pace and make my way toward Central Park.

For the past few days, I've tried to stay busy so I could put Liam out of my mind and get over him, but arriving at rehearsal early and staying late has still left me plenty of time to dwell. Hence, resorting to the ancient torture of jogging as further distraction. It doesn't help matters that things seem to be strained between him and Angel. On more than one occasion, I've seen them have tense words. Josh thinks they're just playing up some relationship drama for the television show, but I'm not so sure. Maybe they're not as happy as they always seem. Could that be the reason Liam's turning to me?

I shake my head and chastise myself. See? My instinct is to dwell, and I really need to stop.

In theory, I should be able to cope with seeing Liam every day by suppressing my feelings. In reality, it's like an alcoholic trying to stay clean by working in a liquor store.

So, now, here I am, concentrating on putting one foot in front of the other and cursing the idiot who thought this sports bra was even close to being supportive enough.

Would anyone care if I just held my boobs as I ran? Because, seriously. Ow.

The first few blocks are okay. The next few are harder. When I get to the park and merge with all the other early-morning joggers, I see just how out of my depth I am. I'm pretty sure one dude passes me five times. Goddamn overachiever.

After thirty minutes, my lungs are burning. After forty-five, I want to die.

When I can't take any more, I collapse onto the grass and try to finish off with some ab crunches. Clearly, my technique is lacking, because a teenager comes over and asks me if I need help getting up. Even calls me "ma'am." Little shit.

I lie back on the grass and huff. Okay, so, this experiment has been mildly successful. Perhaps with more practice, it could actually be a solution.

When I can breathe without it burning, I sit up and look around the park. It's a beautiful day in New York, and people are taking advantage of the mild weather. I watch as the usual cavalcade passes: tourists clicking photos, joggers and cyclists, dog walkers, stroller-pushing parents. Oh, and the lovers. Let's not forget them. They're everywhere, and when you're single, they seem to triple in number, just to piss you off and make you feel extra alone. They stroll by, smugly hand in hand, or with their arms around each other as they chat and laugh, all the while taunting you with their loving glances and easy touches.

I stare at one particular couple who sits on a nearby bench. As the girl tells a story, the boy strokes her face, her neck, her back. He looks at her like she's the sun in his universe, and it's obvious he's just waiting for her to stop so he can kiss her. The girl looks at him the same way. Her eyes roam over his face as she speaks, and sure enough, when the story's done, she winds her hands into his hair and pulls him to her. They kiss slowly. Deeply. Oblivious to everything but each other, as if they had all day to kiss like that.

Assholes.

I want that. That open, easy love. I want a man who isn't already engaged to look at me the way Liam does.

A sharp pang intensifies inside me and I look away.

Sexual frustration is one thing. Relationship frustration is another. Both together make people like me do stupid, desperate things. Things they end up regretting.

To demonstrate my point, I climb to my feet and start to jog again. One foot in front of the other. Over and over again. Until I'm incapable of thinking about anything but my own harsh breathing.

Oh, unholy demons of pain, why? Why do you hate me so?

I hiss as I attempt to grab the stack of company notices that has just slipped out of my hands and fallen to the floor. They scatter everywhere, and I sigh in frustration. There's no way I can pick them up. Thanks to my overexertions yesterday, I'm unable to bend my legs without squealing. Even sitting on the subway this morning wasn't an option.

I wonder if Marco would object to me standing for today's rehearsal. Maybe not, but he would object to me not handing out this important information about costume fittings and tech rehearsals.

Dammit.

Resigning myself to the inevitable, I walk over to the mess of paper and nudge them together with my foot. When I think I have most of them close enough to pick up in one go, I move my legs apart like a giraffe at a watering hole and bend down to try to reach them.

"Come on, arms. Be longer. Just for a few seconds. I swear, I'll never make you do push-ups again if you make this happen."

I grit my teeth as I stretch my fingers out and bend a little farther. *Oh, God. The agony.*

"Liss?" I hear footsteps stop behind me, and I lower my head. Of course Liam would walk in while I was in this position. "Is this some new form of workplace yoga? Or are you dropping the hint that you'd like me to do something very unprofessional with your ass? Because, honestly, the signals you're sending right now are kind of confusing."

I can hear the smile in his voice, and it makes me bristle. After awkwardly pulling myself upright, I turn to him. "Can you please stop smirking and pick these up for me?"

"I'd rather not. Watching you attempt it again seems like much more fun."

I scowl. "I have no idea what I used to see in you. Funny how you go off people."

He chuckles as he walks over, and in one fell swoop grabs all the papers, shuffles them together, and hands them to me. "Care to tell me why you're moving like Frankenstein's monster? It's not still your hip."

"No. I made a stupid mistake yesterday and now I'm paying for it."

"What was the mistake?"

"Jogging."

He genuinely looks shocked. "But your aversion to exercise—"

"Is well-founded. Clearly, I'm allergic to it." I move stiffly to the desk and shove the papers into a folder.

"You didn't stretch afterward, did you?"

"Josh told me to stretch before, not after. Some best friend he is."

"You have to do it before *and* after. You could have come to me if you wanted advice. I'm kind of an expert on exercise, you know."

"Really? I had no idea. You're such an unfit schlub." I take in his ridiculous physique. "I don't know how you cope with that grossness. Thank God I don't have all those weird bulges."

He gives me a long, slow assessment, up and down my body. "No. You don't need bulges when you have those killer curves." As soon as he says it, he drops his head. Like he knows this sort of flirty banter is exactly what we should be avoiding. "I'd offer to train you, but I guess that's not something we could do, right?"

"Nope. Besides, my jogging style can be defined as 'a lumbering seizure.' Don't really need you laughing your ass off at me."

He frowns. "Elissa, you'd be in workout gear. Believe me, I wouldn't be able to laugh if I tried."

A shiver runs through me, and I curse it. I'm trying to suppress these types of reactions, but it's tough when he insists on being so damn sexy. I move away from him and open my laptop. "Uh, anyway, why are you here so early?"

He looks over his shoulder. Angel appears at the far end of the hallway, talking to a good-looking man with dark hair. "Angel and I have an interview this morning. Just for something different."

"In the rehearsal room?"

"Yeah. It was kind of last-minute, but Mary said she'd organize it with you."

In my back pocket, my phone buzzes. When I take it out and look at the screen, I see a text from Mary.

<Forgot to tell you about an interview this morning in the studio. Journalist plus photographer from Moda *arriving at 8. Please provide three chairs. I'll be there soon to supervise.>*

I smile and hold out the phone. "Well, now she has. Better go get set up, I guess." I grab my folder and move past him.

As I come out of the office, Angel sees me and waves. "Elissa! Over here. I have someone I want you to meet."

I try to look normal as I make my way to her, but I can tell how amused Liam is by my stiff-legged walk as he follows behind me.

"Nice work," he whispers. "Toy soldiers everywhere would be proud."

I give him the finger behind my back as I reach Angel and the man she's with. The man looks to be in his mid-thirties, and his handsome face lights with a smile as he turns to me.

"Elissa, this is our agent, Anthony Kent. He's in town for a few days to make sure we're behaving ourselves, which of course we are. Anthony, this is one of the most fabulous women you'll ever meet. Elissa Holt."

I hold out my hand to Anthony and he clasps it. "A pleasure to meet you, Mr. Kent. I'm sure keeping these two in line is like herding cats. I know of some excellent treatments for stomach ulcers, if you need them."

Angel rolls her eyes as he laughs. "Please call me Anthony. And, yes, as long as those ulcer treatments don't interfere with my blood pressure medication, I'm in. A pleasure to meet you, Elissa." His hand is warm, and he gives my fingers a gentle squeeze before he lets go. "Let me guess. You're playing Bianca."

I shake my head. "Thankfully, no."

Anthony frowns. "Really? Why not? Who's your agent? And why the hell aren't they getting you better roles? You'd be perfect for Bianca."

"Anthony," Angel says. "Elissa doesn't have an agent."

He looks at me, then back at Angel. "Bullshit. She's working on Broadway without one?" In a flash, he pulls a card from his pocket and hands it to me. "Well then, this is my lucky day. Sign with me and I'll have you on movie screens in record time. That beautiful face needs to be shared with the world, and I'm just the man to make it happen."

Before I can say anything, Liam steps forward, and I don't miss the tension in his shoulders. "She's not an actress, Anthony, so you can stop hitting on her. She's our stage manager."

Anthony turns back to me. "Seriously? You're hiding yourself backstage?" When I nod, he shakes his head in disbelief. "Look, I don't want to alarm you, but I'm pretty sure depriving hardworking Americans of your kind of beauty is illegal in forty-eight of the fifty states. You may need to get out of town for a while. It just so happens I have a house in the Hamptons if you're looking to hide out in luxury. I'd be happy to harbor you as a fugitive."

I laugh. This guy's pretty charming, even if he is joking. It feels good to have someone I've just met say such flattering things. "I'll keep that in mind."

I notice that Angel is beaming at our exchange. I have the strongest feeling she'll be informing Anthony I'm single as soon as I'm out of ear shot. I'm not sure how I feel about that. Yes, I want to get over Liam and start dating again, but dating his agent probably wouldn't be the best idea.

When I glance over at Liam, his hands are shoved into his pockets, and the glare he's directing at the wall above Anthony's head could blister paint at thirty paces.

Yep. That's what I figured.

I put Anthony's card in my pocket. I'm sure there'll be other handsome, charming strangers with whom I can contemplate moving on. Ones who don't have these kinds of complications.

"Well, if you'll excuse me, everyone, I have to go set up for the interview. Nice to meet you, Mr. Kent. If you need anything while you're here, please let me know."

He reaches for my hand, then places a soft kiss on the back of it. I'm surprised when it makes me tingle.

"I certainly will, Miss Holt. And the pleasure was all mine."

Even though I don't look at Liam as I walk away, I can feel his disapproval.

The following day, I'm in my office working through lunch as usual, when there's a knock at the door.

"Come in."

Liam enters carrying a small bag. He flops down into the chair beside my desk. "Hey." He pulls something from his pocket and places it on the desk in front of me. "I thought you might like this."

I pick up the thumb drive and examine it. "Oh. Wow, Liam. I mean, I know we said we'd keep things professional, but really? You couldn't come up with a better gift? They were out of staplers? Or paper clips?"

He crosses his arms. "Actually, smart-ass, this is a gift you requested."

"It is?"

"It is." He raises his chin. "You asked me to get it because you didn't want everyone to know you'd like to . . . now let's see if I can remember your exact words . . . *'climb me like a tree and bang me like a screen door in a hurricane'?* Do I have that right?"

I close my hand around the thumb drive and sigh. "This is the footage from drunken dress shopping?"

"Uh-huh."

"You didn't have to watch it, you know."

"Of course I did. How else was I supposed to memorize all the things you want to do to me? By the way, I'll be your 'sex stallion' any day, sweetheart." I slap his arm, and he chuckles. "Jokes aside, you'll be pleased to know it won't be appearing in the first episode of our stupid reality show this weekend."

"Thank God. And thank you for helping me out."

"No problem. Can't have you getting fired for your perfectly understandable desire to 'fuck me ten ways from Sunday.'"

I point to the door. "Get out."

He stands and looks down at me. "Is that any way to speak to 'the hottest man you've ever laid eyes on'?"

"Liam!"

He laughs and heads to the door. "Fine. This 'perfect specimen of manhood' is out of here. And don't you dare ogle my ass as I go. Professionalism, please."

I shake my head and try to hide my smile.

Just as he's about to exit, Denise appears in the doorway carrying the most enormous bouquet of flowers I've ever seen. They're arranged in a huge crystal vase.

Liam stares at the flowers and blinks. "Denise, wow. You shouldn't have. I have nowhere to put them."

She gives him a smile. "If I could afford a bouquet like this, do you think I'd still be working for a living?" She puts them down on my desk. "Elissa, a courier just dropped these off for you. Please tell me it's not your birthday."

I glance at the flowers and shake my head. "Believe me, when it's my birthday, you'll know. Gift lists will be distributed and shenanigans will be planned. Thanks, Denise."

She leaves and closes the door behind her.

As I grab the card, Liam frowns at the flowers. "Secret admirer?"

"If they're sending me something this big, they really don't want to remain anonymous." I pull the card from the envelope. *"To the most beautiful stage manager I've ever met. I look forward to getting to know you better. Warmest regards, Anthony Kent."*

Liam doesn't comment, but the tension in the room ratchets up to uncomfortable levels in seconds.

"Well," I say, searching for something to say. "They're certainly . . . extravagant."

Liam swears under his breath.

I raise my eyebrow at him. "What?"

"Nothing. I should go."

He goes to leave, but I grab his hand. "Liam—"

He looks down, and gently removes his fingers from mine. "Liss, I have no right to tell you what to do, and I definitely have no right to tell you who to date. The part of me that's desperately trying to be your friend wants you to find someone and be happy."

"And the other part?"

He stares down at me, and his expression reminds me of a bank of thunderheads right before a storm. "The other part feels like destroying things when I think about you and another man, which is insane, considering our circumstances."

"Yes. It is." I don't mean for it to come out as harsh as it does, but I can't deny that Liam's jealousy regarding my nonexistent love life irritates me.

It must irritate him, too, because he rubs his eyes and lets out a frustrated sigh. "So many times over the years I've typed your name into Google, only to chicken out before I hit 'enter,' because I knew I couldn't handle finding out you were engaged or married. And then I'd hate myself, because if I truly cared about you, which I do,

I should want you to find someone who'll appreciate what an amazing person you are. If I wasn't such a selfish asshole, I'd wish for men to fall all over themselves to be with you. I'd want them to flatter you and buy you presents, and dedicate themselves to making you happy. But every time I have those thoughts . . . every single time, the deepest parts of me know *without a doubt* that the only man on this planet who could ever make you truly, deeply happy . . . is me. Crazy, right?"

I stare at him, and clench my jaw to stop myself from admitting how infuriatingly right he is. "Yeah. Crazy."

He swallows, and glances at the giant flower arrangement. "So, yeah. I'd like to tell you to stay away from Kent, because I don't think he's anywhere near good enough for you, but who the hell am I to talk? He just spent a thousand dollars on flowers for you, and I bought . . . well, this." He passes me the small bag he's been holding since he walked in.

"What is it?" I ask as I look inside. "A T-shirt?"

He shifts his weight from one foot to the other, and I swear, I can see color flare on the tops of his ears. "It's nothing, really. But it reminded me of you, so I had to get it."

I pull out the T-shirt and hold it up. It's bright yellow and reads, SWEET DREAMS ARE MADE OF CHEESE. WHO AM I TO DISS A BRIE?

A rush of warmth hits me. "You bought me a T-shirt about . . . cheese?" For some reason, it makes me want to cry.

I sit there for a few seconds, trying to gather myself together, and when I look up, Liam is frowning. "You hate it."

I hold it to my chest. "Not even a little. It's the most perfect T-shirt in the history of the world. I love it." I swallow hard, because damn him for making a ten-dollar joke shirt seem like the sweetest gift I've ever received.

"You're welcome," he says, before giving me one of those soft, intimate smiles that I know he doesn't give to anyone else. "Okay. I'd better get out of your hair. You should call Anthony. To thank him, or . . . whatever." It's clear that contemplating me doing "whatever" with Anthony makes him want to barf.

As he grabs the door handle, I stand. "Liam." He turns back to me. "For the record, there's no comparison between you and Anthony, no matter how much money he spends. Your present is perfect. For me, anyway. The only thing Anthony has over you is that he's single."

He nods and looks at his feet. "Yeah. Kind of an important trait in a potential relationship, I guess. So, you're going to date him?"

"No."

He studies me for a second. "Why not?"

I shrug and try not to look like the lovesick idiot I am. "He's not my type."

He gives me a bittersweet smile that tells me he sees right through me, then opens the door and disappears down the hallway.

FOURTEEN

CALL FOR HELP

It's the Sunday night before our third week of rehearsal, and I've just settled in for a quiet night stuffing my face with cheese when my phone goes off. A quick look at the screen shows a pretty brunette with the caption—Cassie Taylor, Brother Wrangler and Ethan Tamer. As I answer it, an excited voice squeals, "You're on TV!"

I pull the phone away from my ear. No wonder my brother's fiancée is a great actress. Her vocal projection could shatter glass.

"Hi to you, too, Miss Taylor."

"No, but seriously," Cassie says, and lowers her decibels a little. "Look at you on my TV. You look amazing."

"I'm in the background."

"Yes, but looking *gorgeous* in the background. They've had a couple of shots of you."

The first episode of *Angeliam: A Fairy Tale Romance* airs tonight. Josh is watching it in the living room with a six-pack and a pizza, certain this show will be the beginning of his fifteen minutes of fame.

"There I am!" he yells at the same time Cassie squeals, "Josh! There's Josh!"

"Damn, I look good," Josh calls, and Cassie echoes, "Tell Josh he looks good. Hot geek at his finest."

Who knew a stupid reality show could get people so excited?

I hear my brother's voice mumble something, followed by a cry of pain. Cassie comes back on and says, "Ethan said to tell you that you looked like less of a short-ass on TV, and wanted to know what sort of cutting-edge special effect they're using to make that happen. Don't worry, I've already hit him for you."

I laugh. "I have so much more free time now that you're around to kick his ass twenty-four/seven. Thanks for that."

"Oh, don't worry. I enjoy punishing your brother. A lot."

I hear Ethan call out, "Please don't talk to my sister about our sex life. That shit is private."

Cassie tells him to shush. "Ooh, another shot of you! And there's Marco behind Angel! Aw, we miss you guys."

I'm avoiding watching. I'm glad Liam got my X-rated rant about him cut, but I still don't need to watch an hour of television about his undying love for Angel. Not when I see their intimate exchanges every day, up close and personal.

"Okay, so," Cassie says, reminding me I'm supposed to be talking to her and not contemplating my nonexistent love life. "Dinner, next Sunday. Since you left our show, Ethan and I have hardly seen you, and I need my Elissa snuggles, dammit."

"Fine. Sunday," I say, "but only if Ethan's cooking. Not you."

Cassie is quite possibly the worst cook on the face of the planet. Actually, no, she and her college roommate Ruby would tie. They once invited me over for dinner when we were all studying at The Grove, and I swear to God, my intestines have never been the same.

"Elissa Holt. Are you dissing my culinary expertise?"

"Not at all. Your food does that all by itself."

Cassie gasps dramatically. "Hey! Your mother has been giving me lessons. My cooking is improving, thank you very much."

I doubt it. My mom may run her own catering company, but she's no miracle worker.

"Yeah, Mom told me the fire department was called the other day when she was teaching you how to make toffee."

"That's true, but in my defense, that melted sugar turned to fiery lava in a fraction of a second. I only took my eyes off it long enough to kiss your brother."

"Oh, gross. I can just imagine the grope-fest that was going on while that poor toffee was going up in flames."

Cassie laughs. "I blame Ethan. If he didn't keep distracting me with his hotness, I'd be a gourmet chef by now. Your mom has now banned him from being in the kitchen with me. Man, Maggie can be a killjoy sometimes."

I smile as I imagine how much Cassie's pouting right now. "So to clarify, *Ethan* is cooking on Sunday, right?"

"If you insist. Seven o'clock at our place?"

"Done."

"How are rehearsals going? Is Liam Quinn as gorgeous in person as he is on-screen?"

"Cassie, you're going to marry my brother. You shouldn't be noticing other men."

"Oh, please," she says with a laugh. "As if any man is ever going to compete with Ethan. But a girl can appreciate a fine male specimen, even if she's off the market. So spill. As hot as he seems in *Rageheart*? Or just looks good in demon makeup?"

I close my eyes. Liam did look amazing in his demon makeup. Gray skin, black hair, and bright blue eyes. Rippling muscles that were hardly ever covered by a shirt. Sexy in a fantasy-comic-book kind of way.

But Liam in the flesh is even more stunning.

"Gorgeous," I begrudgingly admit.

"I knew it!" Cassie says. "He looks edible on this show. But please tell me Ethan and I never looked this nauseatingly in love. These two are like Ken and Barbie, if Barbie were a perky redhead and Ken had a penis and sex appeal."

I laugh. If only she knew how much of a penis and sex appeal Liam has. "Yeah, they're pretty gross."

"And what about Angel Bell? She seems like a total sweetheart, but . . . I don't know. No one can be that perfect, can they?"

I sigh. "Apparently they can. She's a doll. She and Liam have amazing chemistry, and that's what people are coming to see."

"Sounds like me and Ethan, then. But it's no secret he carries our show and that I'm just there just to rub myself all over him in front of a theaterful of people. I still don't understand why I get paid for that."

"Oh, shut it. You're an incredible actress, and you know it."

"Eh. I'm all right."

I get another incoming call on my phone, and when I check the screen, my heart skips a beat.

"Uh, Cassie? I have to go. See you Sunday?"

"Yes, see you then! I'll be the one banned from the kitchen. Love you!"

I sign off and answer the other call.

"Liam?"

"Hey." He sounds terrible.

"Are you okay?"

"Not really," he says. "Had a bad day."

"What happened?"

"I don't want to talk about it over the phone. Can you meet me?"

"Where are you?"

"At a bar. A really shitty bar."

"How much have you had to drink?"

"Not enough. Come drink with me."

I almost say "okay" before my common sense kicks in. "I don't think that's a good idea."

"Please, Liss. I need a friend tonight."

"What about Angel?"

"We had a fight. I started it, but still. I need a break. I need *you*. Please."

I sigh and press my hand over my eyes. "Liam, I shouldn't."

"You should. I'm near the corner of Fifteenth and Ninth. It's called the Badger's Den. Just come for one drink, and I'll leave you alone. I swear."

Dammit, I should say no, but I can't. "Fine. I'll be there in twenty minutes."

After I hang up, I get out of my cheese-eating pants and pull on my jeans. Then I freshen up and head out to the living room.

Josh is frowning at his computer screen. "Unbelievable," he mutters.

"What?"

"Just reading the Angeliam hashtag on Twitter. Seems like there are a whole bunch of women who are hating on Angel just because she's with Quinn. Jesus, these comments are harsh." He picks up his phone.

"Who are you calling?"

"Angel. I hope she's not reading any of this, and if she is, she needs to know it's all bullshit." Before he hits "call," he looks up at me. "Where are you going?"

"To meet Liam. He's in a bar. I figure I'll try to get him out of there before someone recognizes him."

"Yeah, good luck with that. This show is going to make him even more of a target. Just make sure you stay out of the way if he starts throwing punches, okay?"

"Deal." I grab my keys off the table and shove them in my bag. "See you later?"

"I'll be here."

As I close the door behind me, I hear him say, "Hey, Angel. It's Josh. You okay?"

Twenty minutes later, I'm wandering down Fiftieth Street looking for the Badger's Den. Turns out, I find it easily. If a lightbulb factory and the Ebola virus mated and gave birth to a bar, it would look like this place.

"Ew."

Against my better judgment, I pull open the door and head inside. It's dark and dingy and smells like stale beer and loneliness. There's a guy sitting near the door watching the TV behind the bar, and the only other people in the place are a middle-aged couple canoodling at a table in the corner. The guy's hand is under the table, and he's either touching his lady friend in special places, or that glass of red wine is *really* good.

Lovely.

I see a familiar figure near the far wall, sitting at a table by himself.

When I walk over to him, he looks up at me and smiles. "Liss." The way he says it sounds like a sigh of relief. "So glad you're here. What are you drinking? Come on, I'm buying."

He gets up and puts his arm around me to guide me to the bar.

The barkeep comes over and acknowledges us with a tilt of his chin. "What'll it be?"

I shrug and gesture to the lady in the corner, who's now making unmistakable moaning noises as she sips from her glass. "I'll have what she's having."

Liam looks over at them and frowns. "That must be some good wine."

"Right?"

Liam orders the most expensive whiskey available, which turns out to cost a grand total of six bucks. When our drinks arrive, we head back to our table.

I sip my wine and study Liam. He looks like he hates the world right now, and I don't know why.

"What's going on with you?" I ask. "You're fighting with Angel?"

"These days I always seem to be fighting with Angel."

"About?"

He shrugs. "The show. The wedding. The ever-present goddamn cameras. All of it."

"You guys seem happy."

He laughs bitterly. "Of course we do. It's required."

His phone buzzes on the table. When he picks it up and taps the screen, a synthesized female voice comes out of the small speaker: *"Liam, where the hell are you? Call me when you get this."*

I frown. "What's that?"

"Text to voice app. Saves me trying to read stuff. It works for e-mails, too."

"That's cool."

"Yeah. It's supposed to be for blind people, but it works for dumb-ass dyslexics as well." He turns off the phone and places it back on the table.

"That was from Angel?"

"Yep. I'm supposed to be at a party the network is throwing for the premiere of the show. Just more photo opportunities. As if the world needs any more goddamn pictures of us. How are people not sick to their stomachs by now? We're like the Kardashians. Fucking everywhere."

"People love you guys. You're inpirational."

He laughs. "People have no clue. If they knew the real us, they'd despise us."

"Why?"

He takes another sip of whiskey. "Soooo many reasons."

"Any you want to talk about?"

"Yep, but I kind of like you looking at me like I'm not a piece of shit, so let's just drop it."

Intriguing. I don't want to push him to talk more about his problems with Angel, because it might make me seem insensitive, but dammit, I really want to know.

A few more people file into the bar. A thirty-something guy scans the room before sitting on the bar stool closest to us.

I sip my wine. It tastes freaking awful. The enthusiastic chick in the corner isn't even pretending to drink hers anymore. She and

Handy Andy are fully making out. It's fascinating, in a train-wreck kind of way.

"Affair," Liam says, pointing at them.

"You think?"

"Yep. This bar? That table? Definitely trying to stay off the radar." He gestures at the rest of the room. "Why do you think I'm in here? No one's looked at me long enough to recognize me. Not one person has asked for an autograph or picture. I'm just a no one here, like everyone else. It's heaven."

I study him for a second. "That's what you want? To be a no one?"

He gives a one-shoulder shrug and swirls his drink. "Sometimes. Actually, most of the time. Things were so much simpler when I was a no one. Now, everything I do is put under the microscope. Every decision. Every piece of personal information is picked over by media vultures desperate to find something to sell their damn magazines and Web sites, no matter the cost." He reaches into his bag beside the table, then puts an iPad in front of me. "This happened today, which is nice considering it's the anniversary of my brother's death."

I pick up the tablet. A popular gossip site is emblazoned with the banner, HOLLYWOOD HEARTTHROB'S PRIVATE HELL.

There's a picture of Liam sitting in front of a gravestone, crying. The caption reads, *"Macho action man Liam Quinn breaks down at brother's grave. Exclusive pics!"*

Oh, God.

I glance over at Liam. His jaw is tight and his eyes are hard. "I went to visit Jamie's grave a few days ago and I guess some piece of shit followed me. By tomorrow, this will be everywhere."

Over the years, there hasn't been much information about Jamie's death in the press. "Killed in a construction accident" is about all that's ever said, but I have no doubt that these pictures will unleash a fresh burst of interest into the death of Liam's twin.

"Liam. I'm so sorry." There are more pictures of him farther down, and I get a hot flash of anger that someone would think to profit off him in his private moment of grief.

"I go to his grave every year," he says. "Sometimes Mom and Dad come with me, but most of the time I go by myself. I like having the time to talk to him. Tell him about what's going on in my life." He looks down at the table, and I reach out and touch his hand. The contact makes him tense, and his breath hitches, but he doesn't look up.

"You don't have to talk about it," I say, "but if you'd like to vent, I'm a decent listener."

He takes a deep, shaky breath and lets it out slowly. "How much do you know?"

"Only that it was on the Mantra project. Five or six people died."

He nods. "Six. Mantra was my dad's construction company. Jamie and I were on his crew from the time we left school. One day, the crane operator forgot to double-check that the anchor points were properly braced. When the crane started lifting two-ton slabs into place, it tipped over and crashed backward onto the apartment block across the street. Jamie and I saw it happen, so we raced to the other building to see if we could help. It was freaking mayhem in there. Debris was falling. People were screaming.

"We headed upstairs and helped a lady and her two boys get out of the wreckage before moving to the top floor where the damage was the worst. It was a stupid move. We could feel the structure was about to go. The crane was too heavy; the walls couldn't support it. Jamie yelled that we had to get out, but I couldn't leave those people there screaming. When I opened the door to their apartment, the crane smashed though the exterior wall. Jamie shoved me out of the way just before it would've hit me. He was killed instantly. So were the people in the apartment. The whole thing happened so quickly, it took me a minute to figure out why the screaming had stopped."

My stomach clenches. "God. Liam." I rub his hand, trying to convey my sympathy.

He shakes his head. "When I saw Jamie there . . . I couldn't move.

I knew it was too unstable to stay, but I couldn't leave. Couldn't take my eyes off him. One second he was my brother. My hero. The next, he was . . . nothing. Just a mess of bone and blood whose face looked nothing like Jamie's. When Dad found me, I was sobbing his name over and over again. It took two firemen to drag me away."

He takes a deep breath, then takes a sip of his drink. I keep rubbing his hand and try to let him know he can stop whenever he wants.

"Mom and Dad were devastated. I mean, there's no way to get over losing a child, you know? Especially when the one left behind looks exactly like the one you've lost. For me, it was even worse. Jamie and I were inseparable from the moment we were born. Mom used to call us the 'cling twins.' Wherever we went, we were a package deal. It was always Liam and Jamie. Jamie and Liam. The Quinn boys. I thought we'd be that way forever, even when we were married and had kids. Then, suddenly, it was just me." He looks over at me. "Afterward, people would forget, and when I'd show up places they'd say, 'Hey, it's Liam and . . . ' then trail off before saying his name. And that summed up how I felt when he died. I was incomplete. An unfinished sentence."

He looks back down at the table, and he's gripping his glass so tightly, his knuckles are white.

"I'm so sorry. I can't even imagine what that must be like."

"After the accident, Mom and Dad were buried under lawsuits. Liability, civil, negligence. The easy road would have been to declare bankruptcy and make it all go away, but Dad would never agree to that. He felt responsible. He negotiated settlements. Sold the business he'd built for forty years, all the equipment, our family home. Paid every cent he could to the families of the victims who were still waiting on checks from the insurance companies. That's one of the main reasons I went to Hollywood. I needed to help them out. All the fees from my first two movies went to paying off their debts."

"Oh, Liam—" I grip his hand, and I can feel his pulse pounding through his fingers, fast and unsteady. I hate that he had to carry around the burden of his brother's death as well as his parents' financial difficulties for so long.

He lets out a shaky sigh and gestures to the iPad. "And every time something like this happens, my first thought is to say screw it, and go live in a cabin in the woods. But then I get a flash of Jamie's face, and it makes me stop, because I feel like I need to be someone, you know? Like my future has to be doubly bright, because I have to make up for him not having one." I see a tear fall onto his cheek as he whispers, "I miss him so fucking much, Liss. Every day."

I reach over and cup his face so I can wipe the tear away with my thumb. "I'm sure if he were here, he'd tell you how proud he is of you. Every day. You're an amazing man, Liam. Your brother knew that."

He closes his eyes and leans into my hand, and I can see he's fighting to keep his breathing steady. I have no idea what it's like to lose a brother, but the mere thought of living in a world without Ethan makes me break into a cold sweat. I can't even imagine the pain Liam must feel without his twin.

"Ever since Jamie passed," he says as he takes my hand away from his face and holds it with both of his, "I feel like part of me is missing. Like I'm always lonely, no matter how many people are with me. The only time I don't feel like that is when I'm with you." He looks into my eyes. "Not Angel. *You.*"

I stare at him for a few seconds as a storm of confusion brews inside me. What does that even mean? I search his eyes, but don't come away with any answers. Right now, he looks just as confused as I feel.

I pull my hand back and look down at the small amount of wine still left in my glass. "So then, why didn't you choose me?"

I can't look at his face, so I watch his hands as they clench around his glass. He's quiet for a long time, and I have a feeling he's trying to find a way to gently tell me the truth.

"Elissa, look at me." When I meet his gaze, he leans forward. "I hate that my actions made you feel second best. You're not. You never could be. Circumstances just weren't on our side, that's all." He looks down and swirls the liquid in his glass. "When I left that message saying I loved you, I meant it. You have to believe that."

I look down at a scratch on the table. "I did believe it. That's why I said it back to you, even though falling in love with you was never a part of my plan."

He looks up at me before he swallows the last of his drink and puts the glass down on the table. "See, that's the problem. Love is an asshole. It doesn't care about people's plans. It's *never* convenient. It crawls inside of you at the most ridiculous times and makes you feel, whether you like it or not. And even long after the time when you *should* have learned to stop loving someone, it just keeps holding on to them. Doesn't it?"

I avoid his eyes and drink the remainder of my wine.

"Liss?" When I look over at him, the intensity of his expression makes my hair stand on end. "Do you still love me?"

Goose bumps break out all over my body. This whole conversation is getting out of control. It's dangerous territory, especially because some part of me is loving the adrenaline rush.

"You know I'm not going to answer that."

He reaches across the table and takes my hand. The soft brush of his thumb makes tingles break out all over my arm.

"If you asked me the same question," he says as he looks down at my fingers, "I'd answer it in a second. And I suspect you already know what I'd say."

He brings my hand up to his mouth and presses his lips gently against my skin. The contact makes me inhale. His lips are warm and soft, and the shock of them leaves me breathless. He's about to say something else when his gaze flickers over my shoulder, and within a second, his expression goes from affectionate to thunderous. "Un-fucking-believable. Prick."

"What is it?" I look behind me.

"Don't worry about it. Wait here." He gets up and stalks over to the man at the end of bar, who's studying his phone. "Did you just take a picture of me?"

The man looks at him in confusion. "What? No. Why would I take a picture of you?"

"I've seen you before," Liam says as he towers over him. "You a reporter? A pap?"

"No. I'm an accountant."

"Then show me your phone."

I walk over and put a hand on Liam's arm. "Hey. Come on. Let's just go."

"No," Liam says. "If this guy has nothing to hide, he'll show me his picture roll."

"I'm not showing you my phone. I don't even know who you are."

Liam goes to snatch the phone, but the guy draws back to keep it out of reach.

"Give me the fucking phone!" Liam's voice echoes through the whole room, and everyone turns to look.

When he grabs the guy's arm, I step between them. "Liam, stop."

"Hey!" The bartender strides down to where we are. "No trouble in here. Take it outside, all of you."

The accountant backs away from Liam and hightails it to the door. "You're crazy, man. You stay away from me. I'll call the cops."

"Good. Then I'll report you for stalking, asshole!" Liam kicks the bar stool the guy was sitting on. It teeters but doesn't fall. "Son of a bitch!"

"Hey, calm down. He really didn't seem to know who you were."

"He was taking pictures of us while pretending to look at something on his phone. It happens all the time."

I look to where the door has just closed behind the guy. "And maybe he was just looking at something on his phone and all the stuff with Jamie has set you on edge."

He drops his head and sighs. "Maybe. I swear to God, being stalked all the time can make a guy paranoid as hell."

"I don't blame you."

He gestures toward the bar. "Do you want one more?"

"Yes, but we have rehearsal tomorrow, so we should get out of here. Also, people are staring. Come on."

I tug on his arm, and after we grab all our gear, I push him toward the door. He doesn't resist.

When we get outside, the humid spring night has given way to a heavy downpour.

Liam turns to me. "Don't suppose you have an umbrella?"

"Don't suppose I do."

"Dammit, Liss. I thought stage managers were like Boy Scouts. Always prepared."

"In a theater, yes. Outside a bar that probably has Nickelback on the jukebox? Not so much."

He looks both ways and then shrugs. "It's only a few blocks to my apartment. Run for it?"

"Okay, but not too fast. Your legs are twice the length of mine."

We rush down the slick pavement. Within a minute, we're soaked to the bone. A minute after that, my shoes are making disgusting squelching sounds every time I take a step, and I squeal when I hydroplane across a particularly slippery piece of cement.

"Wait up," I say, and stop at a small alleyway. "I'm going to kill myself in these things." I walk a few steps into the alley before bending over to pull off my shoes and socks. I know walking barefoot on New York sidewalks is gross, but at least I won't fall and break any bones.

After I shove everything into my bag, I look up to find Liam staring at me.

His posture is rigid, and his face is the very definition of lust.

I follow his gaze down to my chest. My previously white T-shirt and bra have become transparent. I may as well be wearing cling wrap.

I cross my arms over myself. "Shit. Sorry."

He looks up at my face, and exhales. "Every day, I try to ignore my attraction to you. Every . . . damn . . . day. I tell myself I'm over you and can't have these feelings, but it doesn't help. Nothing helps."

His bag falls to the ground as he steps forward and cups my face.

"Liam . . ." Then, he's walking forward, and I'm walking back, and before I know it, I'm against a wall and gripping his sodden shirt. The overhang from the building protects us a little from the rain, but it does nothing to protect me from how I react to him. His wet T-shirt reveals every dip and groove of his physique, and I have to stop myself from pawing him. He doesn't seem to have any qualms. He winds an arm around me and pulls me against his body. He's already hard, and his breathing is shallow as he stares down at me.

Dear God. Aroused men are sexy. Aroused Liam is the equivalent of a metric ton of the world's most potent aphrodisiac.

"I need to kiss you," he says, his voice almost a groan. "Please, Liss."

"Liam, you know why you can't."

"Let's pretend for a moment that Angel doesn't exist and I can. Pretend I didn't go to Hollywood. That I stayed here and made a life with you. One where I could make love to you every day. See you whenever I liked. One where I didn't ache like a part of me is dying whenever I'm not with you."

He's leaning down. So close I can smell him and feel his warm, sweet breath.

"Liss." He cups my face and looks into my eyes. "Pretend with me. Imagine we're in a movie of how our lives could have been. Let me show you what I fantasize about every time I see you. Please."

I want to stop looking at him, but I can't. Just like I can't stop wanting him.

I grip the front of his T-shirt and pull. He takes it as permission, and brushes his lips against mine. Just the lightest touch. My body explodes with sensation. Fierce flutters start in my stomach and spread through all my limbs. When my toes curl, I grip him tighter to urge him closer.

Sweet Jesus, the power of what he does to me. It's been so long, yet everything comes rushing back in knee-buckling detail.

He kisses me again, and a groan passes from his mouth to mine as his lips open and his tongue slides and strokes.

"God . . . this," he whispers against my lips. "You. You're everything."

He captures my lips and sucks gently, then repositions so our mouths slant over each other. We fit together just as perfectly as always, and the soft warmth of his tongue makes me groan. He kisses me again, and again, and each time it's deeper and more passionate, but still not enough. I grab at him and hold on as he lifts me and pulls my legs around his waist. Then I anchor my hands in his hair while he grinds against me, and I'm reminded how he can overload every pleasure receptor in my body in a matter of seconds.

Our hands aren't gentle as we roam over each other. Everything has an air of desperation about it, not only because we're so relieved to finally give in to this unrelenting need, but also because we know this is borrowed time and it won't last. Liam rocks his pelvis against me, stroking and pressing his hard against my soft, hitting all the right places to make me gasp. When I dig my fingers into his shoulders, he makes a noise in his chest. A dark, possessive sound. It makes me kiss him harder and cling to him more fiercely. More than anything, I want to be possessed by this man. Not just physically. I want to belong to him, just as much as I want him to belong to me.

But even through the trembling muscles and low, needy aches, I can't turn off the guilt that comes with kissing a man who isn't mine. An echo of '*This is wrong, this is wrong*' starts in my brain and won't be silenced. Even as I'm gripping his shoulders and pulling him closer, I'm bombarded with images of Angel in her wedding dress, giddy over the thought of Liam waiting at the end of the aisle. The Prince Charming in her ever after.

"Liam." There's barely any noise. Just air. He kisses my neck. Nibbles and sucks. I arch and grip him tighter. "Stop. We can't." I put my hands on his chest and push. He's so solid, I'm sure he barely feels it. He kisses me again, but I pull back and hold his face away from me. "Liam, stop."

He tightens his arms around me as he pants into my skin. "I'm sorry. I wasn't prepared. You still feel so perfect. More perfect than I remembered."

"Put me down. Please." I'm trembling with frustration that my heart still claims him as mine even though he's not. It's trying to convince me that he still loves me, but how can he? After everything he's put me through, he can't. This isn't love. It's lust. And weakness.

He lowers me to my feet, then cups my face in his hands. "What's wrong?"

"I have to go," I say as I turn toward the end of the alley.

"Liss, wait." He grabs my arm but I pull free.

"No, Liam. What the hell are we doing? Pretending we can be together? This isn't a movie. It's my life. And I'm not a goddamn consolation prize."

He exhales and takes a step back, his jaw tight and his hands fisted. "I've never thought of you as a consolation prize."

"You said you didn't want to be one of those assholes who thinks he can have it all, but that's how you're acting. You can't have me *and* Angel. You just can't."

"Then I'll end things with Angel."

My stomach drops. "What?"

He steps forward and takes my hands. "I know the timing sucks, and I'm about six years too late, but . . ." The determination in his expression is unmistakable. "I want to be with you. Wait, that's not right. I *need* to be with you."

I push wet hair away from my face. "Liam, you've been drinking—"

"I'm not drunk. I'm actually thinking clearly for the first time in years. There are so many reasons I shouldn't even be thinking about this. Jesus, more than you could possibly know, but still—"

"Well, now you're really selling it."

He takes a breath and lets it out, then fixes me with a determined gaze. "I know I'm not saying the right things, but . . . God, Liss, I can't live without you anymore, and I'm tired of pretending that I can."

Despite the cold rain drenching every inch of skin, warm hope blossoms in my stomach—followed closely by a sick sense of dread. Now he wants me? He's had years to do this and he hasn't. I can't help feeling like I'm an excuse to escape all the things in his life that aren't working.

"Liam, you're dealing with a lot of stuff right now. Rehearsals, a TV show, your wedding. Not to mention the anniversary of your brother's death. Then, to top it all off, you have paps stalking your every move. I understand that you're feeling . . . fragile . . . or whatever, and I'm here to support you however I can, but this—?"

"You think I'm saying this because I'm . . . what, stressed? Having some sort of breakdown? Jesus, Liss, no."

"I think if you truly couldn't live without me, you'd have found that out years ago, and yet this is the first I'm hearing of it." I try to keep the bitterness out of my tone, but I can't. "I heard nothing from you, Liam. Not a text, or e-mail. Not a goddamn word."

"You don't know the whole story, and I can't tell you everything now. But can you honestly say you don't want more after that kiss? Because I sure as hell can't."

I let out a short, sarcastic laugh. "This is insane!" I don't realize how much panic has leaked into my voice until I see the hurt on his face.

He doesn't let go of my hands, but his grip loosens. "Why are you fighting this? I thought this is what you wanted. Me. *Us.*"

I want to say I don't, because that's the less scary option, but I can't. Of course this is what I want. It's what I've always wanted. But it doesn't feel real. Or right. I'm used to wanting Liam, but having him is another matter. Even now, despite all his declarations, I don't see how it's possible. It's like we're at opposite ends of a maze, and he's saying he can see the exit while I'm still staring at a dead end.

I watch water run down his chest, and clench my jaw against the hopelessness I feel.

He cups my face with both hands and forces me to look up at him. "Liss, the night you went dress shopping with Angel, you sobbed in my arms because I was marrying someone else, and that slayed me. I didn't realize how much my actions have hurt you, and every day I stay with Angel, I hurt you more. I can't keep doing it. I won't."

"Liam, you're talking about turning your whole world upside down."

"I don't care."

"You should. Angel—"

"Will be better off without me. She might not see it like that at first, but eventually she will. She deserves someone who can love her as much as I lo—"

I put my hand over his mouth. "Don't say it. Please."

He kisses my palm before pulling my hand away. "It's true. Why not say it?"

"Because if you do, I'm going to do things I'll regret, and I'm trying to be the voice of reason here." I wipe water off my face and sigh. "Please don't make this decision now. Not in the heat of the moment. Go home. Cool off. Then, tomorrow, if you haven't changed your mind—"

He steps forward. "I'm not going to change my mind. That would imply being with you is a choice. It's not. I've tried to forget about you. To stay away from you. Every single time, I've failed. You know that. Fighting what I feel for you is exhausting, and I can't do it anymore. But the big question is, do you want this?" He takes my hand and weaves his fingers through mine, and the hope on his face melts me. "After all this time, and everything I've done . . . do you still want *me*?"

I look at our hands. "It would be so messy."

"I know. But if we can finally be together, it would be worth it."

I look up into his eyes. "Yeah. It would." He smiles, and even though the rain is still drenching us, I feel like I'm standing in full sun.

I smile back at him, then shake my head at how sappy I must look. "You still need to sleep on it. We'll talk more tomorrow."

He leans down and gives me a soft, slow kiss. "I have some things to work out on my end, but this is going to happen. Trust me."

I pull away, and even though I'm trying like hell to not get my hopes up, the way he's smiling at me is making that impossible.

I pick up my bag and swing it over my shoulder. "I'm heading home. If you figure out how to look Angel in the eye tomorrow after everything that's just happened, let me know. I'll be the one neck-deep in a shame spiral."

I'm almost at the end of the alley when he says, "Liss?" I turn to face him and see that, though the rain has slowed, his hair is still dripping onto his face. "No matter what happens, don't feel guilty about this. I initiated it. Blame me, not yourself."

I shake my head. "It takes two people to kiss like that, Liam. I'm as guilty as you." I turn away from him and trudge to the subway station. My guilt churns through me all the way home.

Later, when I crawl into bed, I dream about a future in which Liam is mine—mind, body, heart, and soul. Even with a troubled conscience, they're the most beautiful dreams I've ever had.

FIFTEEN

SCANDALOUS

Liam and I are making love when something impinges on my consciousness.

It's a song. Tinny and far away.

I try to ignore it.

Liam lifts me until I'm straddling him, and his face melts into pure adoration as I ride him.

"What's that noise?" he asks, as he grips my hips and urges me to move faster.

"Don't know. Don't care. Fuck me."

He flips me onto my back and takes over by pressing my wrists into the bed. He thrusts, hard and deep.

"God, Liam . . ."

"I've been fantasizing about this since yesterday in the alley. Nothing feels as good as being inside you."

He increases his pace. Grabs my leg and pulls it up to his waist. Slides home, time and again.

God, the pleasure. The all-consuming, spine-tingling pleasure.

"Ohhhhh . . . Liaaaaaam . . ."

"Hey, Mona McMoany. Answer your phone." Then someone's shaking me. "Lissa! Wake up!"

I sit up with a start, still in the throes of my dream. Josh is sitting on my bed with my ringing phone in his hand.

I take a quick look at the clock. 4.45 a.m.

"Who the hell is calling at this hour?"

"It's Mary. Please answer it. It's been ringing for five minutes."

I take the phone. "Mary?"

"Finally! Where have you been?"

I rub my face. "Sleeping. What else do you expect at this hour?"

"Well, get up," she says. "We're having an emergency production meeting. Meet us in the conference room as soon as you can."

"Why? What's going on?"

"The shit's about to hit the fan is what's going on. I'll fill you in when you get here."

She hangs up without signing off. A ball of lead falls into my stomach.

Oh, Liam. You did it, didn't you? You've broken up with Angel and told everyone about us. Shit.

I throw my covers back and get out of bed. "Come on, Josh. We have to go."

"Why?"

"Reasons. Move it."

Thirty minutes later we enter the conference room. The whole production team is there, as well as Angel and Liam. Angel looks like she's been crying. Liam looks like he wants to murder someone.

Oh, hell. This is really happening. He told her. I honestly didn't think he would.

I've dreamed about what it would be like to have Liam choose me too many times to count, but not once did I think it would be in such a public way. I sneak a glance at Mary and Marco. They don't seem mad at me. Why don't they seem mad?

Next to Liam, Anthony Kent shuffles a stack of magazines in front of him. "Thank you all for coming on such short notice. We have a situation that needs to be resolved, so let's all get on the same page before a shitstorm of epic proportions lands firmly in our laps."

He passes around the magazines. When one lands in front of me, my mouth goes dry, which is remarkable considering I want to vomit.

The front cover shows a grainy image of Liam kissing a girl. In an alley. In the rain. The angle of the picture hides my face, and my wet hair looks more brown than blond, but still: It's me. The headline reads, EXCLUSIVE SCANDAL! HOLLYWOOD LOVE RAT CAUGHT IN ALLEY CLINCH! Underneath is the caption, *"Trouble in paradise for America's Sweethearts? Cheating Liam Quinn seduces mystery brunette in NYC."*

"Oh, shit," Josh says beside me. He shoots me a sideways glance. He suspects.

"Shit, indeed," Mary says as she takes off her glasses and cleans them.

Across the table, Angel shakes her head. I can barely breathe.

Anthony lays his hand on Liam's shoulder. "This magazine will hit newsstands in a couple of hours, and yes, it looks bad, but we're not here to judge. We're here to go into damage control."

Mary gives Liam a disapproving glare. "What the hell were you thinking, sunshine?"

He doesn't look at her. "I wasn't."

"Who is this girl?" Marco asks. "Will she be an ongoing issue?"

"No." Liam's face is hard. "She's just some chick I met in a bar. I was drunk. I did something stupid. It won't happen again."

Heat engulfs my face as bile rises in my throat.

Opposite me, Anthony crosses his arms. "Liam and I have spoken about this in detail, and he assures me it was just a drunken kiss that meant nothing. He wants to put it behind him and move on."

I swallow down another bout of nausea. It wouldn't hurt so much if I didn't suspect it was the truth. I flip the magazine open to the story inside. There are more pictures. My legs wrapped around Liam.

His hands on my breasts. My fingers gripping his hair. Seeing it like this, it seems so seedy.

"The first thing we do," Anthony continues, "is make sure everyone is clear on the narrative. No one but Mary and I speaks to the media. If we stand strong and united, we'll weather this storm. The woman in these pictures is unidentified, but to America, she's simply a cheap tramp who seduced a famous movie star in the hope of getting her fifteen minutes of fame. Are we clear?"

Everyone nods, even Liam. He's staring down at the table, fists clenched, jaw tight. He can't even look at me.

Angel is also looking at the table. She seems shell-shocked. I curl my fingers into my palms until I feel the sting of my fingernails. So Liam didn't tell her about us and she still gets her heart ripped out? What the fuck is happening right now?

"How can we be sure she won't talk?" Mary asks. "Liam, if you give us her name, we can work out some sort of deal to keep her quiet."

"No," Liam says, roughly. "She's not interested in any of that."

"How do you know? We can draw up a confidentiality agreement. Legally gag her."

Liam shakes his head. "I can barely remember her face, Mary, let alone her name." Now he glances at me. "She won't come forward. Trust me."

I clench my jaw to stop from screaming at him. *"Trust me"? Never again, asshole.*

"The woman isn't part of our strategy," Anthony says. "In a few hours the media frenzy will have reached fever pitch, so we'll need Angeliam to go on television and make a joint statement." Anthony passes Liam a printed speech. "Liam, you're going to say you suffered a moment of weakness. You were nervous about the wedding, but you love your fiancée and deeply regret hurting her in any way. You will be on the verge of tears the whole time and hold your fiancée's hand like it's made of precious crystal, understand? Angel, you will stand beside your man and support him. When he's finished, you will hug him and whisper words of forgiveness. We will manage this disaster with the military precision of the goddamn National Guard. Don't forget, there's no scandal so bad it can't be spun into something good. Except of course if you murder someone or get caught kicking puppies, in which case, you're screwed. But short of that, anything can be turned into promotional gold. We'll get through this."

He keeps talking. Mary chimes in with her opinion. When Marco worries that the backers for the show will pull out, Mary reassures him that this kind of viral exposure will triple ticket sales.

I just keep staring at the pictures and try not to let everyone see how my emotions are strangling me.

So, all that talk about being with me was bullshit. Why do I even bother hoping anymore? It's pointless.

Here I was dreaming about being Liam's girlfriend. Instead, I'm a regret. A stupid, nameless, shameful mistake.

"For the love of God, we blocked this last week!" Marco glares at the actors. "Why the hell are you all in the wrong positions?! Where are your brains, people?"

Since the meeting, everyone's been on edge. The rest of the cast found out about the scandal when the magazine hit the streets an hour ago, and we've been bombarded by phone calls and weeping fans ever since. Down in the street, I can still hear them wailing in disbelief.

"They can't end like this! Their love is eternal! I can't believe Liam would do that. The slut must have made him."

I grind my teeth, and Josh gently touches my leg beneath the table. "This will blow over. Just give it time."

I nod tightly and write notes on my script. "Yep."

He hasn't said anything, but he knows it's me in those pictures. I can feel his disappointment like a vibration in the air. I've been a lot of things over the years, but never the other woman. His affection for Angel makes it even worse. I know he wants to be on my side, but how can he be? I'm the one in the wrong.

"Let's reset please, everyone," I say. "From the top of this scene once more."

Liam looks over at me. I studiously ignore him. In the light of today's drama, the pressure for me to be objective and professional is higher than ever. The cast needs to be reassured that as far as the show goes, everything's under control. It's the old duck illusion: No matter how frantically the legs are paddling below the water, we need people to see us gliding along with serene grace.

"No, Liam! Downstage, dammit! Downstage!" It seems Marco didn't get my memo about the duck thing. "Downstage is *forward*. Upstage is *back*. Do I need to remind you of basic stagecraft, man?"

I put my hand on Marco's arm and whisper, "Please breathe."

Marco pinches the bridge of his nose. Both Liam and Angel are off their games, but Liam's definitely the worse off of the two. There's also an air of resentment from the rest of the cast that he's dropped us all in shit. In my case, the resentment is well-founded.

"Sorry," Liam says. He glances over at me, and I look away.

He doesn't even deserve eye contact.

For the rest of the day, I double-check earlier than usual that all cast members are set for their cues. The last thing I need is for Marco's patience to wear any thinner. Every time I go near Liam, my emotions flare, but I force them down and get on with things.

"Stand by for your entrance, Mr. Quinn. Don't forget to exit downstage left after '*It shall be what o'clock I say it is.*'"

"Liss . . ." He leans down to talk to me, but I cross to the other side of the room to cue Angel.

Poor Angel looks as bad as I feel. Of course, knowing I'm responsible for her misery makes me feel even worse. I've been on the receiving end of this kind of hurt so many times, you'd think it would suck less being the perpetrator and not the victim, but it doesn't.

"You okay?" I whisper.

"I'll be fine."

"I'm sorry." *For lots of things.*

She shakes her head and stares at Liam, who's just entered the scene. "I thought we were always honest with each other. But this . . . My whole family is mortified. My father didn't come out and say it, but I'm pretty sure he thinks all this happened because I'm an idiot who can't keep her man satisfied."

"That's ridiculous. None of this is your fault."

"No. But it does make me wonder what else Liam's been keeping from me." *Rain. His mouth. Hands all over my body.* "He could have been fucking this girl for weeks. He denies it, but I'm inclined not to believe a single word he says anymore."

Me either. I shake my head and check my script. "Okay, stand by for your cue, then exit with Liam downstage at the end of the scene."

"Thank you, sweetie."

"You're welcome. Let me know if there's anything else I can do."

The day drags on. We finish blocking the final few scenes, but the tension in the air negates what little sense of achievement that brings.

By the time I call an end to rehearsal, everyone breathes a sigh of relief. I think we're all emotionally exhausted.

While the rest of the cast leaves, Angel and Liam retreat to the conference room along with Anthony and Mary. Their press conference is in an hour, and Anthony wants to drill them one more time. It's clear a spontaneous and heartfelt apology takes a crapload of rehearsal.

I'm tidying up the production desk when Josh touches my shoulder. "You okay?"

"Yep."

"Want to talk about it?"

"Nope."

He grabs my hands and turns me to face him. I can't look him in the face so I stare at my knuckles instead.

"Listen, I have a date tonight, but if you want me to cancel, I can."

I squeeze his hands. "I'll be fine. I'm used to this, remember? But there is someone who I'm sure could use a friend tonight."

"If you say Quinn, I'm going to punch something. Probably him."

I shake my head and look up at him. "Make sure Angel isn't alone. She doesn't have any friends here, and I'd be with her, but . . . well, awkward."

He nods. "I'll take care of her. Now, go. I'll clean up here." He pulls me in for a tight hug, then passes me my bag.

As soon as I hit the street, I'm accosted by at least a dozen reporters and photographers, all screaming questions as they shove recording devices in my face.

"Any comment on the cheating scandal? How's Angel coping with Liam's betrayal?"

"Is Liam sorry? Has he done this sort of thing before?"

"Can you tell us about the woman involved? Is she an actor, too?"

"If they break up, will the show close?"

I stay silent and push though them. When they start to follow me, I run.

By the time I get home, I'm in need of a Valium, a shower, and tissues. I slam the door behind me, then lean back against it, and when all the emotion I've been suppressing for the past ten hours threatens to bubble out of me in big, frustrated sobs, I let it come.

SIXTEEN

LOVE AND LOBSTERS

Fresh from a hot shower and wrapped in my favorite robe, I flop onto the couch and turn on my phone. Immediately, a slew of message alerts rings out. Most of the numbers I don't recognize, so I figure they're reporters and ignore them. When I see that Liam's tried to call me fifteen times, I grip the phone so hard, I almost crack the glass. I throw the phone onto the couch and head into the kitchen. There's only half a bottle of red wine left, but my name is written all over it. I don't even bother with a glass.

After taking a giant swig, I go back to the couch and turn on the TV. Of course, the first thing that comes on is an entertainment show about the Angeliam scandal.

"Geez, Universe," I mutter at the screen. "I usually like some foreplay before I'm fucked this thoroughly. You could at least buy me dinner."

I sit there like a zombie and watch as the media circus covers the scandal. It's the *Angeliampocalypse*, complete with teary fan interviews, Hollywood insiders speculating about the future of the golden couple, and an actual graph predicting how much retail sales of *Rageheart* will suffer or soar if they split. They'll soar, by the way.

I don't even know why I'm watching. Stupidity? Sick curiosity?

Flat-out masochism? After trusting Liam again, I guess I deserve punishment.

On the screen, Angel and Liam emerge from our rehearsal building and face the barrage of yelling reporters and flashbulbs. They're holding hands. Liam looks gorgeous and contrite. Angel looks gorgeous and devastated. Liam says everything Anthony told him to. He's on the verge of tears the whole time, which leads me to believe he's either genuinely sorry for his actions or needs to win a damn Oscar in the near future.

I hate how choked up I get when he says, "For my whole life, I've only loved one woman. And I'm sickened that my thoughtless and selfish actions have hurt her. I can only hope that one day, she'll understand I just want to be with her, and find a way to forgive me."

He looks right through the camera when he says it, and his performance is so sincere and touching that by the end, even I'm rooting for him and Angel to make it through this clusterfuck.

Jesus Christ, I need more wine.

I take two big mouthfuls, then flip the channel over to a rerun of *Friends*. Phoebe is explaining how Rachel and Ross are soul mates. "She's your lobster," she says to Ross. "It's a known fact lobsters fall in love and mate for life. You can actually see old lobster couples walking around their tank, holding claws."

I wonder what Phoebe would say if I told her that my lobster didn't pick me. He's decided to stay with the gorgeous redheaded lobster whose legs are longer than my whole body. So, do I get to choose another lobster now, or is that it? I'm to go through life forever lobsterless?

Without warning, tears well up and spill onto my cheeks. I swipe them away impatiently. "Fuck you and lobsters everywhere, Phoebe. Fuck . . . you."

I don't know how long I wallow and stare at the television. Long enough to finish the wine, anyway. I'm considering going out to buy more when there's a knock at the door.

Dammit. Josh forgets his key more often than he remembers it. Guess Angel didn't need him to console her after all.

I stomp over to the door and pull it open. "You're hopeless, you know that—?"

Instead of Josh, Liam's standing there, looking more wretched than I feel, if that's possible.

"Liss, you have to know that—"

"Go home."

I try to close the door, but he stops it with his hand. "Wait. Let me explain."

"No need. You've made your feelings clear. It was a mistake. It meant nothing."

"Please, just listen to me—"

"I'm done listening to you, Liam! The only thing listening to you ever got me was hurt. Why the hell do you keep coming back to torture me? You made your choice, and it's not me. Again! I get it!"

"No, you don't! That's the trouble. This situation is complicated."

"Oh, really? Because it seems pretty simple: You're an asshole. And I'm an idiot for believing you. I thought I knew every douche line out there, but you had me totally fooled."

"I wasn't feeding you a line! I meant every word I said to you yesterday. I want to be with you. That's all I've ever wanted."

"How stupid do you think I am? You just stood in front of the *world* and reaffirmed your love for your fiancée!"

He slaps his hands against the door frame so hard it makes me jump. "No I didn't! I don't have a fiancée! I have a fucking contract that forces me to pretend to be engaged to Angel, but that's it! Our relationship is manufactured bullshit!"

He's so worked up he's panting, and my heart is pounding so furiously it takes a moment for me to understand what I've just heard. When it sinks in, a flash of anger runs up my spine. "What?!"

He steps forward, but if he touches me right now, I don't know what I'll do. I turn and walk to the far side of the living room.

"Everything I just said at the press conference," he says, his voice softer as he watches me with wary eyes. "All of that stuff about only ever having loved one woman in my whole life. It was about *you*. God, Liss. Don't you understand? It's only ever been you." He stares at me, as if he's waiting for me to explode. I don't. I'm too shell-shocked to even move, apart from hugging the wine bottle so tightly to my chest it hurts. When the silence becomes uncomfortable, he comes inside and gently closes the door. Then he just stands there for a few seconds, one hand on the handle, his other hanging limply at his side.

"When I got home last night," he says, staring at the floor, "Anthony was waiting with those photos. A friend of his at TMZ had tipped him off they were about to hit, and he was pissed. Seriously pissed. Can't say I blamed him. What I did with you was stupid. Not the kissing part, because I couldn't regret that if you put a gun to my head. But doing it out in the open? That was dumb. After the thing at Jamie's grave, I should have known I was being followed, that that asshole from the bar would have been on us the moment we stepped into the street."

He rubs his face. "Anthony kept drilling me about your identity. Said that if we threw you to the wolves, it would take some of the heat off me. Of course, there was no way in hell I was going to do that, so I denied everything, even though it killed me." He looks over at me, regret coloring every feature. "Anthony's been watching me like a hawk all day, making sure I didn't do anything to make it worse. That's why I didn't warn you. Just before the press conference, I snuck out to the bathroom to try to call you and explain, but your phone was off. I'm so sorry."

I suddenly know how Alice must have felt on the other side of the looking glass. I feel like I'm in Bizarro World. This is completely surreal. "But, you and Angel—"

"Aren't engaged. We never have been. We've never even had sex. The whole thing was set up to generate publicity."

He watches me carefully. Gauging my reaction. I don't know how long I stand there, disbelief all over my face. It must be a while because eventually he says, "Jesus, Liss. Please say something. Anything. Just . . . react."

I take a breath as I attempt to process it all. I can't. It's so ridiculous, my brain has seized. "So you've been *lying*? To me? To the entire world? For *years*?"

"Elissa, I'm sorry."

Incredulity floods my body, followed by fury. Suddenly, I have a lot to say, and all of it is accompanied by huge messy emotions that make my voice loud and my cheeks wet. "Do you have any idea how much you hurt me? How *devastated* I was six years ago when I saw pictures of you and Angel together? How much you hurt me *today* when it seemed you were choosing her all over again? And now you're telling me it was all a goddamn *publicity stunt*?!" I slam the wine bottle down on the table so hard, Liam flinches.

As I try to calm down, he stands there, guilt and regret filling his eyes. When he steps forward, I step back. He puts his hands out like he's trying to placate a wild animal.

"When I was offered *Rageheart*," he says, patiently, "the producers told me I had to agree to their bullshit fauxmance or lose the job. I wanted to tell them to shove it, but I needed that movie to get Mom and Dad out of debt. After all the lawsuits, they were drowning. Anthony assured me this sort of thing happens all the time and would be over before I knew it, so I agreed." He looks at the ground. "I couldn't tell you. The nondisclosure contract was brutal. Plus, I was ashamed. I'd sold out in the biggest way possible, and I knew it."

"That's a piece-of-shit excuse, Liam! You loved me and I loved you. We could have made it work."

His shoulders fall. "No, we couldn't. Can you truly say you would have been happy sneaking around behind the scenes while I pretended Angel was the love of my life? You would have felt like a dirty secret. And after a while, you would have resented me for it."

"So, instead, you decided to rip my heart out? Use my worst fear against me?"

He swallows and drops his head. "I knew signing that contract meant hurting you, and losing you, but my parents had been struggling for years. It was starting to take a toll on my dad's health. And the families of those who died in the accident were struggling, too. I felt like I owed them, for Jamie's sake. In some sick way, I thought the good outweighed the bad. I knew you and I would be miserable, but I also knew that a lot of other people would get the help they needed."

I scrub my hand over my face. "God, Liam—"

"That's why I stopped calling you. I tried to prepare myself for what was coming. Angel and I were tipped off that a photographer was following us, so we played our part. I didn't warn you because . . . well, I thought maybe a clean break would be easier for both of us."

"Easier?" I laugh at that. "You told me you loved me! Why would you do that when you knew you couldn't be with me?"

"I didn't know then. They told me about the contract the day after I called you, and . . . when I heard, I felt sick. Even after I'd made up my mind to sign it, I fooled myself into believing our separation would only be temporary. That when it was all over, I could beg your forgiveness, and we'd get another shot. But then, one movie turned into two, and two into four. The whole thing with Angel turned into this massive publicity gold mine, and no matter how miserable she and I were with the arrangement, the producers wouldn't even discuss breaking the contract. They convinced us the franchise would die if we broke up before the final movie. Everyone who worked on those films had become like our family. If our actions shut it all down, then it would be like the construction accident, all over again. I couldn't live with the guilt of jeopardizing any more livelihoods. Ruining more lives. So we kept going. Then this play came along, but they only wanted us as a package deal. We both wanted to do it, so our purgatory continued."

I think about the hundreds of photographs of Liam and Angel over the years. In cafés. On vacations. Movie premieres. Music festivals. I can imagine how their fans will feel when they find out it's all a sham. It's how I'm feeling right now. Duped. Betrayed. More than a little stupid.

"I believed you two were in love," I say, trying to keep calm. "The way you looked at her. Held her. *Kissed* her . . ." My voice breaks and I bite the inside of my cheek to stop myself from crying.

"Liss, I'm sorry. Our public displays were no different from any other performance, except we improvised the lines. I did my job, and I did it well. None of it was real. How could it be?" He walks over to me slowly. "I've never stopped loving *you*. From the day we met, you've been the only one for me. There's never been anyone else."

I cross my arms over my chest. There's an ache in there that's pushing against my rib cage. A mixture of incredulity and disappointment. But there's also that little spark of hope that's been smothered for so long, it can't decide whether this new information is going to kill it, or shock it back to life.

Liam watches me, and those remarkable eyes are filled with such pain, I have to look away. "Liss . . ." He goes to touch me, but I pull back.

I shake my head. "I can't believe I'm hearing this. Any of it." Tears are falling now. It would hurt too much to try and stop them.

I cross to the other side of the room and stare at the bookcase. He doesn't follow, but when I look back at him, his eyes are wet, too.

"I wanted to tell you the truth so many times over the years, but what would be the point? Even if I did, I couldn't be with you. Not with my life how it is. Every damn day I witness what Angel goes through because people think she's with me. The hate. The bullying. The constant scrutiny and criticism. It eats at her, Liss, even though she's been dealing with that kind of crap since she was a kid. How could I possibly drag you into all that? I loved you too much to even consider it."

"Then why say those things yesterday? Why give me hope that we could be together?"

"Because even though it's selfish as hell to want you in my insane life, I finally realized that by trying to spare you, I've damned you to be just as miserable as I am."

We stare at each other, and I feel like I'm being pulled toward him and pushed away at the same time. So many emotions are twisting through me, I can't make sense of them all.

"My beautiful Liss." He steps forward. "Please say you can forgive me. I keep thinking about what will happen when this show ends. Unless I fix things, we'll go back to our separate lives, me in California and you here, and . . ." He grips his chest. "Fuck. Every time I imagine that, it hurts so much I want to put my fist through a wall." He clenches and releases his hand, and I can feel his tension filling the space between us. "Ask me to give up a limb and I swear, I'll find a way to do it. But don't ask me to live without you anymore. I can't. I'm so goddamn in love with you, it hurts."

For so long, I've dreamed about Liam Quinn standing in front of me, telling me he loves me. In every single one of those fantasies he looked at me like he is now, with obvious, unashamed love. But fantasies don't prepare you for reality. Even though I always thought I'd run into his arms, and cover him in kisses, in actual fact there's more than just him and me to think about. Even if I get past his deception, there's Angel, and the show, and the millions of fans who will be heartbroken when they hear their idol loves a short, blond stage manager instead of their ethereal goddess of the silver screen.

I wipe my face. "What about the contract? Aren't you and Angel still bound by it?"

He doesn't move forward, but it's clear he wants to. "Screw the contract. I've made more money than I ever imagined, and I'm miserable. The only thing I truly want can't be bought. The studio is welcome to sue me down to my last dollar. As long as I have you, I'll be the richest man on earth."

I stare at him as everything he's just said rumbles around in my brain. On one hand, our situation is so unbelievable I want to laugh, but on the other, the deepest parts of me are whispering that everything finally makes sense. For years I've felt wrong. As if I were a stranger in my own life. I've always known it was because of him, but I lived in denial. Pretending I wasn't hollow without him became a way of life. And it seems he was feeling exactly the same way.

Now, we have the opportunity for a second chance, but I have no idea how that would work. His world is full of movie premieres and parties. Beauty and glamor. I spend most of my time in the dark. I'm the person who controls the spotlight, not the one standing in it. In the words of an ancient Chinese proverb, it's all very well for the bird and the fish to fall in love, but where will they make their home?

"Liss?" When I look at him, there's real fear in his expression. He's terrified I'm going to turn him down. He should be. "I understand this is a lot to process, and I know how angry you are with me. And I wouldn't blame you if you told me to go screw myself and never come near you again. But before you do that, please, just tell me this: Do you believe that I love you?"

"Yes." I say it without thinking. Maybe that's the best way to deal with my emotional turmoil. God knows my head and my heart are tying me in knots. Perhaps I should just trust my gut.

I look Liam in the eye. He understands, and his whole posture changes. As if he's holding himself back from following his instinct to show me how he feels rather than tell me.

He takes a breath before he says, "Okay, then. Million-dollar question: Do you love me?"

He doesn't breathe for the three seconds it takes me to make up my mind to be honest. "Despite everything, and even though I'd like to hit you right now . . . yes. Very much."

The moment I say it, he clenches his jaw, and I can tell he's trying to keep himself together. I know how he feels. This is a turning point for us, and I'm running on so much adrenaline, my skin feels too small for my body.

"Liss," he says, his voice rough with emotion. "I know I have a lot of work to do to make up for how much I've hurt you, but . . . do you still want us to be together?"

I have one of those moments where everything other than him retreats into the background and he comes into perfect focus. Beautiful, hopeful Liam.

He swallows hard before continuing. "Think carefully about your answer, because if you say 'yes' . . ." He swears quietly under his breath. "If you say 'yes,' I will never be dishonest with you again. I will never trust my head over my heart again. And I will finally be able to show you the infinite ways I love you."

There are several yards between us, but right now, it feels like there's a steel cable connecting his heart to mine. It's always been there. But now, I'm able to see it as a blessing rather than a curse.

I take a breath and undo the tie on my robe with trembling hands. The heavy fabric falls open, revealing my distinct lack of underwear.

His eyes widen, and his expression immediately turns ravenous. My body responds with an explosion of goose bumps.

"Yes. I want to be with you. Please. Now."

He blinks twice before he mutters, "Fuck, yes." Within seconds he's crossed the room, and he makes a low, possessive sound as he crushes me against him.

Six years of stifled desire and sexual frustration erupts between us. We devour each other, tongues tasting and sucking. My robe is pushed off my shoulders. His shirt is unbuttoned in record time. Everywhere he touches me, pleasure blooms, lush and bright, and I'm breathless with the power of it. I push him back against the wall, hard. The force of the impact causes a nearby picture frame to crash to the floor. Neither of us spares it a glance. He throws his head back as I cover his chest and stomach with hot kisses, tasting the skin I've been able to do nothing but dream about for far too long. His muscles contract in time with his rapid breathing, and he groans when I run my tongue and lips over the delicious planes of his chest. I taste every inch of skin . . . his nipples, his abs. There's nothing delicate or elegant about what we're doing. Everything is urgent, hands moving and squeezing, breaths heavy and moans long. We're so desperate for each other, we're clumsy and rough.

When I come back to his mouth, he moans against my lips and trails his hands down to my ass. With one swift motion, he lifts me, and when I wrap my legs around him he turns and shoves me up against the bookcase. Books and knickknacks spill noisily onto the floor as we press and grind. I reach behind me and hold on to one of the shelves as he kisses down my neck and teases my nipples. I throw my head back and press my chest up to meet him as his hot, beautiful mouth closes around me.

"Oh, God, Liam . . ."

He works my breasts until I'm clawing at him to give me more. Then, he yanks me away from the bookcase and strides over to the couch, knocking over a vase and a floor lamp on his way. He shoves the coffee table with his foot, and the TV remote and a pile of magazines clatter onto the floor.

"Fuck," he says, panting. "Sorry."

"Don't care," I say. "Keep going."

He collapses onto the couch and pulls me forward to straddle him. Every inch of my skin tingles and aches as he traces the curves of my breasts and hips with his fingers.

"God, I've missed you," he whispers against my skin. "This body, your mind, your heart. All of it. Right now, I feel like a kid who's had his Christmas present on layaway for six years and has finally gotten his hands on it. You're so freaking perfect, you blow my mind."

He kisses me again, and his sweet tongue makes me dizzy while his hands set every nerve ending on edge. I can't wait anymore. The only thing that registers through my haze of hormones is an all-consuming need to have him inside me. To claim him as mine again and have him claim me in return.

I climb off his lap so I can undo his jeans. He helps me by pulling off his shoes and socks. Then he stands so I can work his jeans and underwear down his legs.

When he's naked, I have to take a moment, because . . . God. Seriously? He's a walking work of art. If Michelangelo had Liam Quinn as a model, I have no doubt there'd be a whole gallery dedicated to him. Maybe even with a wing just for his spectacular erection.

Liam sits back down on the couch and stares at me with barely restrained desperation. "Come here."

He pulls me down to straddle him, and I use one hand to align us. I look into his eyes as I slowly sink down.

Oh.

Dear.

God.

Both our mouths drop open. Our eyelids flutter. Simultaneous groans fill the apartment as I rock and tilt until he fills me. When we're fully joined at last, I gasp, then sigh. How I can feel so incredibly wired and relieved in the same moment is beyond me. This is what I've been missing for all of these years. Not just the physical pleasure of having him inside me, but the soul-heart connection that joining with him brings. We stare at each other in wonder, in mutual recognition of the fact that even the most vivid fantasies we've had while we've been apart pale in comparison to the spine-tingling reality.

"I love you, Liss," he whispers as he grazes my face with gentle fingers. "I love you so much."

I kiss him. "I love you, too."

I clasp my hands behind his neck and start to ride him, keeping eye contact the whole time. He grasps my hips and guides me into long, deep thrusts. The sensation is so intense, it's almost unbearable. The feel of him. The incredible expression on his face as he watches my every move. Every time I lift my hips he grunts like he's in pain.

When I sink back down, he moans with pleasure. Every movement seems too much for him, and I understand how he feels. After having nothing for so long, suddenly having everything is a shock to the system.

We keep that connection the whole time we make love. Even when I can feel my orgasm building, I don't look away. Neither does he.

I brace myself on his shoulders as I increase my tempo. When my thigh muscles give out, he takes over from below. He thrusts, filling me, over and over again. My orgasm builds quickly, coiling and stretching so tight, I can barely breathe.

I grip his hair as his movements become faster, more intense. He clenches his jaw and groans, as if holding off his own orgasm is painful.

God, the pleasure. The debilitating, breath-stealing pleasure.

When he comes, the noise that pours out of him is beyond passionate. It speaks of a man who's forgotten the extent to which he can feel. Of someone rediscovering how to be real after so many years of pretending.

I make a similar sound when my climax explodes a few seconds later. It's not delicate or pretty, but neither are my feelings about Liam. They're giant, messy, and inconvenient, but I wouldn't give them up for anything.

As our final shudders fade, I collapse onto him, and he wraps his arms around me to bury his head in my neck. Our frantic breathing echoes in the quiet apartment, and we don't move for a long time. When we do stir, it's only because he's hard again, and our second wind ends up turning into a hurricane. Chairs are knocked over. The bathroom door is dented. By the time we retreat into my bedroom, books are all over the floor, plates and bowls have been shoved off kitchen counters, and cushions and clothes litter every inch of the floor. The entire apartment is trashed.

Usually, we both despise mess, but right now, we're too high on each other to care.

After Liam gives me the second orgasm in my bed and the fourth for the night, he collapses onto his back and pulls me onto his chest. He releases a huge satisfied sigh, then closes his eyes. I know we need to talk more about our bumpy road to being together, but all that can wait until tomorrow. Right now, I just want to enjoy being wrapped in the arms of my soul mate.

"Liam?" I whisper, as his breathing evens out.

"Hmmmm?" He's barely conscious.

I can't help but smile as I listen to the hypnotic rhythm of his heart beneath my ear. "Thank you for being my lobster."

SEVENTEEN

COMING CLEAN

The next morning I wake to find Liam wrapped around me like a boa constrictor. I try to ease myself away from him, but his arms tighten.

"No," he says, his voice dark with sleep.

"No, what?"

"Wherever you think you're going that doesn't involve staying in bed with me—no."

"What if I need to go to the bathroom?"

"Hold it."

He throws his leg over me for good measure.

"What if there's a fire?"

"I'm sure New York's Bravest will get here in time to save us."

"Liam—" I squirm, and before I've even registered he's moved, I'm slammed onto my back with my wrists pinned aside my head. When he settles between my legs I'm very aware of how extremely naked we both are. And how impressively hard he is.

"Elissa," he says in a dangerous tone. "This is not up for discussion. I haven't woken up with you in my arms for nearly six years. I'm not letting go anytime soon. You can either get on board with that, or I'm going to have to subdue you. Understand?"

"Define 'subdue.'"

"Kiss you until you submit to my will." He lowers his face so that his lips are almost brushing mine. "Make you come until you can't move."

"And this is supposed to deter me? Psychology—you're doing it wrong."

His face turns dark. "Doing it wrong?" He tightens his grip on my wrists. "Right. That's it, woman. Prepare to be mauled."

He growls and shoves his face into my neck, and I squirm and giggle as he nips and bites. When my struggling gets extreme, he lays his full weight against me to keep me still.

"Concede," he orders.

"Never!" I try to buck him off, but it's impossible. All those muscles weigh a ton. I huff in defeat and go still. "Okay, fine. You win."

"Right answer." He gives me a smug smile before rolling off and pulling me back into the cage of his arms. "On a related note, how suspicious would everyone be if we both called in sick to rehearsal today?"

"Very. But it might be worth it."

He closes his eyes and holds me tighter. "Yeah, it would."

With his right arm wrapped across my chest, I can finally get a good look at his tattoo. It looks like a coat of arms, but instead of animals, it's made up of names. I lightly run my finger across the dark ink.

In the middle, "Jamie" is written in the shape of a heart. On either side, his parents' names, "Angus" and "Eileen," scroll around, and they're surrounded by vines and flowers, just like the pergola Liam built for them. And beneath it all is a banner with . . .

"Oh, my God."

Liam cracks one eye open. "I was wondering when you'd notice that."

"When did you get this?"

"After the first *Rageheart* movie. Hollywood was getting me down, and I . . ." He strokes my back. "I wanted a permanent reminder of all the people I loved who I couldn't be with."

I run my finger over the letters etched into the scroll. At first

I thought it was a generic compliment about his parents and brother: "My Bliss." But then I noticed the capital L.

BLiss

I remember his phone message from years ago. *"My beautiful Liss. My Bliss. See what I did there?"*

He looks down at me. "I thought that if I had you tattooed on my skin, you'd always be with me, one way or the other. Stupid, right?"

"Not stupid. Beautiful." I palm his cheek and kiss him softly.

We just lie there and kiss for a while. The sort of deep, languorous kisses which suggest we have all the time in the world.

"Every day I was away from you," he says, in between teasing me with his lips and tongue, "I've dreamed of this mouth. Every time I had to kiss Angel, I closed my eyes and imagined it was you."

Breathless and horny, I check the clock.

6 a.m.

I'm due at rehearsal at 9 a.m.

"So," I say, and put a hand on his chest to stop him distracting me further. "Have you put any thought into how we're going to handle things today?"

He flops onto his back and pulls me into him. "I've thought about it. Haven't really come up with a solution yet. We'll have to break the contract. There's no way I'm going through with this wedding. I had issues with it before I saw you again. I can't even pretend to marry Angel now."

"What if Angel has a problem with it?"

He closes his eyes and rubs his forehead. "She may be disappointed about not having her princess moment, but realistically, she's a victim in this as well. Neither of us have been able to have a proper relationship since this whole thing started, and I know she really wants one. She's lonely. She wants a man to love her for real, and as much

as I think I'm a great kisser, I can feel she's sick of pretending
with me."

"So you guys have really never . . . ?"

He shifts so he can look down at me. "No."

"Why not? Didn't you ever just want to make the best of a bad
situation?"

He's quiet for a moment, and then he says, "We tried. Once. It was
right after the *Rageheart* premiere. We were both freaking out about
the screaming fans and fame. I think we both figured we'd try to find
comfort in each other, but . . ." He shakes his head. "I couldn't get
you out of my head. Or body. Angel tried her best to make me forget,
but I couldn't . . . uh . . . perform."

I glance down at how tented the sheet is over his crotch. "Seriously?
Because I've never known you to have any problems in that department."

"Yeah, well, that's because you've always made me harder than tita-
nium. But most of the women on this planet don't affect me like that.
Not even Angel. To be honest, I don't think she finds me attractive,
either."

I sit up on an elbow and stare at him. "Are you kidding? She has
eyes and a vagina. How on earth can she not be attracted to you?"

He laughs and smiles at me. "Believe it or not, there are women
on this planet who have zero interest in me."

"Pfft. Lesbians and grandmas, maybe."

"Actually, I'm pretty popular with grandmas."

I smile, then snuggle back down into the crook of his arm. "I'm
not going to lie. Knowing you and Angel have never jumped each
other makes me happy, but I still hate that she was hurt by those pictures yesterday. We need to talk to her. Tell her the truth."

"I agree. She's been my only friend through this whole crazy
ride, and she deserves better. Maybe when I'm out of the picture she
can find a guy who appreciates her. I'll talk to her after rehearsal
today."

"What about the fans? You can't just come out and say, 'Hey guys, guess what? We've been deceiving you for years.' They'd lynch you."

He strokes my hair. "Yeah, the irony is, in order to let them down easy, we'd have to lie to them more. I hate it, but I don't see an alternative. Maybe Anthony will have some idea of what to do."

"What if he tells you to just wait out the contract?"

I feel him tense. "No."

"Liam—"

He pulls away and looks down at me. "*No,* Liss. That means another couple of months of pretending and not having you. No fucking way."

"If you guys break up now, it could hurt the show, and you can't do that to Marco."

He lets go of me and swings his legs onto the floor so he can sit up. I can see the tension in his back as he leans his elbows on his knees and drops his head. "So, what? We just go about business as usual? How the hell am I supposed to hide my feelings for you?"

I kneel behind him and wrap my arms around his shoulders. "You're an amazing actor. You'll find a way. Just remember that I love you."

As soon as the words have left my mouth, he turns to me, and his face goes through a spectacular range of emotions. Finally, his expression melts into one of awe.

"So many people say that to me every day. People who don't even know me. But you . . . you're the one person I crave to hear it from. Before last night, I didn't think I'd ever hear those words from you again."

He cups my face and stares into my eyes. "I used to think that if I just waited long enough, fate would bring us back together. That our stars would align, or whatever, and you'd come crashing back into my life to stay. But that didn't happen. So now I say, screw it. I'm done waiting. Sometimes, fate is what you make it, and I'm making my life with you."

He kisses me and pushes me onto my back, and I gasp as he covers my body with his. Lord, that much Liam is hard to handle. I run my hands down his back and over his magnificent ass. I love feeling his muscles tremble beneath my touch. So much strength wrapped around his sweet heart.

"We don't have long," I say, already breathless. "I have work to do before rehearsal."

He presses his erection against me in ways that make me moan. "Don't need long. Just need to be inside you."

He kisses down my chest, and grinds against me at the same time. Within seconds, every muscle that was complaining about our epic lovemaking of last night is begging for more.

I lift my hips and urge him forward, and with minimum repositioning, he slides into me. When he's fully inside, he lets out a quiet moan before going still.

"Along with you saying you love me, I'm also never going to get tired of this," he says, his voice tight. "Ever."

He moves, slow and restrained, and I breathe in time with his thrusts. "I still find it hard to believe that Liam Quinn, the world's most desirable man, is inside me."

He bends down to kiss me. "And goddamn . . ." He closes his eyes and pants. "The world's most desirable man is about to come in record time because you feel so damn good. God, Liss . . ."

I don't know how long we make love, but I know that it's even better this morning than it was last night. Last night, it all seemed like a dream. Today, it's a very sexy reality. Even though we know we'll have to sort through a massive mess to make it happen, we're no longer going to let anything stand in our way.

I watch, enthralled as a naked Liam trawls through the mess surrounding the couch. "Found my underpants!" he says, holding them up in triumph. "Not sure how they got wrapped around *Cheese Lovers' Quarterly,* but whatever."

I pout as he pulls them on. Thankfully, he ignores the rest of his clothes, which he's already folded into a neat pile on the couch, and begins to clean in just his skintight boxer briefs. We're both freshly showered, and I'm in my robe, and although I would like to stay in bed all morning, knowing the apartment looks like a tornado has ripped through it makes both of us tense. Neat Freaks, Unite!

"I'll do the kitchen," Liam says, and gives me a quick kiss as he passes. "There's broken crockery in there, and I can't have my woman cutting her delicate feet."

I smile at his choice of words. I've never been someone's woman before. I like it.

Liam stops at the hall closet and digs out the dustpan while I start sorting through the mess of books on the floor. Did nothing survive our onslaught?

A shiver runs up my spine as I think about Liam slamming me against walls and counters. *So worth it.*

Liam hums as he cleans the kitchen, and I smile as I concentrate on stacking books on the shelves in my own particular fashion; that is to say, categorized by genre, then author, then color. Kind of sad, but whatever. They're my shelves. I like them to look pretty.

I'm almost finished when I hear voices outside the door.

"Angel, stop."

"No. C'mere, Josh. Jusforasecond."

"I can't hug you and open the door at the same time. Just stand there, okay? And for God's sake, don't puke. I don't deal well with puke."

The door swings open and Josh stumbles in with one arm around Angel. She looks terrible. When they see me and the mess, they both freeze. Angel sways and blinks as Josh turns to me. "What the hell, Lissa?! Did those asshole teenagers from the second floor break in and trash the joint? Because I'd love an excuse to kick some pimply, emo ass."

"Josh, hey. Uh . . . no. Would you believe there was an earthquake?"

"No. What really happened?"

"Elissaaaaa!" Before I can answer, Angel lurches toward me and pulls me into a tight hug. "I love you. I had a shitty day yesterday, but seeing you makes it all better." God, she smells like a brewery. "Will you marry me instead of Liam? He's a dick. He makes me look stupid. He's supposed to be my rock in the stormy sea of life, but he let me drown." She squeezes her eyes shut. "Oh, my God. Someone write that down. I'm so freaking poetic when I'm hammered, it blows my mind."

I glance over at Josh. He holds up his hands, defensive. "You told me to comfort her. She wanted to be comforted by beer."

"Has she been drinking all night?"

He nods. "I tried to stop her, but we both know she won't be argued with. Plus, the more she drank, the more attractive she found me. How could I resist?"

"Ohh," Angel murmurs as she rests her head on my shoulder. "Josh has been lovely, but Lissa . . . you're so soft. This robe is comfy. Let's snuggle."

She leans down and rests her head on my boobs. I hug her and glare daggers at Josh.

He at least has the sense to look regretful. "I'm sorry. She kept flirting with me until I bought her another drink. I'm a weak, selfish man."

"Soon you're going to be a dead man. We have rehearsal in two hours. Marco is going to kill both of us if she shows up like this."

"I know. That's why I brought her here, so you could help sober her up."

I pull back and get Angel to look at me. "Hey, sweetie. How're you doing?"

"Ahmtired. And Josh won't let me have more beer. He's mean. But pretty."

"How about some coffee? And maybe some food to soak up the alcohol?"

I'm about to take her into the kitchen when I remember who's in there. Oh, God, as if this situation wasn't bad enough. At least he has the sense to stay hidden.

"Lissa?" Josh is frowning at me. "Why the hell are there men's clothes on our couch?"

"Um . . ."

Then his eyes go wide, and Angel gasps at the same time. Sure enough, I turn to see Liam standing half naked in the kitchen doorway, looking like a Greek god, except for the dustpan and yellow rubber gloves.

"Hey, guys," he says softly, as he looks between us. "Uh . . . we should probably talk."

Before anyone has time to speak, Angel races to the bathroom and barfs violently into the toilet.

Half an hour and two cups of coffee later, Angel is bleary-eyed, but definitely more sober. Liam and I are fully dressed and have explained our whole story, including our nightly line runs to counteract his secret dyslexia. So far, Angel and Josh are taking it well, all things considered.

"You're an asshole, Quinn!" Josh yells as he paces in front of the couch. Okay, I lied when I said he was taking it well. "Not only do you dump Elissa for this bullshit PRmance years ago, but then, when you knew you were having feelings for her again, you didn't even think to warn Angel about the approaching shitstorm? How fucking selfish are you?"

Liam shakes his head. "Josh, I understand why you're pissed—"

"Good. Because your actions have hurt two of the most amazing women I know, and if I wasn't terrified of physical violence, I'd be kicking your ass all over this apartment right now!"

When he stops in front of Angel, she gently takes his hand. "Josh, please calm down before Liam squashes you like a bug. Also, you're too loud. Could you grab me some painkillers?"

Josh throws Liam a final glare before heading into the bathroom. Angel rubs her temples, and when Josh returns with two Advil and a glass of water, she quickly swallows them down.

"Okay," she says with a sigh. "So, I guess we need to figure out what to do, right? I'm not going to lie. The thought of breaking the contract gets me all kinds of excited, but we know that can't happen. Not right now."

Josh sits next to her and lays his arm along the back of the sofa. "So what's the plan, then?"

"Personally," I say as I grip my coffee cup, "I think the wise choice would be to pretend Angeliam is business as usual until the fuss from the alley pictures dies down. When the media circus packs up and goes home, we'll work something out."

Liam crosses his arms over his chest. "I don't like having to wait, but I agree it's probably for the best. I need to talk to Anthony about possible exit strategies, but he's got his hands full right now. He's already left six messages for me today. It seems we've had over two hundred interview requests since the press conference last night. This thing isn't going away easily."

Josh frowns. "So in the meantime, you and Elissa think you're going to sneak around behind the scenes and sex each other up without anyone noticing?"

"Sex would be nice," Liam says with a shrug, "but I'm not counting on it, no. I just know I've been away from her for six years and I'm not doing it for another damn day."

"And you expect Angel to be okay with that?"

Liam glances over at Angel, who holds up her hands in surrender. "Hey, don't look at me. As long as you two spare me the horny details, I don't want to know what happens behind closed doors. Just promise me you'll be extra careful. Everyone is going to be watching us like hawks from now on, and I already look like the clueless girl-friend. Even the slightest hint of another scandal will have the press swarming both of us like flies on roadkill."

"I promise, we'll be discreet." He gives Angel a warm smile. "Thanks for understanding."

Angel stands and gives him a hug. "You're welcome. At least one of us is getting laid. It's been so long for me, I've almost forgotten what a penis looks like."

Josh clears his throat. "May I interest you in a high-quality selection of dick pics, delivered straight to your phone? Elissa can attest to the fact that they're quite artistic."

Angel raises her eyebrow at me. "Do I want to know why you've seen pictures of Josh's dick?"

"No," I say with a laugh. "You really don't."

Liam frowns at me. "Do *I* want to know?"

"It was an accident, trust me. Now, maybe you and Josh can go and grab something for us all to eat. We have to head to rehearsal soon and I'd like Angel to get some rest before we go."

"Sure." He gives me a quick kiss. "We'll be right back. Unless Josh decides to beat me up on the way, in which case . . . well . . . We'll be right back."

Josh gives him a disdainful look. "There's a lot of traffic in New York, Quinn. Wouldn't it be a shame if Hollywood's leading meat-head got hit by a car?"

Liam laughs, then opens the door. "Okay, tough guy. Clearly I need to buy you a bagel to purge your rage."

"A bagel *and* a cookie," Josh corrects. "And a crapload of very black, very strong coffee."

"You drive a hard bargain. Fine. Get your keys and let's go."

Liam heads downstairs, and after Josh grabs his keys off the table, he turns to Angel. "Just so you know, I was joking about the dick pics. Mostly. But I am here for you if you need me. I know you're probably hurting about this whole situation, and sometimes it's best to get over someone by getting under someone else, you know? Rebound sex can be very cathartic."

Angel tilts her head, a bemused smirk on her face. "Liam and I were never in a proper relationship, Josh. No rebound necessary."

"So you say. But Magic Mike and I are available if you happen to change your mind."

"Magic Mike?" When I snort, she smiles. "That's . . . sweet, Josh. Thanks."

"No problem. Anytime."

When the door closes behind him, I shake my head. "My best friend, ladies and gentlemen."

"You have great taste in friends," Angel says, then yawns. "Just look at me."

She rubs her eyes, and the apartment is engulfed in silence. I know Angel seems to be coping with the situation, but if I were her, I'd have a healthy dose of resentment over the whole thing.

"So," I say, as I turn to her. "How do you really feel about me and Liam? Honestly."

She shrugs and flops back onto the couch. "Honestly? It's hard to tell. I'm still extremely drunk."

"Do you want to hit me?"

"No."

"Not even a little?"

"And ruin my manicure? That's crazy talk." She gives me a smile. "More than anything, I'm angry at myself for not seeing it coming. I could tell he was weird around you; I just didn't know why. In all our time together, Liam refused to talk about past relationships. The closest he came was one night when were both tanked and jet-lagged, and he muttered a remark about how he'd done something unforgivable once upon a time and lost the love of his life. I never suspected he'd dumped his one true love so he could pretend to be in love with me. That's new information."

"Are you mad?"

"No. Just disappointed he didn't tell me that he's been pining for you all these years. I mean, we've been through all this craziness together from the moment we both signed on to *Rageheart,* and even though he's endured countless hours of me whining about my issues with my dad and my sister, he never once confided in me about what he was going through with you, or his dyslexia. It makes me feel like crap, you know? I thought we were closer than that."

She looks down, and I put my hand over hers and squeeze. "I'm sorry."

She takes a sip of her drink. "I'll get over it. At least this stupid charade is coming to an end. The only man I've had between my legs in recent years is my waxologist, Hernando, and he's gay. I'm jealous Liam's finally getting some relief."

"Liam told me that you guys tried to . . ." I look down at my hands. "Make it work once?"

She laughs. "God, it was so bad. Awkward as hell. I mean, Liam's gorgeous and everything, but he does nothing for me. I love him like a brother. Weird, right?"

"Not really. That's exactly how I feel about Josh."

She screws up her face. "Seriously? You've never wanted to throw that hot geek down and fuck him?"

Now it's my turn to laugh. "Never."

"Well, that's just bizarre."

"Hey, you just told me you have no vaginal impulses toward 'People's Sexiest Man Alive' three years running, but you're surprised I don't want to do my best friend?"

"Well, yeah. Liam's good-looking and all, but Josh is *hot.* I'm considering taking him up on his offer for sex, even if it's only so I can break my dry spell." There's a mischievous glint in her eye I've seen too many times to trust.

"You fake me out so often, I have no clue if you're joking or not right now."

She shrugs. "Me neither."

I give her a quick hug, then pull her up to standing. "Come on. You can sleep in Josh's room for a while. I'd offer my bed, but . . . well—"

"Your sheets are covered in the evidence of Liam's luuuuurve?"

I screw up my face. "Angel—"

"The salty seed of his desire?"

"Stop."

"The sticky-whiteness of his everlasting devotion?"

I clap my hand over her mouth. "Stop talking or I'll hurt you. Seriously."

She giggles as I lead her into Josh's bedroom. It's not super-tidy, but Josh isn't a slob. Living with me has rubbed off on his sense of cleanliness.

Angel looks around. "Hmmm. The Josh Cave. Interesting."

I pull back the quilt and urge her to get in. "I saw him change these sheets yesterday, so you're pretty safe." After she settles in, I pull the sheet up to her chin and stroke her hair away from her face. "Try to get some rest. I'll let you know when the boys are back with the food."

As I go to stand, she grabs my hand. "Elissa . . . ?"

"Yeah?"

She looks down at my hand as she strokes it. "I feel like I owe you an apology as well."

"What for?"

"Ever since we met, I've been shoving my magical wedding and hottie fiancée down your throat. I even made you come dress shopping with me, for God's sake. I've been a total asshole. I hope you don't hate me."

I laugh. "Actually, I love you, despite thinking you'd stolen the man of my dreams. You're just that adorable."

"Well, yeah. Tell me something I don't know." She blinks a few times, then her eyes drift closed. "I just want you to know that I'm glad you and Liam have found happiness with each other. You're both amazing people, and you deserve it."

Before I can tell her she deserves happiness, too, she's asleep.

EIGHTEEN

WORKAROUND

Four Days Later
Pier 23 Rehearsal Rooms
New York City

"Angel! Liam! This way! To your left!"
  "Over here, guys! Please! Over here!"
  "Can we get a few words?! How are you today?"
  "Angel, have you really forgiven Liam for making out with another woman? Is the wedding still on?"

A burly team of security guards parts the rabid media throng, which has completely blocked off the entrance to our rehearsal space for the fourth day in a row. Yet again, vans and equipment trucks are everywhere, and it's brought traffic in front of our building to a standstill. Add to that the dozens of passionate fans who believe screaming at their idols will save their relationship, and it's safe to say our current address is West Bedlam Street, Crazytown.

Before I even have to ask, Josh is on the phone to the local precinct to get the cops on-site. He knows the drill by now. We might have to live with this madness, but we can at least keep it a little more under control.

Angel and Liam push through the crowd with as much composure as they can, but I notice they're both finding it more difficult to keep up the charade these days. Especially Liam.

"You guys okay?" I ask as I usher them inside the foyer and lock the glass doors behind them.

"Just great," Liam says through gritted teeth. He smiles and flips the bird to the photographers, who are now pressing their lenses against the glass. "Haven't punched anyone out yet, which I'm claiming as a win."

Angel grabs his arm and pulls him up the stairs. "Yeah, but you're getting that look that means you're close to it. Just chill, dude. This can't go on for much longer. When the buzzards fly away, we'll magically fall out of love with each other, go our separate ways, and start macking on people we actually want to bang."

I notice her eyeball Josh at the end of the hall when we reach the top of the stairs.

"Do you have anyone in particular in mind when you say that?" I ask.

"No," she says with a flick of her hair. "Just general people. No one you guys know."

Josh glances over and gives her a tilt of his chin. The smile that spreads across Angel's face is brighter than the sun. Josh frowns at her. For all his bluster and bravado, I don't think he ever truly expected Angel to think twice about him, and he probably believes she's only paying attention to him now as a practical joke. I'm tempted to let him know that Angel finds him hot, but it's much more fun to watch him squirm.

"See you guys in the production meeting," Angel says, not sparing me and Liam a backward glance as she heads over to talk to my bestie.

Once she's gone, Liam surprises me by grabbing my arm and pulling me down the hallway to my office. When we're safely inside, he locks the door and shoves me against the wall in a crushing kiss. For a couple of minutes, we're a mess of urgent, needy hands and mouths, and when he finally pulls back, we're both panting way too loud considering there are other people in the building.

"Not seeing you every night is killing me," he says as he cups my face. "Didn't Anthony get the memo that I'm owed six years of Elissa time? Why the hell is he torturing me?"

All week, Liam and Angel have been putting in overtime for their PR appearances. It's meant we've barely seen each other outside rehearsal, and neither of us is coping with that.

"Let me ask you this," he asks, assessing my skinny jeans and combat boots. "How feasible would it be for me to fuck you right now? I know we have the production meeting in five minutes, but I promise, I could be done in two. Maybe less."

I fist his T-shirt. "I'm sorry, but the standard procedure is *seven* minutes in heaven."

"Not sure I can last that long. I fantasized about you all last night."

"Wasn't that awkward, considering you and Angel were having a very public romantic dinner? Right in the front window of one of New York's trendiest restaurants."

"Saw the pics, did you?"

"Of course. How convenient the paps knew you'd be there. I assume Anthony tipped them off? That kiss was very believable, by the way. And seemed to go on forever."

"The funny thing is, our mouths weren't even touching. I put my head in front of hers and then pretended to kiss her while we had a conversation about how to get you into my apartment without anyone seeing you. Eventually we decided you're small enough to fit in a suitcase. We can load you into the car here, then get you to my penthouse through the service lift in the garage. We also planned a citywide chase scene in which paps on motorbikes swarm us before dying in horrible ways. On a related topic, don't ever piss off Angel, or she'll invent a grisly end for you, which will include having to sit through a Broadway musical composed entirely for banjos and bagpipes. I mean, no one deserves that sort of torture. Not even paps."

"You spoke about all that while you were pretending to kiss?"

"We're multitaskers."

"Prove it."

He kisses me again, and what he's doing with his hands at the same time makes me seriously consider taking him up on his offer of two minutes in heaven. He's undoing the top of my jeans when there's a sharp knock at the door.

"Elissa? You in there? It's Anthony." We jump away from each other at the sound of Anthony's voice. The door rattles. "Hello?"

I straighten myself up as Liam looks around for somewhere to hide. I shove him behind the door, then unlock it and open it a crack.

"Anthony, hey. What can I do for you?"

Anthony looks over my head and frowns. "You okay? Why is your door locked?"

"Uh . . . I'm on the phone. With my . . . gynecologist." I inwardly cringe, but what else can I say that won't invite further questions? "Did you need something?"

He hands me a piece of paper. "Just wondering if you could photocopy this agenda for our meeting."

"Sure. No problem."

"And have you seen Liam? I thought I heard him arrive a few minutes ago, but now I can't find him."

A warm, giant hand closes over my left boob, which is thankfully hidden by the door. My eyelids flutter as Liam gently kneads my nipple. "Uh . . . um . . . no. I haven't. Seen him, I mean. He's here. I saw him arrive. But I don't know where he is now." Liam's other hand cups my ass. A breath gushes out of me.

Anthony looks at me with concern. "Elissa, is everything all right? I hope the phone call isn't bad news."

Liam slides the hand that was on my boob down between my legs and massages me in the most arousing way possible.

"No," I say, and my voice breaks. "Everything's great. Down there. Uh . . ." I wave the piece of paper he gave me. "So, I'll photocopy this for you and see you in the meeting in a couple of minutes, okay? K, bye."

I close the door, then lean back against it as Liam continues to work his magic.

"At least not everything you said was a lie," he whispers, and his lips brush the shell of my ear. "Everything *is* great down there. So fucking great I want to rip these jeans off you and bend you over your desk."

"You've evil," I moan.

He presses harder, and I stop breathing. "Then it seems you have a thing for evil."

"I do. Oh, God. I really, really do."

I'm squeezing my eyes closed and waiting for my orgasm to hit when suddenly Liam takes his hands off me and steps back. I open my eyes and stare at him in shock.

"But here's what *true* evil looks like: You need to do your photocopies and then we need to go. Anthony will be pissed if we're late."

I take a moment to realize he's serious about depriving me of my orgasm, then I shove him in the chest. "You're mean!"

He chuckles as I turn away and run off copies of Anthony's meeting agenda.

"God, you're hot when you're angry," he murmurs as he lays soft kisses along my neck. "Remind me to piss you off more often."

A few minutes later, Mary and Anthony call everyone into the conference room. The meeting begins with Mary giving an update on how everything's tracking with the Angeliam "crisis." As she predicted, presales for the show have gone through the roof thanks to the massive amount of publicity.

"With numbers like these," she says with a smile, "we could extend the run by weeks. Even months. Imagine, we might run so long, we could hold the wedding on the stage. How beautiful would that be?"

Liam's face darkens. "No."

Mary frowns. "I beg your pardon?"

I shoot Liam a look, and he drops his scowl to give Mary a dazzling smile. "Sorry, Mary. That was rude. I meant 'Fuck no.' Thank you."

Angel puts her hand over Liam's. "What my beloved is trying to say is that we already know what we'd like to happen over the next few months, Mary, and getting married in a theater isn't really part of the plan."

"Of course," Mary says, chastised. "I understand. I'm sure you have it all worked out."

Liam glances at me. "Not quite. But we're very close to getting exactly what we want."

When we get into the rehearsal room, I do my best to not look at Liam. Since our reconciliation, this is how I have to play it. I'm not an actor, so I don't know how to stop every emotion he brings out in me from showing on my face. Thank God I have Josh on my side. Whenever he finds me staring for an obvious amount of time, he gives me a gentle nudge. Hopefully the rest of the cast can't tell how often I end up in fantasy land.

At the end of rehearsal, Angel comes over to the production desk as Josh and I are packing up.

"Hey," she says quietly. "I have an idea. If you want to spend time with Liam without ending up in a suitcase, follow my lead."

"What?"

She looks around before saying in a loud voice, "Hey, Josh and Elissa. I can't believe you guys finally gave in and started dating. That's awesome! Why don't you come over to our place tonight and party with me and Liam? We've always wanted another couple to double-date with."

Liam looks at us in shock for a few seconds before catching Angel's drift. "Oh . . . uh, yeah. Come over. Both of you. We'd love to . . . hang out. With both of you."

Josh is more than happy to play along. He puts his arm around me. "Aw, thanks, guys. That'd be great. Since Elissa gave in to her overwhelming attraction to me, she's been very demanding. Sexually. It'll be nice to leave the bedroom for once."

The rest of the cast seems perplexed. Marco couldn't look more confused if he tried. "I have no idea why you're all acting like you're in a Victorian melodrama, but please stop. It's off-putting and wrong."

Wrong or not, Angel has just given me and Josh a perfect excuse to be seen entering and leaving their apartment building whenever we like. No suitcase or paparazzi chase required.

Thank God.

"See you in a couple of hours," Josh says as he and Angel exit the elevator at her floor.

"Have fun!" I say, hoping against hope that tonight is the night Josh mans up and kisses Angel for the first time. Thanks to Angel's smoke screen, we've spent the last few nights coming here after rehearsals. It's clear Angel and Josh have the hots for each other, and yet they both seem incapable of making the first move. They've been dancing awkwardly around each other like freshman at a prom, and the sexual tension has reached such epic levels, I don't know how they stand it. Probably the same way Liam and I coped with being in close proximity before we started seeing each other naked. Which is to say, not at all.

I look over at Liam. He's staring at the floor with a deep frown on his face.

I put my hand on his arm as the elevator moves again.

For the past few days, our nightly routine has been blissful. Liam's assistant is still in England caring for his sick dad, so I help Liam with his e-mails and correspondence, in addition to running lines when necessary. I also help him with orgasms. Many, many orgasms in lots of different positions.

Most nights, after we get our filthy lust out of the way, we order in food and eat it naked. We watch movies, or talk, or I read to him. It's the best time of my life. I never realized I could be so happy. I'm so crazy in love with this man, it makes me giddy.

But tonight is different. Because of the punishing schedule of the upcoming tech week, this is the last time we'll see each other for six days, and the thought of going back to not seeing him every day makes me want to punch things.

"It's only a week," I say, trying to convince myself as much as him.

He lets out a short laugh. "You say that like it's possible. Six years? No problem. Six days? No fucking way. Tell me again why this has to happen?"

"You know what tech weeks are like. Josh and I are going to be locked in the theater all day and night. We have to oversee sets, costumes, props, lighting, sound. Basically, we're going to work our asses off so that when you and Angel swan in like the Hollywood brats you are, everything goes off without a hitch."

He slips his hands in my hair and grips it hard enough to make me moan. "I'd rather a whole damn set fall on my head than be without you."

"Yeah, but Marco doesn't see it like that. He'd like a complete lack of sets falling on his stars' heads. He's old-fashioned that way."

The elevator doors open, and Liam grabs my hand before striding down the hallway.

"Hey, short legs here," I say, scrambling to keep up. "Slow down."

"Can't. Need to get you inside. And get inside you. Immediately. Sooner if possible."

He doesn't slow down, and his dark determination makes my thighs tingle.

When he reaches the door, he presses me up against it as he fumbles with his keys.

"Fine," he says, irritated. "A week. I'll deal with it. But as soon as Anthony gets back from L.A., we're sorting out when to burn that damn contract. As soon as the show opens, it's done." He cups my face with both hands and kisses me deeply. As usual, the feel and taste of him leaves me breathless and high.

"Great. Now, open the damn door. And your pants."

He shoves the door open so hard, it slams into the wall. Neither of us cares. He walks me backward and kisses me again. His leather jacket is warm in my hands as I grip him. I think my body has already started missing him, because now it blazes to life with fresh intensity.

As soon as we're inside, he kicks the door closed and presses me back against it. I'm dizzy and breathless, turned around by his desperation, as well as my own. I want to fold time around us and live in these long moments of him pulling at my clothes. I love how feral he becomes when he roughly unbuttons and unzips until his fingers are able to push into places that make me gasp.

"Oh, Liam . . ." By now he knows every single secret my body has been hiding. Each sweet spot and erogenous zone. He makes all of them scream for his touch.

The spinning tension inside me makes me moan. I tug at his jacket, his shirt, his pants. He joins me, desperate to get everything but naked flesh the hell out of the road.

"I love you," he says in a tight voice with short breaths. "I can't wait until everyone knows that. Until I can take you out in public and show you off." He yanks down my panties, then his jeans and boxers. "I need to show everyone you're mine. And I'm yours. Finally."

He presses my back into the wall and pulls my left leg up to his hip. When he bends his knees and pushes inside me, everything I'm feeling becomes too much. I cling to his shoulders as his hot kisses smother my moans.

"God, Elissa. A week without this? Impossible."

He moves in and out in slow, strong strokes. Every thrust pulls me tighter, and for the longest time, I just hover, impossibly high, just stretching and stretching and squeezing my eyes shut as I fight to get enough breath.

"You know you ruined me the first time we made love, right?" Liam says as he increases his pace. "Look at me."

I can't. I really can't. He has me flying so high I'm terrified to crash back down to earth.

"Liss. Look at me."

With effort I lift my head away from the wall and look at him. His face is magnificent. Flushed and glorious.

"Look what you do to me." He clenches his jaw, and it's like he's trying to show me how I affect him while trying to hide it from himself. "You're everything to me. You always have been."

He kisses me again, then he moves so fast and hard I can't hold off any longer. I cry out as the coiled tension snaps, and the most intense orgasm I've ever had crashes through me.

"Fuck, yes," Liam murmurs. He grunts as he thrusts a few more times, then he freezes, and groans against the hot skin of my neck.

We stand there for a few minutes until our breaths become less harsh and shallow. When we can move again, we untangle ourselves from our mess of half-removed clothing.

"Are you hungry?" he asks before pressing soft kisses against my lips.

I run my fingers through his hair, just enjoying having him close. "Only for you."

"Bed, then?"

"Yep."

We head into the bedroom, and feast on each other until Josh texts me that it's time to go. After cleaning up and reluctantly getting dressed, I head to the door. Liam follows, dressed only in his boxers. He opens the door just as Josh is about to knock.

Josh drops his hand and turns to me. "Are you trying to give me an inferiority complex? He can't ever say good-bye to you with clothes on?"

I slap his arm. "Shut your filthy mouth. If I had my way, he'd never wear clothes." I turn to a bemused Liam and stretch up on my toes to kiss him. "See you next week. I miss you already."

He shrugs. "Eh, I've decided not to miss you. It's not convenient for me. Sorry."

I laugh and kiss him again, then head to the elevator with Josh. Liam watches from his doorway, and yells, "I'll call you," just before the doors close and deprive me of his half-naked glory.

Good to his word, Liam calls me several times a day while I'm imprisoned in the theater. He leaves me a ridiculous amount of messages, and each one makes me miss him a little more.

As for Josh and me, we spend every waking moment working: overseeing set construction, cleaning and outfitting dressing rooms, labeling and organizing props, and of course, sitting in the auditorium for hours taking endless notes as Marco and the lighting designer plot every cue in the show.

By Sunday night, I'm exhausted. I've just collapsed onto my bed when my phone rings.

I check caller ID and smile. "Hey, handsome man."

He exhales in relief. "Hey. God, I miss you."

"Me, too."

"How's everything going at the theater?"

"Fine. Long hours, but we're all set up and ready for tech runs tomorrow. How was your day?"

"Good. Kind of. I finally convinced Anthony to have lunch with me. I broke it to him about Angel and me wanting out of the contract after the show opens."

A flutter of nerves hits me. "And?"

He sighs. "He was shocked. A bit pissed, I guess. He's been orchestrating our love affair for so long, I think he's actually going to miss it."

"But he agreed to talk to the producers about the contract?"

"He did, but he thinks it's a mistake to break the contract. He said we'll have our asses handed to us because the agreement is watertight. I told him I don't care, that I want out and I'll do anything to make that happen."

The sound of his voice soothes me so much, I can't stop my eyes from drifting closed. "So how did things end up?"

"He said he'd figure something out. After all, he still works for me. He has to act in my best interests, right?"

"Right."

I try to stifle a yawn, but it happens anyway.

"You should sleep," he says, and even though I want to talk more, I can't deny I'm barely conscious.

"Okay. I'll see you tomorrow, yes?"

"Yep. I'll be there at nine. Probably salivating at the sight of you. You in early again?"

"Uh-huh. Seven a.m."

"Okay, get some rest. I love you."

"Love you, too."

I hang up and start to tell myself to get up and brush my teeth, but I'm asleep before I even finish the thought.

NINETEEN

ONE SMALL PROBLEM

The next morning, Josh and I have just arrived at the theater when Marco finds me backstage and takes my arm.

"Elissa, you need to come with me." His expression is grave. I tense up, because I get the impression something is very wrong, and I don't have time for screwups today.

I follow Marco into the production office, where Ava and Mary are waiting. Ava gestures to the chair opposite her at the small meeting table.

"Elissa, have a seat."

I do as she asks, and Marco sits beside me. Now I'm really worried. Ava and Mary look even more stressed than Marco.

"Elissa, I've had a disturbing e-mail this morning from an anonymous source, and I need you to clarify some things."

"Okay."

"An accusation has been made against you regarding your level of professionalism on this show. Now, as you know, we've already been plagued by scandal, so the last thing we need is for any other indiscretions to be made public. You understand what I'm saying?"

The question takes me by surprise. As soon I fully comprehend what she's said, a thick knot of dread coils in my stomach.

I look from Ava to Marco, and then to Mary. "Ava, I'm not sure what you're referring to."

Ava links her fingers together. "Is it true that you've been visiting Liam Quinn in his apartment every night after rehearsals?"

Adrenaline shoots through every vein. I'm lost for words. I'm always super-careful to be strictly professional on my shows, so I've never had reason to be questioned like this.

Well, now there's reason. And if it got out, it would be the scandal that echoed around the world.

"Josh and I have been socializing after rehearsals with Angel and Liam," I say, being selectively truthful.

"That's not what I'm taking about. I mean you and Liam alone in his apartment. Has that been happening?"

I'm careful to keep eye contact. "Yes."

"Why?" Mary asks. It's clear she's nervous about my answer.

I take a deep breath. I can't tell them about the PR contract, or Liam's dyslexia, or that he and I are in love. None of those things are my secrets to tell, and I don't want them to think our stars are anything but what they appear to be. "In our second week of rehearsals, Mr. Quinn admitted he was having trouble learning his lines. He requested I run lines with him each night to prepare for the following day. I agreed."

Marco nods. "I can attest that Liam was having trouble with his lines. After Elissa intervened, he seemed much more at ease."

"Why would he need you to run lines?" Ava asks. "Surely he has an assistant for that sort of thing."

I clasp my hands together so hard, my knuckles crack. "His assistant had to return to England unexpectedly. Sick father. Mr. Quinn asked me to help in David's absence."

Mary breathes a sigh of relief. "Oh, thank God. I thought for a minute we were in trouble. I'm sorry, Elissa. I should have known better than to doubt you."

Ava cocks her head. "I still don't understand why *you* had to undertake a task that any number of people could have done."

"Mr. Quinn has worked with me before. I guess he felt comfortable around me. I was hesitant to agree because I knew it would look bad, but Marco advised us to keep our stars happy at all costs, so I didn't feel refusing would be appropriate."

"And that's all you did? Worked on lines? There was nothing else going on?" I feel like Ava is trying to see into my soul.

I keep my face passive. "I tried very hard to keep our sessions as short and professional as possible."

"And did you succeed?"

I swallow. My face is hot. I can't sit here and lie to these people. I really can't. I'd never be able to live with myself.

"No. I didn't."

Marco's shock is audible. So is Mary's.

Ava seems satisfied that I just admitted something she already knew. "Thank you for being honest, Elissa. I should mention that the e-mail came with this attachment."

She holds up an iPad and presses "play." Footage of Liam and me kissing in the rain comes into focus. It looks like it was taken from across the street, but whatever device recorded it had a mighty zoom. The footage goes from a wide shot to a close-up in seconds, and if there was any doubt about the identity of the "nameless brunette" in the magazine pictures, there isn't anymore. There's my face, clear as day. When Liam picks me up and presses me against the wall, Marco drops his head and rubs his eyes.

Mary utters a quiet, "Shit," and shakes her head.

"What possessed you to do something like this, Elissa?" Ava asks, incredulous. "With an engaged man? On a show you're *running*? I've never known you to behave in such a reckless and unprofessional manner."

I look at the floor and shake my head. Even if I could tell them the truth, it wouldn't excuse what I've done. I've broken every one of my professional rules of conduct, and now I'm paying the price.

"I'm sorry." I hate that I can feel the force of their disapproval hanging in the air. "I've behaved shamefully, and I apologize unreservedly for my actions. You all put your faith in me and I've let you down."

Ava nods. "I appreciate your apology, but given the circumstances, I'm afraid you can't continue working on this production. You're fired."

Marco flinches. "Ava, no. I need Elissa. Despite her admission, she's still the best stage manager around."

"We have no choice," Ava says. "The threat in the e-mail is to fire her or the film clip will be made public. You tell me, which one is going to be more damaging to our show?"

"So we're going to give in to anonymous threats now?"

"How would you suggest we handle it, Marco? Ignore it and hope it doesn't happen? Liam will be reviled if it comes to light that this wasn't an isolated incident. He's been carrying on with Elissa behind Angel's back for *weeks*. All those tickets we sold because people wanted to see a changed man back with his one true love will be *canceled* in the blink of an eye. People will stay away in droves and our show will close. You know it as well as I do."

My throat is tight and my breathing is shallow, but I refuse to cry. I made my bed, and now I have to have the grace to lie in it without becoming a whiny little bitch.

I put my hand on Marco's arm. "The show will be fine without me. I'll make sure Josh is up to speed on everything, and Denise can step in as his assistant. He won't let you down, I promise."

Marco doesn't say anything. He just clenches his jaw and nods. I hate seeing him so upset. "I'm sorry, Marco."

"As am I, dear girl. You will be missed."

I give his arm a squeeze, and stand. "I'll need an hour or so to wrap things up and hand over the reins to Josh, then I'll leave. I have no doubt you'll have an amazing season. It's a wonderful show. You should all be proud."

As I head to the door, Ava says something about a severance package, but I barely hear her. I wander backstage in a daze until I find Josh.

"Hey. We need to talk."

After I explain the situation, he reacts precisely as I would have predicted.

"This is bullshit, Lissa! They can't fire you for banging a man who's not even really engaged."

"They can, and they did. And I don't blame them. Based on the information they have, they're doing the right thing. For everyone."

He slumps back against the wall and swears again. "But you and I are a team. I don't want to run the show without you."

"You have to. You're the only one who can. Now come on. We have a lot to do and not much time to do it."

I try to keep as calm as possible as I hand over control of all the spreadsheets and cues. Josh listens in stony silence as I explain some of the trickier transitions. As furious as he is now, I know he'll rise to the challenge.

He curses under his breath as he heads off to brief the crew for the tech run. I've just finished transferring all my files to his computer when there's a knock on the door of our tiny backstage office.

"Come in."

The door opens to reveal Anthony Kent. He looks pissed. Guess he's heard, too.

"What the *fuck* were you thinking?"

"The short answer is, I wasn't. The long answer has a truckload of swearwords directed at *you* for making Liam sign that stupid contract in the first place."

"Like it or not, that contract is what made him a star. Do you think he'd be where he is today without Angel and their fairy-tale love story? He should get on his knees and thank me for that contract. *Not* be making noises about tearing it up and ruining the best thing that's ever happened to him."

"But where does it end, Anthony? If he goes through with the fake marriage, and afterward fake divorce, *then* can he get on with his life? When will he have some privacy so he can have something real?"

"*Never*. He's a star. Stars don't get privacy." It's clear he's agitated. "Like it or not, Elissa, Hollywood is a business. It's *my* business. I'm there to make money, and the only way I can do that is to ensure my clients get top dollar every time. Liam is *my* brand, and I'm going to do whatever's necessary to ensure he continues being valuable to me. Because rest assured, the moment he becomes a liability, I will end him and his career in the blink of an eye."

A sickening realization washes over me. "*You* sent that e-mail. You wanted to get me away from Liam."

"You're damn right I did. He's not jeopardizing everything I've worked for just to nail a nobody who gives me zero promotional traction."

I've never wanted to punch someone before, but man, right now, I'm itching to smash my fist into Anthony Kent's nose. "Why bother being anonymous? You're a big-shot agent. You could have demanded I be fired."

He leans against the door frame and sighs. "I could have, but then pesky questions about where that video came from would have cropped up, and admitting I had someone follow Liam to keep tabs on him would have seemed . . . questionable, at best."

Liam was right. He was being stalked. He just didn't know his agent had arranged for someone to do the stalking. "I'm betting all those videos of Liam getting into drunken fights were sold to TMZ by you too, right?"

He shrugs with not a hint of shame. "Someone needs to profit off the bottom-feeders. Might as well be me."

"Unbelievable." Hot anger rises up my neck and sets my face on fire.

Anthony looks at me in mock sympathy. "Did you really see this thing with Liam working out, Elissa? Honestly?" The condescension in his tone makes me even angrier. "Can you imagine yourself on the red carpet next to him? I mean, come on. You're beautiful, but irrelevant. In every single shot you'd just be a hand whose body is cropped out, because people don't give a shit about you. The best you can expect is to be ignored, but most likely, you'd be hated. All the women who want to beat off to images of Liam would see you as an obstacle to their fantasy."

"And Angel isn't an obstacle?"

"No, because Angel *is* the fantasy. You're the reality. And let me tell you, in Hollywood, the fantasy is going to win out every time. The best thing you can do right now is put this whole thing behind you and forget about Liam. The contract will stand, the wedding will happen, and if you do a single thing to fuck with me, I'll destroy Liam and take you down with him. And just in case you doubt me, I made this little teaser for you."

He slaps his phone onto the desk and hits "play." A montage of me pops up onto the screen with the caption, AMERICA'S MOST HATED WOMAN.

He's gone to the trouble of producing a whole news report, complete with voice-over.

"Broadway stage manager Elissa Holt is tonight being hailed as the most hated woman in America amid revelations that she has seduced *Rageheart* superstar Liam Quinn and convinced him to break off his engagement to Hollywood's sweetheart, Angel Bell. Industry insiders say the ambitious blonde has been obsessed with Quinn for years, and that during rehearsals for his latest venture she pursued him relentlessly, despite his fiancée's presence."

It cuts to a shot of me standing next to Angel in a wedding dress.

Then there's a close-up of me with Angel's head in my lap. "Angel, your fiancé is the hottest man I've ever laid eyes on. He's a perfect specimen of manhood. If he wasn't engaged to you, I would climb him like a tree and bang him like a screen door in a hurricane."

Bile rises in my throat. He's cut out Angel demanding I say all those things. Instead it closes in on her teary face as she says, "Why would you say that? I thought you were my friend."

He's made me look like a first-class bitch.

Next is footage of us in the bar. I'm touching Liam's face, then he takes my hand and kisses it. It doesn't matter that I was consoling him about his brother. It just seems like two people having a hookup in a seedy location.

"Sources close to Quinn say the star hasn't been himself since associating with the woman, and suggest the two may have bonded over illicit drugs. Whatever the reason, it's clear that the brazen blonde has had a major hand in destroying what some commentators call 'the most iconic couple in Hollywood's history.' Rumors imply that Quinn may have killed his career along with his relationship, with many producers now reluctant to work with him."

The clip finishes, and I'm too shocked to speak. I feel sick. And furious.

Kent looks down at me in smug triumph.

"One word from me and that story hits every news outlet on the West Coast within five minutes, along with the video of you two in the alley."

"You've taken everything out of context. That's not how things are."

"It doesn't matter how things *are*, Elissa. All that matters is how they *seem*, and I'm an expert at making people believe whatever the hell I want."

"You're disgusting."

He's still smiling, but I can feel the venom behind his words. "What I am is protecting Liam and his career. Stay away from him. If you visit him, I'll know. If he visits you, I'll know. The one call you're allowed to make is to tell him it's over and he should ride out his contract with Angel. Be smart, Elissa. You know it's the only thing you can do."

He leaves and closes the door behind him.

I sit there and stare blindly at my computer screen for a long time as white-hot fury pounds behind my eyeballs. Getting fired was bad enough. Add to that having my professional reputation trashed and I already want to inflict massive amounts of physical pain on Kent. But more than that, this asshole is messing with our lives. Our happiness. He has to be stopped.

One reason I'm such a good stage manager is that I excel at assessing problems and finding ways to fix them. I have to approach Kent in the same way. Right now, he has leverage over all of us, and unless I can figure out how to reverse that, Liam, Angel, and I might as well forget about our happy ever after.

By the time I've packed up all my belongings from my office, news of my departure has filtered down to the crew. They've been told I'm leaving "for personal reasons," and thankfully, no one is brash enough to ask what those reasons are. After I bid them all good-bye, I head over to Liam's dressing room to wait for him. Even if he is being followed, unauthorized personnel can't get into the theater. And there aren't many places for a paid stalker to hide back here anyway.

When Liam enters his dressing room and sees me, he beams, but his smile quickly fades when I give him a rundown of the morning's events.

By the time I've told him about my conversation with Kent, he's trembling with so much rage, I fear for Anthony's safety.

"Calm down," I say, and stroke his arm. "We'll figure this out."

"No need," he says, quiet and intense. "I know exactly what to do. I'm going to murder that motherfucker."

I pull his head down and kiss him. He's tense for about three seconds before he kisses me back, and then we both forget about everything but each other until the speaker above the door crackles with Josh's voice.

"Ladies and gentlemen of the *Taming of the Shrew* company, this is your half-hour call until places for the tech run. Thirty minutes. Thank you."

I make Liam look at me. He seems calmer, but not by much.

"I don't want you to be distracted by this," I say, looking into his eyes. "You have opening night in a few days, and your head needs to be in the game. Okay?"

"Can't guarantee that."

"You need to. Do you trust me?"

"Of course."

"Do you love me?"

He pulls me against him and rests his forehead on mine. "More than anything."

I stroke his cheek. "Then just concentrate on this show, keep up your act with Angel, and stay away from me for a while."

"Okay to the first two things. *Fuck no* to the last one."

"Liam, we can't give Kent any reason to screw with us. Just give me some time. I'll find a way to take that asshole down or die trying. If he thinks he can bully and intimidate me into giving up the only man I've ever truly loved, he's in for a world full of hurt."

I kiss Liam again, and make it a good one. If this is the last time I see him for a while, I'm want to be sure we both remember it.

TWENTY

DIRTY RAT

I'm bent over my laptop scouring the Internet for dirt on Anthony Kent for the third day in a row when I hear the front door slam. Five seconds later, Josh walks into my bedroom and face-plants onto my bed.

"How's it going?"

"Peachy." His words are muffled by my duvet. "Third preview is done and I only screwed up five cues."

"Much better than the nine from last night."

He flips onto his back. "Right? I think I should get a bonus or something. To be honest, I think my choice to not bring up Liam's spotlight for his first entrance was bold and unexpected."

"I'm sure Marco didn't expect it."

"Yeah, he yelled at me. A lot. See, this is why I like being second-in-command. When I'm in the background there are fewer people kicking my ass."

"Have you kissed Angel yet?"

He looks over at me and scowls. "Are you seriously asking me this? The woman who's drilled into me since we were teenagers that I'm not allowed to mess around with girls on the shows we're running? Just because you didn't have the willpower to resist jumping Quinn doesn't mean I have to travel that slippery slope."

"She still scares the crap out of you, huh?"

He throws his arm over his eyes. "She's just too goddamn perfect. It's intimidating."

"Poor baby." I finish scanning the article I'm reading and grunt in frustration. "Dammit! Anyone as sleazy as Kent must have some skeletons in his closet, but I'm coming up empty."

"So your revenge plan is still a bust?"

"So far. But I'll get there, don't worry. It's just a matter of how and when. Do you have something for me?"

"Oh, yeah." Josh pulls his phone out of his pocket and hands it over. Since Liam and I can't see each other, and we have no idea if his phone is being monitored, Liam has been videoing himself on Josh's phone. It's not as good as a phone call, but at least I get to hear his voice and see his face.

I bring up the latest entry. He appears on the screen in his costume. He must have filmed it straight after exiting the stage tonight. God, he looks sexy in that leather doublet.

"Hey, Liss. Hope you're having a good night. I freaking miss you. So much. The previews are going well, but it's not the same without you. And if Josh forgets to bring up my spotlight one more time, I'm going to kill him." Josh grunts and waves his hand. "If you're listening, Josh, I'm not kidding. Get it together, man."

I smile as Josh flips him the bird.

Liam leans his elbows on his knees and sighs. "Anyway, I can't believe I still have to go through the motions with Angel as we leave the theater every night. She says hi, by the way. She said she misses you and she's pissed about you getting fired. She also wants to pull out Kent's toenails with rusty pliers. Keeping up the charade isn't fun for either of us anymore, and now, there doesn't seem to be an end in sight. To make things worse, Angel won't shut up about Josh. It's boring as hell."

Josh sits straight up and frowns at the phone. "What the . . . ?"

"Josh is freaking out over that piece of information, isn't he?"

Both Josh and I say, "Yes."

Liam chuckles. "I can just imagine. Now that he's running the show, he has a new air of authority, and I guess Angel finds it hot."

Josh puffs up like a peacock. "I have an air of authority? Hell, yeah."

"Now, Josh," Liam says. "I need to say something to Liss alone, so do me a favor and get the hell out, okay?"

Josh sighs and stands. "Fine. I'll take my air of authority and go. Guess I can be all hot and authoritative somewhere else."

After Josh closes the door behind him, Liam exhales and looks into the camera. "I really hope he's gone or this is going to get awkward, real fast. I fucking miss you. Everything about you. I miss your face. Your lips. Your body. God, Liss, I'm dying to see you. Not even sex. I just need to hold you. Can't we just meet up somewhere for a few hours?"

He drops his head. "I know we can't, but I really want to. Did you hear that Kent has organized an interview on Sunday night for us with Angel's sister Tori? An exclusive live chat so Angel and I can re-affirm our love and assure everyone we're stronger than ever. I don't think I can do it. I really don't. I'm so tired of pretending. I can't wait until all this is over and I can tell the world I'm in love with you. For real."

There's a noise behind him, and he looks over his shoulder. "K, I'd better go. I have to get changed and go sign autographs at stage door with Angel. It's *required*." He looks back at me, and smiles. "I'll talk to you soon, okay? I love you."

He reaches forward, and then the screen goes black.

I lie back on the bed and close my eyes.

Kent is such a prick for making them do that interview. It's like rubbing salt into their wounds.

My need to take him down intensifies.

Apart from a few incriminating posts about him on a site called *Agents Behaving Badly*, the Internet has been a bust, so if I want to put this guy in his place, I'm going to need to think creatively.

I deepen my breathing and concentrate. In order to catch a rat, I need to think like a rat.

If Kent were me, what would he do?

I go through several different scenarios until a kernel of an idea hits me.

Oh. Wow. Could that actually work?

I think it through some more, and when I'm done, I feel myself smiling. It's so simple, it's genius.

They say you have to fight fire with fire? Fine. That's what we're going to do.

I sit up and yell, "Josh!"

Within seconds, he's poking his head around the door. "You bellowed?"

"I have an idea, but it's risky. And it's going to take all of us to pull it off."

Josh flops onto my bed with an excited expression on his face. "Sounds pervy. Count me in."

TWENTY-ONE

THE STING

I put the finishing touches on my lipstick and step back to assess the result.

Not bad.

When Marco called and said he wanted me at opening night, I was so happy, I cried. I'd invested so much hard work in this production, it devastated me to think I wouldn't get to see it come to life. I was also happy because it helped solidify my plan against Kent.

When Liam found out I was attending, he sent me presents. Lots of them. The first was a vintage midnight-blue Givenchy gown. Corseted bodice. Full skirt. Absolutely beautiful. He also sent a stunning diamond-and-sapphire necklace with matching earrings, a glittery clutch that's probably worth more than my MacBook, and red-soled shoes that are so pretty I feel bad wearing them; they should be on a shelf somewhere, being admired.

I've never received anything so extravagant. With my hair curled and my makeup completed, I feel like the 'after' photo in one of those jaw-dropping makeovers. Even though I know Liam and I won't get to spend much time together tonight, I have to admit, I can't wait to see his reaction. I think he'll be pleased.

"Lissa! The car's downstairs. You ready?"

I throw my lipstick into my clutch and head out to the living room, where Josh is waiting. He looks beyond handsome in his tux, and his wild hair is tamed for once. Very sleek. Angel's eyes are going to bug out of her head.

When he hears my footsteps, he turns. I smile when his eyes go wide and his mouth drops. "Oh. Fuck. Me."

"I don't think Liam would agree to that, but thanks for the offer."

He looks me up and down several times before speaking again. "Okay. So, yes. Well done. Hotness achieved. Quinn may actually shoot his load in his pants when he sees you. Better take some tissues."

I laugh and grab my keys. "Come on. They're waiting for us."

When we get down to the street, a stretch limo is waiting. As we approach, the driver opens the door, and Josh and I climb in. Angel and Liam are already inside, and when Liam sees me, his reaction is similar to Josh's, but even more extreme. I react to him in the same way. As Josh and I sink into the plush leather seats opposite him and Angel, I can't help but stare. Although I've seen him in a tux dozens of times on the Internet, I've never experienced it up close, and let me tell you, the power of him in the flesh is a totally different experience. If the definition of hotness ever took human form and walked the earth, it would look like Liam right now. Add that to having not been this close to him for nearly a week, and I'm not prepared for how violently my body reacts.

"Hi," I say as I drink in his appearance. Every ounce of saliva in my mouth has dried up.

"Hi." Liam's voice cracks. He seems to be having the opposite problem. He swallows and tries again. "Sorry. Hi." His voice cracks again. "Dammit. I feel like a teenager. You look . . ." He shakes his head, then wipes his mouth. "I'm actually drooling. That's how good you look."

Angel rolls her eyes. "God, Liam. Gross." She holds out her hands, and I take them. "Hey, my darling friend. I've missed the hell out of you. And P.S.—you're stunning. As disgusting as Liam's salivation is, I can't say I blame him."

"Thanks, Angel. You look incredible." She really does. She's wearing a pale, crystal-covered halter dress that hugs her in all the right ways. It's crazy how beautiful she is. Inside and out.

Angel squeezes my hands, and when she lets them go, she turns to Josh. As soon as her eyes settle on him, her smile fades into something more lustful. "Hello, Joshua."

Josh clenches his jaw and nods. "Angela."

Angel takes in a short breath. "No one but my father calls me Angela."

"I've decided I'm going to. Get used to it." Damn. Josh has game with this girl. Air of authority, indeed.

Angel blinks a couple of times, then licks her lips. "Okay."

So, the sexual tension in here has just gone into overdrive. And don't even get me started on Liam's expression. He looks like he's about three seconds away from turning the very expensive dress he bought me into confetti.

I take a breath and let it out. As distracting as the man-god opposite me is, we don't have much time, so I smooth my dress and get down to business.

"Okay, so everyone knows the plan?"

They all nod.

"You got my package?" Liam asks Josh.

Josh winces. "Please rephrase that to be less weird."

Liam rolls his eyes. "You got the package I sent you."

"Yes. It's all charged and ready to go. I even know how to use it. I guess all those hours in high school AV club are finally paying off." He shoots a glance at Angel. "Actually, forget I said that. I was too cool for A.V. club. They *wished* I spent most of my lunch hours there."

Angel tries to stop herself from smiling. "That's a shame. Geeks are sexy."

Josh tilts his head. "Is that right?"

"It is."

After a few more seconds of them staring each other down, I clear my throat. "So, Angel, you sure you're okay with your part in this?"

"Absolutely," she says. "Hell, I'd let Kent go all the way if it meant getting us out of this situation. Besides, I paid a crapload for these boobs. Might as well get my money's worth."

"What if he calls our bluff?" Josh says. "You'd be in the firing line with him."

She smiles. "Oh, don't worry about that. After being saved by Liam in four movies, I'm great at playing the victim. If Kent insists on doing anything but killing Angeliam when my sister interviews us tomorrow, I'll make sure he regrets it for a very long time."

"My offer stands to murder Kent," Liam says, his face tight with anger. "I have experience pouring concrete, and plenty of contacts in the New York construction scene. His body will never be found."

I glance at Angel. "Can we swap seats?"

"Sure."

After a mid-car mess of dresses and limbs, we swap positions, and when I'm seated next to Liam, I take his hand between both of mine.

"This will all be over soon," I assure him. "One way or another."

He brings my hand up to his mouth and presses warm kisses against it. "I know. I just hope this works."

We all go quiet as the limo gets closer to the theater. We're all thinking the same thing. It has to work.

There's no other option.

Because Josh and I can't be seen fraternizing with the stars of the show, the limo drops him and me off at the back of the theater before driving Angel and Liam around the waiting throng of press and screaming fans. By the time we get to the front, the celebrity arrivals and red carpet are in full swing. It's not as lavish as a film premiere, but Broadway still knows how to throw a party.

"Is all your gear inside?" I ask as Josh scans the crowd.

"Yep. Set up and ready to go. As soon as Liam and Angel finish with the press line, I'll go get into position."

"Make sure he can't see you."

He rolls his eyes. "You act as if I've never taken secret blackmail photos before. I got this."

We stand to the side and watch as New York's elite schmooze with one another and pose for the cameras. When waiters appear with trays of champagne, I almost break a heel getting to them in record time.

"Lissa. Look." Josh gestures toward Angel, who's rushing down the red carpet, ignoring all calls for her to stop. She shoots us a wink on her way past.

"Showtime," Josh whispers, then follows her into the foyer of the theater.

I down my champagne in two mouthfuls. "Okay. Let's do this." The trap is set. Now we just need to wait for our prey.

I'm halfway through my second glass of bubbly when Anthony Kent appears beside me.

Speak of the devil and he shall appear.

"Miss Holt. I didn't think you'd be here tonight."

"Marco invited me. Is that all right? Should he have asked your permission? I can leave if you like."

He gives a slight smile, then looks me up and down with a predatory expression. "On the contrary. I'm glad you're here. You look ravishing."

"Thanks. You look like a snake in a suit."

He laughs and moves closer. "I'm pleased to see you heeded my advice about staying away from Liam."

"You didn't give me much choice."

A photographer steps in front of us. "Mr. Kent. A photo with your date please."

I'm about to spit that I wouldn't date this man if you put a gun to my head, but Kent blithely puts his arm around my waist and pulls me closer. "Of course. Smile, darling."

I think I smile. I'm not sure. Maybe I just bare my teeth in a horrifying way.

The photographer clicks off a few shots. "Wonderful. Thank you." He moves on to his next victims.

When I squirm away from Kent, he chuckles. "I can see what Liam sees in you. Beautiful. Feisty. Intelligent. I like you, Elissa. Current circumstances may be painful, but there's no need for things to become unpleasant between us."

I give him my most condescending smile. "They don't need to be, but they are. That's what happens when you ruin my professional reputation, get me fired, blackmail me and my friends, and try to keep me from the man I love."

He shrugs. "It's just business. Nothing personal."

I lean into him, and touch his chest. "Well, since business is so important to you, perhaps you'd be interested in a proposal I have to offer."

He looks down at my hand before returning to my face. "I'm listening."

"Can we meet tomorrow morning? The conference room at the rehearsal venue?"

He frowns. "What is this about?"

"You'll have to show up to find out." I give him what I hope is a sexy smile. "But I promise, it will be worth your while."

"Well, that's sounds too intriguing to pass up." He leans down, his face close to mine. "I'm looking forward to finding out more."

I hide my disgust as Mary rushes up to him. "Anthony, where the hell is Angel? She ran straight past all the interviewers. We need her."

Mary rushes off in a panic, and Kent looks around. Liam is about halfway up the carpet, smiling and doing his duty by answering questions and signing things for fans. When he glances over, a frown passes over his features as Kent mouths, "Where's Angel?" Liam shrugs and shakes his head.

"Shit." Kent pulls out his phone and dials her number. He taps his thigh as he waits for her to answer. "Angel? Where are you?" He frowns and looks back at the theater. "Is it broken?" He looks at me. "Okay, fine. Wait there. I'll get help."

He hangs up. "The strap on her dress has broken. Could you go help?"

I half shrug. "Sorry, but I don't work here anymore. Guess you'd better do it yourself."

"What the hell do I know about fixing dresses?"

I reach into my clutch and pull out a safety pin and some double-sided tape. "This will fix pretty much anything short of an eight-cylinder engine. Knock yourself out, MacGyver."

"You just happened to have these in your purse?"

"I carry them everywhere I go. Stage manager, remember? Always prepared. There are bound to be wardrobe malfunctions at these things."

He smiles. "You really are remarkable, aren't you? You know, if you're ever looking for a replacement for Liam—"

"Not if you were the last man on earth."

He chuckles. "Okay, enjoy the show. I'll see you tomorrow morning."

As he heads into the theater, I whisper, "Yes, you will," and muster up what I hope is an evil-mastermind smile.

Ten minutes later, Angel and Kent emerge from the theater, and he escorts her to her rightful place next to Liam. As Kent walks away, Angel glances over at me and smiles. I raise my glass to her. A few minutes later, Josh slinks out of the theater and stands next to me. His face is bright red.

"You okay?" I ask.

"Fine." His voice is tight, and the muscles in his jaw are working overtime.

"Josh?"

He pushes out a short breath. "He had his hands all over her, Lissa. It was disgusting. Mission accomplished, I guess."

"Jealous?"

"Of course not. But I'm starting to think Quinn had the right idea in murdering him. Just give me ten minutes alone in a room with him. They'd have to use dental records to figure out who he used to be."

"Sure you're not jealous?" He shoots me a glare. "Okay. Fine. But you got the money shot, right?"

"Oh yeah. I got more money shots than a feature-length porn film."

I drain the rest of my champagne and smile. "Then stick a fork in Kent. He's done."

TWENTY-TWO

THE LAST STAND

Thankfully, opening night goes off without a hitch. Liam and Angel are magnificent, and the audience screams through five curtain calls to show just how much they loved the show. It's officially a hit.

At the after-party, all I want to do is throw my arms around Liam and tell him how proud I am, but I feel Kent watching my every move. I settle for giving Liam the most loving smile I can when he glances at me from across the room. After that, Josh and I head home early.

On Sunday morning I'm as nervous as I've ever been. What happens today will either ensure future happiness for me and my friends, or tear our worlds apart.

I'm gambling everything on it being the first option.

When Josh and I get to the rehearsal venue, we set up my computer in the conference room, and then I lay out a plate of Danish before brewing fresh coffee.

"I can't believe you bought pastries for that douche," Josh says with a hint of disgust.

I shrug. "It's all well and good to destroy an evil, money-hungry dickwad, but we don't have to be barbaric about it."

It's not long before Liam and Angel arrive, but I don't even have time to hug Liam before Kent strides into the room. He looks around at the others.

"Elissa, I'm disappointed. I thought this was a private invitation. I was looking forward to some quality alone time with you."

I swear to God, I hear Liam growl.

"Please," I say, keeping my eyes on Kent as I put a hand on Liam's arm. "Take a seat."

When Kent sits, I pour him coffee and offer him a Danish. He munches on the pastry and gives me an inquisitive eyebrow.

"Okay, so, I'm here. What's this about? We need to make it quick because I still have to brief Liam and Angel on their interview tonight." He gives us a smug smile. "Against all odds, the saga of their Epic Love continues."

"Actually, that's what we're here to discuss."

I gesture to Angel, and she steps forward. "Anthony, I know you think you're acting in our best interests by keeping up this facade, but enough is enough. We want to use the interview tonight to break up. We can say we've drifted apart. That working and living together has taken its toll. Let the fans down gently."

Kent stops chewing and stares at her. Then, he frowns. "Um . . . okay. Let me think about this for a second." He swallows. "No. Next topic of conversation."

Liam takes a step toward him, but I grab his arm. He jabs a finger at Kent. "We're not your puppets, you piece of shit."

"Yes you are," Kent says, infuriatingly calm. "And you'll dance until I tell you to stop or I'll make sure you never work again. *I* made you and Angel stars. *Me.* You'd both still be doing soda commercials if I hadn't come along."

"And we're super-grateful, Anthony," Angel says, matching his snarky tone. "But we made you, too. You've gotten *very* rich by exploiting us, so forgive me if I don't feel bad for telling you to go fuck yourself. You're fired."

Liam crosses his arms over his chest. "After today, we never want to see you again."

Kent laughs. Actually *laughs,* like he's having a good time. "I'm not sure how else to say this to get it through your thick heads. No, you're not firing me. No, you're not breaking up. No, to all of it. Capital N. Capital O. I'd write it down, but Liam wouldn't be able to read it."

Everyone in the room tenses, and Josh has to physically restrain Liam, who snarls at Kent, "You prick!"

I stand in front of Liam to calm him down, but really, I'd like nothing more than to watch him smash his fist into Kent's bastard face.

Instead, I take a deep breath and plaster on a smile.

"Okay, Anthony, so, this is how it's going to work. Either Angeliam breaks up tonight in an exclusive heartbreaking interview with Tori Bell, or we give her this."

I press a button on my laptop, and a film clip starts. Kent isn't the only one who can create fake news reports.

"Hollywood is reeling tonight amid allegations that high-powered Hollywood agent Anthony Kent has been demanding sexual favors from his famous clients. After revealing photos emerged of Kent in a clandestine clinch with megastar Angel Bell, a Hollywood insider has revealed that Kent is well-known for using his professional influence to manipulate young actresses into fulfilling his voracious sexual appetite."

Pictures come up on the screen showing Anthony and Angel in what seems like an intimate embrace. One of his hands is on the back of her head, and the other is grasping her breast. The expression on Angel's face suggests she's not enjoying it. More photos appear, and in each one Kent appears more aggressive.

"The high-profile agent was caught cornering Miss Bell on the opening night of her Broadway debut, despite Bell's fiancée being only yards away. The photographer who took the pictures said Kent physically intimidated the actress before pawing her roughly. After several tense minutes, he let Bell go, and she quickly escaped to take her place back on the red carpet. If these allegations turn out to be true, Kent could be blacklisted by his big-name female stars, as well as being liable for various criminal charges."

When I turn to glance at Kent, I'm thrilled to see he's gone as white as a sheet.

"This is bullshit," he says. "I was helping fix her dress. Nothing more."

I pause the clip on a particularly incriminating shot in which it seems as though he's tugging Angel's head back and kissing her throat. "As some wise man once told me, it doesn't matter how things *are*, just how they *seem*. How do you think people are going to perceive you after this?"

Kent exhales and runs his fingers through his hair. His face has gone from ghost-white to completely red, and for the first time since I've met him, his composure has slipped.

"Of course," Liam says with a smirk, "you can still walk away with zero consequences *if* you agree to kill our PR contract. Simple."

Kent stares daggers at him. "You wouldn't dare release this. If you did, I'd tell the world you've been lying to them for years about your relationship with Angel. You'd be blacklisted. No agent would touch you."

Liam gives him an incredulous smile. "I don't know if you're aware of this, but there are many, *many* people in Hollywood who hate your guts. A lot of them are fellow agents. I'm sure if Angel and I offered to sign with them in the process of taking you down, they'd throw us a damn parade."

I can see Kent's gears spinning. He's used to being the smartest one in the room. The one holding all the cards.

Well, you've just been trumped, bitch.

"In tonight's interview," Liam says patiently, "Angeliam is breaking up, one way or the other. You get to choose if we go out quietly, respecting our fans as best we can, or if we drop a giant shitbomb that will take you down in the messiest way possible. Your call."

"What if my business partners won't agree to void the contract?"

"They will. You've told me for years that you're the best negotiator in the business. Convince them it's in their best interests to drop it."

Angel steps forward. "Either way, better get them on the phone. You're running out of time. Tori needs to be briefed on what we're saying in tonight's interview, and trust me when I say my sister does *not* like to be kept waiting."

Kent glares at each of us before picking up his phone and jabbing some buttons. "It's Kent. Get me Davis." He stands and heads toward the door. "I don't care if he's sucking the president's balls. Get him on the damn phone. Now!"

Tension fills the room as we listen to Anthony's voice reverberate in the corridor. Whoever's on the other end of the phone is putting up a fight.

None of us talks. I glance at Liam. His shoulders are bunched and his hands are shoved in his pockets. Angel is next to him, arms crossed, gazing at the floor. They look like prisoners on death row waiting to hear if their sentences have been repealed.

After about ten minutes of tense conversation and some flat-out yelling, Kent comes back in. His usually perfect hair is disheveled, and he has a light sweat all over his face.

"It's done." He shoves the phone into his pocket. "All obligations have been fulfilled. Go fuck whoever the hell you like. Preferably yourselves. I'll have the appropriate paperwork sent to you later today."

He goes to leave, but I step in front of him. "Oh, one more thing. When you leave here, I expect you to have a private conversation with Ava, Mary, and Marco in which you explain about Liam and Angel's relationship and clear my professional name. I don't need my job back, but I do need them to know I'm not the horny home-wrecker they currently believe me to be."

He crosses his arms over his chest. "I'm not admitting to the blackmail."

"I don't care about that. Just clear my name. And keep in mind, if you even *think* about starting a smear campaign against Liam and Angel, we have no problem leaking rumors that you have your own clients followed. And considering that what you've been doing is actually illegal, you have a hell of a lot more to lose than they do."

He tenses his jaw so hard, he's actually trembling. "Screw you, Elissa."

Liam steps forward and puts his arm around me. "Sorry, asshole. That's my job. Now, get out before I give you a reason to sue me for grievous bodily harm."

Kent gives each of us one final glare before stalking out.

After the four of us release a collective exhale of relief, Angel squeals in triumph and pulls us all into a group hug.

"Hell, yeah! We did it! Free at last!"

After much jumping and laughing, Liam turns to me and takes my face in his hands. "You're brilliant. You know that, right?"

I run my hands over his chest. "It was a group effort. It seems the four of us make a good team."

"Yes, we do." He lowers his head, and I'm holding my breath in anticipation of his lips when there's a crash beside us.

We turn to see Josh pressing Angel up against the wall and kissing the hell out of her. For her part, Angel is kissing him back like her life depends on it.

"I hated seeing that asshole's hands on you," Josh says in between kisses. "I wanted to break all his fingers."

Angels grips the front of his shirt. "Then show me what you've got, Kane. God knows I've waited long enough for you to put *your* hands on me."

Josh makes an animalistic noise and spins her around so he can lift her onto the conference room table. Angel opens her legs and he quickly steps between them before kissing her again.

Liam and I look at each other and smile.

"Do you think they even know we're still here?" he whispers.

"No. And damn them for getting to the giant table first. I had plans for that."

He takes my hand and leads me out just as Angel starts pulling at

Josh's clothes. "I have a giant dining table in my apartment. Big. Expensive. Sturdy. Let me show you all the ways I can defile you on it."

"Sold."

We nearly run down the stairs and out to the street to grab a cab. It might be my imagination, but just before I close the cab door, I swear I hear Angel scream Josh's name.

EPILOGUE

Six Months Later
St. Patricks's Cathedral
New York City

A storm of nerves churns in my stomach as I look down the aisle. The church is packed with friends and family, and down in the front, I can see that my mother is already crying.

God, Mom. No. It's a happy day. Please don't cry or I'll follow, and then my makeup will be ruined for the photos.

I take a deep breath and glance down at the bouquet in my hand. The symmetrical beauty of the flowers calms me a little, and when I look back up the aisle, Liam's handsome face gazing back calms me even more. He looks at me with so much love, my heart swells.

I step away from the door and turn to Cassie, who's waiting nervously behind me. She looks absolutely stunning in her ivory form-fitting gown and long veil. I always knew she'd make a stunning bride.

"Everyone's seated," I say, and take her hand. "Ready to make an honest man out of my brother?"

She nods, and I can tell she's fighting back tears. "I've been onstage in front of thousands of people, and yet I've never been this nervous before. As soon as I see Ethan at the end of the aisle, I'm going to be a sobbing mess. You know that, right?"

"Yep. Don't worry—I'll be right there with you."

Ruby, Cassie's best friend from college, steps forward. "I have tissues and a flask of vodka. Don't panic, girls. We got this." Ruby's a nice no-nonsense counterpoint to Cassie and me. We all take a deep breath and share a group hug.

When the music starts, we do last-minute checks before taking our positions, then it's time to take the long trek down to the altar. I go first, followed by Ruby, and then Cassie.

At the end of the aisle, my brother turns. As soon as he catches sight of his bride, his jaw clenches and his eyes fill with tears.

Oh, Ethan.

I well up just looking at him. I can't remember the last time I saw my brother cry. He used to be so closed off and damaged, and now look at him. I never thought I'd see the day he'd stand in a church and take a wife, looking so handsome in his suit, with so much love on his face I can't even deal with it.

Beside him is Tristan, Cassie's other best friend. Tristan is huge, exotic, and gorgeous, and he isn't even trying to hide his tears. Behind me, I hear Ruby and Cassie sniffling as well.

Man, we're all going to look like raccoons in the wedding pictures.

As I pass Liam, I reach out and he gently grazes my hand. That tiny touch brings everything into sharp focus. How lucky I am. How lucky my brother and Cassie are. Even Josh and Angel are here. As I make my way to the front of the church, I see old friends from The Grove: Miranda, Aiyah, Lucas, Jack. Zoe is here with a boy who's mildly famous. Connor Baine, who loved Cassie from afar for years, seems to have a new girlfriend. Even Erika Eden, the head of acting at The Grove, is here. She grips Marco's hand and lays her head on his shoulder as they catch sight of Cassie in all her glory.

As we take our positions at the end of the aisle, I float between grinning and weeping during the whole ceremony. Ethan and Cassie recite vows they've written themselves. By the time they're done, there's not a dry eye in the house.

What is it about weddings that reduces us all to romantic saps? Is it the presence of such incandescent happiness and love? The miracle of two souls finding perfection in each other when so much in this world is imperfect and wrong?

Whatever it is, everyone in the church feels it today. Having Liam here after so many years of struggling without him, I feel it more than most.

After the ceremony, everyone decompresses with lots of hugging and laughing, and then we all pose for photos until our faces ache. Cassie and Ethan are radiant in their happiness, and every now and then I see them gaze at each other, and I know that for those few seconds, no one else on the planet exists for them except each other.

I feel the same way when I gaze at Liam. It's like everything else fades into hazy black-and-white while he glows in brilliant color.

It's not until hours later, when I finally have my arms wrapped around him on the dance floor, that I can take a moment to just exhale.

"Have I told you how beautiful you look today?" Liam asks as he strokes my cheek.

"Just a few times," I say. "Well, that makes number twenty-seven, but who's counting?"

"Hmm. Only twenty-seven? I'm slipping."

He tightens his arms around me.

In the six months since the news that almost broke the Internet aired on prime-time television, it's been a long road to get to where we are now.

Mayhem erupted after Angel and Liam "broke up." The interview that had been hailed as their phoenix moment ended up being their swan song. When they both admitted to having fallen out of love with each other, the whole country gasped. They vowed to remain lifelong friends, but they announced that the wedding had been canceled.

Liam was being sincere when he said he'd always love Angel. In a way, Angel is Liam's Josh. She'll always be in his life, come what may.

Of course, the fans were devastated. Some of the YouTube reactions were extreme. Blame was thrown everywhere, but mostly onto Liam. "If only he hadn't cheated!" they cried. Conspiracy theories flourished, with some clever commentators doubting the relationship was ever real. And yet, to this day, some die-hard fans still believe the breakup was a smoke screen to cover up the fact that they married in secret and are expecting their first baby.

Ah, sweet delusion.

"Hey. Are you asleep?" Liam asks with a low chuckle as he strokes my back.

"No. Just resting my eyes and thinking."

"About?"

"You. Me. You know, the usual."

"Hmmm." He rests his cheek against my forehead. "You and me is my favorite thing to think about, too."

I open my eyes and smile up at him. He rewards me with the world's softest, yet most arousing kiss.

"Aw, get a room." I look over to see Josh and Angel dancing beside us.

"We've got one," I say. "It's right next to yours. And that leads me to ask if it's absolutely necessary for you two to make quite so much noise when you're expressing your physical love."

"It's all Josh," Angel says with a roll of her eyes. "I've tried to get him to be quiet. He sounds like I'm murdering him, for God's sake."

I give her a wry smile. "Oh sure. So I know that you call him Mr. Jackhammer because you're so quiet?"

She giggles and leans over to kiss my cheek. "Shut up. You're making me horny."

"So, Lissa," Josh says, trying to ignore the fact that his girlfriend is now nibbling on his earlobe. "Are you going to put on your big-girl panties and stand beside your man at his fund-raiser tomorrow night?"

Liam looks down at me. "Good question. Are you?"

One other thing the Tori Bell interview did was enable Liam to tell the world about his dyslexia. Now, he's the founder and CEO of the James Quinn Foundation for Dyslexia Research, named for his twin brother, and he's garnered the support of dozens of other celebrities who've followed his example and admitted to their disorder. The foundation's inaugural fund-raiser is tomorrow night, and he's been trying to convince me for months to let him show me off for the first time as his girlfriend. Every time I think about that level of scrutiny, however, it gives me the heebie-jeebies. I adore Liam with all my heart, but revealing myself as the woman who's replaced Angel in his affections is going to get me swift and vicious hate mail. Still, I realize we can't hide our love forever. And I do want to be there to support him.

"Tell you what," Josh says. "I'll bring Angel. Then we can all walk the red carpet together, and everyone will realize Angeliam has well and truly moved on. I even volunteer to let Angel kiss me with full visible tongue in front of the paparazzi."

"Do you now?" Angel asks with a raise of her eyebrow.

"Yes. I'm selfless like that."

"Such a giver."

"Come here," he says, and cups her cheek. "We should practice." He kisses her deeply, and it makes me smile. I was starting to doubt I'd ever see him so in love. He deserves someone amazing, and Angel is all that and more. I love them both like family.

When I look back at Liam, he's smiling at them, too. He glances at me before saying, "Hey, Josh. Mind if I steal your girl for a dance? I barely get to see my ex-fiancée these days. I miss her."

He kisses me before handing me over to Josh, and I admit, I'm glad I get some alone time with my bestie. I miss him.

I clasp my hands around Josh's neck and he puts his arms around my waist.

"So, things with Angel are getting serious, huh?"

"I guess. She asked me to go back to L.A. with her next week."

I look up at him. "To live?"

He frowns. "Yeah."

A lump forms in my throat. I can't figure out if I'm happy or sad. "What did you tell her?"

"That I'd have to think about it." I'm having trouble deciphering his feelings as well. "Leaving New York. Leaving . . . you. It's . . . I don't know, Lissa. Every time I think about it, I get angry and I don't know why."

"Change is scary. Fear makes us angry."

"Yeah. I guess." He's quiet for several seconds, then he exhales and says, "For as long as I can remember, I've been in love with you. You had to know that, right?"

I look down at his chest. "You always played it off like a joke, but . . . I suspected. You don't know how many times I wished I was meant for you."

"But you weren't. And for a long time, it didn't matter—what we had was enough for me. That's why I dated girls I knew wouldn't last. Being emotionally unavailable didn't matter when no one was in it for the long haul. But then . . ."

"Angel came along."

"When I first saw pictures of her, it was lust at first sight. But I wasn't prepared for how she made me feel when we actually met. It was like . . . God, how do I even describe it?"

"Like there was a stranger standing in front of you who felt like home?"

His expression melts into a soft smile. "Exactly. You felt the same way about Quinn?"

I nod.

He looks down. "I thought no woman would ever measure up to you, but Angel does. In so many ways, she's just like you, except for the fact that she actually wants to jump my bones on the regular. I don't know that I deserve someone as sweet as she is, but I'm sure as hell going to try to make her happy."

I hug him. "I've known spotlights that beam less than your girl-friend. Trust me: You're knocking this boyfriend thing out of the park."

We sway to the music for a few minutes, and I know he's made up his mind about going back to L.A. with her. I'm happy for him, but it doesn't mean I don't already miss him.

"Is there a way for me to go with Angel and still stay here with you?" he asks, his voice low.

"No, but that's okay. It doesn't matter if life leads us down differ-ent paths. We'll always come back together. You're my bestie, Josh. Now and forever. No amount of miles between us will ever change that."

We dance in silence for a while, and when the song finishes, Angel and Liam appear next to us. Judging from their expressions, they've just had a conversation similar to ours. Liam's decided to spend most of his time in New York from now on. I'm thrilled about it, but I have no doubt Angel is going to miss him.

When the next song starts, we share a group hug and sway in uni-son. It might be the last time we're all together like this for a while, and we need to make the most of every moment.

The morning after the wedding, I open my eyes to find Liam already awake. He's sitting up against the headboard in just his underwear, looking ridiculously sexy in his new glasses as he frowns at the book in front of him. I smile when I see what he's reading. *The Outsiders*. It was one of my favorite books when I was growing up. When I first read it, I loved it so much I bought a copy for Ethan. He ended up loving it every bit as much as I did, maybe even more. So when Liam told me he wanted to test out his new dyslexia-busting, high-tech glasses by reading a book for the first time in his life, I thought it only fitting to buy him a copy. Easy to read and short enough to not give him a headache, it's the perfect introduction to the world of classic literature.

"Hey," I say, my voice husky with sleep.

"Hey, sleepyhead." He leans down for a soft kiss. "Just so you know, I've been sporting the world's most painful boner for the past half hour and I plan to fuck you to within an inch of your life very soon, but I need to see what happens in this scene first. The Socs have just cornered Ponyboy and Johnny in the park, and if either of them gets murdered, I swear to God I'm going to launch this book off the top of the Empire State."

I glance at the clock. It's only 7.30 a.m. "How long have you been awake?"

"A couple of hours. Worked out. Showered. Now I'm reading. Shush."

I smile and watch as his eyes scan the page. It's hard to believe that this is the same man who used to avoid looking at the printed word as much as possible. His new glasses have dark rims, and the lenses glow with faint light. The difference they've made in his life has been immediate and remarkable. I love watching him read. I mean, any man who reads is sexy, but Liam reading is off-the-charts hot.

I move over and kiss his shoulder. "You're enjoying it?"

"Sssh. They're shoving Ponyboy's head into the fountain. They're going to kill him, aren't they? Goddamn rich, entitled assholes."

I kiss his shoulder again, and this time I add a flick of tongue.

He sucks in a sharp breath. "Hey. I'm trying to concentrate here. You're making that impossible."

"I'll save you the time. They kill Ponyboy and everyone's sad. The end."

He slaps the book down and glares at me. The way the light of the lenses reflects off his incredible eyes makes me warm all over. "You'd better be joking right now, lady. Seriously. I will take you down."

I lean over and kiss his neck. "As if I'd ruin it for you. But let me give you a spoiler alert about what's going to happen in this bed right now—I'm going to lick you. Everywhere. Brace yourself." I start with his neck, and God, he tastes good. I kiss and suck my way down to his chest. I don't miss the way his breathing speeds up, or the way his boxer briefs now seem a whole lot fuller.

"Uh . . . is this going to happen every time you see me reading?"

"Probably. It's super-hot."

"Then I'm never going to get through my reading list."

"Oh, sweetie. No one ever gets through their TBR list. For every book you finish, you'll add five more. That's just the way it works."

He groans as I graze my fingers over his abs and finger the edge of his underwear. "In that case, maybe I'll take a break."

"Awesome idea."

He places his glasses carefully on his nightstand before pouncing on me. In a matter of seconds, he's yanked off my nightie and settled between my legs.

"Now, how should I punish you for your heartless Ponyboy joke?" He grinds against me. God, he's so hard. So arousing.

I swallow. "Well, usually the sentence for false reports of character death is mind-blowing oral sex. Just saying."

"Is that right?" He circles his hips. I pant and grip his shoulders. "Why is it that every evil thing you do is punishable by oral?"

"Hey, I don't make the rules."

"Lucky for you, I'm more than happy to punish you as often as you like."

He kisses me before moving down my body, setting every piece of skin he touches ablaze with his mouth and hands as he goes. My breasts get special attention. I close my eyes and moan. This man is a foreplay genius. Within seconds my whole body is aching for him. By the time he starts kissing up the insides of my thighs, I'm already half gone. When he closes his mouth over me, I bury my fingers in his hair and gasp. *Sweet Jesus*. He growls against me, and I have enough experience to know that when he grips my hips like that and pulls me to the end of the bed, there's nothing I can do but try to keep breathing and hold on for the ride.

A few minutes later, I'm arching off the bed and screaming his name.

"God, I love you," Liam whispers as he yanks down his underwear and climbs on top of me. "I seem to love you more every day. How is that possible? It's driving me insane."

When he pushes inside me, we both let out a sigh of relief. My whole body seems to melt around him.

Being together like this isn't optional. It's essential, like breathing. There's nothing else in the world as miraculous as having Liam Quinn inside me. I knew it the very first time we made love and I know it now. How we both survived without each other for so many years, I'll never know.

Liam takes his time as he makes love to me. Neither of us wants it to end.

We end up making love all day. We punctuate it with eating, sleeping, and reading, but barely a moment goes by when we're not touching each other.

In the late afternoon, we shower and get ready to go to his foundation's fund-raiser. He's in his tux and ready to go within five minutes. I take over an hour to bring my hair and makeup to a red-carpet standard. The pressure is extra high, because it's our first public appearance together. I just hope I don't get rotten tomatoes thrown at me.

I finish up, and when I ask Liam to zip up my dress, he presses soft, warm kisses to my neck and shoulder. "I have something I want to give you before we go. When you're ready, come out to the living room, okay?"

I turn and give him a gentle kiss. "Okay."

It takes me only a few minutes to put all the essentials in my clutch and step into my shoes, and by the time I get out to the living room, there are two bright gift boxes sitting on the coffee table.

Liam leans back on the couch and appraises me as I sit next to him.

"What's this?" I ask.

"A game."

"Pick a box?"

"Something like that."

"How does it work?"

"You pick a box. That's pretty much it."

"Huh. Sounds boring." He gives me a smile that tells me he's not buying my nonchalance. "Okay, I'll take the one on the left."

"Are you sure?"

"I think so." There's a smugness to him that's making me nervous. He was smug the very first time I met him, and he's even smugger right now. Considering he changed my life all those years ago, I can't help but wonder what the heck is going on.

"What if the one on the right contains something amazing?" he asks.

"Then you should have put it on the left 'cause that's the one I'm choosing."

"Don't want to change your mind?"

"Nope."

God, he's bought me a car, hasn't he? Although I have no idea why he would. I've lived in New York my whole life. I can't drive.

"Okay, then." He passes me the box on the right. "First of all, let's see what you're missing out on."

I open the box. Inside is a joke check for a million dollars and a card written in Liam's messy handwriting: *Thank God you didn't choose this box. This box sucks. Really. Out of all the boxes in the world, this one is the worst. P.S. I love you.*

I look at Liam and smile. "I love you, too."

"Good. Now, you can choose to keep that check for a million dollars, or stay with the other box."

I laugh. "Hmmm, let me think if I should keep the bogus check."

He says nothing and smiles. I look down at the small piece of paper. "Oh my God, Liam, this is a *real* check for a million dollars?! What the hell?"

"Does that change your mind about choosing the other box?"

I fan myself with the check. "No."

"You sure about that?"

I just about scream in frustration. "Liam!"

"Okay, fine. Here." He passes me the box. "Just remember, you turned down a million dollars for this box. I couldn't be happier with your choice. I just hope you'll feel the same way."

I take a deep breath and let it out. When I lift off the lid and peer inside, my breath catches.

Oh, God.

Inside is a black velvet ring box. A very *expensive*-looking ring box.

I look up at Liam, and he smiles. "Take it out."

I clasp the tiny box with trembling fingers and pull it out.

Oh my God. He bought me a ring. And knowing Liam and his generosity, it's going to be a monster.

Okay, Elissa, just breathe. Don't pass out when you see he's bought you something that makes the Hope Diamond look like a Cracker Jack prize.

I take a deep breath and exhale.

I'm not prepared for this. Not even a little. It's not that I haven't considered marrying Liam, because I have. I still get embarrassed about how passionately I pictured myself walking down the aisle to him when I was trying on wedding dresses with Angel. I just didn't think it would happen so soon.

Liam leans over and presses his lips against my ear. "So are you going to open that thing or just hold on to it all day?" There's the smugness again.

I close my eyes as I open the case. When I open them, I can't believe what I'm looking at.

"Uh . . . wow. Okay." It's not a ring. It's a quarter nestled in the place where a ring should go. "I'm so confused right now. You said the box containing a million dollars sucked, but you're happy I've chosen the one containing . . . twenty-five cents? Is it just that you've saved yourself a whole bunch of cash, or . . . ?"

Liam reaches over and takes the coin. Then he gets down on one knee and pulls another ring box from his pocket, and this one doesn't contain a coin. It contains the most stunning engagement ring I've even seen. Emotion knots in my throat as he takes my hand and kisses it.

"Elissa, I love you more than anything in the world and desperately want to be your husband. I've wanted it for a long time. And yesterday, seeing you walk down the aisle in that church . . . I've never seen anything so beautiful in my entire life. I want to be yours, and for you to be mine. And even though I'm certain you want that, too, I know your sensible side will try to argue that it's too soon. That the world's not ready to see me committed to another woman. So, I'm going to challenge you to leave it up to fate. What can be more random than a coin toss, right? Five flips. If it comes up heads every time, you wear that ring to the fund-raiser tonight. You don't have to make a big announcement or anything, but if anyone asks, you tell them we're engaged. And if I lose, well then—"

I stop him with a kiss. The kind of kiss that tells him I'm not interested in flipping a coin to prove how much I love him. My love isn't based on chance or luck. It's a fact. Solid and irrefutable. I'll shout it from the rooftops if that's what he wants.

"Put that ring on my finger," I say, holding my hand out as I pull back. "It would make me the happiest woman on the planet to be your fiancée."

He beams at me, and I feel like my heart and my eyes are about to overflow. With the care of handling something precious, he slides the ring onto my finger. When it's on and glinting in the light, he lets out a shaky sigh of relief.

"You okay?" I ask.

He nods, and I can see how emotional he is. "I wasn't expecting